ML

APR 2019

# Advance Praise for
## *Beyond the Point*

"In *Beyond the Point,* Claire Gibson writes a stellar trio of heroines—women I want to hug, women I want to befriend, women I want to be. Hannah, Avery, and Dani enter the male-dominated world of West Point as very different personalities, but they all prove tough as their Army boots as their friendship weathers the tests of school and life, faith and loss, love and war. An inspiring tribute to female friendship and female courage!"

—Kate Quinn, *New York Times*
bestselling author of *The Alice Network*

"As the wife of a veteran of the Iraq war, I sometimes feel it's hard for others to understand the sense of duty and honor that prompted him to enlist after 9/11. Especially since he was married. Especially since he was a father. *Beyond the Point* is the rare novel that allows you to feel the importance of family, friendship, and patriotism simultaneously. This compelling read includes poignant reflections on femininity, the vicissitudes of life, the gravity of war, and cost of freedom. Plus, it also offers hours of page-turning fun with believable women . . . women you know . . . women you are . . . women you want to be."

—Nancy French, author of *Home and Away:*
*A Story of Family in a Time of War*

# BEYOND THE POINT

# BEYOND THE POINT

*A Novel*

## Claire Gibson

WILLIAM MORROW

*wm An Imprint of HarperCollinsPublishers*

P.S.™ is a trademark of HarperCollins Publishers.

BEYOND THE POINT. Copyright © 2019 by Claire Gibson. All rights reserved. Printed in the United States of America. No part of this book may be used or reproduced in any manner whatsoever without written permission except in the case of brief quotations embodied in critical articles and reviews. For information, address HarperCollins Publishers, 195 Broadway, New York, NY 10007.

HarperCollins books may be purchased for educational, business, or sales promotional use. For information, please email the Special Markets Department at SPsales@harpercollins.com.

FIRST EDITION

Designed by Diahann Sturge

Title page art © Lauren Ledbetter

Library of Congress Cataloging-in-Publication Data has been applied for.

ISBN 978-0-06-285374-5 (trade paperback)
ISBN 978-0-06-288433-6 (hardcover library edition)

19 20 21 22 23    LSC    10 9 8 7 6 5 4 3 2 1

*To women on every battlefield, in every uniform.*
*You are not alone.*

*When the angel of the Lord appeared to Gideon,*
*he said, "The Lord is with you, mighty warrior."*
*"Pardon me, my lord," Gideon replied,*
*"but if the Lord is with us, why has all this happened to us?"*

Judges 6:12–13

# BEYOND THE POINT

# PROLOGUE

*November 10, 2006 // Tarin Kot, Afghanistan*

Assuming her gear scared him, Hannah Nesmith took off her helmet and sunglasses and placed them on the ground.

"*Da sta lapaara day,*" she said. *This is for you.*

The boy couldn't have been much older than seven. He wore navy blue pants and a threadbare shirt, both at least two sizes too big. Dirty toenails peeked out of his sandals, and his heels threatened to strike the rocky ground. Every student at the school was dressed this way. Nothing fit. Everything was covered in sand. His arms and neck and face were tanned and smooth. Any other day, in any other country, Hannah would have been tempted to reach out and stroke his head. He was just a child.

A U-shaped concrete building stood behind them, seemingly in the middle of nowhere, surrounded by large rocks the color of the desert. There were no roads. The infrastructure for education had crumbled under Taliban rule, which had turned this area of Afghanistan into a haven for opium production and sharia law.

Hannah wondered how far these children had to walk to school, what their parents did all day, and whether or not there was even food at home when they returned at night. In Afghanistan, the average life expectancy was only fifty years. Nearly half of the population was younger than fourteen. And these children were caught in the crossfire.

The battalion commander, Lieutenant Colonel Markham, sent Hannah's platoon on humanitarian missions like this specifically because she was a woman. He said her presence would put the children and teachers at ease. But these students would think she was a Transformer robot before they believed she was a female. She wore an ID patch on the bicep of her uniform and an M16 slung over her shoulder. A Kevlar vest flattened her chest, and before she'd taken it off, her helmet had hidden a bun at the nape of her neck. But surely this boy could overlook her dirty-blond hair and blue eyes for the sake of a free, fully inflated soccer ball, Hannah thought. When their convoy had pulled up an hour earlier, the children were using a ball of trash tied together with string.

She gripped the soccer ball in her hands and raised it a few inches higher. The boy took two steps backward, his mouth closed tight, like he was trying to swallow something bitter.

"For you," she repeated in English, wishing once again that she'd listened to Dani.

Sophomore year at West Point, her closest friend had tried to persuade her to take Arabic instead of Spanish. Of course, Afghan people spoke Pashto, something Hannah hadn't known until she arrived in March. But she wished she had familiarity with the tones and rhythms of Middle Eastern languages, and would have, had she listened to Dani. But the add-drop period for classes had ended in August—two weeks before the towers came down. The Arabic department at West Point was inundated after that. But the truth was, even if she'd known the future, she probably would have stuck with Spanish. West Point was hard enough without adding another challenge to her schedule. Plus, even if they could speak the same language, the boy wasn't listening.

Hannah wiped a stream of sweat from her forehead. Heat dragged its fingers up the sleeves of her uniform, down her back, against her neck. It was hard to breathe here. Hard to think. She recalled watching heat waves rise from the ground on her grandfather's ranch every summer of her childhood, distorting her vision, like transparent oil in the air. But this—one hundred and twenty degrees—was a formidable home-field advantage.

The heat made the days run together. Hannah had arrived in Afghanistan eight months earlier, in March. She'd taken two weeks of rest and recuperation in the summer with Tim, and now was staring down the barrel of seven more months in the Middle East. She closed her eyes and imagined her husband out kayaking on the water.

*Husband.* That word sounded as foreign in her mouth as any word of Pashto. The time they'd spent together on Jekyll Island during her R & R was a memory Hannah could hold on to until they were together again. She could still feel the grit of sand in his hair, taste the salt of his skin. She'd never seen him so tan.

People constantly asked her how they did it. By "it" she assumed they meant the deployment, the Army, or long-distance marriage. But to Hannah, it was just part of the package. She wouldn't have wanted to be married to anyone else. So if this was what it took to be Mrs. Timothy Nesmith, then so be it. No part of her felt resentful of the path they'd chosen. Somehow, it felt right for them—even if it was hard. Maybe specifically because it was. Their time apart intensified their time together, making every moment that much more romantic, that much more precious. They were like a magnet and steel: they felt the pull when they were apart, and when they were together, they couldn't be separated. The sacrifice was part of the sacrament.

She had a canned response ready to dismiss people's concerns. "We just try not to think about it," she'd say with a shrug.

But the truth was, she thought about the calendar all of the time. She counted down the days, the months. June 2007 lingered in the future as though it were their wedding date—even though they'd already had one of those. In less than a year, they'd be back together again. It wasn't that long, really. Not when you compared it to forever. If they could just endure, all would be well in the end. And as the days ticked off of her deployment, moving her closer to home, Hannah had never been more confident that the waiting would be worth it.

The little boy had started to cry. He looked back over his shoulder at his classmates, who were busy running after Private Murphy and Sergeant Willis. Willis and Murphy were terrible at soccer, bobbling around with the ball, holding their M16s to the side so they wouldn't swing around their backs. The children were laughing. It had turned into a game of chase.

"Look," Hannah continued. "See?"

When he turned back to look at her, the little boy's eyes narrowed with hate. Before she could move out of his way, a loogie of spit flew out of his mouth and landed on the shoulder of her uniform. Then he wiped his mouth, ran across the schoolyard to his classmates, and put his hands in the air. The boy was yelling. He pointed back toward Hannah, then at the soldiers, at the sky. Everyone froze, watching the veins in the boy's neck pulse. Wetness spread across his cheeks as deep guttural screams flooded out of his throat.

Slowly rising from the ground, Hannah put her helmet back on her head and had a dismal thought.

*How were they supposed to win the war if they couldn't even give away a gift?*

**INBOX (7)**

**From:** Avery Adams <averyadams13@yahoo.com>
**Date:** November 16, 2006 5:36 PM EST
**To:** Dani McNalley <danimcnalley@yahoo.com>
**Subject:** hi

I just heard. call me.

**From:** Wendy Bennett <wendy.l.bennett@hotmail.com>
**Date:** November 16, 2006 6:24 PM EST
**To:** Dani McNalley <danimcnalley@yahoo.com>
**Subject:** Hannah

D, we just heard. Please let us know when the funeral is set. We will be there.

We love you.

**From:** Locke Coleman <lockestockand@hotmail.com>
**Date:** November 16, 2006 02:59 AM EST
**To:** Dani McNalley <danimcnalley@yahoo.com>
**Subject:** r u ok

this is so fucked up. r u ok?

**From:** Eric Jenkins <ericbjenkins144@aol.com>
**Date:** November 16, 2006 5:58 PM EST
**To:** Dani McNalley <danimcnalley@yahoo.com>
**Subject:** My deepest sympathy

Dani,

I'm not sure if you remember me, but I was Class of '03 at West Point, and Tim and I were both on the parachuting team. I'm stationed at Fort Bragg and my wife and I live right down the street from them. I got your e-mail address from Avery Adams.

We've decided to stay here through Thanksgiving. I just wanted to let you know that everyone here is in shock. They were an incredible couple. Again, I am so sorry for your loss. It's a loss for all of us.

Eric B. Jenkins
Captain, US Army
82nd Airborne Division

**From:** Sarah Goodrich <goodrichs129@hotmail.com>

**Date:** November 17, 2006 1:26 AM HST

**To:** Dani McNalley <danimcnalley@yahoo.com>, Avery Adams
   <averyadams13@yahoo.com>

**Subject::**-(

I can't believe this is happening. Has anyone heard from Hannah's family?

**From:** Avery Adams <averyadams13@yahoo.com>

**Date:** November 17, 2006 4:37 AM EST

**To:** Dani McNalley <danimcnalley@yahoo.com>

**Subject:** re: re: re: **hi

I have a key to the house. Tim gave it to me before he deployed.

**From:** Laura Klein <laura.klein@egcorporation.com>

**Date:** November 20, 2006 05:59 AM GMT

**To:** Dani McNalley <danielle.mcnalley@egcorporation.com>

**Subject:** Bereavement Leave

Technically, you only get two weeks of bereavement leave. But that's only for immediately family members. You should check with HR.

Can you resend me your latest draft of the insights deck? I can't find it in my inbox.

Also, for future reference, if you need to leave a meeting, please say so. We have processes in place for emergencies.

I'm sorry to hear about your friend.

                                                                LK

# BEFORE

*Senior Year of High School*

*Winter 2000*

1

*Winter 2000 // Columbus, Ohio*

From the beginning, Dani McNalley wanted to be known for more than basketball.

Her father had introduced her to the sport in the driveway when she was three years old, teaching her the mechanics of dribbling and switching hands and dodging defenders. She'd grown used to the feeling of thirty thousand little bumps under her fingertips and the hollow sound of the ball hitting pavement. Over the years, she'd advanced from the driveway to club teams, from club teams to a travel squad, and from the travel squad to the roster of the top point guards in America. College scouts had written Dani McNalley's name on their recruiting lists as early as her thirteenth birthday. That she would play NCAA Division I ball was a foregone conclusion—everyone said it was her destiny. What they didn't know was that while athletics was a big part of her life, it certainly wasn't her whole life.

That's why, on a cold February morning of her senior year in high school, Dani didn't feel nervous at all. What was there to be nervous about? She'd get up, go to school, go to practice, and then come home. Sure, there would be news crews, photographers, and a dotted line to sign. But once she announced what she'd decided, the story wasn't going to be about basketball. Not anymore.

Her small-minded suburban town of Columbus, Ohio, had tried to put her into a box. After she'd earned a near-perfect score on the PSAT, a reporter from the *Columbus Dispatch* named Mikey Termini had arrived at her house with a camera and a recording device. He'd only asked her about basketball, and the photo that ran in the cover story was of her shooting baskets in her driveway. He'd buried the fact that she was a National Merit Scholarship finalist below a list of her basketball accolades, and when she'd tried to take him inside to talk, he'd stopped her and said, "I can't take a picture of you doing calculus. People want to see you play."

It was the same story everywhere she went. But Dani worked too hard to believe in foregone conclusions. Anything was possible. Even now, she knew she could surprise herself and change her mind at the last minute. But she wouldn't. Whether she wanted to admit it or not, deep in her psyche, there was something about this day that felt as though it had already happened. Like she could remember it if she closed her eyes and imagined herself from the future.

Grabbing a Pop-Tart from the counter, Dani stuffed her AP Physics homework in her backpack and took the keys to the family sedan from the hook by the door.

"I'm going!" she yelled to no one.

At that moment, her mother, Harper McNalley, shuffled into the kitchen and looked her daughter up and down with the warm disdain of a woman who thought she'd raised her child better. Five foot nothing, Dani's mother had metal-rimmed glasses and facial expressions that spoke louder than words. Her eyes grew large as she scanned Dani's choice of wardrobe: sneakers, jeans, and a loose-fitting Nike T-shirt.

"What?" said Dani, sticking her hip out.

Harper reached for the coffee carafe and filled her travel mug. "Why don't you do something with your hair?" She swirled the carafe through the air, indicating her daughter's head. "Fix that situation."

Ever since she was young, Dani had worn her hair in a spiky ponytail. The edges near her forehead were frayed and broken, but athletic pre-wrap headbands did a decent job of keeping the wild parts off her face. She knew her mother was annoyed she hadn't made an appointment to get her hair relaxed at the salon. But there was no time for that nonsense. Dani didn't have the patience to sit in a chair and have her head doused with chemicals. There were better things to do with her time. Plus, if they were going to put her picture in the paper, it might as well look like her. Afro and all.

"Go on," her mother said, pressing her. "Comb it. They should at least know you're a girl."

Begrudgingly, Dani ran back upstairs to the hall bathroom, dropped her backpack by the door, and stared at the light-skinned black girl in the mirror. A constellation of freckles graced her face, as if God had decided at the last minute to splatter dark paint against a light brown canvas. Eighteen, with the attitude and swagger to go with it, Dani pulled a brush through her tangled hair and smothered the ends with oil.

*They should at least know you're a girl.* Of course they knew she was a girl! She had boobs, for God's sake. She played women's basketball. Just because she didn't wear makeup or wear skirts didn't make her less of a woman. Her mother of all people should have known that. Harper McNalley was a chemical engineer—a black woman at the height of a white man's profession. At times, Dani thought her mom was the wisest, most progressive person in the world. Then she'd go and say a thing like that.

A heavy fist pounded against the bathroom door three times in a row. *Bang, bang, bang.*

"Just a minute!" Dani shouted.

"Dani, I've got to go!"

High-pitched and incessant, her little brother's voice had yet to change. She could imagine Dominic standing outside the door with his little Steve Urkel glasses, holding his crotch and crossing his ankles. Dominic was a confident little boy, always reading some book too advanced for his age. A few nights earlier, he'd recited a Shakespearean soliloquy for the family at dinner. She loved him for how fiercely he chose to be himself. Of course, their father would have liked it better if their talents had been switched at birth, Dani knew. Tom McNalley had hoped to have an athletic son and an artistic daughter. But realizing there was no changing his children, he'd enrolled Dominic in every music lesson, acting class, and audiovisual club the greater Columbus area had

to offer. And when Dani showed promise on the driveway basketball court, he'd signed her up for club teams, private coaches, and
ultimately, the AAU team that had shaped Dani into the point
guard she was today. All opportunities available to white children were equally available to the McNalleys: Tom and Harper
had worked hard for that to be so.

Dani knew the stories. Her parents had both grown up in the
South—her mother was among some of the first children to inte-
grate her white North Carolina elementary school. After meeting
at Howard University in the late 1970s, Tom and Harper uprooted
and replanted in Ohio, hoping to chart a new future for their
family. They lived in a gated community, the children attended
great public schools, and they had two cars in the driveway. By
every measure, they had "made it"—whatever that meant. Dani
still wondered sometimes if they'd swung the pendulum a bit too
far. They were the only black family within a twenty-mile radius,
and though it didn't bother Dani to be different, she wondered if
there was something she was missing, some experience that she'd
lost, in the shelter of their suburban zip code.

"Dani, I must say, I've never seen a black person with freckles,"
her friend's mother had said once, as if Dani were a new species
at the local zoo. "Where does that come from? You know, in your
gene pool?"

At the time, Dani just shrugged it off and said she wasn't sure.
But if she were asked that same question today, she would say,
"Mrs. Littleton, no offense, but I would never ask about your gene
pool." Or, more likely: "That's easy. One of your ancestors probably raped one of mine."

Smiling, Dani would of course add that she was joking. But every joke comes with a dose of truth, and sure enough, when Dani's aunt had dug into the family history several years earlier, it turned out their great-great-grandmother, Scarlet McNalley, had birthed eight children with her slave owner's son. That was why light skin ran in the family genes.

Most people in the community had pigeonholed Dani as a superstar athlete. She couldn't really blame them, since her most public achievements took place on the court. But when she earned a near-perfect score on the PSAT, suddenly, Dani was being recruited by the Ivy League for her brain even as state schools chased her for her brawn. People kept assuming that Dani was going to UConn or Tennessee. But that's what made today so exciting. Because while everyone in the community thought they knew where this shooting star was headed, they were wrong.

*Bang! Bang! Bang!*

"Open up, D!" her brother shouted. "I'm going to wet myself!" Opening the door, Dani stared straight ahead at her little brother, dressed in long khaki pants and a maroon shirt, the uniform for the arts school he attended. He pushed his glasses up his nose. "I don't really have to go. Mom just said to—let me see if I can do this right." Twisting his face and sticking out his hip, Dominic pointed a finger toward his sister and turned his voice into his mother's. "Get your ass out the door or you're going to be late!"

Wrapping her little brother's head under her arm, Dani rubbed his cranium with her knuckles until his glasses nearly fell off. "Well why didn't you say that, bro?"

THE COURSE OF her fate had changed last fall, when a thin brunette woman arrived at the Lincoln High School gymnasium. Though she hid in the shadows, the woman's tall and thin silhouette was the picture of pure authority. Her dark hair was sliced with streaks of silver and cut short for easy maintenance. Close-set blue eyes with raised eyebrows made her look strangely alert. Her nose was small and upturned, softened by rosy lips and a quick smile. The femininity of her facial features was offset by the rest of her body: ungraceful and bony arms and legs mimicked the sharpness in her fingers. She was a beautiful woman, but intense, for sure. A hunter.

Unlike other university recruiters who'd leave halfway through practice, Catherine Jankovich stayed to the very end, through conditioning. When she stepped out of the shadows and introduced herself as the head women's basketball coach at West Point, Dani was impressed by her stature.

West Point. Standing in front of the coach, Dani racked her brain to remember how she'd heard of it before. Eventually, a picture from her AP history textbook surfaced in her mind. Thomas Jefferson and George Washington had chosen West Point as a strategic position during the Revolutionary War. A hillside overlook onto a narrow hairpin turn in the Hudson River, West Point was the perfect position from which to capsize British ships as they tried to navigate north from New York City. Against her better judgment, she was intrigued.

"West Point?" repeated Dani. "Is that a high school?"

"No. It's a college," the coach said.

"They have a women's basketball team?"

"Would I be here if we didn't?" the coach said, setting her jaw slightly. "I know you've got a lot of other colleges trying to get you to pay attention to their programs, Dani. And that's great. You deserve those choices. You've earned them. But I happen to think you need to go to a school that will serve you athletically, academically, and personally. West Point is not exactly a normal school. But I have a feeling that you're not necessarily a normal girl."

That in itself might have been enough to convince Dani to pack her bags and buy a pair of combat boots. But when the coach explained how West Point operated, Dani felt transfixed. An interested applicant couldn't just apply—she first had to interview with her congressman or senator to receive a nomination. With that nomination in hand, an applicant could send on essays and transcripts and SAT scores to West Point's admissions office. But even then, only 10 percent of applicants were accepted. Of those, less than 15 percent were female. As a university, West Point had a reputation for excellence, and its students went on to leadership in business, military, and government sectors. It wasn't a normal school. It was better.

Coach Jankovich had insisted on flying her in for an official visit, and three weeks later, when she stepped on campus, her decision was made.

That day, the Hudson River was like a long glittering road, reflecting mountains on the east and granite on the west. Gray stone buildings towered over a green parade field, oozing with history and dignity. The campus teemed with handsome, athletic students in gray uniforms walking to class with full backpacks and square jaws. There were kids of every race, and girls like

Dani, who didn't seem to mind that they were wearing the same uniform as the guys.

Dani's mother had never been the type to cut out newspaper articles about Dani's successes. Her ribbons and trophies had been lost or thrown away, not displayed around the house. "Let someone else praise you, and not your own mouth," was Harper's favorite proverb, a biblical reminder to her precocious daughter not to become a braggart. But walking around campus at West Point, Dani met the gaze of every cadet that passed her by, and saw in their eyes a familiar self-assuredness, like she was looking in a mirror. Here, confidence wasn't a quality to hide; it was essential to survival.

For twenty-four hours, a sophomore on the basketball team named Sarah Goodrich showed Dani around, answering her questions and introducing her to everyone they passed.

"What's it like playing for Coach Jankovich?" Dani asked, right when they started walking to class.

"I don't know. I haven't played for her yet," explained Sarah. "You know, this is her first year. You're her star recruit."

With dark black hair, fair skin, and striking green eyes, Sarah looked like Snow White in a military uniform. Over lunch, she told Dani that she was one of five siblings who had all attended West Point, and that even though she'd been recruited by a different head coach, she would have played for anyone, just to say she played at Army. A psychology major, she planned to be an intelligence officer in the Army after graduation.

"But that's still two years away," Sarah said knowingly. "A lot can change in two years."

At other colleges, kids wore pajamas to class. Here, they wore "as for class"—a uniform of dark wool pants, a white collared shirt, and a flat wool cap with a shiny black bill.

"Then there's gym alpha," Sarah had continued, counting off the uniforms on her fingers. "Gray T-shirt, black shorts, ugly crew socks. Most of the time, I'm wearing gym-A. BDUs—that's 'battle dress uniform,' and they're the most comfortable. Then you've got full dress gray, which is the whole shebang, brass buttons, maroon sash, big feather on the hat. Sorry, am I going too fast?"

"Nope," said Dani.

"Some girls take their uniforms home to get them tailored, but I don't care that much. You get over it pretty fast. Looking like a dude."

Dani laughed at the casualness of Sarah's confidence. Her face shined with the kind of dewy skin normally seen in celebrity magazines, and when Sarah talked about West Point, it was like she was in some kind of secret club where everything had a code name. There were so many inside jokes and terms, Dani wondered if she would ever learn them all.

After shadowing her classes, Dani followed Sarah back to her dorm room, which was about as barebones as any Dani had ever seen. Two single beds sat on opposite sides of the room, wrapped tightly in white sheets and green wool blankets. Sarah explained that she rarely slept under the covers, since it took so long to make up her bed to regulation standards. Instead, she and her roommate both slept on top of the sheets with blankets they kept stowed in their trunks.

Two desks held identical government-issued desktop computers, part of every cadet's incoming equipment. Sarah and her roommate both had wardrobes that housed their uniforms, hung in perfect order, the hangers evenly spaced two inches apart. Everywhere they went, doors opened and people shouted Sarah's name—like she was famous.

"Is there anyone here you don't know?" Dani asked. They were on their way to dinner in the mess hall, guided toward a pair of arched wooden doors by a row of lights and a stream of students. The autumn air felt just cold enough for a jacket, but Dani's whole body felt warm and alive.

"That's just how it is here. Four thousand students isn't really all that many. You'll see," Sarah answered, reaching for the iron door handle. She paused and gave Dani a mischievous look. "You ready to see something crazy?"

Dani nodded and Sarah pulled the door open, revealing an expansive room of wood and stone. Inside, the mess hall walls stretched thirty feet high and were covered with golden lamps, state and Revolutionary War flags, oil paintings of epic battle scenes, and towering stained glass windows. The hall spanned the length of two football fields and it overflowed with the raucous, jovial sound of four thousand people breaking bread all at once. Cadets were seated ten to a table and there were 465 tables in perfect rows across six wings, likely in the same place they'd been for centuries. Each wing bustled with clinking plates, glasses, and silverware. Steaming dishes passed from one hand to the next, family style. One homemade pie rested in the center of every table, waiting for a knife.

"Come with me," Sarah said in Dani's ear. "We've got to get all the way to the back."

In the back wing of the mess hall, the noise increased by a few decibels. On the far left, Dani identified the football team: hefty boys nearly busted out of their uniforms and chairs, shoveling food into open mouths. The men's and women's lacrosse teams sat on the right, the boys leaning back in their chairs, roaring at some joke, the girls leaning forward, rolling their eyes. Sarah guided Dani toward a sundry crowd of girls—some tall, some muscular, some white, some black—that filled three tables in the center of the wing.

"Save yourself!" someone shouted from another table. "You'll hate it here!"

"Ignore them," Sarah said. "Of course everyone hates it here. But we love it too. It's hard to explain."

When Sarah introduced Dani to the team, they quickly pulled out a chair for her to join them.

That's all it took. An invitation and an empty chair. In that moment, Dani watched her future unfold before her. Wearing a uniform, joining the military? All that was secondary to the things she saw in the eyes of her soon-to-be teammates. They were like her. From that point forward, imagining a typical college, with its redbrick buildings and kids wearing hoodies and jeans, seemed lackluster. Boring, even.

And so, when she returned to Columbus two days later, Dani canceled every other college visit she'd scheduled. Her parents tried to encourage her to keep her options open, but there was no need to look anywhere else. She'd found her path. Her future existed in the Corps Squad wing of Washington Hall.

It was just like Coach Jankovich had said. At West Point, Dani could be all of herself. Not just a part.

DANI SAT AT the center of a table in the Lincoln High School gymnasium, staring at a gathered crowd of parents, students, and reporters. Two football players sat on her right side, hefty and smiling, while two cross-country runners sat on her left, emaciated and frail. Each of the five athletes had a contract and a ballpoint pen waiting in front of them. Dani read the page for what felt like the millionth time.

*I certify that I have read all terms and conditions included in this document . . .*

When she looked up, she saw Mikey Termini, the short, balding reporter, in the front row rubbing the lens of his camera with a cloth. He'd written more stories about Dani's basketball achievements over the years than she could count, and seeing her smile, he snapped a photo of her, checking the light in the room.

"So where's it going to be, Dani?" he asked. "UConn? Georgia?"

"Ah, come on, Mike. You know I can't tell you that for another . . ." Dani checked the clock on the gym wall. "Thirty seconds."

The crowd laughed. Dani's parents stood near the back of the gym, their smiles only dimly hiding what Dani knew was a growing sense of dread. They were nervous, understandably. Dominic was seated behind them, his legs crossed in a pretzel shape underneath him, reading a book, as if all this fanfare was beneath him. In the moments that remained between her past and her future, Dani replayed all the reasons she'd made this decision, and all she felt was confidence.

"Athletes, it's time."

The boys on either side of Dani quickly picked up their pens and scribbled on the page, exactly what everyone already knew they would write. Dan Williams had committed to play football at Auburn. His tie was blue and orange. Tyler Hillenbrand had signed to play for Miami of Ohio—though Dani wondered if he'd ever see the inside of a classroom. The other two, both runners, had pledged to go the distance at Ohio State. Dani waited for the hubbub with the boys to pass. Then she leaned over, pen in hand, and carefully filled in the blank.

She paused before the waiting crowd. Mikey Termini snapped a photo, sending a flash of light throughout the quiet gymnasium. Then Dani picked up the contract and read the final line.

"'This is to certify my decision to enroll at the United States Military Academy at West Point.'"

A gasp emanated from the crowd, followed by a roar of applause and a whistle from her father—the tallest man in the room, forefinger and thumb in the shape of a circle under his black mustache. Dani smiled, the freckles on her face nearly jumping with excitement. Classmates shook her hand. A line of adults formed around her to ask questions and offer hugs and well wishes. While the boys still had nine months before they headed to college, Dani had to report to West Point for Reception Day on June 29. As she scanned the room from right to left, she tried to etch the scene into her mind, so she could remember it forever.

If this was her destiny—if this was her fate—then so be it.

**2**

*Winter 2000 // Pittsburgh, Pennsylvania*

S now fell from a charcoal sky, sticking to the ground and melting on the surface of a hot tub full of teenagers. Underneath the surface, legs and arms tangled, while above it, Avery Adams closed her eyes and swayed to the sounds of Third Eye Blind coming over the radio.

Wisps of platinum-blond hair curled at her neck, which was encircled by the black strings of her bikini top. The warmth of alcohol inched toward her cheeks and the smell of chlorine seeped into her skin, while inside Kevin's house, the party grew louder. Though she could have stayed here forever, eyes closed, muscles relaxing in the Jacuzzi, Avery knew she needed to get out before the steam and alcohol went from her cheeks to her head. She was an experienced enough drinker to know when she'd hit her limit.

As she stood, Avery's body emerged from the heat into the cold, drawing the eyes of every high school boy at the party. Toned shoulders, slender stomach, muscular legs—she had the body of an athlete, hewn from years sprinting up and down basketball courts, encouraged by the voice of her coach on the sidelines, shouting: "Faster, Avery! GO!"

She shivered, quickly realizing the difference in temperature between water and air.

"Hey, hand me one of those," she ordered.

A football player named Marcus Jones reached over the side of the hot tub and grabbed a folded towel from a plastic chair. "Where do you think you're going?" he asked as he passed it over.

"Inside," Avery explained, then shook her cup. "Time for a refill."

"Here," he said, reaching for her cup. "I'll get it for you. Stay."

"I can take care of myself." Avery stepped over the edge of the hot tub. Her mother always told her never to take a drink that someone else poured; it was one of the few rules Avery actually followed. "Plus, I wouldn't want your pruney hands all over my cup, anyway."

"These?" he said, raising his palms out of the water—they were large, wide-receiver hands, dark on top and pink on the undersides. "You and I both know what these hands can do."

The rest of the guys in the hot tub laughed, while the girls seemed to share a collective sigh of relief that Avery was leaving. Her presence attracted attention from the boys that they hated to share, Avery knew. But she was used to both responses—the attraction and the jealousy. She wavered, sometimes relishing her role as queen bee, and sometimes trying to shrug it off her shoulders, a weight she'd never intended to carry in the first place.

Ignoring Marcus, Avery wrapped herself in the towel and weaved her way through the warm house, between people dancing. A crowd encircled the dining room table, watching a group of guys who were in the middle of a game of flip-cup.

"Go! Go! Chug!"

Avery rolled her eyes. She was so ready for high school to be over. Senioritis felt like sitting in a brand-new car with no gas: all of the promise, none of the horsepower. Kids from her high school talked a big game about going to college out of state, but in the end, they'd all end up at the University of Pittsburgh. The boys would play the same drinking games in college until they were fat and bald. The girls would join sororities and attend themed parties until they gained communications degrees or engagement rings or fetuses—whichever came first. It was sad, Avery thought. So predictable. So convenient. So *not* her future, if she had anything to say about it.

She'd seen what the American dream achieved—and it wasn't happiness. Her mother and father coexisted in their house. Other than attending Avery's basketball games as a pair, they might as well have been strangers.

Avery's relationship to her parents was like that of a business owner to a bank. At the beginning, they were happy to finance her way to big dreams. Hank and Lonnie Adams justified the money they spent on private coaches and summer basketball camps with the assumption that Avery's future would be financed by her skill in basketball. But the more time passed, the more the pressure built for Avery to perform, and the more uncomfortable they looked writing the checks. Every day, her mother asked whether or not any college coaches had called, and while she waited for an answer, Avery could see her mother doing math behind her eyes. *Have you been worth it?*

Walking toward the kitchen, Avery held up the towel around her body and filled her empty cup with water, guzzling it quickly to counteract the anonymous pink punch she'd imbibed earlier. A cooler of beer sat on the counter and the smell of weed wafted in from outside, pungent and earthy. She wasn't much of a smoker, especially not during the basketball season—it took away her edge—but the smell sent her shoulders rolling down her spine. Maybe she would stay a little while longer. After all, what good was having an edge if she was just going to end up in the same place as everyone else?

"Yo, Avery!"

Turning, Avery spotted Kevin Walters across the kitchen, holding a corded telephone in his hand. The plastic spiral dangled from the phone to the floor and back to the wall, where it was plugged into the base. Rotund and jovial, with bright red cheeks and dark brown hair, Kevin had avoided years of bullying by making fun of himself before anyone else could, gathering friends by the dozen. It also helped that his parents were frequently out of town and chose to ignore the signs that he held ragers in their absence.

"Phone's for you," he said. He held a puffy hand over the receiver and extended it toward her.

Avery's thin, tweezed eyebrows immediately crunched together in confusion. Who in the world would be calling her here?

Swallowing hard, she walked across the kitchen, still barefoot, aware of the sticky layer of smut she was accumulating on the pads of her feet.

It couldn't be her parents.

Definitely not. In four years of high school, they hadn't once asked where she was going. They never waited up on the couch when she didn't come home by curfew. She wasn't even sure she had a curfew. If she did, her parents had never enforced it. Maybe that was because they'd assumed Avery would be like her older brother, Blake—bookish and square. At sixteen, her younger brother, Caleb, had only had his driver's license for a month. Plus, it wasn't like he had anywhere to go. Caleb was a sophomore with nerdy friends that were always watching sci-fi movies or playing board games, the names of which Avery couldn't pronounce. Settlers of Catan. Dungeons and Dragons.

But as lame as Caleb Adams might have been, at least he could keep a secret. Any time Avery arrived home from a party in the single-digit hours of the morning, smelling of guilt, her little brother would pretend not to notice. Bleary-eyed and drunk, Avery would place a single finger over her mouth in the universal symbol for "shhh," and then tiptoe up the stairs to her room. It was their secret. Don't ask; definitely don't tell. And Caleb never told.

She took the phone from Kevin.

"Hello?" Avery plugged her other ear with a finger, trying to block out the sound of Dave Matthews in the background.

"Avery?"

The voice on the other end of the line was quiet, shaking—and unmistakable.

"Caleb? Are you okay? What's going on?"

"I need you—" her little brother said, hiccupping like he'd been crying for hours. "I need you to come get me."

"Okay," she said, quickly trying to assess whether or not she was sober enough to drive. "I'm on my way. Where are you?"

"The Riverview police station—"

"The what?"

"—on the parkway. Hurry, Avery. They say they're going to call Dad."

SEVERAL HOURS LATER, Avery's little brother sat in the passenger seat of her beat-up Honda Civic, his Kurt Cobain hair hanging like a sheet in front of his eyes.

A six-inch piece of duct tape held a rip in the back seat together and the left rear window hadn't rolled down in more than a year, but there was no money to get this piece-of-shit car fixed.

"It has four wheels and an engine," her father had said. "Be grateful."

For her eighteenth birthday, Avery's mother had given her one of those cassette tapes with a cord that attached to her portable Discman, so at least she could play her CDs. That fact alone had bought the car another few years of life. Plus, she wasn't about to ask her parents for anything else. Not before, and definitely not now. Sitting in the driveway looking at the split-level house in front of them, she realized that this night would destroy any chance she'd ever had at getting a new car.

"Shit, Caleb," Avery said. "Do you even realize how much a lawyer costs?"

"I'm going to be sick," he said.

"Oh God. Not in the car. Open the door!"

And he did, spilling the contents of his stomach onto the concrete in the driveway.

Avery's jeans and black T-shirt were wet from the bathing suit she still wore underneath, and she shifted uncomfortably in her seat. Her brother sat up again, wiping his mouth with the back of his hand.

"Dad's going to kill me." A moment passed, and then he leaned forward, his head in his hands. "How could I have been so stupid?"

"If you'd just set the beer down, they probably would have let you go with a warning," Avery said. "Why did you run to the car? Why'd you take the keys?"

Caleb turned his gray-blue eyes on his sister, looking like a hurt puppy. Saliva gathered at the corners of his mouth. "How was I supposed to know, Avery? I've never even been to a party!"

"Shhh, shhh. Calm down." She worried his shouts might wake the neighbors. She looked at their house—every light was on. "It's going to be okay. Just . . . when we get inside, go to your room. I'll deal with Mom and Dad."

"He's going to kill me, Avery."

"He's not going to kill you. It's going to be okay."

She wasn't certain it would be. But, assuaged by her promise, Caleb walked up to the house, through the front door, and disappeared down the back hall. The bathroom door slammed hard behind him, followed by the sound of a loud retch. Liquid splattered against porcelain, then she heard the toilet flush.

At that moment, Avery's mother, Lonnie, appeared in the hall-way, her shining face and worried eyes showing all that Avery needed to know. Her mother tightened the red terry-cloth robe around her waist.

"How did this happen?" her mother snapped. Her voice was as thin and cold as the snowflakes still falling outside. "Were you with him?"

"No . . . he called me from the station. Seriously, Mom. Every-thing's fine."

Moving past her daughter, Lonnie hustled down the hall to-ward the bathroom and began to bang on the door. "Caleb! Caleb! Open up. Now!"

From the front door, Avery could see into the kitchen, where her father, Hank, paced back and forth across the linoleum floor, holding the cordless phone to his ear. Lean and imposing, Hank Adams had dark features and a permanent five o'clock shadow that looked as though he'd spent his life in a coal mine, which, to be fair, he would have, if he'd been born a quarter century earlier. He was fit, though, with muscles that hadn't diminished over the years since he'd played football at Notre Dame. And despite the fact that he spent his life above ground, selling coal, there was always dirt under his fingernails, always a rasp in his voice, like he carried an aluminum pail to work every day. Avery felt the same grit in her blood, just underneath the surface, trying to break free. Coal was stubborn that way. It stayed in your veins.

"Sure," Hank was saying. "Can we do it in installments? Oh. Okay. Understood. Well, then, we'll get the retainer to you to-morrow. All right, Dan. We'll see you Monday."

Slamming the phone on the base, Hank turned to look at Avery, who put her chin up, pretending to be calmer than she felt. She'd never seen her father's eyes look so intense, his pupils so small. The dark hair on his forearms seemed to stand on end.

"Two thousand dollars, just to take on the case," her father told her.

A silence filled the room, so thick Avery struggled to breathe.

"Dad . . . I—"

"He watches you, you know," her father said. His lower lip quivered. "You go out. Drink. Carry on. And what happens? You get voted homecoming queen. He does the same thing, and his life is fucking ruined."

"Dad." Avery nearly felt like crying. "His life isn't—"

"What exactly do you think you know about life, Avery? Huh? I'm sorry to break it to you, but beauty doesn't exactly pay the bills. And you have the audacity to tell me about life? That's rich."

He paused his rant, rubbed his temple.

"All I know is, you better be on your knees thanking God that this wasn't you. Because you and I both know, it could have been."

He pushed past her and down the hall. "*Caleb!* Open the damn door!"

ON MONDAY, HER parents took her little brother, dressed in an oversized suit and tie, for their first meeting with the lawyer. Avery drove herself to school and pretended to pay attention in class, when in reality, all she could think about was the disappointment painted all over her father's face as he'd yelled at her Saturday night, and as he'd ignored her the next morning. For years, Avery had lived her life without fear of any consequences. But watching her brother suffer because of her bad example, she suddenly felt like she'd swallowed a toxic cocktail of anger and shame. Anger that her father would accuse her of causing Caleb's mess; shame that he was probably right.

ON FRIDAY EVENING, the gymnasium doors opened at five o'clock, sending a flood of light and a pack of girls into the darkened parking lot. They walked slowly under the weight of their backpacks, chatting idly while parents pulled up to pick up the freshmen. Soaked in sweat that defied the near-freezing temperature outside, steam rose off of Avery's bare limbs into the cold.

"Great job at practice today, Mandy," Avery said to one of the more promising freshmen. "I liked that little behind-the-back pass you did."

Mandy quickened her pace to catch up to Avery's side. "Thanks. Hey . . . I was going to ask, are you going to Kevin's tomorrow night?"

Avery walked with her chin up, blond hair glistening with sweat. She knew instinctively that Mandy Hightower wasn't looking for information; she was looking for an invitation.

"Doubt it," Avery replied flippantly.

She reached for the keys in her backpack before remembering with a surge of anger that they weren't there, and wouldn't be for another week. In a rare feat of parenting, her father had grounded Avery from driving—for what she wasn't quite certain. It wasn't like *she* was the one who'd been arrested. As she made her way across the parking lot, Mandy followed, hoping, Avery assumed, for the invitation that wasn't going to come.

"I've got a shit-ton of homework this weekend, Mandy," she said by way of explanation, "and nothing good happens at those—" She was going to say *parties*, but at that same moment, she noticed a dark and hulking figure standing in the middle of the parking lot. So instead she said, "Shit."

Following Avery's gaze, Mandy's eyes filled with concern. Standing on the passenger side of Avery's black Honda Civic, a short and stocky man waited with his arms crossed over his chest.

"Who's that?" Mandy asked. "He's hot."

With a sigh, Avery shifted the backpack on her shoulder and started walking faster toward her car. "That's my dad."

"Oh. Well, call me. Maybe we could go to Kevin's together on Saturday!"

When she reached her car, Avery rolled her eyes.

"You don't have to make such a scene, Dad."

Avoiding her father's gaze, she threw her backpack in the backseat and reached for the handle of the passenger-side door.

"Ah, ah, ah!" he said. "We had a deal."

Next to each other, Hank and Avery looked nothing alike. Avery was ethereal and glowing, her father earthen and rugged. But they shared a competitive spirit, or a persistent stubbornness. And any time Avery reached a goal Hank set for her, he raised the bar higher.

"*We* never had a deal," she said. "*You* had a deal."

Starting Avery's freshman year, Hank had driven up to the school like all the other parents, pretending to pick his daughter up from basketball practice. But instead, he'd instruct her to throw her backpack in the back of his car, start a timer, and send her on the three-mile run home. Each day she tried to beat the previous day's time. He'd presented it as a game—a way for Avery to work on her endurance.

Within a few months of starting high school, Avery could run a six-minute mile without breaking much of a sweat. Her father's mantra rang through her head as she ran: *The only way to run faster is to run faster.* In four years, Avery had learned that she could outrun just about anything. She could outrun her teammates. She could outrun the competition from other schools. She could even run the insecurities right out of her head, if she was willing to go hard enough. It was easy to be confident when you were faster than the boys.

The game had ended last year, when she'd started driving herself to school. But now, here he was, looking at the watch on his wrist. "You better get going. Clock's started."

"Dad," Avery said, her voice sounding desperate. "Coach made us do thirteen suicides at the end of practice. I can't."

Hank laughed out loud. "This from the girl who applied to West Point? It's hard enough to imagine you with a gun, Ave. But you gonna say 'I can't' when they hand you a fifty-pound rucksack and say *go*?" His tone turned dark. "You've gotta get serious."

Staring at his dark features, Avery knew suddenly why he was here. This wasn't about her future in Division I basketball, or even the long-shot application she'd mailed to West Point six months earlier, which he was now apparently using against her. This was about Caleb.

The parking lot cleared of cars, leaving rectangular imprints outlined with dirty snow. Avery stood in silence until she realized her father wasn't going to back down.

"I'll be in counseling someday talking about how you made me run three miles home every day like a maniac."

"Nah." He waved a hand through the air. "You love it." He unlocked the door of his daughter's car and jumped inside, immediately starting the engine and the heat. His hands slapped together, rubbing out the cold. "Better get moving."

"Hold your horses!" She pulled off her sweaty jersey, grabbed a dirty long-sleeved fleece from the backseat of her car, and yanked it over her head with force. Then, shooting her father a murderous look and a middle finger, she took off running.

Fury drove her legs over and over again against the cold. Tucking her fingers into the sleeves of her shirt, Avery pushed the pace. From her high school to their home was exactly 3.4 miles. She'd measured it at least ten times with her car odometer, hoping it would get shorter, which it never did. Wind whipped over her ears and eyes, giving her a slight headache. *Note to self,* Avery thought as she hit her stride, *tomorrow, pack a hat.*

Once her breathing steadied, she settled into a rhythm. That was the sole benefit of these long runs: they provided time alone, time to clear out the clutter in her mind.

First and foremost—she hated the fact that her father was using West Point against her. Back in the fall, her AP history teacher, Ms. Williams, had forced her classes to fill out West Point's initial screening form online. In the library computer lab, Avery typed out her GPA, SAT scores, list of extracurriculars, without thinking twice. But that night, the phone rang, and suddenly there was a deep-voiced man on the other end of the line, asking Avery a series of questions with military precision. When she'd placed the phone back on the stand, Avery stared at it for a long time before her mother's quiet voice broke through the silence.

"Well?" Lonnie Adams had asked. "What was that all about?"

Avery's parents were sitting still at the kitchen table, their forks suspended in midair. Oblivious to the phone call that had just taken place, Caleb shoveled a bite of spaghetti into his mouth.

"That was an admissions officer from West Point," Avery had said. "They want me to apply."

"You?" her father had grunted. He shook his head and went back to eating. "Will they let you wear your tiara while you shoot your gun?"

"West Point?" her mother repeated. "Do they even admit girls?"

The disbelief in their eyes was all it took for Avery to decide to apply. In the weeks after that phone call, Ms. Williams had helped Avery navigate the application. She explained that the U.S. Military Academy wasn't just an athletic and academic powerhouse of a school—it was also *free*. Free. As in zero dollars. That fit into Avery's framework. She didn't want to owe her parents anything anymore. And she was smart enough to know that they didn't have savings just lounging around in some bank account.

After some research, Avery learned that in exchange for that free education, West Point graduates committed to serve for five years as officers in the U.S. Army. But that didn't sound like that bad of a deal. She had a cousin who'd joined the military and got stationed overseas in Italy. So, a free education *and* a guaranteed job after college, possibly in an exotic location? To Avery, that seemed like the deal of the century.

Almost too good to be true.

After Avery passed the Candidate Fitness Assessment—the push-ups, sit-ups, and shuttle run came easy—Ms. Williams told Avery that she needed a nomination from a congressman, a senator, or the vice president.

"Uh," Avery had said with a laugh, "my family doesn't know anyone in politics."

In response, Ms. Williams set up an interview for Avery with the famed Pennsylvania senator Arlen Specter. When his nomination came in the mail, Avery started to think that she might just have a chance. On her own, she'd reached out to the women's basketball coach, a woman named Catherine Jankovich, whose e-mail address had been listed on West Point's athletic website. She'd mailed the coach videotape of games and practices, as requested. The coach had offered Avery a position on the team if West Point offered her admission, but Avery noticed she'd placed particular emphasis on the word *if*.

"Unfortunately, there's really nothing I can do to stamp your application through," Coach Jankovich had said over the phone. "It's quite competitive. We'd love to have you, of course, but I can't make any promises."

It was just the kind of challenge that Avery lived to overcome. *You say I'm not strong enough? Watch me flex. You say it's competitive? Watch me compete.*

And yet, February had nearly come and gone. A cloud formed in her chest, which distracted Avery from the tears in her eyes. Why hadn't she heard anything from West Point?

*They probably don't want you,* Avery told herself, in a voice too brutal to be her own. The voice was right, though. West Point was a *reach*. A long shot. Who was she to think she was special? Who was she to think she could get out of Pittsburgh? She was going to have to tell everyone that she'd been rejected, and everyone would secretly laugh, knowing she'd never had a chance all along.

She tried to ignore the voice in her head by moving faster. The harder she pushed, the more pain she felt, which released her emotions through sweat, rather than tears. It was simple math. By wrecking her body, she didn't have to face her wrecked soul.

But her father's words cut through the ache in her muscles, whispering like wind into her ears. *He watches you.* Was he right? Had Avery ruined her little brother's life, simply by setting a bad example?

She wanted Caleb to see her do something good. Something responsible. Something important. But time was running out. And she couldn't slow down. Not now.

Not ever.

Streetlights drew Avery westward, spilling an orange haze on bare tree limbs. She pushed to the top of the hill with long, purposeful strides, listening to her own breath: in through her nose, out through her mouth. The cold dried the sweat on her face and her slender legs flew past fences, children in white yards, and half-melted snowmen. The smell of wood-burning fireplaces filled her head as she sucked air and heaved toward the finish. She leaned forward as she passed the mailbox in front of the home at the end of the cul-de-sac. Her father was standing on the stoop, holding his stopwatch.

"Twenty-five thirty-two. So much for that six-minute mile pace."

"I'll get it back, Dad," she yelled, placing her hands on her head. "I'll get it back."

"That's my girl," he said, leaving her out in the cold.

Exhausted and sweating, Avery walked toward the mailbox, just in case. Inside, there was a stack of mail: a circular of flimsy coupons, a pink envelope with the words *Final Notice* printed on top, a *People* magazine, and a large manila envelope with West Point's gold crest glittering in the top left corner.

"Dad!" she shouted, ripping through the paper. "*Dad!*"

Her father stepped back onto the porch. The rest of the mail fell to the ground. Avery held her breath, frantically opening the leather-bound announcement.

"I got in," she mumbled to herself. Then, raising her eyes to her father, she screamed, "I got in!"

3

*Summer 2000 // Austin, Texas*

After dinner, they sat on the back porch and waited for pie.
There was always pie.

Hannah Speer leaned her head back and breathed in the smells of the night. This was her very last dinner at her grandparents' ranch and she wanted to take it all in. Barbecue ribs, smoked on her grandfather's grill, had left a sticky brown residue under her nails. A light lemon-garlic dressing had been slicked across baby spinach and chard, the bowl dusted with Parmesan cheese. Soft salted butter had been spread on crusty homemade baguettes. Hannah had eaten three slices before her grandmother warned her to save room. It was a perfect meal, washed down with sweet tea, served on toile china. Every bite closer to her last.

Tomorrow, an airplane would transport her family from Texas to New York and time would speed up, racing toward West Point's Reception Day for the incoming class of 2004. Her duffel bag waited on her bedroom floor, stuffed tightly with the things she'd been instructed to pack: underwear, socks, an assortment of first aid gear, a pair of brand-new leather combat boots. Her grandfather had explained how to mold them to her feet: "*Lace them up, wear them in the shower, and don't take them off until they're bone dry*," he'd told her. Hannah had spent the day walking around her house in a pink robe and combat boots. She hated to imagine having blisters all summer, just because she didn't break the boots in correctly.

Blisters and combat boots were still two days away. At the moment, the fertile smell of cow manure wafted in from the fields. Above her, the porch's tin roof reflected a string of twinkle lights, and just beyond the roof, a dark sky hovered over the pasture. The stars looked like the scene at a jewelry shop: tiny diamonds strewn across black velvet. Staring at this view, Hannah couldn't help but imagine a Creator who'd spread this tableau of jewels just for her. She gripped the cross pendant on her neck and slid it back and forth along its chain, her own secret signal, a prayer of thanks. Life was so beautiful, so vast.

Lowering her eyes from the sky, Hannah watched her grandfather walk up from the yard. Gates Speer was a young-looking sixty-seven, with a full head of white hair and tan skin that had held up to age. He pinched a piece of grass between his fingers, then let it fall to the ground.

Though he'd lived on the ranch full-time for the last five years, he still carried himself like he was walking through the halls of the Pentagon. Shoulders back, chin up. Hannah wondered if U.S. Army generals ever lost their military bearing. She imagined that even when they buried her grandfather someday, his muscles would be clenched. But underneath that rigid exterior, General Speer had a softness that few outside of his family had ever seen. Hannah knew she was one of the lucky ones.

He took a seat on the porch swing next to her, slid his arm around her shoulders. His scent was a mix of Old Spice and fresh-cut grass, the way a man was supposed to smell. But her grandfather wasn't a cowboy. He didn't have dirt under his nails or an unkempt shirt. "I judge a man by three things," General Speer often said. "His clothes, his posture, and his handshake."

If she wanted to see someone lackadaisical about his appearance, Hannah only needed to look a few inches over, to her father, Bill. He sat in a rocking chair and alternated between picking his teeth, scratching at his mustache, and adjusting the ball cap on his head. That's why Hannah had never understood the phrase *"The apple doesn't fall far from the tree."* It was a terrible analogy. Couldn't people see that a tree and an apple are nothing alike? Of course one came from the other, but one was round and sweet, and the other was tall and stoic. She tried to imagine the tree and the apple having a conversation. It would probably go about the same way as tonight's chat between General Speer and his son.

"Goats would do it," her father was saying. "Six or seven. You wouldn't have to mow ever again."

"Well, I like mowing," her grandfather replied. "I like making all those straight lines. Plus, if I had goats then I'd have to take care of the goats. There are no shortcuts. You're gonna work hard, one way or another."

Hannah's sister, Emily, snorted a laugh. She was swaying on a swing on the opposite side of the porch next to their mother, Lynn.

When they stood side by side, the three Speer women looked like triplets. Lynn appeared only slightly older than her daughters, a few wrinkles at her eyes. Emily's hair was lighter than Hannah's dirty blond. They all had sky-blue eyes, dimples, and sharp chins.

"I bet if Grandpa had goats, he'd end up chloroforming them all," Emily said, her voice flat.

The whole family broke into laughter, including the general.

At that moment, Hannah's grandmother emerged from the kitchen holding a pie plate and a ceramic pitcher.

"Oh Lord, not that story again."

Nearly as tall as her husband, Barbara Speer was a formidable woman. Hannah had always thought she looked a bit like Geena Davis in *A League of Their Own:* glamorous with gusto. Had she been born in a later generation, Barbara might have become the CEO of a major international company, but instead, she'd raised five children and successfully negotiated life as a general's wife. Entertaining heads of state had become second nature: she could hold her own with First Ladies, UN ambassadors, and senators. She read three newspapers every morning and could speak as many languages. To Hannah, her grandmother was like royalty, but to the rest of the world, she was simply a retired general's wife.

It was Barbara who had convinced her husband to transform their hundred acres into an organic cattle ranch. Now that he was retired from the Army, her grandfather had finally agreed, and the business was growing faster than anyone had predicted—anyone except Barbara.

"This pie is going to get cold if he starts telling stories," Barbara said.

"I'll do it," said Emily. Then, channeling her inner Jimmy Stewart, Hannah's sister began telling the tale, speaking as if she were holding a cigar in her mouth. "Now, *you see*, those Navy midshipmen had us beat down. Mentally. Physically. Spiritually. Emotionally! We were done for. Kaput! If West Point had a fighting chance, we had to do something. Something big."

They were laughing too hard for Emily to continue, but of course she didn't have to. They all knew the story by heart. In 1954, Gates Speer was a Firstie at the U.S. Military Academy at West Point—a senior. It was his last year at the academy, and he couldn't bear to watch the football team lose to Navy one more time. So in a moment of desperation, he and a group of friends decided it was up to them to turn the tide: they were going to steal Navy's mascot, a hundred-and-fifty-pound goat with massive curved horns that spanned more than five feet across. To successfully kidnap the mascot and transport him back to West Point, her grandfather hatched a plan that included a rag, a can of chloroform, and his roommate's convertible drop-top. They'd snatched the goat, heaved his passed-out body into the backseat of the convertible, and then put the roof up, speeding away from Annapolis in the dead of night.

"Damn if that goat didn't wake up," her grandfather said, picking up the story. "We stop at a gas station to fill up. And suddenly, Bill the Goat is ripping through the convertible top with his horns, trying to break loose. I jump on top of him and have to wrestle him all the way back to West Point. Scariest day of my life."

Of course, they all knew that it wasn't the scariest day of the general's life. Her grandfather had fought in the Korean War as a second lieutenant. He'd spent four years in Vietnam, too. A lieutenant colonel then, he'd been in charge of a large regiment of officers and soldiers and had probably seen a lot of terrible things happen, Hannah assumed—things she couldn't even imagine. But then again, she wasn't certain. He never told those stories.

"Of course, West Point isn't all just stealing goats," he said, clearing his throat. Suddenly, she felt her grandfather's arm stiffen. His teeth clenched behind his cheeks and he shook his head, like he was trying to shake a memory.

"Let's not get into all that," her grandmother said gently. "We've got pie!"

Barbara Speer placed the pie dish on the table and opened her hands over it as if to say, *Ta-da!* The sweet aroma of fruit and butter mingled with the tension in the air.

"Strawberry rhubarb," she announced. "Who wants more tea? Hannah, have I told you how much I love this pitcher? I get compliments on it all the time."

Hannah smiled humbly. The pitcher was a product of the one elective class she'd taken during her last semester of high school. The body of the pitcher was tall and slender, with a perfect triangle spout and a curved handle. As much as her grandmother entertained, Hannah had known it would get good use.

"It looks great, Barb," said Lynn. Hannah watched her mother stand up from the swing, raise her eyebrows, and make strong eye contact with the rest of the family.

"I'll grab the plates," her dad said, straightening his ball cap. "Emily, why don't you get the ice cream?"

Suddenly, the porch cleared, leaving Hannah and her grandfather alone on the swing. The exit had clearly been planned, because at the last minute, Emily turned back to Hannah and mouthed, "*Sorry.*"

*So that's what this is,* Hannah realized. *An ambush.* She felt the muscles in her throat tighten. She didn't like to be taken by surprise.

"Two days, huh?" her grandfather said solemnly.

"Yes, sir," she started. "But you don't need to worry. I broke my boots in just like you told me."

It was impossible to reassure a man who needed no reassurance. Arms crossed over his chest, he turned to her with his blue eyes, looking down at her the way she expected he'd looked down on so many of his subordinates over the years.

"It's not too late you know," he said. "Your dad knows the coach at UT. There are opportunities all over the place. Not just there."

Hannah bit the insides of her cheeks hard. Her grandfather had never encouraged his grandchildren to join the service. On the contrary, he'd almost downplayed the significance of his contributions to America. Hannah had to beg her father to tell her the truth: How, when he was a lieutenant, her grandfather had single-handedly saved his platoon from capture in North Korea. How he served as an Army liaison for the space program. How without him, Neil Armstrong might not have walked on the moon. He had medals that he wouldn't pin to his uniform, even though he'd earned them. To Gates Speer, wearing all the pins you'd earned was the antithesis of humility, and if he was anything, he was humble. That was the Speer way. Stay modest. Never claim credit. Avoid talk about politics and religion. Always smile demurely, even when inside, you're beaming with pride. Stay married for the long haul. Make pies. But couldn't her grandfather see?

As the second child, she'd spent her childhood watching Emily get into trouble for talking back, sneaking out, and getting bad grades. That was why Hannah had been so compliant: she'd learned early that it was easier to follow the rules than to break them. And the rules worked. If she studied hard, she aced the tests. If she went to bed on time, she felt refreshed in the morning, just like her parents promised. There was no need to rebel when following the rules worked in your favor every time. West Point's offer of admission was the direct result of all the success Hannah had accumulated by following the rules. Hannah was confident that she was making the right choice, and of all the people in her family, she'd assumed her grandfather would understand her decision. She'd expected him to look at her with joy and pride and respect. Instead, the worry in his eyes stretched across the swing, cutting Hannah like a knife.

"You don't think I can do it," she said, more of a statement than a question.

Her grandfather reached over and grabbed Hannah's hand. For the first time in her life, she realized that his skin was *old*— paper-thin, with veins pulsing purple below the surface. But his grip hadn't lost its strength: his long fingers wrapped around her palm and squeezed warmly.

"It's not a matter of capability. I know you *can* do it. I just don't think you should *have* to."

The cross on her necklace slid up and down its chain as Hannah prayed for the right words to land on her tongue. How could she make him understand?

When Hannah was in sixth grade, her grandparents had taken her to West Point for her grandfather's fortieth class reunion. They took a tour of campus, ate dinner in the mess hall, cruised the Hudson River on a party boat. Hannah watched white-haired men shake hands and retell old stories while their wives stood behind them, smiling with patience. Watching, Hannah decided she never wanted to stand on the sidelines as her husband told his stories. She wanted stories of her own. She loved her grandmother, but she didn't want to spend her life serving pies; she wanted to serve *people.*

Soon after that trip to New York, a neighbor in Austin had invited Hannah to church, and the preacher spoke at length about being "on mission" for God, helping the poor and defending the defenseless and living up to the call God had placed on your life. While he preached, Hannah felt a burning in her heart and remembered experiencing that same thrill at West Point. She took that sermon, that feeling, as a sign, and hid it away in her heart.

Though Hannah was new to faith, she knew that people who believed in the eternal could be unattached to outcomes in a way that perplexed people who didn't. The more you believed, the more you were willing to sacrifice. It was how someone like Mother Teresa could spend her life among lepers. It was how someone like Martin Luther King could risk his life marching for a dream. It's how Hannah could sense the concern in her grandfather's eyes and decide, in a moment, that she was okay if he never understood.

The general stood up from the swing and rubbed Hannah's

shoulder. "If you want to go to West Point, there's probably nothing I can say to stop you. But there are things I've endured that no woman should have to endure."

And then he rubbed his hands together, in anticipation of pie, as if he'd just had a conversation about the weather.

THE NIGHT BEFORE Reception Day, most incoming cadet candidates booked cheap hotel rooms for their families outside West Point's gates. But a member of the women's basketball team, Sarah Goodrich, had connected Hannah's family with a free place to stay on campus. Apparently, one of Sarah's professors, Colonel Mark Bennett, and his wife, Wendy, often hosted families for R-Day.

"The Bennetts live just a few hundred yards from the stadium," Sarah had told Hannah over the phone. "Wendy is amazing. You'll see. She's just like Martha Stewart. They're excited to have you."

As active-duty members of the military, West Point's faculty lived on campus in houses maintained by the Army. Quarters on other Army posts looked like prefabricated boxes, Hannah knew, because she'd visited her grandparents at Fort Leavenworth and Fort Knox, when he was still a lieutenant colonel. But West Point's housing matched its historic greatness.

At the center of campus, just in front of the granite barracks, stood a statue of George Washington, looking out over a green parade field known as the Plain. On the north side of the Plain, the superintendent's whitewashed mansion sat next to the commandant's home, a Tudor. Next to that was the massive redbrick mansion of the academic dean. Hovering behind the barracks, up a hill, was the towering Cadet Chapel, a reminder to Hannah that God was above it all. In another area of campus, there were tightly packed neighborhoods for junior faculty members, apartments for bachelor professors and TACs, short for "tactical officers." Within West Point's stone gates, a mini self-sufficient community existed solely to serve cadets.

The Bennetts lived in Lusk Area, a wooded neighborhood of high-ranking professors, comprising two-story redbrick homes, situated behind Lusk Reservoir and Michie Stadium. To Hannah, the homes looked like a string of paper dolls—each one a mirror image of the one that came before. American flags flew from each front stoop. Doorsteps displayed black and white placards indicating the name of the family who lived inside. *COL. Carter's Clan. Team Turner. The Bostwick Brood.* Hannah's parents sat in the front of the rental car, while she and Emily sat in the back, and when they pulled up to the right address, Hannah noticed the straightforward placard waiting in front of them. It simply read, *The Bennetts.*

Before they could unload their luggage from the car, the front door opened, and a petite woman with short brunette hair stepped outside. She wore dark jeans and a casual white button-up shirt with the sleeves rolled up, like she'd been washing dishes just before they'd arrived. As for makeup, Wendy Bennett didn't seem to wear much—mascara laced her lashes; a natural shade of mauve lipstick graced her lips. She smiled and waved.

"Come on in!" Wendy shouted. Her voice carried a slight Southern accent, the likes of which Hannah hadn't expected to hear this far north of the Mason-Dixon Line. "Y'all must be exhausted."

Wendy looked nothing like Martha Stewart, Hannah decided, but was a dead ringer for Sally Field, with the same bright eyes, high cheekbones, and easy smile that had made her America's sweetheart. But as soon as Hannah crossed the threshold, she realized why Sarah had made the comparison.

The Bennetts' house oozed comfort and gentility. Antiques graced every room, complemented by inviting upholstery. The house smelled like a cake was finishing in the oven, all sugar and butter and vanilla. Hannah caught herself breathing in the scent and feeling surprisingly at ease in this stranger's house.

In a flash of hospitality, Wendy took drink orders, showed Hannah's parents to a guest room, directed Hannah and Emily to another spare bedroom, and arranged three different kinds of cheese on a platter. Later, even Hannah's father, Bill, seemed relaxed, sipping a beer and helping Colonel Bennett tend the grill. Breathing in the scent of charcoal and grass in the Bennetts' well-manicured backyard, Hannah tried not to let her nerves about the following morning spoil her last night of summer. But every ten minutes, a wave of nausea crashed on her stomach, reminding her that the time was ticking away, bringing her closer to the end of one life and the beginning of another.

"How are you doing?" Wendy asked as Hannah refilled a glass of water at the sink. The cake was iced now, waiting to be cut. "Are you nervous?"

Hannah considered lying. She imagined shrugging her shoulders and pretending that everything was fine. But seeing the look of honest concern in Wendy's eyes, she exhaled instead.

"Completely," admitted Hannah. "I doubt I'll sleep at all tonight."

Wendy nodded, pursed her lips in a way that communicated deep understanding, then reached out and touched Hannah's arm, as if they'd known each another for much longer than a few hours.

"I want you to know that if you need *anything*—and I mean *anything*—all you have to do is ask," Wendy said. She grabbed a scrap piece of paper and wrote her phone number on it. "I know we just met. But I mean it."

"Okay," Hannah replied, receiving the paper from Wendy's hand. She folded it, tucked it in her pocket. "Thanks."

"Now," Wendy said, clapping her hands together. "How about cake?"

WHEN THEY LEFT the Bennetts' house the following morning, bellies full of homemade cinnamon rolls and strong coffee, the Speers walked across a stone bridge that traversed Lusk Reservoir and ended right at the entrance to Michie Stadium. Hannah shifted her black duffel bag on her shoulder, feeling the weight of everything she'd packed. It struck Hannah then that aside from bras and underwear, she hadn't brought any clothes. Unlike other college students who arrived to school with bedding and lamps and decor to "liven up" a dorm room, candidates for West Point showed up with nothing but the clothes on their back and faith that all of their needs would be met.

Ignoring the sound of yelling already coming from the other side, Hannah led her family beyond the stadium's stone facade, though its iron gates, and toward the beginning of the rest of her life.

## 4

*Summer 2000 // West Point, New York*

Dani lay prostrate on the ground, her finger wrapped around the trigger of an M16.

*Movies make this look easy,* she thought, feeling frustration crawl up her spine. Her elbows dug into the soft ground, along with a vertical pistol grip, creating a tripod for the weapon. She had to keep her knees, hips, and abs engaged to hold her body straight, low to the ground, and yet upright enough to see the target and shoot with accuracy. It was far harder than she'd anticipated. Any time she pulled the trigger, the kickback pummeled into her shoulder. She had bruises.

"*Miss,*" a voice said above her as the bullet whizzed past the target, wide by several inches. "It might help if you open your eyes, McNalley."

"And it might help if you shut your mouth, Nesmith," Dani replied.

She wiped her dirty hands against the legs of her green and brown combat uniform and let her platoon mate help her up. Eighteen, with dark hair buzzed completely to the scalp, Tim Nesmith had quickly become Dani's favorite person in their platoon, and one of the few reasons she hadn't quit. Had she been attracted to the all-American look, Dani might have had a crush on him. But she'd seen him pee in the woods more times than she could count, which meant that Tim had moved firmly into the friend zone. During breaks, Tim would lounge against the trunk of a tree, in the shade. He spent half the time sleeping; during the other half, he and Dani drilled one another on the inane definitions they'd been told to memorize out of a book called *Bugle Notes*.

"Definition of leather."

Tim would pause before saying, "'If the fresh skin of an animal, cleaned and' . . . oh God . . ."

"'Divested . . . ,'" Dani would hint.

"'. . . divested of all hair, fat, and other . . . uh . . . extraneous matter . . . be immersed . . .'" Tim would groan, rolling over onto his stomach and pummeling the ground with his fist.

But if Tim was horrible at memorizing useless trivia, he more than made up for it with the kind of outdoorsy knowledge that was completely foreign to Dani. When orienteering, Tim naturally knew which direction was north. A week earlier, when their platoon had prepared to walk through a concrete bunker called the *House of Tears*, Tim had shown Dani how to tighten her gas mask.

"Don't worry," he'd whispered, ensuring that their platoon leader didn't hear him talking. "It's just tear gas."

*Just* tear gas? Dani had looked at him like he had three heads. That was like saying the flu was *just* a virus.

Every person in the platoon had lined up with their hand on the shoulder of the person in front of them, like elephants linking trunks to tails. When Tim placed his hand on Dani's shoulder, he'd squeezed it twice, as if to say, *You've got this.*

As soon as they were inside and told to remove their masks, a stinging sensation exploded into Dani's nose and mouth and eyes, clawing at her insides. Water, mucus, and sweat poured out of every orifice imaginable, like the tear gas was somehow melting her face. Not a second too soon, a door at the front of the room had opened, and the platoon had filed out quickly into the fresh air, all hacking and coughing and spitting into the grass.

"Wave your—*cough*—arms!" Tim had shouted at Dani, windmilling his arms through the air. She'd followed his instruction, mostly because she didn't know what else to do, and soon, it seemed the motion had circulated fresh oxygen over her body. Snot covered her upper lip and tears ran down her cheeks, but surprisingly, she was laughing. They all were. This, she was learning, was what West Pointers called "type two" fun. It wasn't fun while you were having it; it was fun later, when you could look back on it.

After they'd recovered, Dani asked Tim how he knew to circle his arms through the air. He'd just shrugged.

"Seemed like the right thing to do," he'd said.

That was the way it was with Tim. Everything came naturally to him. He never seemed flustered with the training, and not once had Dani seen him lose his cool or bite the insides of his cheeks to keep from showing emotion. The insides of her cheeks, however, were a disintegrating mess of flesh. She'd chewed them so hard in the last three weeks, trying to hold her tongue, that she was afraid she'd have a hole in her cheek by the time Beast Barracks was over.

They switched positions, Dani holding the clipboard while Tim took the prone on the ground. He shot three times in quick succession and hit the target in a perfect isosceles triangle, right in the center.

"Show-off." Dani took the weapon from him and went back to the ground, ignoring the growing pain in her lower back. It felt like her hip might snap out of its socket. But she knew better than to complain. Last week, the only other girl in Alpha Company had fallen out of a two-mile run with what she'd said was a sprained ankle. Soft in the face and around her middle, the girl looked genuinely in pain to Dani, but she'd watched as the men in her platoon rolled their eyes and groaned, as if she were faking the injury to slow them all down. The girl had quit three days later, packing up her gear and heading back to Arizona. Dani didn't blame the girl for quitting any more than she'd blamed the guys for rolling their eyes. If you wanted to be comfortable, you shouldn't have come to West Point. But now, the lone female in their platoon of twenty, Dani was highly aware that she was being watched. Any misstep, any wince, would confirm her status as the weak link.

The morning she'd reported to West Point, Dani's body felt perfectly ready for any challenge, bolstered by a rush of adrenaline. Through the night, Dominic had punched her in the side, annoyed by her relentless tossing and turning. But Dani didn't care. Dominic would be able to go back to sleep this afternoon. She, on the other hand, wouldn't get much sleep for the next six weeks.

The McNalleys had left the hotel an hour later, Dani carrying a black duffel bag over her shoulder, stuffed with everything that had been on the short packing list. Sarah Goodrich had told her to pack extra bandages, blister pads, moleskin, anti-friction gel, and foot powder, saying they might come in handy. Dani had shivered imagining how her feet might look at the end of Cadet Basic Training, torn up, blistered, and bloodied. But thankfully, the moment she shivered with fear, a fresh rush of energy soared through her veins. She could feel the thrill in her neck, her fingers, her toes. Her abs tightened. It was amazing how the body could sense impending danger and release a chemical to help carry you through the fear. At times, the body was smarter than the mind.

Her hair slicked back into a dark bun, black Nike sneakers looking sharp against her mocha legs, Dani walked through the gates to the stadium.

As they found their way to an area overlooking the fifty-yard line, the McNalleys joined other white families, black families, an Asian family, and even a few families that weren't speaking English. Most boys had preemptively shaved their heads, but several had grown their hair out long and bushy, knowing that at some point in the next few hours a barber would shear it off. Once they found their seats along the aluminum bleachers, Dani leaned forward and pressed her elbows into her knees. Everything in her body was on extreme alert—like she was about to run a marathon. Instead, she had to sit still and wait. On . . . *what*? An announcement? Someone to start yelling at her to do push-ups?

Just before the welcoming ceremony began, a tall blond woman had appeared beside Dani's mother. She was beautiful, with a sharp chin, brilliant blue eyes, and a Southern accent as smooth as Dani had ever heard. Behind her, there were two blond girls that looked like twins and an older man with a graying mustache, wearing a burnt-orange University of Texas ball cap. The woman pointed at the aluminum bleachers and smiled.

"Can we slide in?"

"Of course!" Dani's mother said. "Scoot down, Dani."

"It's so quiet," the woman said to Dani's mother as her family slid onto the row. "You'd think we're at a funeral."

Harper McNalley laughed out loud. "*My* funeral. Still can't believe my baby is going to college. *This* college."

"Is she your youngest?" the woman asked.

"No." Dani's mother pointed down the line to Dominic, who pushed his glasses up his nose. "Dominic will be a sophomore in high school this fall. Dani's our oldest."

"Oh, well then, you'll still have one at home," the woman said. "I'm about to have an empty nest."

Soon, Harper and this woman were chatting like old friends. Dani sometimes hated the fact that her mother had never met a stranger. They could be standing in line at the grocery store, and before they'd checked out, Harper would have a list of prayer requests from the person in front of her and the one behind her. Dani, on the other hand, would have been content to stay quiet, waiting. It wasn't like she would ever see these people again. Then again, she thought, there weren't going to be that many other girls in the class of 2004.

Dani locked eyes with her new classmate, and together they rolled their eyes at their respective mothers. A beat passed as the two memorized each other's faces. Without a doubt, she was a natural beauty: tall, with dirty-blond hair and dark blue eyes. Her face carried a carefree expression that would have filled the room with warmth, if they weren't sitting outside. And most notably, she looked comfortable in her own skin, which seemed like a commendable feat of bravery to Dani, considering the faint sound of yelling coming from the other side of the stadium.

"We're from Austin," the girls' mother said, answering Harper's latest question. "I'm Lynn Speer. And that's my husband down there with the mustache. Bill. Our daughter Emily, she goes to the University of Texas. And this is our daughter Hannah."

The beautiful girl extended a long hand toward Dani. They shook and shared a sigh of anxiety.

"Do you play a sport?" Hannah's mother asked. "Hannah's here to play basketball."

Dani's eyebrows crunched together in shock. "Really? Me too." *What are the odds*? She shifted forward excitedly on the bench. "What's your position?"

"Post," Hannah offered with a chuckle. "I actually thought I recognized you. Coach Jankovich sent me a newspaper article when you signed. You're from Ohio, right?"

In the quiet moment that passed, all the plays they could run together moved through Dani's mind. Hannah was so tall and

Dani so short; there were a lot of ways they could maneuver around another team's defense. They were going to be unstoppable! Dani was surprised to find that that little connection—that tiny, imperceptible moment of contact—had calmed her nerves. Though it was unspoken, Dani knew that she'd just made her first friend. It didn't matter that she didn't know much about this girl. They were going to be on the same basketball team, and that was enough.

"I need to get your phone number," Harper McNalley said to Lynn Speer. "I have a feeling you and I might need a support group."

She reached in her purse for a piece of paper and a pen, but before they could exchange information, a lone snare drum began to beat.

"Here we go," said Dominic, pushing his glasses up his nose again. "The show begins."

As a group of five cadets in uniform marched through a stadium tunnel and into the stands, the entire crowd went silent, listening to the sharp *tap, tap, tap* of their feet against the aluminum bleachers. All five cadets looked identical, stiff from the top of their hats to the bottom of their shoes. They wore starched white pants and crisp white overcoats, cinched at the waist by white belts with gold buckles. Suddenly, everyone in the stands seemed shabbily dressed by comparison. An officer in a navy uniform stepped forward to a microphone.

"Ladies and gentlemen . . . friends and family. Welcome to the U.S. Military Academy at West Point."

A collective sigh released from the crowd into the air as his voice echoed across the stadium, toward the reservoir. Then they all held their breath again.

"Today, you embark on the six-week journey known as Cadet Basic Training. CBT is rigorous and it is demanding. It will require every bit of personal fortitude, discipline, and determination you can muster. The people next to you—your family and friends—have helped you to get this far. But in just a few moments, you will say goodbye, and you will be going on alone."

Someone sniffled. In her periphery, Dani saw Hannah's father wipe his eyes. West Point's first captain, a senior who held the highest rank in the Corps of Cadets, introduced the rest of the CBT leadership, called Cadre. There were a few more speeches. And then, the officer who had started it all walked back to the microphone.

"Parents, family, and friends, please prepare your final good-byes. Candidates, you will be moving out in ninety seconds."

The shock of that statement seemed to hit everyone in the audience at once. A beat passed and they stood up to exchange hugs and tears and goodbyes, grasping for the seconds even as they disappeared into the past.

Dani felt the pressure of her mother's arms around her body, the softness of her father's lips against her cheek, the punch of her brother's fist against her shoulder.

"Go get 'em, D," Dominic said.

And then, with no opportunity to look back, she'd followed Hannah and several hundred other eighteen-year-olds down the stairs and onto the football field. They proceeded to the fifty-yard line and waited for their first instruction, their parents standing behind them watching in silence. In that moment, Dani's back stiffened, and her neck grew tall and straight. A cloud hovered above, threatening to pour rain on their heads.

"Cadet candidates," a cadre shouted from beside her. "Move your bags to your left hand. And move."

IN THE HOURS, days, and weeks after that moment, so much had happened, Dani could barely remember it all. In the first hour, they'd issued uniforms, inspected everyone's body for tattoos, and led every candidate through a barbershop, where the boys had their heads sheared like sheep. Hair covered the floor like in an image Dani had seen at the Holocaust Memorial Museum, and she'd fought the urge to gag. By the afternoon, they'd taught her to salute, to stand at attention, to march. By the time the sun had set, Dani didn't know if it had been six hours or six days since she'd said goodbye. The mediocre sleep she got every night felt like naps in one never-ending day. Cadre quickly started calling Dani "Head-lights," simply because her eyes were permanently stretched wide, always on high alert. And her eyes weren't the only thing that had changed. Within the first week, she was speaking an entirely new language.

*CBT* stood for "Cadet Basic Training." If someone "smoked you," it meant he beat you in some kind of competition. "Racking" was sleeping. To "police" your area meant to clean up. But all that language was for the future, because as a plebe, Dani was only allowed to speak one of four responses:

*Yes, sir.*

*No, sir.*

*No excuse, sir.*

*Sir, I do not understand.*

The boys looked infantile, their heads shaved to the skull. The girls were scattered among the boys, hard to pick out since they were so few. The teammate she'd met on R-Day, Hannah Speer, had been assigned to a different company, and even though Dani kept her eyes peeled—*Headlights!*—she hadn't seen Hannah once. Dani wondered if the girl from Texas had already quit, but hoped she hadn't. When Dani felt the urge to give up, when she felt pain growing in her body, she imagined Hannah out there facing these same obstacles and tried her best to be strong.

"YOU'VE GOT TO breathe, McNalley," Tim Nesmith instructed her. He bent down in a low squat and repositioned the rifle to better aim it at the target. "Breathe in. And when you breathe out, right at the end of your breath—when you have nothing left— that's when you pull. Keep your eyes open. Trust yourself. You can do this."

As she found her position, Dani realized that his instructions— Breathe. Give it all you've got. Trust.—were basically what she'd been doing her whole life. But if that was the case, why couldn't she hit this stupid target?

Back on the ground, Dani inhaled, feeling her chest expand. The air smelled of spent ammunition, a combination of tin, mud, and grass. She exhaled, kept her eyes open, squeezed the trigger, and watched a rip the size of a quarter open in the outer ring of the target.

"I hit it!" she yelled, standing up, exultant.

Tim offered her a high five, and they laughed together until they saw their platoon leader, Mike Wilkerson, approaching them from down the field. Wilkerson was a Cow—West Point speak for a junior. A former football player who'd quit after his first season, he had a thick neck, big ears, and hair cut so short, he looked bald. For the last three weeks, he'd been staring over Dani's shoulder, constantly hazing her and refusing her any moment of rest. Before Wilkerson spoke, Dani already knew that he was coming for her. Her head, neck, and shoulders ached from the strain of feigning confidence.

"New Cadet McNalley," Wilkerson said as he stopped in front of them. "Recite 'Duty, Honor, Country.'"

Dani swallowed. Tim had worked hard on this one. And listening to him repeat it over and over again, she was confident she'd memorized it, too.

"'Duty, honor, country,'" she began. "'These three—'"

"Incorrect," the cadre spat. "Not *these three*. *Those* three. Attention to detail, New Cadet McNalley. Twenty push-ups, and then start again."

Dani went to the ground, performed the push-ups with ease, then stood, breathless, and began again.

"'Duty, honor, country. *Those* three ... uh—'"

"I don't recall General Douglas MacArthur stuttering," Wilkerson spat. "Forty this time. Then start again."

Beads of sweat gathered along the top of Dani's cotton under-wear after she completed the push-ups. There was nothing she could do except try again until either she got it right or Wilker-son had mercy. He seemed to be enjoying her discomfort, even as he looked impressed by her ability to complete forty push-ups without pause. Closing her eyes for a moment, Dani tried to apply Tim's instructions for hitting the target. She inhaled, exhaled, and started again.

"'Duty, honor, country. Those three hallowed words reverently dictate what you ought to be, what you can be, and what you *will* be.'" She paused, then stared Wilkerson in the eyes. "'They are your rallying points: to build courage when courage seems to fail; to regain faith when there seems to be little cause for faith; to create hope when hope becomes forlorn.'"

When she finished, Dani held her breath. Wilkerson stood in front of her with a look of shock and admiration on his face. He raised his eyebrows.

"Wow," he said. "Nice job, McNalley. Not to sound racist, but normally black kids can't memorize shit."

Dani bit her cheeks harder than she ever had before, the tinny taste of blood spreading across her tongue. Later, she would cycle through all the things she wished she'd said to him—*What, so you've met* all *black kids?* or better, *And what about you, Wilkerson, how'd you do with plebe knowledge?*

But plebes were only allowed to speak one of four responses. So Dani lifted her chin, set her jaw, and chose the only one that applied.

"Sir, I do not understand."

Wilkerson offered her a half smile. "You did good. I'm giving you a compliment."

Dani's body went hot with rage. Most often, racism was expressed in small, imperceptible movements of distrust: in glances, in grabbing purses tighter, in moving to the other side of the street. Rarely was she confronted with a blatant admission that someone assumed she would be less capable, simply because of the color of her skin. She seethed. But thankfully, before she could react, the upperclassman moved on.

"I can't believe he said that," Tim said. "Are you okay?"

"Yeah," Dani answered firmly. "I'm fine."

Once again, she knew she couldn't complain. Not about her pain. Not about what Wilkerson had said. The look on Tim's face was one of compassion and sadness. He obviously understood that there was a lot she wasn't saying. But there was no use in dwelling on Wilkerson's ignorance. She remembered the words her mother had spoken once when she was younger: "*They're ignorant, Dani. So they think you're different? They're right! You are different. You're better.*"

"I think I'm ready to shoot again," she said with confidence.

"I should say so." Tim handed her back the weapon. "Let's go, soldier."

Dani found her spot on the ground and shot the target straight in the center three times in a row. This time, with her eyes wide open.

5

*Fall 2000 // West Point, New York*

Twelve thirty on a misty afternoon in early September, four thousand cadets gathered in the mess hall, eating pierogies and passing plates of lemon-pepper chicken counterclockwise around the tables. Avery Adams rolled her head from side to side, trying to work out the tension that had appeared overnight. Plebes weren't allowed to speak at meals, and since they only had fifteen minutes to jam food into their mouths before jetting off to classes, everyone kept their head down, stuffing their face as quickly as possible. It was disgusting. Like they were a bunch of farm animals at a trough.

In August, all of the new cadets that had survived basic training had put on their as-for-class uniforms and joined the Corps of Cadets for the regular academic year. Training would commence again next summer, but until then, they were students. Writing assignments replaced weaponry. Homework took over hazing as the heaviest burden, and every weekend, the campus came alive with school spirit for the Army football team, which still hadn't won a game. Avery dreaded the uphill walk to Michie Stadium, where she was forced to stand and freeze while the quarterback threw interceptions for two hours straight. Games were mandatory fun, and she hated every second.

Avery caught herself staring at the bespectacled cadet seated in front of her, whose face was as pale as the white uniform shirt he was wearing. He ate so fast, it was a wonder he had time to breathe. Shaking her head in disgust, she looked back down at her plate and sighed.

Six months ago, she'd screamed and celebrated, having received her acceptance letter. The summer had introduced her to camouflage, ruck marching, orienteering through the woods, and the joys of memorizing useless trivia. Thanks to all the running her father had forced her to do leading up to R-Day, she'd quickly risen to the top of her platoon, scoring the highest possible marks on the Army Physical Fitness Test. In separate two-minute drills she could complete seventy-five push-ups and a hundred sit-ups. And when they sent her off for the two-mile run, Avery always returned within thirteen minutes flat. She hadn't just met West Point's standards; she'd exceeded them.

The guys in her platoon had wavered between seeming annoyed that a girl had outperformed them and grateful to have her strength among their ranks. Avery had seen some of the other girls in other platoons. There were the butch ones, who'd cut their hair into pixie-like styles before R-Day to prove that they were serious. Then there were the unathletic ones, who failed to keep up with the guys and so immediately lost their respect. Girls who were pretty *and* athletic were the fewest and farthest between. For that reason, Avery knew that her stock was high, and the attention gave her a rush. Every sideways glance, every prohibited flirtation, helped her breathe just a little bit easier. She was wanted, and that made her feel powerful.

Of course, she couldn't fully savor the extra attention. West Point followed a strict "ninety-degree" rule—if two people of the opposite sex were in a room together, the door had to be open at a ninety-degree angle. It was so antiquated, so ridiculous, and yet, everyone seemed to follow the rule with religious precision. If a male and female cadet were found together with the door closed, it could mean long hours of walking back and forth along cadet area in full regalia. Marching tours were West Point's favorite mode of punishment. Her TAC had explained that the rules existed to keep them focused on their academic and military instruction. To Avery, it all felt like a waste of her college experience.

But sure enough, once the academic year began, her schedule grew so hectic, she didn't have time to worry about West Point's outdated rules of decorum and chastity. The Corps of Cadets reported every morning at 0630 for formation, standing at attention in silence, watching their breath enter the freezing morning air, four thousand miniature clouds. West Point required plebes to take at least twenty-two hours of classes, meaning that Avery had eight courses to keep up with, including chemistry, Spanish, calculus, and a class in the Department of Military Instruction. Plebes weren't allowed to talk as they crossed campus between classes, and she had to address every upperclassman she passed with the proper rank and greeting. Her head moved on a constant swivel.

"Beat Rutgers, ma'am," Avery said to a Firstie who passed her way, naming Army's next opponent, as required.

An upperclassman who happened to be in her company, G-4, whose mascot was a gator, walked by her, and she quickly stammered, "Go gators, Sergeant." She moved past him in case she'd used the wrong rank. Was he a sergeant? Or a sir?

In high school, Avery had regularly worn blush and foundation, but West Point prohibited her from hiding her flaws, even the ones on the surface. Female plebes could wear light tinted moisturizer, but the standard for what constituted too much makeup was subjective and judged mainly by men. She'd risked concealing the pimples on her chin and the dark circles under her eyes only once. On that same day, she'd watched an upperclassman force a plebe who'd denied having makeup on her face to wipe her eyes on a towel. Smudges of beige and black streaked across the white fibers, and the upperclassman shook his head three times. Rumor had it, he'd reported the girl to the Honor Committee for lying. Avery had immediately rushed to the nearest bathroom and washed her face with harsh hand soap, wiping her eyes with a rough paper towel. If she was going to leave West Point, it was going to be on her own terms. Not because she'd used a little Maybelline.

That afternoon, Avery's turn had come up to be the "minute caller"—a job she'd been dreading since her first day at West Point. Ten minutes before lunch formation, she'd taken her place alone in the hallway announcing a list of memorized information, speaking loudly, slowly, and in a low monotone, like a man, so every cadet on the hall could hear her. Any slip-up or stumble would draw unwanted attention, and so Avery had studied the script for nearly an hour before stepping into the hallway and beginning.

"Attention all cadets . . . there are . . . *five minutes* . . . until assembly . . . for lunch formation."

"Don't mess up, Adams," an upperclassman had taunted, prowling around her like a predator.

"The uniform is . . . *as for class* . . ."

"Oh. I see you smiling. Don't slip up. I'll make you start over."

"For lunch we are having . . . lemon pepper chicken . . . pierogies . . . and Gatorade . . . I repeat . . . *Five minutes remaining* . . ."

Cadets underwent daily inspections for shined shoes and polished brass buckles. Upperclassmen could stop and check that her uniform was properly "dressed off," meaning tucked into her wool pants at a perfect forty-five-degree angle. At random intervals during the week, plebes were required to sort, fold, and deliver laundry to the upperclassmen in their company. In addition to all of her coursework, Avery had to memorize the names and room numbers of more than one hundred people, in order to properly deliver laundry and avoid hours of unnecessary hazing.

"Do I LOOK like a *female*, Cadet Darby?" she'd heard a Cow shouting at a plebe last night. He'd held up a gray skirt. "This isn't even my SIZE!"

To complete all of her military duties and not neglect her homework, Avery had taken to staying up far past taps. When her roommate, a girl from California named Nadine, complained that the light was going to get them in trouble, Avery had started using a small flashlight instead.

Streaming through the darkness, the small spotlight shined on chemistry equations while Nadine snored on top of her cot. Avery's notebooks filled with little lists, outlining her days in fifteen-minute increments, as if, by scheduling each minute, all the tasks she'd been assigned could possibly be completed. Meanwhile, she found herself daydreaming about her friends back home, friends who were probably sleeping late, skipping class, and attending parties on the weekends just because they *could*.

When Avery considered adding practices, games, and a hectic basketball travel schedule to her already-packed daily itinerary, it made her want to be sick. Last week, the team's captain, Sarah Goodrich, had sent out an e-mail inviting all the new recruits to an "optional" practice that clearly wasn't optional, since she'd couched *optional* in quotation marks. And when Avery wrote the practice on her calendar, she realized that something was going to have to give. What, she hadn't decided. Perhaps she'd have to stop sleeping altogether.

Her decision to come to West Point was beginning to feel like an exercise in pride that had bitten her harshly in the ass. Who *chooses* to enroll in a prison? It was a cruel bait and switch, to tell prospective students West Point was prestigious, only to treat them like shit once they got there.

The mess hall filled with a cacophony of sliding chairs, stacked plates, heavy feet leaving for class. Avery looked at her plate, still full of food. How had fifteen minutes already passed?

"That's it, plebes," her table leader, John Collins, said. He checked his watch, then put his fork down on his plate and gave Avery a wink. "Time to get your ass to class."

LATER THAT AFTERNOON, Avery made her way to the Holleder Center, a large complex that housed coaches' offices and a basketball arena for the men's and women's teams. She arrived twenty minutes early, hoping to shoot a few baskets before the rest of the team showed up. She'd expected the locker room to be empty, but when she turned the corner, Avery found herself face-to-face with a girl who was standing in front of a locker, completely naked.

"Oh God." Avery averted her eyes. "I'm so sorry."

"It's all good," the girl answered. If Avery wasn't mistaken, the girl chuckled, apparently amused by Avery's blushing cheeks.

Dropping her hand from her eyes, Avery tried to act cool, but it was hard to ignore how stunning this girl was. She had smooth brown skin and dark freckles across her face that looked like a map of the constellations. With a small waist and muscle definition, she looked like she could be on the cover of *Sports Illustrated*. Avery felt suddenly mediocre by comparison.

"You should see your face right now," the girl laughed as she put deodorant under her armpits.

"No. It's no big deal." Avery found her way to an open locker. "I just wasn't expecting anyone to be here."

The girl smiled wide. "I'm Dani."

"Avery," she replied. "So you're here to play basketball?"

"Oh, because I'm black?"

"No . . . ," Avery said slowly. She laughed. "I assumed you're playing basketball because you're in the women's locker room before basketball practice."

Dani smiled like Avery had just passed a test she hadn't signed up to take. "That's good detective work. Good *attention to detail.*"

"I guess that means you're a plebe too."

"I consider slitting my wrists most nights, so yes."

They laughed, then dressed in silence for a while. But soon, Avery could no longer handle the quiet. It was hard to admit, but she knew it was true. After nearly ten weeks at West Point, Avery was desperate for a friend.

"So what position do you play?"

"Point guard. You?"

In that moment, it felt as though a hot knife had sliced through Avery's gut. She busied herself fixing her ponytail, hoping that Dani wouldn't notice her disappointment.

"What?" Dani asked.

But Avery didn't answer, because right at that moment, another group of women flooded through the doors, and Avery took that opportunity to exit into the gymnasium.

*It's all right,* Avery thought, trying to coach herself as she walked out onto the court and started to stretch. *So what? So Coach Jankovich recruited two point guards. Who's to say she's any good?*

THREE MINUTES INTO their "optional" practice, Dani had made it abundantly clear to everyone in the gymnasium that the team was only going to need one point guard. Time and time again, when they went after the same ball, Avery ended up on the floor, while Dani sprinted upcourt for an easy layup. The girl was fast and nimble. She dribbled the ball like it was tied to the center of her palm with an invisible string. Dani couldn't have been taller than five foot four, but somehow, even her petite frame worked to her advantage. She kept her center of gravity low, fooling even the most seasoned defenders. Worst of all, the girl was obnoxiously confident, quickly aligning herself with Sarah Goodrich and the other Firsties, throwing high fives and patting butts, as if they'd all known each other for years.

"What's her deal?" Avery said breathlessly to a new teammate, Hannah, when they'd both taken a moment to get water. Hannah Speer was also a plebe, and impossibly tall. When she looked at Avery like she didn't know what she meant, Avery jutted her chin out in Dani's general direction. "McNalley. She's been showing off this whole time."

Hannah just shrugged. "Everyone wants to make a good first impression. Can't blame her for that."

Avery found herself retreating to the bench for water more often than normal, simply to gather the emotional wherewithal to continue. There's nothing worse than believing you're talented, only to encounter a greater talent. And as the practice went on, Avery grew more and more despondent. Her performance went from lackluster to awkward, from awkward to embarrassing. And just when she thought things couldn't get worse, she looked up into the stands to see a thin woman sitting in the shadows.

Even from so far away, Avery could see the whites of the coach's eyes, trained on the court. Her long and slender fingers, wrapped around a pencil, were writing on a page on her clipboard.

The NCAA had strict rules about preseason practices—coaches weren't supposed to be at practices until the regular season started. That's why Sarah Goodrich had organized the practice instead of the coaches, and why she'd strategically added the word *optional* in the e-mail. But staring up at the coach in the stands, Avery's ears turned red with frustration. So it was an ambush. This "optional" practice was, in fact, an exhibition.

AFTER PRACTICE, THE locker room filled with steam. The black and gold striped carpet hid years of sweat and smelled dank with age. Maybe the girls were tired, or, Avery thought, maybe they'd noticed Coach Jankovich in the stands, too, because other than the sound of water spraying out of the showerheads, it was quiet. Surely the coach would take into account the fact they'd been at Basic Training all summer—naturally, they were all a little rusty. Avery had nearly convinced herself that everything would be okay—that she would have another chance to prove her skill—when the locker room door creaked open.

Coach Jankovich walked in, wearing a navy pantsuit and black high heels. A rush of cold air entered the locker room with her. Without speaking a word, she taped two white pieces of paper to the cinder-block wall by the door, and then left the way she came—in silence.

THE GIRLS STOOD like statues, each afraid to be the first to speak.

"Well I'll look," said Avery. Ignoring the growing dread in her stomach, she walked to the wall as if she didn't give a damn and stared at the papers, covered in Coach Jankovich's barely legible handwriting. "You've got to be kidding me."

"What?" asked Hannah.

At that moment, Dani walked out of the shower wrapped in a towel, surrounded by a cloud of steam. She wiped the inside of her ear with her pointer finger. "What's going on?" she asked.

"They're . . ." Hannah had walked up behind Avery and was staring at the pages, her voice full of shock. ". . . rosters."

Avery laughed sardonically, turned to grab her gym bag, and shook her head at Dani, who stood stunned in the middle of the room.

"Glad to know I survived Beast for *this shit.*"

The two pages fluttered as Avery blew past them and out the door. The first page had "JV" written at the top, and below it, a long column of names. The other page said "Varsity" and listed only one.

BY EARLY OCTOBER, the trees on campus had turned from green to orange, like the whole place had been lit up in flames. At breakfast, Avery took her seat at her table and stabbed at her eggs with murderous rage.

"Someone piss in your pancakes, princess?"

The upperclassman at the head of the table, John Collins, offered her a wide smile. A Spanish major with green eyes and wavy black hair, Collins was handsome, funny, and extremely bored it seemed, since he was surrounded by a table of plebes who weren't allowed to talk.

"No excuse, sir." Avery faked a smile, took an oversized bite of eggs.

But she did have an excuse. She had a million excuses.

After the first few varsity basketball games, Dani McNalley had become something of a celebrity on campus. Avery didn't need a crystal ball to predict how her career as an NCAA athlete was going to unfold. Dani was going to secure every possible minute of playing time for the season—maybe even all four years. Avery would ride the bench.

She felt trapped, like Coach Jankovich had promised her a place on the team, only to abandon her to the sidelines. In light of her rejection, everything about West Point chafed against her. She had to check the hall for upperclassmen before darting from her dorm room. Plebes were forced to walk like Pac-Man, in straight lines, only taking right-angled turns. You could spot plebes at West Point, walking along the perimeter of the hallways, squaring off with their eyes straight ahead, trying not to be noticed. By contrast, upperclassmen walked wherever they wanted and spoke freely among themselves. It was enough to drive Avery crazy, watching them flaunt their freedom. Every time someone yelled at her, the voice inside Avery's head repeated their instructions with an added layer of sarcasm.

"Adams, move to the wall!"

*You move to the wall,* she would rant in her inner dialogue.

"New Cadet, stop right there and recite the 'Alma Mater.'"

*You recite the fucking alma mater!*

Instead, she'd bite her tongue and do as she was told, allowing the anger to boil inside of her, unsure of when it might explode.

Avery placed her fork on her plate.

"Okay," Collins announced suddenly, breaking the silence.

"New rules. As long as you use your radio, you can talk. New Cadet Willis," Collins said, addressing the plebe who sat across from Avery midbite. "Your call sign is Trojan, because you'll never need one."

Avery fought back a laugh. He went down the table, assigning nicknames. When he got to Avery, he stopped, looked her up and down. "Adams. Your name is About-Face, because all you ever do is sulk, and if it's the last thing I do, I'm going to get you to smile."

"*Chhhhh*—ah, Eagle for About-Face. Come in, About-Face," he started, pretending to hold a radio in his hand. "What's your twenty?"

Avery rolled her eyes.

"*Chhhh*—sorry, About-Face, I'm not getting that. Check your radio."

With her hand curled around an imaginary radio, Avery decided to play along.

"*Chhhh*—roger that, Eagle, I'm downwind of Trojan. Smells like he's looking for a place to defecate, sir. Over and out."

The table erupted in laughter, Trojan included. Satisfied, Avery offered a flirtatious wink to Collins, then picked up her fork and kept eating.

MIDTERMS SWALLOWED WHOLE weeks of October. Cadets attended nonstop review sessions and banged out sixteen-page research papers, and a chemistry exam nearly flattened Avery with its intensity. When she wasn't at basketball practice with the JV team, Avery was buried beneath her books, trying desperately to stay afloat. Her GPA was a sorry 3.2, and with that, Avery was happy. Then all the leaves detached from their branches, glittering through the air like falling gold. They'd gathered in rotting piles on the ground before Avery could appreciate the beauty of their death.

After that, campus went gray. People had warned her about this: during the winter, West Point was a depressing palette of black and white. Charcoal river, stone buildings and roads, slate uniforms, cloudy skies. Barren and lifeless, the whole place felt like Siberia, and the thin wool coat Avery had been issued over the summer suddenly didn't stand a chance against the wind chill.

"Attention all cadets . . . there are *four minutes* . . ."

"Today's uniform . . . is *battle dress uniform* . . ."

As the weeks passed, Avery's life fell into a rhythm that, if not enjoyable, was at least predictable. At practice, Dani McNalley barely spoke to Avery. Instead, that girl spoke exclusively to upperclassmen—as though if she separated herself from the plebes, she would no longer be one. Sarah Goodrich and her friends adopted Dani into their fold, and had even invited Dani to some *Bible study* they attended, an invitation Avery would never receive, but would have liked to turn down.

She tried her best to ignore her growing jealousy by taking long runs around campus whenever she had a spare thirty minutes. The only reprieve from the madness had become her twice-daily meals with Collins and his imaginary radio. West Point explicitly prohibited plebes from dating upperclassmen, but somehow, the fact that he was off-limits made Collins that much more attractive. By mid-November, she'd moved to the seat directly next to his, letting her leg brush up against his under the table. That went on for a few days, until he responded, clutching his hand around her upper thigh. She felt her eyes roll back in her head at the warmth of his touch.

It was innocent, she told herself. A game she knew she could win.

ON THE SECOND Tuesday in November, the day before they left for Thanksgiving break, Avery sat on a cold metal chair outside of Coach Jankovich's office, waiting her turn. The coach had scheduled one-on-one meetings with her players, called "MSTEs," short for "midseason team evaluations," which made Avery roll her eyes so hard, she thought they might disconnect from her brain. It was clear that Jankovich had worked hard to create an acronym of her own, as if West Point hadn't already filled their lives with an alphabet soup of abbreviations.

Fifteen minutes after Avery's scheduled MSTE, Coach Jankovich's office door opened, and out came Dani McNalley, holding a folded piece of paper. She made eye contact with Avery, her eyes full and intense—like two headlights on the front of a car, barreling through the night. Avery couldn't quite decipher whether Dani was angry or sad. It didn't matter.

"Adams," Coach Jankovich barked from inside her office. "You're up."

Inside, the office felt cold and lifeless. Empty plastic water bottles and stacks of paperwork covered her desk, unattended and unorganized. *No way this place would pass inspection,* Avery thought. It was a wonder Coach Jankovich still had a job at a place like West Point. Her players had to keep their beds made with hospital corners, their mirrors devoid of a single speck of dust, and yet, her office looked like a tornado had just passed through.

"Take a seat," the coach said. Her dark brown hair, streaked with white, gave her the appearance of a skunk, and for some reason, Avery suddenly felt on edge, like Coach Jankovich had caught her doing something illegal and couldn't wait to show off all of her evidence. Shifting in her seat, Avery opened her mouth, but was cut off before she could say a word.

"This is your midseason report. You can see here, you're fifty-two percent at the line. Not great. You've outpaced Hannah Speer and Lisa Johnson with your defensive rebounds, which isn't bad. But I think we both know you're not where you need to be. You had great stats in high school, but here, you've haven't exactly reached the right level of play."

Avery's body filled with heat, and she struggled to breathe, like a heavy cloud had formed in her chest.

"When I compare your stats with varsity, I mean . . . it's just impossible to compare." Coach Jankovich focused on the page in front of her, avoiding the eyes of her player. "For example, Dani McNalley hit seventy percent of her free throws."

Avery cleared her throat, trying to regain her confidence. "That's actually what I wanted to ask you about. Dani. I'd like a chance to play against her. I mean, she's great. I know that. But I've improved a lot since September. And I think if you gave me a shot, you'd be—"

"We don't reward players for being the most improved," Coach Jankovich replied. "We reward players for being the best."

"Okay," Avery said, swallowing the hurt. She'd never not been the best. The words that came next sounded foreign coming out of her mouth. "So what do I need to do?"

"Well, Avery, you just don't have the edge. And unfortunately, that's not something I can teach."

The hair on the back of her neck stood on end. Staring at this woman—this person who had convinced her that West Point was *the best option available*—Avery felt something deflate inside of her. "So that's it?"

Avery couldn't fight the tears any longer. "I'm sorry, but, if you're not going to give me a chance to play, why am I even here?"

Coach Jankovich crossed her arms over her chest and sighed. "To be frank, Avery, we assumed one of you would quit during basic training." She held out a tissue box, but Avery refused to take it from her. "I'm just being honest with you. With McNalley here I doubt you'll see much of the court. That's just the way it is. So you can come, participate in practice, and be part of the JV team. Or you can quit now, take a red shirt, and transfer to some other school, where you can play in a year or two. It's your choice."

The coach handed Avery the paper printout, then turned to look at her computer.

"Send in whoever's next."

AVERY EXPLODED OUT of the Holleder Center into the wintry air, breathless and angry. *We assumed one of you would quit.* Was that what she was to them? A backup plan? Not worth coaching? *You just don't have the edge.* What did that even mean?

Avery had ignored Hannah on the way out of the Holleder Center and ran back to cadet area, letting the wind freeze the tears on her cheeks. *It's just not enough.* That's what Coach J had said. And she was right. As fast as Avery was, there would always be someone faster. As pretty as she was, there would always be someone like Hannah, who was downright *angelic*. What was the point of trying to be good? She'd tried. And she was tired of trying.

When she found her way back to the barracks, Avery knew exactly what she was doing. It didn't matter that she was covered in sweat and tears and that she hadn't showered. His room was two floors above hers, she knew because she'd delivered his laundry just last week. If she was lucky, he would be there when she arrived, rules be damned.

She stood in the hallway outside of his door, her heart racing in her chest, looking to her left and to her right before she raised a fist to knock. If his roommate answered, she would be ruined. She had no way to explain why she, a plebe, needed to see Collins, a Cow, at ten thirty on a Tuesday night. But thankfully, when the door opened, the green eyes and half smile of her table leader were there, accompanied by a half-hearted laugh.

"About-Face?" he said, shocked. "What are you . . ."

Avery peered behind him, saw that his roommate was not there, and then stepped into his room, closed the door, and turned the lock. Breathless, she pulled her shirt off over her head, and savored the look on his face as his eyes dropped in awe.

"Get undressed, Collins," she ordered.

And he obeyed.

6

*Spring 2001 // West Point, New York*

I assume you're all ready for today's discussion?"

There was a quiet murmur of assent from all of the cadets in the room.

Hannah sat front and center, wearing BDUs and lining up her pens in a perfect row like soldiers. Red for the most important notes. A highlighter for text in the book. Black gel for transcribing portions of Colonel Bennett's lecture. There was little about West Point that Hannah could control, but at least in the classroom, she knew how to excel. The spiral notebook in front of her was full of notes from the semester, with dates written in perfect cursive handwriting at the top right of each page.

"Good, good." The professor dropped a copy of Plato's *The Republic* on his podium and smiled. "Before we cut into this juicy piece of philosophical goodness, let me check with our section marcher. Mr. Arant?"

While the cadet in charge looked around the room to take roll, Hannah looked at Colonel Bennett. He wore a green uniform with an eagle emblem on the lapel, showing his rank. He was in his midfifties, with peppery brown hair and the clean-shaven face of a man who'd been in the military for most of his life. At the beginning of the semester, when Hannah had walked into his classroom, she'd immediately recognized him. Colonel Bennett and his wife, Wendy, the couple that had hosted her family the night before R-Day, also had season tickets to all of West Point's home basketball games. During the varsity games, the JV players sat in the bleachers in the row just in front of the Bennetts.

"You doing okay?" Wendy would always ask Hannah at some point during each varsity game.

"Yes, ma'am," Hannah would assure her, even if it was a lie. "I'm doing good."

The piece of paper with Wendy's phone number on it was stuffed in the back of her desk somewhere. Hannah had never used it. More than once, Hannah had promised to try to attend the Bible study Wendy hosted at her house, but every Wednesday night, she'd find herself buried under a pile of homework, simply trying to keep up.

"You coming?" Sarah Goodrich had asked the previous Wednesday, popping her head into Hannah's barracks.

"I can't," Hannah had said, gripping the silver cross necklace in her hand and surveying the pile of textbooks and assignments in front of her. "Sorry . . . I just . . ."

"Books don't love you back, you know."

Guilt had washed over Hannah in that moment, and she'd groaned, putting her head on her desk. Against her better judgment, she let Sarah drag her out of the barracks and up a steep, snow-covered staircase to Lusk Area, where she'd defrosted in front of the Bennetts' fireplace, eating homemade chili followed by brownies and ice cream. It had been a moment of calm in a world of constant discomfort.

Now, waiting on Cadet Arant to finish taking attendance, Hannah flipped through the first few pages of the book, frantically trying to remember anything she'd read the night before. Passages were underlined and highlighted, but the words meant nothing to her. She wondered if overexercising could cause temporary amnesia.

After losing three games in a row, Coach Jankovich had transformed her practices from predictably horrible to outright sadistic. At the previous night's practice, it had been easier to name the girls who *didn't* throw up than those who did, and sadly, Hannah was among the latter.

"Do you *want* to lose?" Coach Jankovich had shouted after the varsity team lost on the road at Rutgers. She'd lined them all up on the baseline of the opponent's gymnasium, long after the stands had cleared of fans. Hannah saw the Rutgers janitor standing at the door, waiting to wax the floor. But Coach Jankovich didn't seem to notice him, or if she did, she didn't mind making him wait. She blew her whistle ferociously, sending them sprinting across the court, watching the Rutgers logo pass beneath their feet. Hannah and Avery hadn't even been a part of the varsity squad that had lost the game, and yet, they sprinted. Jankovich's shrill whistle pierced Hannah's ears. It echoed through her dreams.

"This can't be normal," Avery had whispered under her breath to Hannah on the flight back from Colorado last week, after they'd watched the varsity team lose to the Air Force Academy. In the last seconds of the game, Coach Jankovich had lost her cool, screaming maniacally at a referee. As punishment for the loss, the players were told to spend the flight back in silence.

"What if we all just quit?" Avery continued. "If we all quit at the same time, they'd *have* to fire her."

Hannah just shook her head and went back to doing her calculus practice problems, hunched over her tiny airplane tray table.

The truth was, there was nothing normal about Coach Jankovich. Hannah had spent the season trying to understand the woman's tactics, and the best she could come up with was that Coach Jankovich was simply scared of losing her job. As the first woman to ever hold the position of head women's basketball coach at West Point, she had a lot on the line, Hannah knew. Coach Jankovich hadn't shown her players a single moment of vulnerability—hadn't once provided an inspirational quote or a pat on the back. Instead, it seemed that the only way Coach Jankovich maintained her confidence was by belittling her players and reminding them of her authority. She was paranoid, Hannah thought, the kind of coach who believed she could shame her players into greatness, as if having all of their flaws exposed would suddenly make the players feel motivated to improve.

Hannah wondered if Coach Jankovich had always been this way, or if she'd adopted some twisted militant coaching philosophy when she'd arrived at West Point, imagining that her boss, a three-star Army general, would expect her to be tough. But the hazing Hannah endured in the barracks felt more productive than what Coach Jankovich put them through. At least the upper-classmen acknowledged Hannah's effort. At least they all laughed from time to time. Yes, the cadre in her company had broken her down, but were just as intent on building her up.

The only player who didn't put her head in a trash can at last night's practice was Avery, the second-string point guard from Pittsburgh. Early in the season, Avery had mentioned that she felt Coach Jankovich wouldn't care if she quit. Hannah didn't see that. Sure, Coach J was hard on them, and yes, splitting them into two teams was unexpected. But what else could they do? At least they got to play—even if it was just JV games.

But by the second semester of their plebe year, halfway through the basketball season, Hannah had started to notice that the harder Avery worked on the court, the harder Coach J worked to ignore her. Once, Hannah had literally watched the coach turn her back when Avery sank a three-point shot. Another time, when Avery recovered an impossible rebound in midair and threw it back into play before touching her feet out of bounds, Coach said *nothing*. It was strange. Neurotic, even.

Coach's willful disdain for Avery and some of the other play-ers had started to bother Hannah, if she was honest. She found herself worrying about Avery off the court too, the way a mother might worry over her rebellious daughter. Cadets savored stories like sweet and satisfying grapes plucked off of the vine of campus gossip. And with Avery, it seemed the harvest was plentiful.

"I heard she's slept with ten guys. All upperclassmen."

"I heard it was twelve."

"No, it's just one guy, but twelve times."

"I heard they did it on the roof of the library."

Hannah wasn't one to indulge in gossip, but there were too many stories being passed around for all of them to be false. Clearly *something* had happened with *someone,* because when Lisa Johnson had confronted Avery about it in the locker room, she'd just grinned and put a single finger over her lips, and said, "Don't ask, because I won't tell."

The whole exchange had made Hannah supremely uncomfortable. Did Avery *really* think that sleeping with some guy in the first few months of college was a good idea? Plus, if Avery was sneaking into an upperclassman's dorm room at night, as the rumors alleged, she was putting her entire future at West Point in jeopardy, let alone her reputation. Last semester, a couple in Hannah's company had been found making out behind closed doors, and they'd both been given a hundred hours of walking tours. For the next ten Saturdays, Hannah had watched them both walking back and forth along the concrete of cadet area, wearing full dress gray uniform, carrying their rifles against their shoulders—rain or shine. It was medieval punishment, all that walking. But it was better than the alternative, which was to be kicked out of the academy. It wasn't that Hannah was a prude, but she worried that Avery wasn't thinking clearly. Sooner or later, all those bad decisions would catch up to her. To Hannah, nothing was worth the risk of losing her Saturdays. After all, without her Saturdays, when would she get all of her homework done?

Cadet Arant had just read out the name *Nesmith,* bringing Hannah out of her thoughts—but as usual, there was no response. The professor paused. "Anyone seen Tim?"

The classroom door opened, and a tall, olive-skinned cadet hustled through, checking the clock to ensure he'd beat the buzzer, which he had, by mere seconds. Hannah sat up a little taller in her seat. Tim smiled, flashing a perfect row of white teeth to the class. He had one dimple in his right cheek.

"Sorry," the cadet said. "No excuse, sir."

"Isn't that what you said yesterday, Nesmith?" a classmate called out.

"Take your seat," Colonel Bennett said. "You're playing with fire."

Hannah watched Tim unpack his backpack and ask his neighbor for a pencil. Then, nonchalantly, he pointed at the book on Colonel Bennett's podium and turned his lips into a frown, like he was surprised to find that they'd moved on to another book. Hannah looked at the notebook in front of her, full of quotations that she'd jotted down while completing the assigned reading, and shook her head. She couldn't fathom being nearly late and so unprepared for class so many days in a row. But this kid? This Tim character? Nothing seemed to faze him.

She'd watched him out of the corner of her eye for weeks now, studying him as closely as she'd studied Plato. He was muscular but not bulky, tall but not gangly, with a stately jaw and that one dimple that indented his cheek every time he smiled. When he walked into the room, the energy shifted toward him, like he was the sun and they were all those jungle plants that grow at odd angles simply to catch a ray. Tim's humble charisma had even charmed their professor into letting his near-tardiness slide.

Hannah knew she shouldn't be attracted to him—he was a mess. Yesterday, he'd come in with toothpaste caked in the corner of his mouth, and she'd noticed the small black outline of a tattoo peeking out from under his short uniform sleeve more than once. She'd *never* been attracted to a guy with a tattoo. How could someone mark something so permanent on their body? Didn't he worry he'd regret it someday? And yet, there was something about Tim's smile that made her constantly look at him. He was interesting. Like a puzzle she wanted to solve.

Colonel Bennett wrote a question across the whiteboard with a red dry-erase marker.

"The rest of the semester, we will tackle this book, and its central question." The teacher pointed at the board.

## WHAT IS JUSTICE?

The room was silent while Colonel Bennett walked through a comprehensive timeline of Greek philosophy. Hannah looked down at her notes and stared at the question, which she'd written at the top of a fresh page in her spiral notebook. *Justice.* She thought of *Law and Order* on television, bad guys getting what they deserve. She thought of a gavel slamming against wood and a widow receiving help from her neighbors. She thought of D-day and American soldiers liberating France from German occupation during World War II. These were examples of justice, weren't they? But she was pretty certain that wasn't what

Colonel Bennett wanted to hear. He wanted a definition. And all Hannah could think was that justice came from God. She wouldn't dare say that aloud.

The officer began pacing the room, shiny black shoes carrying him back and forth. He pointed at the board.

"So. What is it?"

A cadet to Hannah's left lifted his pencil. "Justice is doing the right thing, even when no one is looking, sir."

"Okay. Good. That's a fine place to start." The professor added *Righteousness* to the board. "Anyone else?" he asked.

Tim Nesmith cleared his throat and raised his hand. The professor pointed at him, giving him the floor.

"With respect to my classmate," Tim began, "all people have different definitions of what they see as *right*. For example, for some people, doing the right thing means following the law. But if there's an unjust law on the books—think Jim Crow South— wouldn't the right thing be to ignore that law? So, in my opinion, justice can't be defined as doing what's *right*. Because who defines *rightness?*"

The class grew quiet again. Hannah fought the urge for her jaw to drop, amazed at his confidence. Who was this kid?

"And if I may be so bold," he continued, "Army soldiers and officers are given permission to do something that in all other circumstances is considered morally *wrong*. Was it right in World War II to kill Nazis? Yes. But I'm certain the Nazis told their soldiers the same thing about killing the Allied forces."

"Mr. Nesmith makes an excellent point," the professor said. "Socrates points out that laws, even laws that we create for ourselves, can be unjust, with or without our knowledge." Colonel Bennett took a meaningful pause and then continued. "What are you going to do if the government you've taken an oath to serve asks you to do something that isn't just?"

"Civil disobedience," someone said.

"Conscientious objection," added another.

"Resistance," said Tim.

A slick of sweat took up residence on Hannah's palms as she considered whether or not to raise her hand. She hated speaking in class and rarely took the risk. It was an easy equation: if she never spoke, she'd never say something stupid.

But Tim had touched a nerve. Of *course* it was right to kill Nazis. Just because someone *claimed* that they were right didn't *make* them right. In Hannah's heart, she knew that justice existed far above any human opinion. But rather than bring her faith into the conversation, Hannah looked through her notes from the night before, searching for something to say. At West Point, she'd learned, you couldn't get by with simply nodding along. A good portion of her grade was participation, and with only twelve students in the classroom, there was nowhere to hide. Timidly, she put her hand in the air. Colonel Bennett looked her way.

"Miss Speer."

"On page one ninety-seven, Socrates says that stealing a weapon from a madman is actually the right thing to do. So— stealing might be wrong in most contexts, but stealing a weapon from someone threatening to harm himself or others is the *right* thing to do. I guess what I'm trying to say is that I . . . I think we're all born with a sense of right and wrong. We know what's right, deep down. And just because two people—or two countries—claim to be right, doesn't mean they're both right. There is such a thing as *right*, objectively."

Tim Nesmith shook his head. "But who gets to determine who's *actually* right?" he said. "You can't define a feeling."

Hannah felt her face flush red. Shut down, defeated, she sank back into her seat, desperately trying to disappear into the linoleum floor. Did this guy really believe that there was no truth at all?

"Fair enough, Mr. Nesmith," Colonel Bennett said, "but Miss Speer brought up a good point. And at least we know she completed the reading."

The class laughed in unison, and this time, it was Tim's cheeks that turned pink. But then he shrugged, laughing at himself. Moving back to his podium, Colonel Bennett picked up *The Republic* and held it in his hand.

"For students at other colleges, philosophy may seem theoretical and arbitrary. But the way that you answer this question will impact your life in real and tangible ways." He paused, put the book down, and then continued. "In just a few short years, you're going to be officers in the U.S. Army. Unlike those kids at other schools, you're going to be leading soldiers and making decisions that could have life-or-death consequences. As leaders of the U.S. Army, we must believe that justice is a concrete, definable concept, and we must always be striving to live our lives in line with that ideal. At the end of the day, we must be able to say with certainty that the Nazis *were* wrong. And although they might have made the same truth *claims*, in the end, it was the right thing to do to defeat them. Yes, Miss Speer?"

Hannah had lifted her hand again, which seemed to shock everyone in the room, especially herself.

"Sorry, I had one more thought."

"Never apologize for thinking."

"You asked us what we would do if our sense of justice conflicted with our sense of duty. What I was trying to say earlier was that if you believe in justice, you have to risk being wrong for the sake of what's right. You have to choose."

Nodding, the professor turned the back of his green Army uniform to the class. On the board, he wrote *CHOICE*. On another part of the board, he wrote *RISK*.

"Very good, Miss Speer," he said respectfully. Moving back to his podium, he picked up *The Republic* and continued lecturing, as his pupils scribbled frantically in their notebooks, trying to keep up. Asking more questions, prodding them further, the professor walked them through the rest of the reading, until the clock ran out on class.

"The next reading assignment is listed in the syllabus," he said. "And your first reflection paper is due next week, too. Don't forget. Class dismissed."

Chairs squealed against the floor and all the cadets stood up and adjusted their uniforms. Hannah packed her backpack quickly, hoping to reach Tim before he jetted out the door. Taking a risk had worked during class, and she was hoping it would work with him, too. Across the room, he slid his backpack over his shoulders, revealing the lean muscles in his arms and releasing a fleet of butterflies into Hannah's stomach. She was two steps behind him, about to reach out and touch his shoulder—to say what, she hadn't decided—when she heard her name.

"Hannah," the professor said, calling her back toward his desk.

All the courage she'd mustered fell apart as her arm lowered. Another opportunity, missed. She turned back and smiled at Colonel Bennett, trying to hide her disappointment.

"I just wanted to check on you," he said. "My wife and I were at that last game. I was sorry to see that you didn't get a chance to play."

"Oh, that's all right," Hannah said. "The older girls really are good. For some reason it's just not clicking yet. Actually, I have to get going." She pointed at the door. "Coach J makes us run if we're late to practice."

"Well, I don't want to hold you up, but I did want to say that we're here for you. Keep it up. I know it's hard to believe, but plebe year is almost over."

"Thanks, Colonel Bennett," said Hannah sincerely.

"And great job today," he said as she headed out the door. "Someone's got to keep that Nesmith on his toes."

RUNNING BACK TO the barracks, Hannah dropped off her schoolwork and picked up her basketball bag, certain she would be late to practice. As she sprinted uphill toward the Holleder Center, where the men's and women's basketball teams practiced, the first hints of spring called for her attention. Small packs of daffodils popped through the grass like little trumpets, heralding the end of winter. Buds on the trees outlined every limb with a hint of green. The brutal winter temperatures were finally break-ing, and even though she was late, she loved the sensation of the first hints of warmth on her skin. The season always reminded her that no matter what, change would eventually come. Things could look absolutely dead—completely hopeless—and yet, the future always held the promise of new life.

Fearing Coach J's fury, Hannah picked up her pace and tried not to be distracted by the flowers in bloom. As she entered the gym and jogged down the hall, she quickly tucked her silver cross necklace into her T-shirt and checked her watch, which told her she was three minutes late. The next thing she knew, Hannah looked up, expecting to push through the door to the women's locker room, but instead crashed into a guy standing in the doorway.

"Whoa, whoa," he said to her, putting up a hand between them. "Slow down, plebe."

The cadet wore black gym shorts and West Point's typical gray T-shirt with his last name blazoned above the school crest. Hannah read it quickly, the way you'd read the license plate of a car in the midst of a hit-and-run. *COLLINS.* It sounded famil-iar, but Hannah couldn't exactly pinpoint where she'd heard the name before. The cadet had sharp green eyes, wavy black hair, and a smile that made Hannah feel unsettled. He was standing too close to her.

"Sorry," Hannah said, though she wasn't sure why she was apologizing—*he* was the one standing in her way.

"No problem," he said with confidence. "I was just checking on your TP supply. Someone said you guys were running low."

Something about his story didn't exactly add up. Hannah had never heard of a cadet working at the Holleder Center—and didn't they have janitors to resupply toilet paper? Perhaps he'd been in trouble with his company or sports team. Could he be cleaning as punishment? If she'd had more time, she would have asked him. But she was already late.

"Oh, okay. Thanks," she said, stepping around him to push through the locker room door. "See ya."

"Yep," he said. "See ya."

In the empty locker room, Hannah dropped her bag, changed clothes, and quickly forgot about Collins. It didn't matter why he was snooping around the Holleder Center. She needed to get out onto the court, and fast, before Coach J had her running suicides until she puked. Again. On a normal day, being this late would have put her in a panic. But Hannah couldn't help but smile, thinking about Colonel Bennett's last words before she'd left his classroom.

*"Someone's got to keep that Nesmith on his toes."*

He was right. And something inside Hannah's heart told her she just might be the perfect girl for the job.

## 7

*Summer 2001 // West Point, New York*

H ere's your bay number, Cadet McNalley. Grab your rucksack from the truck. Cross over the gravel road. Bay number
eight is a half mile up the hill to the left. Next."

Camp Buckner, part of West Point's military training ground,
was located five miles from campus in the middle of the woods.
It looked like the set of *Dirty Dancing,* only Patrick Swayze had
been replaced by countless other shirtless boys, pretending to be
on a mission. A group of guys commanded the volleyball court,
already midgame. Another group carried kayaks out onto the
lake. Cicadas, mosquitoes, and gnats buzzed around her, adding
to the hum of the afternoon. *Now, this is college,* Dani thought to
herself as she received her packet of information from the cadet
behind the table and then moved back outside into the mid-July
heat. A closed-lipped smile spread across her face.

Of course, all the fun happening today would end abruptly tomorrow when training began.

IN ONE YEAR at West Point, Dani had already learned that friendships born in comfortable circumstances rarely last when times get tough. Her friends from high school just didn't understand. There was something about being dirty, wet, and exhausted that forced two people to look one another in the eye and burst out laughing. When you get to the end of your rope, and the person next to you is at the end of theirs, it's possible to find a secret joy that you're simply surviving together. It was how she and Tim had become such great friends last summer, and how the entire varsity basketball team had bonded, over their shared hatred of Coach Jankovich.

People assumed they would have better friends if they hosted better parties. But the opposite was true. Shared suffering led to unshakeable connections. Pain wanted you to stop. Give up. Quit. But the truth was, you could go so much further than your body said you could, because when the body quit, the heart took over, and the heart was far more powerful than any muscle in the body. It had led women to lift cars off children. It had led men to sacrifice their own lives for their friends—even some for their enemies.

You couldn't teach that kind of strength. You had to live it. You had to believe what others who had been to that dark place told you. In whispers. In silence. "Trust me. There's joy down there."

You could believe them, but you still had to live it.

For the next eight weeks, the entire class of 2004 would live it. Together, they would learn to fire cannons, care for the wounded, shoot live rounds, complete urban missions, overcome a water obstacle course, and navigate through the woods with nothing but a gun, a compass, and a map. The entire place was like a little boy's dream camp, filled with real tanks, helicopters, and even a handful of enemy combatants—enlisted soldiers from nearby Fort Drum who would dress up like rebel fighters. Buckner would be far better than last year's Basic Training because she could talk, and because she no longer walked around with eyes permanently bulging. All of the upperclassmen had promised this would be the best summer of her life. And even though their words were drenched with sarcasm, Dani knew they were right.

A year ago, her idea of a dream camp had included a basketball, a hoop, and maybe a few good-looking coaches thrown in. But the Army? Field training? *When did I become so gung-ho?* Dani wondered. But she didn't have enough time to consider what a difference a year makes, because at that moment, an Army Humvee arrived, stuffed to the brim with rucksacks—one of which was hers. She needed to find it and go claim a bunk bed before the only one left was above a girl who snored.

AS SHE APPROACHED the truck, three boys opened the hatch and climbed up to start unloading. The tallest of the group was an African-American kid Dani hadn't seen before. He wore his camouflage pants high on his waist, with a belt cinched tight around his hips. There was something otherworldly about him;

his dark hair had been shaved close to his head, and he maneuvered the heavy luggage with ease. The more he worked, the silk-
ier his dark brown skin looked in the sun, and Dani felt suddenly
embarrassed. She wasn't normally one to gawk—but, *Lord*, she
thought, *he is not normal.*

"Hey!" she shouted toward the shirtless marvel. Up close, he
looked like an action figure. "You see McNalley up there?"

Turning, he wiped his forehead and shouted back, "You seen
some patience?"

"Nope. Not lately," replied Dani.

"Why don't you come up and look for it," he said, offering her
his hand. She took it, and in one motion, he hoisted her up onto
the back of the truck, like she weighed nothing at all. For a moment, they were inches apart, Dani staring into his deep brown
eyes, shocked by his disarming smile, punctuated by a gap between his front two teeth.

"Locke Coleman," the guy said, then opened up his hands as if
to tell Dani that the truck was hers to explore. "You might as well
look for mine while you're at it."

"Your patience or your bag?"

"I've seen you before," he said simply. "Aren't you that point
guard?"

"That's right," said Dani, flattered that he'd seen her play.

"Sucks to lose, don't it?" he said jokingly. "Y'all had a rough
season."

"Thanks for the pep talk."

"No disrespect! I play football. I'm familiar with the losing
feeling."

"We're going to change that this year, Coleman," another cadet on the truck shouted. "Fuck Navy. Hey, what'd you say your name was?"

"McNalley," Dani answered.

A rucksack flew through the air and she caught it against her chest.

"Thanks, guys. See you around."

She and Locke Coleman exchanged one long moment of eye contact before she jumped off the truck and quickly walked off across the gravel road toward the bunkhouses. The pressure of his palm against hers had sent an electric shock up her spine. She didn't want to forget that feeling anytime soon, and yet, she didn't want to read too much into their interaction, either. Guys always loved to hang out with her, but they rarely saw her as *"girlfriend material."* It was her constant relationship kryptonite. She was one of the boys.

BUNKHOUSE NUMBER EIGHT smelled like summer camp: a hopeful combination of sweat, sunscreen, and plastic mattresses, worn out by years of use. Down the narrow hallway, girls were hugging, laughing, and unpacking unnecessary toiletries. Boys roamed the hall half-dressed, checking out who would be living in close proximity for the next eight weeks. Dani shook her head, surprised by the insanity of the premise: West Point put a thousand nineteen-year-olds in the woods for a summer, crossed their fingers, and hoped for the best. It was like a social experiment, created to determine how much sexual frustration you could stuff into one square mile.

Suddenly, a girl with dirty-blond hair dressed in black shorts and a gray T-shirt stepped into the hallway. Dani immediately recognized Hannah Speer and felt a surge of gratitude fill her chest. Straightforward and honest, Hannah had spent last year working hard on the JV basketball team, never once complaining or holding a grudge against Dani for her success on varsity. Minutes earlier, Dani had had no idea who she'd be forced to live with, but now, seeing Hannah's bright blue eyes and easy smile, she knew she'd have at least one friend this summer.

"McNalley!" Hannah shouted. "Get down here!"

Trotting quickly, Dani arrived in the doorway and peeked inside. Five bunk beds lined the walls, leaving a square space on the floor. Smiling, Dani surveyed the girls in the room and realized she recognized every single face—the entire sophomore class of female basketball recruits. Lisa Johnson and Megan O'Leary had claimed the bunk by the back wall. Kate Shoemaker's rucksack waited on the bottom bunk near the door, and above that, Dani spotted a bright-blond ponytail hanging down from the top bunk, as if Rapunzel were letting down her hair. The girl turned over and looked down, her eyes assessing Dani with sharp disdain.

Avery Adams let out a loud sigh, then rolled back over. "Oh great. Gang's all here."

Dani looked to Hannah, who quickly waved Avery off with a gesture that said, *Ignore her.* But the moment was hard to disregard. If she was going to live in this tiny room, crammed with ten girls for the entire summer, Dani at least wanted to feel welcome.

"Is there a problem, Adams?" she said. "Because we can address it right now, if you'd like. Unless you'd rather go across the hall and sleep with the offensive line?"

"Excuse me?" Avery snapped, closing the magazine. "They don't have enough room over there for you? Your *ego* take up too much space?"

"Hey, hey, hey," Hannah interjected, putting her hands up. "Just everybody chill out, okay? Geez. We just got here."

Avery looked down at Hannah, who offered the same wave of the hand that minutes before she'd given Dani. Though she could have been pissed, the whole interaction made Dani laugh. Hannah was clearly the mother of the crew—already fulfilling her role perfectly.

Though Dani had never noticed it before, Avery and Hannah looked like they could be sisters. Avery's hair was lighter and Hannah was taller, but side by side, they looked like opposing reflections in a mirror. It was fascinating to Dani that two people who looked so alike on the surface could be so different beneath it. Avery cussed quickly and often, while Hannah's favorite curse word was *shenanigans*. Avery held her body like she knew how to use it, while Hannah bumped into things clumsily, like a little girl who still wasn't used to having an adult body. Appearances could be so very deceiving.

For the time being, Dani decided to follow Hannah's advice and ignore Avery's rude behavior. To room with the girls' basketball team all summer was far better than getting stuck with a bunch of random girls she didn't know. But West Point wasn't keen on giving out pleasant surprises. There had to be a catch.

"So is this a mistake?" Dani asked rhetorically. "Would they really put us all in the same room?"

"I unpacked as fast as I could," laughed Hannah. "Before they realize what they've done."

"No one's asking any fucking questions," Avery said, her eyes buried again in the *People* magazine photo spread of Brad Pitt and Jennifer Aniston.

"If it was a mistake, it's a good one," said Lisa, from the other side of the room. Taller than any girl on the team, Lisa Johnson had a head full of cornrows and long fingers that she presently used to point in all their faces. "I'm with Avery. No one talks."

"So what does this mean?" Dani asked, taking a seat next to Hannah on the bottom bunk. "Are we in the same company too?"

"Charlie," Hannah answered in the affirmative.

"The guys too," Lisa said, pointing across the hall toward the room of football players. "All Charlie Company."

Dani quickly realized her luck: if all the football players were in Charlie Company, that meant Locke Coleman—the guy she'd met just a few minutes ago out among the rucksacks—was going to be near her all summer.

"Oh snap!" Dani shouted excitedly. "If we're in the same company as those guys, then no one else stands a chance! We're the most athletic girls in our class, by far. And they're some of the most athletic guys. Our company is going to crush this!"

"Ooh," Avery cooed from the top bunk, raising an eyebrow. "Aren't we cocky?"

"I'm cocky because I know how awesome we all are," Dani replied. "And that includes you, Adams. You're fast as hell."

That seemed to soften her, because in that moment, Avery turned her gaze from the magazine and looked at Dani straight in the eyes, as if to determine whether or not the compliment was genuine.

"That's not what Coach Jankovich thinks."

"Yeah, well, screw Coach J."

"Can we *not* talk about her this summer please?" said Lisa from her bunk. "Thanks."

"I thought you two were like, best friends," Avery added to Dani.

"Are you kidding? That woman is the most racist person I've ever met."

"Here, here," added Lisa from her bunk.

"I'm beginning to doubt if she ever even *played* basketball, let alone if she can *coach it*," Dani said. "She is so horrible. You know she's as bad to us as she is to you guys on JV. Maybe worse."

"*See*," Hannah said to Avery, as if she'd been trying to convince her of the truth before Dani had arrived. "I told you."

IN DARKNESS, DANI heard whispers.

"Shh!"

"Dani," Avery whispered into the top bunk. "Get up. Get your shoes."

Stumbling out of the bed, Dani rubbed her eyes until they adjusted. Avery and Hannah stood in the doorway, lit by the moonlight and waving her into the hall.

"What's happening?" asked Dani, her voice as quiet as she could muster.

Shaking her head, as if to say they couldn't talk, Avery tiptoed down the hall and carefully pushed the screen door at the end of the bunkhouse. It screeched open, threatening to wake everyone and blow their cover, but closed without a sound.

"We're meeting the guys," Avery said once they were outside, her eyes focused directly on the lake in front of them.

Hannah crossed her arms over her chest and kept looking back at bay number eight, where they were supposed to be sleeping. "We could get in trouble, Avery. It's the first night."

"Exactly," she said. "They won't expect us to sneak out on the very first night. That's why it's perfect."

At that moment, Dani heard a branch snap in the woods. She imagined an officer walking out of his bunkhouse and catching them in the act, and so grabbed Avery and Hannah's arms, pulling them to hide behind bay number six.

"Shh!" she said. "I heard something."

And at that moment, six guys emerged from the woods. Locke Coleman stood at the very center of the group, his gap-toothed smile shining through the darkness.

"We can see you," Locke said, and the girls stepped out from behind the shelter.

Without warning, Avery took off jogging toward the water's edge, followed by several of Locke's teammates. Clothes littered the sand under a grove of trees, and Dani tried to keep her composure as she watched Locke Coleman drop his shorts and tiptoe toward the water, wearing only boxer-briefs. He offered Dani a smile, then raised his eyebrows at Avery's pale body in the middle of the lake, as if to say, *Your friend's got balls.* Dani shook her head and shrugged, as if to say, *I'm not sure she's my friend.*

"I'm not getting *naked* in front of those guys," Hannah said under her breath. "We're going to get caught!"

"Come on," Dani said without breaking a sweat. "It'll be so fast. They're not even looking."

"Oh lord," Hannah groaned. "You two better not get me kicked out of this place. My grandfather would never recover."

OVER THE NEXT few weeks, it seemed that Avery warmed up to Dani a little bit more every day. Once, she'd even laughed out loud at one of Dani's jokes. It was small, but to Dani it felt like progress.

*Baby steps.*

During the day, their company soared to the top of the pack, always crushing the other companies in physical fitness tests. Soon it was clear that Avery had made a full 180-degree turn. When Dani and Hannah struggled to learn how to disassemble and reassemble their M16s, Avery came to the rescue, teaching them every step their platoon leader had glossed over.

"Do you think it's true?" Hannah had whispered to Dani once Avery had stepped away, leaving them with their weapons. "All those things people said last year?"

Turning her lips into a frown, Dani shook her head and shrugged her shoulders. "Does it matter?"

"I guess not," Hannah answered. "I'm not judging her. I'm just worried about her."

Dani worried about Avery too, but not for the reasons Hannah did. Hannah worried about the consequences—that Avery's reputation would be sullied, or that she'd get kicked out of the academy. Dani worried about the feelings Avery hid beneath the surface. Avery rebraided her hair every few hours. She applied concealer to the minuscule imperfections on her face before they left the bunkhouse every morning. And Dani observed these little tics, gathering them up as evidence of the truth. For all the defiant confidence Avery wore on her face, she was supressing a whole lot of self-doubt, just beneath the surface.

As the days passed on, their company passed first aid training with flying colors, and with any moment of free time, Dani and Locke held their positions as reigning beach-volleyball champions. The only son of a single mother, Locke was from Brooklyn, and had an encyclopedic knowledge of soul music. He'd taken it upon himself to educate Dani at night, starting with James Brown's *Live at the Apollo* spinning in his portable CD player. She relished the moments together, lying on his bunk side by side, with one earbud in his left ear, and the other in Dani's right. His finger tapped the beat out on her thigh.

*"See? That riff? That's what I'm talking about."*

The only possible threat to Dani's summer was the growing discomfort in her right hip. It wasn't something she wanted to complain about, but at times the dull ache would give way to a sharp, slicing pain in her back that stole her breath. The only person who had noticed a grimace on her face was Hannah, but Dani told her not to worry. As long as she popped a few preemptive Advil every morning, she could endure. She had to endure. She'd never quit a single thing in her entire life, and she wasn't about to start now.

THE MORNING OF the final field exercise, water poured out of the spout of an Army-green water buffalo into Dani's canteen. The four-hundred gallon tank on wheels had been marked on the map she carried in her hands. They'd been in the woods for two days straight. She was dirty, tired, and thirsty, and even in the shade of the trees, sweat poured from her forehead, smearing the camouflage paint on her face, stinging her eyes.

"Too bad you can't camouflage your blond-ass hair, Adams," Locke said jokingly to Avery, who was waiting for Dani to finish at the spigot.

"*Shut up, Coleman,*" said Avery, stepping to fill her canteen. "Dani, can you get your boyfriend to leave me alone? I can't get rid of him."

"You know Navy's not doing this shit," Locke said, changing the subject. "They send us out to the woods with nothing but a compass and a map. Haven't they heard of a GPS? Meanwhile, those Navy guys . . . they're cozied up with some private chef bulking for the season. I'd put money on it. No wonder we can't beat them. Have I told you? I've already lost—"

"Fifteen pounds. Yeah, you've told us, Coleman," said Avery. "Do you think there's a correlation between the amount of weight you lose and the age you act? Because . . . honestly . . . there's an uncanny . . ."

"Oh?" Locke raised his eyebrows. "D, your friend's a comedian!"

"Hush, you two," Dani said. She fiddled with the radio in her hand until she heard static. "Get your water. We've got to get back."

Together, the three of them tromped through the woods in a row, holding their M16s at the ready like they'd been taught. The entire day had gone by without a hitch, which worried Dani more than she wanted to admit. In the morning, before the sun came up, they'd met their company commander at a small outpost near the woods and outfitted all of their M16s with laser attachments. He'd passed out a bunch of folded "injury" cards, which they were supposed to unfold if the laser sensor on their chest was hit. Then he pointed into a glorified sandbox where a scene of wooden figurines illustrated the area they were meant to protect. An outhouse stood on the south side next to a general purpose medium tent, stretched out for shade where they'd been told to convene for lunch. The water buffalo station was a half mile to the north. A safe zone existed in the eastern section, up a tall hill, near a make-believe Red Cross station. They had from dawn until dusk to maintain the area while keeping a lookout for the OPFOR—a fake opposition force made up of soldiers from Fort Drum. They all knew the ambush was coming, but so far, there was no sign of them. Dani knew they needed to get back to the rest of their platoon, and fast. Out here alone like this—she felt suddenly like they were being watched.

Dried leaves crunched under their feet. Branches snapped, far louder than they should have.

"Shhh, Coleman," Dani whispered. "Walk lightly, dude."

Perhaps they should have returned to the rest of the platoon by a different route than the way they'd come, Dani thought to herself. If anyone had seen their tracks, walking toward the water buffalo, they could have staked them out, easily. As soon as Dani had considered that possibility, Locke stopped in his tracks. Silent, Dani gripped her rifle even tighter. She knew it was all in fun—just practice—but her heart was still pounding in her chest. She checked the laser attachment on the end of her gun, to make sure it was ready to fire.

"Do you hear that?" Avery asked, her voice a whisper. She stood right behind Dani, breathing like she'd just run a 5K. In the distance, a faint echo of loud voices rose into the trees.

"Turn up the radio, D," whispered Locke to Dani.

Dani turned the volume up slightly, just as she saw a man dressed in black behind a tree. He raised his rifle and aimed it directly at them.

"GET DOWN!" shouted Dani.

*Pow! Pow! Pow!*

"MAYDAY! MAYDAY! MAYDAY!" yelled Dani into the receiver of the radio. *"COME IN, SPEER! WE NEED BACKUP!"*

"Oh shit!" yelled Locke, seeing a whole new crew of men dressed in black moving their way. "Run!"

Avery took off sprinting through the woods, separating from Locke and Dani just enough to provide them cover from behind a rock. Out of the corner of her eye, Dani spotted another man in black, and she shot—hitting him square in the chest. *Take that!* Dani thought. *I'm a sniper!* At that moment, another enemy combatant emerged from behind a tree and took aim at Locke's back.

"Coleman! Get down!" Dani called out, then she fired her gun. The enemy fell to the ground, his laser attachment lit up in red.

Dani smiled. But turning back to look at Locke, she realized her shot had come a moment too late.

"He's hit! I've got your cover, Dani!" shouted Avery from across the woods. "Go! Go! Go!"

Her legs flew across the expanse of leaves and shadows. When she arrived at Locke's side, he held up the white injury card in his hand. "Head wound," he said. "Traumatic brain injury."

"Okay," panted Dani, trying not to panic. She tried to remember the first aid training she'd been given the week before. "We've got to keep your neck stabilized and get you to the safe zone."

The reality that he was nearly twice her weight suddenly struck Dani in the gut. How was she going to get him through a half mile of woods without getting shot? And how was she going to do it with this pulsating pain flaring up in her back? She looked around her and realized there was only one option. Dani struggled, shifting his weight from the ground to her back. Once she had him on her back, she began walking, one hobbling step at a time. Her hip screamed out in pain, like all the cartilage in her joints had disappeared. Bone rubbed against bone.

"I need cover!" Dani shouted to Avery.

"Go!" shouted Avery. "I've got your cover! Go!"

"Oh my God, Locke. Why do you have to be so huge?" she said. "I thought you said you'd *lost* weight."

"You got this, McNalley."

"Shut up. You're dying. Save your energy." She felt him laugh.

When they finally reached the hill, Dani watched the rest of her female company mates zigzag across the valley, providing cover fire and dragging the rest of the guys in their platoon, with their various feigned injuries, up to the safe zone. Apparently the ambush had been swift and fierce. Bodies were strewn every-where. The girls had all survived, while the boys in their platoon had all been taken out of the game. Apparently the boys had been a bit overly aggressive; the girls had the presence of mind to assess the threat before taking action. Clearly, that was why they were the ones who had survived.

"GO, DANI! GO!" Hannah shouted when she saw Dani ap-proaching the bottom of the hill. The final few OPFOR combatants exchanged fire with Hannah as Dani heaved as fast as she could up the hill with a two-hundred-pound football player on her back. When her legs gave out, she put Locke on the ground and pulled him up the hill by his foot, sliding him into the safe zone like a sack of heavy potatoes.

"I'm going to go out on a limb and say we failed this mission," Locke commented. "I had a head injury and you pulled me up the hill upside down, McNalley. I'm pretty sure I bled out."

Breathless, Dani tried to stand up, hoping to go rescue another fallen comrade. But the pain in her hip suddenly exploded into her back and skull. The woods went white in her eyes, and she cried out before hitting the ground. With her eyes closed, all Dani could hear were voices in the dark.

"We're in the safe zone, D," someone shouted. "You don't have to pretend to be injured."

"What's going on?"

"Hey, I think she's hurt."

"What's her card say?"

"No, dumbass!" Someone shouted back. "She's *actually* injured! Hey, someone call a medic!"

The next thing Dani heard was the loud peal of a siren over her head.

Eyes open, trying to focus through the pain, all she could see was blurry faces surrounding her in a small white room. Or was this a vehicle? Her body felt as though someone had taken a hammer to her lower back, crushing every bone into a million pieces. How would they ever put her back together again? The thought forced her to close her eyes and bite her cheeks. She tasted iron and smelled the scent of hospital bandages. They were driving fast. It was definitely a vehicle. An ambulance.

Faintly, she recognized the sound of Avery's voice.

"It's going to be okay, D."

A warm hand squeezed her upper arm, and opening her eyes, Dani saw a blond angel looking down at her. *Avery*.

"I'm here with you. I'm not going anywhere."

"Call Wendy," Dani said through clenched teeth.

"Who?"

"Wendy Bennett."

"I'm putting in an IV," someone else said. "Quick pinch. There you go. We're going to get you hydrated and figure out what's going on. A little ibuprofen in there to help with the pain."

Relief suddenly spread through her veins. Her body relaxed; it stopped fighting. And her mind wandered into a blackness that felt like bliss.

8

*Fall 2001 // West Point, New York*

On a clear Tuesday morning in September, every blade of grass at West Point looked like a tiny saber, reaching for the sky. The color turquoise stretched overhead without a single cloud to interrupt its hue, and as Avery moved toward Thayer Hall, her dark gray uniform shirt tucked into wool pants, all she could think about was how quickly life can change. All it took was an instant.

She'd seen it with her brother, Caleb. In one moment, he was an innocent sophomore on the way to acing Algebra I; the next, he was wearing an orange vest, picking up trash on the side of the highway for community service. She'd seen it this summer with Dani, too. With one misplaced step, she'd morphed from point guard to patient, undergoing emergency surgery to repair what the doctors had determined was a torn ligament. It was awful; Avery had never seen someone's face so contorted in pain.

That day, the EMTs had loaded Dani's body into an ambulance and drove her from Camp Buckner to Keller Army Hospital, which looked more like a Gothic castle than an infirmary. Without asking permission, Avery had hopped in the back of the ambulance and refused to leave Dani's side until the nurses wheeled her back for surgery. For hours, Avery sat in the hospital's cold waiting room alone, until the woman Dani had told her to call, Wendy Bennett, had arrived. She'd only met the woman a handful of times, at basketball games, but her presence somehow forced a crack in the dam Avery had constructed to keep her emotion in check. Still dressed in BDUs, her face painted green and black and brown, Avery had fallen into Wendy's motherly embrace, smearing camouflage face paint against the woman's white shirt.

"It's okay," Wendy had said. "It's going to be okay."

"I was horrible to her last year . . . I—"

"Stop that. People remember who showed up for the crappy moments far more than they remember who showed up for the party. And you're here, aren't you? You're *here*."

If she was honest, Avery still felt ashamed of how she'd acted toward Dani last year. Bitter and resentful, she'd isolated herself, choosing to believe that she had enemies rather than risk being rejected by new friends. But the summer had proven her wrong. Eight weeks had multiplied—breaking into tiny fragments, like the loaves and fishes from that old Bible story—until they'd spread into a million moments, some bitter, some savory, and some sweet. Time was malleable that way. Weeks could feel like years, if you filled them to the brim. A day could manufacture memories to last a lifetime.

During a late-night game of Never Have I Ever, Avery had even admitted to Dani and Hannah that she'd slept with John Collins last year. While Hannah winced, as if Avery's fornication had caused her physical pain, Dani didn't seem shocked or appalled; she just laughed and shook her head, which helped Avery feel at ease for once. They'd never spoken of it explicitly—Dani had never asked for an outright apology—but somehow, over the course of the summer, her fiercest competition had become one of her closest friends.

After the surgery, the commandant of cadets had agreed to let Dani move into a spare bedroom at the Bennetts' house while she recovered. Wendy's daughters were all in college, leaving three empty bedrooms and three empty seats at the dinner table, where Avery and Hannah would often join Dani, savoring Wendy's cooking. Vegetable lasagna. Roasted chicken with tabbouleh. Grilled salmon with mango slaw. There was always a gallon of cookie dough ice cream in the freezer, and Wendy would present it nightly with a pile of spoons, as if bowls were an unnecessary step between their stomachs and delight.

If Avery had ever felt embarrassed by Dani's nudity, all that dissipated as she and Hannah took turns helping Dani into the Bennetts' guest bathroom shower. Tears came often for Dani in those days, and not just from the physical pain. It was hard, Avery knew, for this former powerhouse of a woman to be so powerless. Everyone wants to be the friend who helps. No one wants to be the friend who needs the help.

"Shit, Dani, do you have to be as thick as a horse?" Avery had said once as she lifted Dani off her wheelchair and into the shower. Dani had clung to Avery's shoulder, and in the end, they both ended up drenched in soap and water.

"This is what I like to refer to as karma," Dani had replied.

Spending time at the Bennetts' was just one of many new privileges they had, now that they were sophomores, also known at West Point as "Yuks." The academic calendar boasted six B-weekends, when upperclassmen could leave campus in civilian clothes and pretend to be free for a while. And while Yuks still were low on the totem pole, they had far more freedom than they'd had the year before, and Avery relished every opportunity she had to leer at new plebes whenever they called minutes in the hallway.

"Attention all cadets . . . there are . . . *three minutes remaining . . .* until breakfast formation . . ."

At West Point, you couldn't escape the constant reminder that time was moving forward, counting down, drawing to a close. Urgency was the only operating mode because time was Avery's only resource and her greatest enemy. West Point operated on a true meritocracy. A cadet's academic and physical performance, measured by GPA, PT scores, and other evaluations, converted to class rank, which would eventually dictate her future.

A year earlier, Avery had watched from the wings as Sarah Goodrich leveraged her high class rank to receive an assignment to her desired Army branch, Military Intelligence, and to select the most coveted Army post: Oahu, Hawaii. Rain had poured over the class of 2001 at their graduation ceremony, their white hats soaring into the gray downpour. And though legend had it that any class that graduated in the rain would go to war, Avery would have done anything to trade places with Sarah. In a feat of personal achievement, she'd transformed her time at West Point into a one-way ticket to paradise.

As the days ticked by, Avery grew more uncertain that Dani could recover in time for the basketball season. Large inflamed patches appeared under Dani's arms where crutches had worn her skin raw. The four-inch incision across her right hip remained red and irritated, like an angry half-moon. Even when she'd moved back into the barracks, daily physical therapy sessions seemed ineffective in rebuilding strength in Dani's hip and back. Everywhere they went, she limped, crutched, and smiled. And Avery had never felt worse. A year earlier, she would have given anything to be on the varsity women's basketball team. But now, the inevitability felt suffocating. Like her envy had willed Dani's injury into existence.

Three days earlier, at the team's annual "optional" season-opening practice, Coach Jankovich had written Avery's name at the top of the varsity roster, relegating another plebe recruiting class to JV. Guilt, shame, and excitement had appeared in equal force as she read her name on that piece of paper. Her dreams for the basketball season only existed because Dani's had been torn apart—ripped to pieces like the ligament in her hip.

It was a cruel twist of fate. Loaves and fishes, in reverse.

One dream broken, so another could survive.

WALKING INTO THAYER Hall, yellow spots appeared before Avery's eyes as she adjusted from the brightness outside to the academic building's dim corridor. Normally, the hallway was abuzz with cadets rushing to class, hanging their hats on the hooks outside the doors, chatting before they shuffled through into the classrooms and into their seats. But today, the hallway was empty and silent.

Her freshly shined black shoes clicked against the linoleum floors for twenty paces, until she reached the door to the lecture hall. She'd expected her Physics professor to be standing at the front, handing out the midterm packets, while cadets frantically used the last minutes they had to finish studying. But instead, every person inside the classroom was statuesque, staring at a television screen that had been rolled to the front of the room.

Life could change so quickly. All it took was an instant.

Turning to look at what held their attention, Avery's stomach lurched, like she'd just stepped off the edge of a cliff. On the screen, two silver buildings glittered against a blue sky. The same blue sky she'd just been admiring outside. But something wasn't right. The buildings were on fire, gashes cut into their sides, flames spilling out. Black smoke pooled above the towers, reaching higher than the tallest buildings in the world. Smoke signals.

"Two planes. Back to back. Flew right into the buildings," the cadet standing next to her said.

"On purpose?" Avery asked, incredulous.

He nodded.

"Did they . . ." Avery stuttered. "Did they get everyone out?"

The cadet didn't answer, but simply turned to look back at the screen.

The news flickered between images of the World Trade Center and a confused anchor, frantically trying to assess what had happened in the world around him. When the room let out a gasp, Avery closed her eyes and tried to pretend that the *slam* she heard through the television speakers was something else. Anything else.

Only one thought went through her mind, circling and circling, like a plane waiting to land. Like the dress of the woman who'd just jumped.

*Oh my God. Oh my God. Oh my God.*

*This changes everything.*

"THIS IS WAR," Avery said, breaking the silence. "That's what I keep thinking. It's . . . just . . . I can't believe it."

The entire women's basketball team had gathered in Wendy Bennett's living room. Paper bowls of half-eaten chicken pot pie littered the floor, and were stacked on the coffee table. The team huddled under blankets, interlocking arms and passing around a tissue box. All twelve pairs of eyes were puffy and red. Women at West Point learned quickly to hold their emotion in check— never to shed a tear. But that unspoken rule had shattered to the ground, falling with the towers.

All day, people had speculated about what might happen next. Would they cancel school and send them all immediately to the Middle East? Avery heard more than one person say they wanted to go down to the city to help search for survivors. And though she didn't say it out loud, she wanted to remind them that two 110-story buildings had collapsed. From what they were showing on television, it looked like a nuclear bomb had gone off in the middle of the city. There weren't going to be any survivors.

"I just don't understand," said Hannah, wiping tears from her cheeks. "Why would anyone do something like this?"

"They're saying it's al-Qaeda," Dani explained. "Terrorists."

"But what do they want?" said Lisa Johnson. "What does killing thousands of innocent people accomplish?"

Avery had chosen a spot on the couch between Dani and Hannah, while the rest of the girls spread out throughout the room—some seated by the fireplace, others on the floor. Five plebes—girls who'd graduated high school a mere four months ago—sat in the corner, white faced. *Time to grow up*, Avery thought to herself. They would no longer get the liberty of treating their training like a joke. And Avery wished, suddenly, that she hadn't either.

At the beginning, she'd wanted to come to West Point to prove something: maybe to her father, maybe to herself. But the sound of that body hitting the ground had knocked her motivations completely off balance. Could it be possible that *this* was the reason she was here? That the universe had conspired to get her to this house, in this moment, with these people?

She shuddered, afraid of what that might mean. Dani was a natural leader. And Hannah was selfless, to a fault.

*But what about me?* Avery wondered. *Am I really cut out for war?*

*Do I even have a choice?*

Wendy sat on an ottoman with her hands resting in her lap. The television was still on, flashing scenes that made Avery cringe. People had walked out of lower Manhattan covered in white dust, their cheeks tear stained, their bodies hunched over in defeat. It was hard to watch. And yet, she couldn't turn her eyes away from their faces.

Wendy sighed deeply and looked around the room, as if she was trying to imprint the moment into her memory. Then she grabbed the television remote and pressed a button. The screen snapped to black.

"What does Mark think?" Dani asked suddenly.

Wendy's husband wasn't home tonight. Tonight, he'd gone to meet with the men's basketball team, who were likewise in shock. Avery felt oddly jealous of the familiar way Dani had called Colonel Bennett by his first name. She knew the Bennetts had a special bond with Dani after she'd lived here, recovering from surgery. But as Wendy stared across the room, eyes trained to the freckles on Dani's face, Avery felt a deep pang of sadness that she didn't have that kind of close-knit relationship anywhere, with anyone. Wendy, with her pearl stud earrings and tattered Bible, had probably heard the gossip. *She probably thinks I'm a lost cause.*

"He's in shock. Just like the rest of us," answered Wendy.

"Does he think we'll declare war?" Lisa asked timidly.

"I don't know."

Wendy paused, her chin quivering. "You know, a lot of people may not understand how people of faith—people like Mark and me—could choose to be in the Army. But what those men did today is evil. It's pure evil—killing innocent people. And I know that Mark feels honored to be part of a team that wants to rid the world of that kind of evil. It's an honorable path you girls have chosen. But it won't be easy." She dabbed a tissue under her eyes, then cleared her throat. "I've been thinking about you girls all day, and how scary this must feel. It's scary for everyone—it's scary for me too. But for you—this day will change the course of your lives forever. Maybe in ways we can't even predict."

Avery knew that was true. Already, she'd run through the memory of the morning countless times, and when she closed her eyes, the images wouldn't stop assaulting her brain. She'd never forget the color of the sky—an aggressive blue. The smell of fresh-cut grass in the air. The eerie quiet in the hallways before she turned and saw both buildings collapse, right there on television. Maybe that's what made a memory powerful. Not that it happened once, but that it happened over and over again on the screen of your mind.

They sat in silence for a long time before Wendy offered to pray. Around the room, all of her teammates had their eyes closed and they were nodding along, wiping their tears and noses.

What did they think all this prayer would change? Avery wondered. *Did they actually think someone was listening?*

"For some reason, I keep coming back to this story," Wendy said, once she'd finished her prayer. The pages of her Bible flipped back and forth, thin and worn, like she'd done this a lot. Her finger landed in the middle of a page.

"I'll paraphrase," she said, slipping on round tortoiseshell reading glasses. "Jesus was with his disciples and he got word from Mary and Martha that one of his best friends, Lazarus, was sick. And this is what blows my mind. It says, '*Now Jesus loved Mary and Martha. So, when he heard Lazarus was sick, he stayed where he was two more days.*'"

Wendy put her glasses down. "Doesn't that seem strange? He loved them, *so* he waited? When I think about love, I think of someone jumping on the first plane to come see me when I'm in trouble. But by the time Jesus arrives, Lazarus has already been dead for four days. *Four days!* He's already in a tomb; Jesus missed the funeral." She paused, letting that information sink in.

"And when Jesus finally arrives, Martha doesn't say, 'I'm so sorry you missed the funeral.' *No.* She says, *'If only you had been here, none of this would have happened.'* She's basically saying, 'You could have prevented this, but you didn't.' It's faith mixed with total confusion. 'I believe, but I have no idea what you're doing.'"

The silence was almost too much to bear. Avery wanted to jump out of her chair and scream: *EXACTLY!* If God had been there, all those people in those buildings and planes wouldn't have died. But God wasn't there, because there was no such thing as God. Tragedies happened *every single day.* To believe that God could prevent those tragedies but didn't? That wasn't confusing. It was offensive. That meant God wasn't loving—it proved He was cruel.

"I'm sorry," Avery snapped. "But I don't see what this has to do with anything."

Wendy closed her Bible. "Martha's prayer is one of the most honest, raw prayers I've ever read in the Bible. *'Lord, if you had been here, none of this would have happened.'* It's her cry from the trenches. And Jesus doesn't get angry with her. He doesn't walk away. He cries with her."

And suddenly, much to Avery's amazement, the girls were talking. Sharing. Dani said that she'd constantly felt that way about her injuries—that she wanted to believe there was a reason, but she couldn't understand what God was doing in her life. Lisa Johnson brought up Coach Jankovich. The woman grew worse and more vindictive with every passing day, and Lisa wondered how much more she could stand. Avery pressed her fingers into her eyes and felt wetness. She hated to cry. But somehow, she couldn't make the tears stop. She wanted to feel angry at God. But you can't be angry at a God you don't believe in.

"Let me get this straight. These assholes fly planes into buildings full of people," Avery cried. "And what? We're just supposed to trust that God has some bigger plan for all this? What's the point?"

Wendy took her glasses off. "That's a really important question, Avery. Keep going."

"Keep going?" Avery cried. "What else is there to say? It's bullshit."

Dani squeezed Avery's arm tight, and when Avery turned to look at Dani's face, there were tears streaking down her freckled cheeks, in heavy lines.

Wendy didn't respond immediately. Instead, she simply nodded her head, letting the sound of Avery's harried breathing fill the room.

"Yeah. It is," Wendy said finally. "It is bullshit. And I think that's why I love this prayer from Martha so much. She's saying, 'Where the hell were you, Jesus?'

"It's dirty. It's ugly. But it's faith, just the same."

9

*Spring 2002 // West Point, New York*

I have nothing to wear."

"That's not true," said Avery. "Here, try this." She threw Hannah a black dress.

Pulling it over her body, Hannah stared at herself in the mirror hung on the back of one of the wardrobe doors. The dress hugged her in all the wrong places.

"Um, no." She pulled it off her head. "That looks like I'm going to a funeral."

Her small dorm room was littered with clothes. Sequined skirts, spaghetti-strap shirts, Daisy Dukes, and dresses fit for nights of dancing were scattered across the floor. Since they were only allowed to have a few select civilian clothes in the barracks, Avery kept her stash in a trunk in the basketball locker room, where she would not get caught. For this occasion, she'd carted the trunk back down to the barracks. A pile of rejects draped the back of Hannah's desk chair.

They were allowed to wear civilian clothes only on the rarest of occasions: on infrequent Thursday night spirit dinners, B-weekends as they traveled home or to the city, and select events on campus. Thick with muscle, her thighs looked larger than she remembered, and her arms, though toned, looked strange against the pastel colors of Avery's clothes. To Hannah, dressing like a girl felt pointless, and suddenly, she understood why no guys at West Point had dared to ask her out. Who needed a ninety-degree rule when you had a wardrobe full of high-waisted wool trousers?

Propelled by a surge of anxiety, Hannah fell face-first onto her bed, wishing that she'd never agreed to let Avery Adams play stylist. How did Avery fit into these clothes anyway?

In high school, Hannah always got asked to dances. The student body had voted her homecoming queen, and the quarterback of the football team was her boyfriend for two solid years—that is, until they'd disagreed about sex. He'd wanted it; she'd wanted to wait. The relationship had ended abruptly and without much fanfare. And though she'd never been afraid of being alone in the past, with Avery around, Hannah couldn't escape the daily reminders that she was desperately, permanently single.

"You seen Avery?" a guy from the lacrosse team had asked last week, popping his head into her room.

"Nope, not here."

"Adams around?" ventured a dark-haired Latino cadet Hannah had never seen before.

"Sorry."

"Where's Avery?" John Collins would demand, for what felt like the millionth time. He was the only one Hannah knew for certain Avery was trying to avoid. Apparently, she'd broken off their fling, and the green-eyed Collins had gone green all over.

"Beats me, Collins. You might try *her room*," Hannah had said.

The last time he'd come around, Collins had thrown his fist into the cinder-block wall and Hannah thought she'd heard his knuckle crack.

"You should talk to him," Hannah had suggested a few days later in the women's locker room. She and Avery were both cleaning out their lockers after the season ended. "It seems like he might need some closure."

"Closure?" Avery said. "How much more closure can you get? I told him it's over."

As one of her closest friends, Hannah had a front-row seat to Avery's pattern of ups and downs, which started with Avery's pronouncement that she'd found *the one* and ended with her sobbing in the fetal position, because the guy had decided to date a cheerleader—better known as a Rabble Rouser—instead. The drama had grown predictable, and Hannah worried constantly that Avery would get caught behind closed doors, putting her entire future at West Point in jeopardy.

"Don't worry," Avery had said that night as they'd walked back to the barracks. "I'll take care of Collins. He won't bother you anymore."

IN THE SEMESTER that had passed since September 11, every-thing had changed at West Point.

As soon as the towers came down, West Point had increased security, outfitting every campus entrance with bomb-sniffing dogs and military police, fully armed with automatic rifles. Where once there had been open roads, spike strips now con-trolled the flow of traffic. Visitors used to be able to walk through the gates simply by showing their ID. Now they had to submit to background checks.

Conversation had changed too. Once a far-off land few could pinpoint on a map, Afghanistan had become the center of most discussions on campus. The name Osama bin Laden could be heard in the mess hall and between classes. At Grant Hall, cadets shared slices of pizza and opinions about military strategy. You couldn't turn on the news without seeing grainy images of the world's most wanted criminal: a thin, gray-bearded man seated in a cave. Whenever she saw Bin Laden's face, Hannah shud-dered. But her unease was always short-lived. Perhaps because she imagined men like her grandfather at the Pentagon planning the response, she felt confident that the U.S.-led retaliation would be over quickly. After all, America's army was the strongest in the world. Its most recent military conflict, Desert Storm, had only lasted six months.

How long could it take to find and kill one lone terrorist?

But while headlines raged, the daily proceedings of college life had moved forward as usual. Professors went on teaching. Sports teams went right on practicing. Leaves fell into piles of gold on the ground, and soon, the sky turned the color of wool. With Dani still recovering from her surgery and the loss of last year's class of seniors, Coach Jankovich promoted Hannah to the varsity team, along with Avery and Lisa Johnson. During a basketball game over the Thanksgiving holiday against Cornell University, Hannah scored twenty points, and Avery hit a half-court three-point shot in the last second to win the game. The entire arena had erupted in chaos. Hannah had never seen Avery's face so lit up with joy. Even the Cornell fans celebrated, as if West Point's ability to win a women's basketball game somehow correlated with their future ability to take out terrorists.

When they weren't on the road, they were in the gym, listening to the shrill sound of Coach Jankovich's whistle reverberate across the court. Last year's losing season meant this year, her antics had risen to a fever pitch. She was extremely hard on the plebes, Hannah thought, and had replaced her hatred for Avery with ceaseless criticism of Lisa Johnson.

"LISA!" she'd screamed a few weeks earlier, throwing her clipboard to the ground. "THOSE CORNROWS TOO TIGHT? Maybe if you'd loosen them, you could actually *think!*"

The more Jankovich yelled at Lisa, the more Dani crutched to the sidelines to give her teammate quiet pep talks. Hannah marveled at Dani's ability to motivate her teammates, despite her injuries. She called out ideas for plays during time-outs, whispered tips to Hannah during games. And rather than see her as an asset, Coach Jankovich often sent Dani out of practice for speaking out of turn.

It didn't make sense to Hannah. The fact that the players had respect for Dani didn't mean they had less for their coach. Respect wasn't pie. But Coach Jankovich's unrelenting paranoia had turned into a self-fulfilling prophecy. Team morale had never been lower.

Even Hannah, who hated conflict, had ventured to ask for a change. Practices ran late every single day, leaving the girls little time to rush back to their dorm rooms before dinner. In January, when Hannah had asked Coach Jankovich to consider ending practice promptly at six o'clock, like other coaches, she'd offered only a thin-lipped smile in return.

"So you can spend more time *IM-ing* your boyfriend?" the coach had snapped.

Hannah didn't have the heart to tell her coach that she didn't have a boyfriend, and—as long as she was at West Point— probably never would.

It seemed ridiculous that while the world was on the brink of war, Hannah's thoughts veered so often to *guys,* but she couldn't help herself. Rooming with Avery during the spring semester had put a magnifying glass on Hannah's chief worry: not a single guy had expressed an ounce of interest in her since she'd stepped foot on campus at West Point. Least of all, the one she wanted.

Ever since Colonel Bennett's philosophy class, Tim Nesmith had been like the wind—blowing past, never knowing that he'd touched her. She'd see him in the library, poring over an Arabic textbook, refusing to look up from the page. In the fall, at home football games, cadets in the stands would point up at the sky while Tim parachuted with the rest of the skydiving team into the stadium. During Christmas dinner, held every year the week before cadets went home on break, a crew of cadets in Santa out-fits had picked up a table off the floor, as five others holding ever-green branches climbed up and built a human Christmas tree on top. Sure enough, when Hannah turned to watch the spectacle, it was Tim, dressed as an angel, who crowned the tree. From that perch, he'd led the corps in a rousing rendition of "The Twelve Days of Christmas," moving his arms like a conductor.

She couldn't escape him, and yet he still hadn't noticed her.

By April of her Yuk year, Hannah had given up all hope of having a date during the entirety of her college career. Basketball season had ended and Hannah had nothing to fill her newfound free time. A week earlier, in a striking role reversal, it had been Hannah on the bed in the fetal position.

Dani had just taken a seat in Hannah's desk chair, snacking from a box of Cheez-Its, when Avery walked in from class.

"What's with her?" she'd asked Dani, pointing at Hannah and dropping her backpack.

"Nervous breakdown number six of the semester," Dani had said casually. "Standard issue."

"I've told you a million times, Hannah, no one is ever going to ask about your GPA once we're out of here."

Hannah had rolled over and narrowed her eyes.

"It's not about grades, Avery. It's about . . ." She'd paused, then groaned. "Ugh. It's about the two of you."

Dani had laughed, pointing at herself as though she were completely innocent. "What did I do?"

"You're always off with Locke," Hannah had said, then pointed at Avery. "And *you*! There's practically a line of guys outside your door every day, there to pay homage. Seriously. Have you checked lately? Someone's probably out there right now."

Avery had laughed, while Hannah pulled herself dramatically off the bed and stuck her head into the hallway. Dani chuckled and dug her hand back into the bag of Cheez-Its.

"She's losing it," Dani had said.

"Come on, Hannah. It's not that bad."

"Yes it is! This place is swarming with guys. I'll never have odds like this again! And still . . . I haven't been *touched* by a guy in two years. TWO YEARS! What is wrong with me?"

Avery raised an eyebrow. "Nothing is wrong with you. Maybe something's wrong with *them*."

In a flash, Hannah had crossed the room, lifted the window, and stuck her head into the balmy April air, looking down to the darkness of cadet area below. Around the concrete courtyard, the barracks squared off, every window lit up with golden lamplight.

"WHY WON'T ANYBODY DATE ME?" she'd screamed, her voice echoing off stone.

Someone walking across cadet area whistled up toward her.

"HELLO!" Hannah had shouted. "Hey! You! WILL YOU GO ON A DATE WITH ME?"

Soon, all three girls were in hysterics on the floor, laughing.

When they'd wiped the tears from their eyes, Avery said, "Hannah, we can get you a guy, if it's a guy you want."

"She doesn't want *any* guy," Dani had said knowingly. "That's the problem. It's a specific guy."

With a deep sigh, Hannah had nodded, dropping her head into her hands.

"So what's his name?" Dani had prodded.

"I just have this feeling."

Avery had let out an impatient groan. "Okay, okay. What's his name?!"

"Tim Nesmith." Hannah had fallen again on her bed, cradling her pillow against her face.

"The guy on the parachute team?" Avery had asked, scrunching her eyebrows together in surprise.

Wrangling the bag of Cheez-Its back into its box, Dani had wiped her hands against her black shorts and then slapped them together. "Hannah. Why didn't you say something sooner? Tim was in my Beast squad. We're like this." She crossed her fingers tight.

Against her better judgment, Hannah had permitted a bubble of hope to rise in her chest and dropped the pillow from her face. "Really?"

"Yes." Dani limped over to Hannah's computer, and spoke with full confidence. "You and I both know I can make this happen."

West Point's event calendar populated the screen, teeming with possibilities—concerts at Eisenhower Hall, half-price tickets to Broadway shows in the city. But apparently, as Dani scanned the options, her eyes landed on a recurring meeting in Cullum Hall, scheduled by the Cadet Hostess.

While social etiquette was dying everywhere else in America, West Point had to ensure the nation's future leaders didn't embarrass themselves at a dinner with a VIP guest, or at a ball with a foreign dignitary. That's why West Point kept their very own Emily Post on the payroll, also known as the Cadet Hostess. The hostess's office offered frequent classes throughout the year, in table manners, chivalry, and decorum. On the docket for April were six weeks of ballroom dancing lessons—free for any cadet who wanted to participate.

Convinced that it was the perfect cover, Dani had sent a series of instant messages to Tim that night, each message fired off faster than the one before. Hannah had watched over Dani's shoulder in horror.

**BBALL4EVA:** Tim.

**TIMNESMITH66:** Hey Dani. what's up. long time no see.

**BBALL4EVA:** Hey—Locke and I are doing ballroom dancing lessons this semester—and I need one more guy to join our crew. You interested?

**TIMNESMITH66:** ballroom dancing?:-/

**BBALL4EVA:** tuesday nights in Cullum Hall. Six weeks.

**TIMNESMITH66:** six weeks?! wtf. i don't know mcnalley . . . I'm not the greatest on a dance floor.

**BBALL4EVA:** even more reason to come.

**BBALL4EVA:** and before you go giving me some crap excuse, might I remind you that without me, you never would have made it through Beast.

**TIMNESMITH66:** that's not exactly how I remember it.

**TIMNESMITH66:** who else is going?

**BBALL4EVA:** just us and my friend Hannah.

**BBALL4EVA:** She's awesome. You'll like her.

**TIMNESMITH66:** the tall girl you're always with?

**BBALL4EVA:** possibly. I travel with a lot of tall girls. comes with the territory.

**TIMNESMITH66:** six weeks, huh?

**BBALL4EVA:** what else are you going to do on a Tuesday
    night??? Plus. You know Locke and I will make it a blast.

**TIMNESMITH66:** all right. I'll do it.

**BBALL4EVA:** I'll e-mail you the details. No backing out.

**TIMNESMITH66:** why do I get the feeling I'm going to regret
    this?

**BBALL4EVA:** NONSENSE. I've got you. It's going to be great.

"I'm not going," Hannah said now, her voice muffled by the
pillow.

She had nothing to wear, let alone the confidence to make it
through the night without puking. Dani, dressed in a V-neck
T-shirt that exposed just the right amount of cleavage, dug
through Avery's trunk, pulling out more slinky dresses and tank
tops.

"What about this?" she said, holding up a miniskirt.

"Oh my gosh, not that skirt," Avery said, pulling it back. "Bad
high school memories."

Dragging herself back to the mirror, Hannah tried another
dress and held her hair off her shoulders to see if that helped at
all. It was a bright red number that clung to her hips and waist
obscenely. "Nope." She dropped her hair. "Not gonna work. Plus,"
she said, pointing at Dani, "why does *she* get to wear jeans?"

Dani opened her mouth to speak, but Avery held up a hand to
stop her.

"Dani doesn't think dancing with Locke is a date. And she's
*barely* off her crutches, so let's give her a break, shall we?" She

plunged her head deep into her trunk. "There are very few chances to look like a real girl around here, Hannah, and I'll be damned if I'm going to let you walk out of here looking less than perfect."

Hannah groaned. "I'm so screwed."

"One can only hope," Avery laughed.

Standing up, she pulled a cotton dress that tied at the waist from her trunk. Hannah assessed its maroon color, knee-length hem, and perfect cut—and gasped.

"Wow," she said. "Give me that."

DANI HAD ARRANGED to meet the boys on the flat stone walkway called the Apron, near General George S. Patton's statue overlooking the Plain. The sky turned red, the final light of the day dying in a flash of beauty. Locke looked like he always did: shoulders broad, muscles bulging. The gap between his two front teeth conspired to make his hulking figure far less intimidating, Hannah thought. Next to him, Tim stood with his back turned to them, his hands stuffed in the pockets of a camel-colored jacket. He wore a white collared shirt and dark jeans paired with leather loafers. He looked like a Ralph Lauren model—casual and handsome. Locke pointed over Tim's shoulder, and he turned, his face breaking into a sincere smile. Nearing the boys, Hannah inhaled the spicy scent of Tim's after-shave and felt her stomach drop. *Why does he have to smell so good?*

"It's about time!" Locke said to Dani. He checked his watch. "We're going to be late."

"Calm down," Dani shouted back. Just as they began walking

toward Cullum Hall, the streetlights flickered on, and Hannah looked up, grateful for the distraction from Tim's gaze. Locke and Dani were already several paces ahead of them before Tim cleared his throat and stroked his chin.

"So, how'd she rope you into this?" he said. "Blackmail?"

"Oh yeah," Hannah laughed. "You should see the dirt she has on me."

"Well, I hope you're ready to lead. I don't know the first thing about dancing."

"Where I come from, leading is the guy's job."

"Where are you from? Mayberry?"

"Austin."

"Close enough." He smiled.

She wanted to die. He'd just put his hand on her back, guiding her up the steps toward Cullum Hall. In response, all the blood in her body had rushed to that very spot. He dropped his coat on a hook outside the ballroom door.

"What about you? Where are you from?" Hannah asked, even though she already knew the answer. Dani had told her Tim had grown up on a farm in Maryland.

"California," he said.

"Dani said you were from Maryland."

"Then why'd you ask?" he said with a grin.

Hannah blushed.

"I was born in California, so I like to claim it," added Tim. The dimple in his right cheek appeared as he smiled.

"So when did you move to Maryland?" asked Hannah.

Tim raised an eyebrow, as if to do the math. "When I was . . . let's see . . . ten days old? My parents had to get special permission for me to fly on the plane because I was so little." A moment passed, and then he explained, "I was adopted."

At that moment, Hannah suddenly knew exactly why she'd been attracted to Tim in the first place. He had a certain confidence in the way he walked and talked that she wasn't used to seeing in the South. And yet, since he'd been raised on a farm in Maryland, he had all the qualities that Hannah had grown to respect in a man, thanks to her father's and grandfather's examples. Hard work. Intensity. Determination. He was the perfect combination of the familiar and the mysterious, the relatable and the unknown. She wanted to step closer to him, and yet felt an equal desire to step away, for fear that he might sweep her up in a wave she couldn't control. She tried to imagine what his birth mother must have felt, handing her child over to a stranger. And yet, she was grateful. Because of that brave woman, he was here. Loved by his adoptive parents into the kind of man that would attend West Point, even if he bucked the system every now and then. It all made sense. He made sense.

"You're quiet," he said.

"Sorry," she answered. "I was just wondering. Do you think you'll try and find your birth parents someday?"

He shrugged. "I doubt it. I had a great family growing up. If I wonder about anything, it's what it would have been like to grow up on the West Coast. I feel like there's this surfer in me just dying to break out. But that's enough about me. What about you?"

"Hm." Hannah thought. Compared to his story, nothing about her seemed all that interesting. "I grew up in Texas. My grandfather went to West Point."

"Is that why you came?"

"No. Actually he didn't want me to come."

"But you came anyway."

Hannah smiled. "I came anyway."

"Good for you," he said, then asked with excitement, "Hey, what did you get for the summer?"

West Point had just handed out summer assignments. Hannah would only get one week at home, before reporting for Airborne School at Fort Benning, Georgia. After that, she'd return to West Point and lead plebes through basic training.

"I've got Airborne School. Then Beast Two. I get to walk plebes through the House of Tears."

"You ever jumped out of a plane?"

"Not yet," Hannah admitted. "But I've seen you do it. At the football games."

He smiled broadly. "You're going to love it. It's terrifying. But the rush you get is incredible. Like you're flying."

"Are you ever afraid?"

Someone inside the ballroom clapped their hands loudly, so rather than answer her question, Tim offered her the crook of his arm.

"Believe it or not, I'm more afraid of what we're about to do in there."

She'd never been drunk before, but Hannah was certain this must be what it felt like. Warmth passed from his body to hers and she tried not to think too much about it. If she did, her hands might start sweating.

Cullum Hall boasted cherry floors and warm wooden beams that rose all the way to the ceiling. The ballroom looked almost candlelit, with sconces glowing against the wood and portraits of famous generals spaced evenly along the walls, like they were spying on the future. The parquet dance floor filled with cadets—upperclassmen laughed and whispered at the back of the hall—while Yuks like Tim and Hannah ventured toward the front. The instructor, a short, burly-looking man with a singsongy voice, clapped his hands, gathering the attention of the room.

"Okay, people!" he shouted over the din of voices. "Who's ready?"

There was a lackluster hoot from around the hall.

"All right, fine! Act cool now. I'll have you spinning like teacups at Disneyland before the end of the night."

The instructor pointed toward the back, where a woman wearing loud pink lipstick turned a dial. Suddenly the room filled with the sounds of classical instruments. The instructor looked annoyed, then pumped his thumb in a downward motion, telling the woman to decrease the volume, which she promptly did.

"The waltz . . . ," bellowed the instructor as he pranced through the room, making eye contact with each pair of dancers, "is about forbidden romance."

The students giggled.

"Laugh all you want, but it's true. If you're uninterested in seducing your dance partner, I'd suggest you leave. Perhaps there are shoes that need shining back in the barracks."

More laughter. But at this point, Hannah knew, he'd gained the respect of the room.

"That's what I thought." The instructor bellowed over the soft hum of violins. "The waltz was the predecessor of rock and roll, if you will. Just imagine!" he gasped dramatically. "Men and women twirling on the dance floor so close together and so fast! How vulgar! How positively sinful! In those days, men and women weren't even allowed in the same room together unchaperoned—"

"Sounds familiar!" a male voice behind Hannah shouted. It was Locke. Dani smacked him with her hand. The laughter in the room sounded like the ocean, coming in regular waves.

"Well then, I guess you don't have to imagine." The instructor grinned. "For the Austrians, the waltz was this sensual break from oppressive aristocratic rules . . . in three-quarter time. Now, each pair find a square!"

Tim and Hannah realized they were standing on top of a white square, which had been taped to the floor before their arrival. The instructor stopped just in front of them.

"Now, men, wrap your right arm around your partner's back and give her a nice squeeze."

Tim slipped his right hand between Hannah's hip and arm, and pulled her in tight. Their bodies were so close, she could feel him breathing. His breath smelled minty, but as she'd expected, the rest of his body smelled like spice and cologne.

"Now, turn your faces to the left, and stand cheek to cheek."

For a moment, Hannah felt a magnetism pull her closer and she thought she might collapse into him if she didn't concentrate on holding herself upright. When the instructor glided away from them, they both broke the pose. Around the room, laughter spread until most couples had stepped away from each other.

"Not easy, is it?" the instructor said. "I've always said if we could harness sexual tension at the United States Military Academy we could power New York City for a century. Am I right?"

"This guy," Locke whispered, rolling his eyes. He and Dani had sidled up to them, looking confident with their arms wrapped around each other. "And you said this is six weeks?"

"Yes, and you're going to love it," Dani ordered.

"Is she always this bossy?" Tim asked Hannah.

"Sometimes worse," Hannah whispered in his ear.

"Let's start with a basic box step," the instructor announced. "Gentlemen, face your ladies. It's just three steps. That's it. Toes pointed toward toes, please!"

Hannah and Tim both looked down at their toes at the same time, and their heads crashed together.

"Sorry!" said Tim, rubbing his head.

"First, gentlemen, we're going to start with our feet together. Forward with your left foot, to the side with your right foot, and then close your feet together. Left, side, close. Got it? Then you do the same thing with your right foot. Right, side, close. Right now, just focus on moving forward! Ladies, same thing, only you're going backward, and mirroring the gentleman's moves. Now give it a shot!"

Tim and Hannah took the first steps together perfectly. Soon, all around the classroom, couples were waltz-stepping like pros.

"Good. One, two, three! One, two, three!" the instructor shouted. "Keep moving!"

"Wait," Tim said, looking down at their mismatched feet, "I think I—"

"This way," Hannah laughed, pulling him back.

"And that is the waltz!" The instructor smiled, looking at all his progeny. "Wonderful, just wonderful! Linda! The music!"

The song started with long slow notes, filling the ballroom with orchestral formality. Meanwhile, the instructor moved from couple to couple, eyeing them with disdain and pride, depending on their performance.

"No, no, no! *Stop*," the instructor barked once he'd reached Hannah and Tim.

He grabbed Tim by the hips and Tim's eyes bulged. Moving them like a unit, the instructor pushed and pulled Tim's hips until they'd completed one perfect waltz step. All the while, Hannah tried hard not to break into hysterics. As soon as the instructor moved away, Tim's foot landed hard on top of Hannah's.

"Oh—God. Are you okay?" He winced, as if it were his foot that had been crunched.

"I'm okay," Hannah said, rubbing her foot. "I think he meant your other left."

Looking over Tim's shoulder, Hannah watched Dani and Locke, already twirling and box-stepping around the room like pros. Tim looked at her with big, puppy-dog eyes, then looked toward the exit door.

"I guess I suck at this, huh?"

They didn't move for a while, just stood there, looking at each other. His eyes were a hazel color, Hannah realized. Brown with flecks of gold scattered throughout.

"You know," he said, "I keep looking at you and wondering how I didn't notice you last year. How is that possible? Dani said we were in a class together . . . but for the life of me . . ."

"I didn't talk much in class," Hannah said. "You, on the other hand . . ."

"Yeah, I've never been one to shut up." He laughed. "Well. It's possible I'm sucking so bad because I'm so distracted. I wish we'd met a long time ago."

The compliment came out of nowhere. Equally genuine and playful, it sent blood rushing to Hannah's cheeks.

"It's hard to focus on my feet, when I'd rather look at this beautiful girl I just met."

"No, no, no," Hannah said with a smile, feeling her insides ache with joy. "You're not getting off that easy. We've got six weeks of this, mister, and flirting won't get you out of it."

"Oh, you thought I was talking about you?" he said. "I was talking about Linda."

They both turned to look at the pink-lipped woman in the back of the room, who was bobbing her head along with the music. They broke into laugher, then spent the rest of the class stepping on each other's feet and smiling uncontrollably. Hannah loved the pressure of his hand on her back, the brightness of his smile, the jokes he kept throwing out to distract her from how bad he was at dancing. She felt the muscles underneath his shirt flex and move with the music. Then she felt the pang of something else— something invisible taking root in her heart.

Love starts in the body. It starts with the tingling of toes and the rushing of blood and the lightness in the head. It feels a lot like pain, Hannah would realize later that week, as she and Tim shared slices of pizza in Grant Hall, and three weeks later, when they took a five-mile run together up Bear Mountain. There are convulsions, nausea, heartburn, and breathlessness. There is a physical ache you feel when you're falling in love. It's your heart making room for someone else, like a gardener is there, digging out a hole for a new plant. There is pain, and there is fear. The fear that the hole might stay forever.

10

*Spring 2002 // West Point, New York*

F ourteen days, D. Fourteen days and we're out of here."
A barbell loaded with two fifty-pound plates dropped from
Locke Coleman's hands to the gymnasium floor with a loud
crash. In the mirror, Dani watched him slide the large weights off
and move two forty-five-pound plates onto the sides.

"Here," he said. "I think you're ready for one thirty-five. Do a
clean."

For the last few months, Locke had made it his personal mission to help Dani fully recover from her injuries. He told her what
to eat, how fast to run, how much to bench-press. And now he
was monitoring how much weight she could lift from the ground
to her shoulders. With a heave, she completed the move, in one
snap of the wrists and hips.

She hadn't told him that the old familiar twinge was back
again—that ache in her right hip. But it was possible that the dis-

comfort was just residual scar tissue from last fall's surgery, or a by-product of doing cleans with the wrong form. Plus, if she ignored the static in her joints, she could lift nearly as much weight as she had this time last year, and that was something.

Three months earlier, at the last practice of the season, the entire women's basketball team had written the name of the player they wanted to serve as captain next year. Coach Jankovich read the votes out loud with growing disdain.

*"Dani McNalley... Dani McNalley... another for McNalley..."*

Normally, the team chose a rising Firstie to be captain. And since Dani had truly only had *one* season on the court, this vote felt particularly kind. So she *had* to be better by next season—there were no excuses.

Releasing the bar, Dani looked at herself in the mirror. Her muscles had returned, arms sculpted, quads toned and strong. The scar on her hip had faded from red to dark brown, just a few shades darker than her skin. She finally looked like an athlete again, and not a moment too soon. This summer—in fourteen days, in fact—she and Hannah were headed to Airborne School. At times, the image of her body falling out of a plane with nothing but a parachute made her shiver with nerves. According to Tim, the biggest obstacle to overcome wasn't getting used to the height, or the equipment, or the risk. It was getting used to the fear.

"Everyone's scared," he'd explained a few nights earlier, while cooking a pot of spaghetti for Hannah on a hot plate in her room. "Everything in your body screams at you to step back from the edge—your palms sweat and your heart rate goes up, and everything in your head shouts that this is suicide. But once you're actually in the air—once you've jumped—all that fear goes away and you just fly. It's crazy. Most people never step over the boundary of fear."

Dani liked having Tim Nesmith around. Ever since ballroom dancing, he and Hannah had been inseparable. West Point's newest poster couple were nothing alike, of course. Tim was loud, opinionated, and spontaneous; Hannah was quiet, reserved, and thoughtful. But somehow, together, they were like opposite sides of a magnet that refused to separate.

"They're so attractive, it's annoying," Avery had whispered to Dani a few days earlier when they were passing between classes. Tim and Hannah were ahead of them, allowing the backs of their hands to touch every few steps. Academy rules prohibited holding hands.

"It's like, I can't decide who to look at," Dani said. "Him or her? They're both so beautiful."

They'd cracked up, mostly because it was true. The lovebirds looked like a Hollywood couple that had accidentally put on uniforms, and while Dani could admire their newfound love without growing a root of jealousy, she was pretty certain that it was becoming a difficult feat for Avery. It seemed hard for Avery to be content when faced with evidence that Hannah was happier with Tim than Avery had ever been with her fleet of boyfriends. Three weeks earlier, disregarding Hannah's new relationship status, Avery had planned a girls-only trip to New York City.

"We deserve this," Avery had said. And knowing it was their last B-weekend of the year, Hannah and Dani had complied.

Wendy Bennett had dropped them at the Garrison train station, and they'd taken the commuter train into Grand Central Terminal, stepping off the train and into the dirt, grime, and electricity of the world's most beautiful city.

"Soho," Avery had said decisively while they were on the train, pointing to the southwest corner of Manhattan on her map. "Then Greenwich Village or midtown. There are supposed to be some great clubs around there."

"The clubs all ID," Dani had said.

In response, Avery displayed a collection of freshly laminated driver's licenses like playing cards. "Here you go, Agatha. And you." She passed one to Hannah. "Juliette Ramsey."

"I don't know about this," Hannah had said. She turned her head to the side to inspect her alias.

"We won't use them unless we have to," Dani had said to Hannah, warding off Avery's annoyance. "And if we get some better clothes in Soho, I'm guessing we won't have any trouble getting into the clubs."

After a hearty brunch of French toast and coffee at a bakery on Bleecker Street, they'd meandered in and out of the stores in Soho, purchasing clothes that they'd later change into in the bathroom of a Starbucks in the Flatiron District. At Express, Avery had chosen a slinky black dress. Dani replaced her jeans with a tight miniskirt, to show off her newly sculpted legs. A fire-engine-red dress had called Hannah's name, and even though she'd cringed at the amount of skin it exposed, the girls had forced her to carry it to the checkout line.

They spent the night dancing, and when a limousine of FDNY

firefighters pulled up next to the club they were trying to get into, Avery had talked her way into their party, securing their entry into every club for the rest of the night. Because of their heroic efforts after the attacks on September 11th, the city still treated firefighters like celebrities, keeping their drinks full and their tabs on the house. At two A.M., Hannah had started to grow weary, rubbing her heels and staring at Dani pleadingly.

"Let's leave," she'd shouted over the music. "I'm ready to go back to the hotel."

"No, no, no," Avery had interjected. "Rally! Come on. This is our one chance to be in the city."

Hannah asked for a bottle of water from the bartender, who rolled his eyes as he delivered it to her hand. "Tim's going to love hearing that I partied 'til dawn with a bunch of bachelor fire fighters."

"Well—with all due respect—Tim can suck it," Avery had shouted back over the din of the music. "You're not doing anything wrong. And we've earned a little fun."

"She's kind of right," Dani had said, pinching Hannah's elbow. "Be a college kid for once. You can go back to being responsible tomorrow."

Hannah shook her head and chugged her water. Then she said, "It already is tomorrow."

"He's going to hold her back," Avery told Dani once they'd returned to life in uniform the following week. "They're both so serious."

"They're seriously in *love*," Dani had replied. But the explanation fell on deaf ears.

Lately, Avery had been sneaking around with God knew who at God knew what hour of the night, as if by the sheer volume of people she dated, she could find what she was looking for. Dani had started to wonder what had happened in Avery's past to make her so ravenous for attention. She was like a diabetic, only instead of sugar, she couldn't absorb love. Or, maybe, she absorbed it too quickly, and constantly felt the need for more. Whatever the problem, Dani wondered how long Avery could go on like this. Rather than dealing with her deficiency, Avery kept running, working hard to prove her worth and amass awards and achievements and admirers. But to Dani, all that effort seemed exhausting. She wondered if Avery would ever stop running. She wondered if she'd ever have the courage to stand still.

If she needed any advice, Dani knew where she could turn—after all, she was becoming an expert at being single.

"That looked good," Locke said, bringing Dani out of her thoughts. "Go again."

She picked up the bar, completed another perfect clean, and let the bar drop to the floor.

AFTER DINNER, THEY went back to Locke's dorm room to study for West Point's Term End Exams, known as TEEs. *The Miseducation of Lauryn Hill* played from Locke's computer speakers, mingling rhymes of revolution with Dani's pack of physics problems. While she measured velocity and torque, she grew distracted by other sounds coming from Locke's computer. A door creaking open or slamming shut. The sound of a loud *cha-*

*ching,* indicating that someone special had come online. The constant *ba-da-bing* of an incoming AOL instant message.

"You're popular tonight," Dani said, putting her pencil down on the paper in front of her. "What's happening up there?"

In truth, she worried Locke might be chatting online with some other girl, even while Dani sat comfortably on his floor. In the last six months, he'd had countless opportunities to make a move. Throughout the ballroom dancing lessons, they'd moved across the dance floor with more chemistry and ease than anyone in the room. She'd grown tired of feeling his hands spotting her in the gym, rather than reaching for her to pull her in for a kiss.

A few weeks earlier, Dani had been sitting in Wendy Bennett's kitchen, talking about this very thing, when Wendy had firmly set her coffee cup on the counter and sighed.

"You're going to drive yourself crazy waiting around for him to make a move."

Tears had welled in Dani's eyes, as if the truth had unlocked some inner door, letting the emotion free. A tissue box appeared on the kitchen table, but swallowing hard, Dani forced the tears back to where they came from.

"That's not true," she'd insisted. "Locke and I *are* friends. I don't want to lose that."

"You're going to lose him one way or another. One of you will start dating someone else. Someday you'll both be married. It won't be like this forever."

"So what? Stop being friends now because maybe someday we'll marry other people?"

"No. I'm saying you should tell him how you feel."

"It's not that easy."

"Of course not," Wendy had said. "Doing the right thing never is. That's how you know it's the right thing."

Locke's broad shoulders hunched over his keyboard, his eyes trained on the computer screen. And suddenly, the thought of spending two more years in relationship purgatory overwhelmed Dani with frustration. Wendy was right. She deserved an answer, but she would never get it waiting around on Locke's dorm room floor.

"Hey, Locke," Dani started. "I think we need to—"

"Oh man," said Locke, interrupting her. "D, you've got to come see this."

The somber tone of his voice and the shock on his face sent Dani's eyes directly to his computer screen. There, a collage of images assaulted her—pale white limbs, curves, pink nipples. Dani pushed Locke out of the way. She scrolled quickly, her eyes reflecting the bright light of the computer screen, the images of one naked female body, over and over again. Locke stood behind her, biting his lower lip.

"Where did these come from?" Dani snapped. She looked back at Locke, who raised his hands in the air—*Don't shoot.*

"Someone on the football team just forwarded them to me. It was a zip file. I didn't know . . . I . . . What are you doing?"

Clicking maniacally, Dani toggled through the photos, pressing *Print* on each one. She snatched the photos off Locke's printer. The pages felt warm in her hand.

"What are you going to do?" he repeated. "Where are you going with those?"

Without answering him, Dani limped out the door. As she made her way down the stairs and outside, Dani couldn't stop thinking about Lisa Johnson. Three weeks earlier, she'd found Dani in the library and tearfully admitted that in the fall, she was transferring to Tulane.

"I can't do it," Lisa had said. "I can't go to war, D. And even if that wasn't happening . . . Coach Jankovich. She . . . she's ruined this place for me."

For her part, Coach Jankovich had acted as if it was a personal victory. "*It was only a matter of time,*" she'd said in response to the news, as if Lisa had finally been outed as a weakling, rather than acknowledging her role in breaking her down so far that Lisa no longer saw a future for herself at West Point. Dani had spent hours trying to convince Lisa to stay, to no avail. It felt like a personal failure, losing a teammate. Her first failure as the next team captain.

And she wasn't about to let these photos be her second.

IN THE HOLLEDER Center, most offices were reserved for football coaches. Since spring football practice was in session at Michie Stadium, and the rest of West Point's coaches were on recruiting trips, the entire place was empty and quiet. Unfortunately, it was harder than ever to recruit competitive players, now that the U.S. was engaged in an all-out war on terrorism—*whatever that meant.* Dani still didn't understand the long-term strategy of a war against a network of people that had no flag, no country, no identifying characteristics other than hate.

*How do you defeat fear? How do you defeat evil?* It seemed like a never-ending task that could lead to never-ending conflict. *How would they ever know that they'd won?*

But the war was only one reason that recruiting had become so difficult. Fluorescent lights lit the corridor outside of Coach Jankovich's office, and one flickered, like a fly had been caught in its electrical circuit. It couldn't hurt to change a lightbulb or put a little effort into updating the facilities, Dani thought. But West Point wasn't like other colleges; they practically needed congressional approval to turn up the air-conditioning. And if recruiting had been difficult for Coach Jankovich before, it was about to get much harder. No one wanted to send their daughter to a place where she'd be treated like a piece of meat.

Taking a deep breath, Dani knocked on the coach's office door.

MINUTES LATER, THE printed photos were spread out over Jankovich's already-crowded desk, an array of identical bodies, like images from a crime scene.

"How did you get ahold of these?" the coach asked.

Each photo showed the same person from a different angle, decapitated by the top edge of a camera lens: light skin, thin waist, round breasts, hairless between her legs. A headless body—bare for the entire corps to devour.

"My friend received them in a forwarded e-mail."

"How do you know this is our locker room?" she asked, lifting one photo in her hand.

"The carpet, see?" Dani pointed to the distinguishing black and gold lines. "And the . . . well. I know it's ours, because I know who that is."

Blood rushed to Dani's extremities as she watched the coach inspect the photos, turning them from side to side. *What is she looking for?* Letting out a massive sigh, Coach Jankovich ran a hand through her short hair, and it stood askew, pointing in different directions. She suddenly looked Dani directly in the face, her steel-blue eyes narrowing.

Silence spread between them, leaving the room devoid of oxygen. Dani coughed, took a breath, and tried again.

"I think we should report this. Someone hid a camera in our locker room and is now—"

"The damage is already done, wouldn't you say?"

"Coach, I—"

"Doing that is going to cause a huge scandal. There will be news crews. A massive witch hunt. We have a hard enough time recruiting girls without something like this. Every one of our recruits will renege on their commitment, Dani. Is that what you want?"

"No. But this isn't about basketball—"

"Of course it's about basketball! So someone snapped a few nudie photos in the locker rooms. Big deal. It's not exactly rape we're dealing with here."

"Does it have to be, for it to be wrong?"

The coach steeled her gaze.

"Whoever did this used a digital camera," Dani continued pleadingly. "The angle is bad. That's why you can't see the face.

They were taken from above—like someone stashed a camera above our lockers or something. And they're not photos. You see the time stamp here? They're *still shots*. Whoever did this has *video footage*. The camera could still be there."

"Well, then, we will remove it."

"We can't just do that, Coach . . . if it's there, it's evidence." Dani hated how exasperated she sounded. She wanted to reach across the desk and shake her coach into caring. Into understanding.

"Jesus, Dani. You sound like you think you're on some crime show or something. We'll deal with it internally and move on."

There was a long pause, and in it, Dani knew she had to make a decision. She could walk away, or she could push back against what was an obvious attempt to brush this under the rug. Without a doubt, if she made any demands, her relationship with Coach Jankovich would never be the same.

After taking a deep breath, Dani decided to push forward.

"As the team captain, I felt it was my duty to bring this to your attention before I take it up the chain of command," Dani said with authority.

"Oh my *God*! You people!" Coach Jankovich laughed derisively. A square smile appeared on her face that looked forced and awkward. She stood from her chair, narrowed her eyes until they were dark slits. "I don't know what you're playing at here, but I can guarantee one thing. If you think you can come in here and make *threats*, you can think again. What did you do? Did you tell them all to write your name down, so you could lead your little revolution?"

"What?"

"You and your little *cult*. I bet you did this. Put the camera there. Sent the e-mail yourself."

"Coach, you and I both know that that's ridiculous."

"The only thing that's ridiculous is the fact that all of my work is going to go down the drain because of this trash." Picking up the photos off her desk, she gripped them tight, crushing the pages.

Dani bit the insides of her cheeks, hard. *How could someone be this paranoid? This blind?*

"What makes you so scared of the truth?" Dani asked boldly. "That's one of your *players*. And when she finds out what's happened, she's going to be *crushed*. Don't you care? Aren't you concerned about her at all?"

"I'm concerned about the big picture," the coach said.

"You're concerned about yourself."

They stood, facing once another across her desk, refusing to blink.

"You're dismissed."

Dani turned to leave. She took a halting step, feeling a surge of pain.

"And you can forget about being captain," the coach said, then lifted her chin toward Dani's hip. "That is, if you can even play anymore."

LATE THAT EVENING, Dani sat next to Hannah on her bed, the two of them poring over the photos. By this point, every male on campus had received the zip file, of that much Dani was certain. It was only a matter of time before the women on campus started to get wind of the fact that naked photos of a female cadet were being passed around like common pornography.

"We have to tell her," Dani said to Hannah. "Before we do anything else. We have to tell her."

Hannah shook her head and groaned. "This isn't going to go well at all."

"Where is she?" asked Dani.

"I don't know. I never know."

"Well then, let's go to her room. We'll wait."

# WEST POINT ALMA MATER

*

*Hail Alma Mater dear, to us be ever near*
*Help us thy honor bear, through all the years.*
*Let duty be well performed*
*Honor be e'er untarned*
*Country be ever armed,*
*West Point, by thee.*
*Guide us, they sons aright, teach us by day by night,*
*To keep thine honor bright, for thee to fight.*
*When we depart from thee,*
*Serving on land or sea,*
*May we still loyal be,*
*West Point, to thee.*
*And when our work is done, our course on earth is run*
*May it be said, "Well Done, Be Thou at Peace."*
*E'er may that line of gray*
*Increase from day to day*
*Live, serve and die we pray,*
*West Point, for thee.*

# BETWEEN

*Three Months After Graduation*

*Fall 2004*

**11**

*Summer 2004 // Fort Bragg, North Carolina*

Avery woke up naked in bed with a twenty-six-year-old enlisted soldier named Josh Ramirez. Pushing a white-blond hair off her face, she stared at the Tilt-A-Whirl ceiling, wondering how much she'd had to drink the night before. She'd lost count somewhere around her seventh gin and tonic. A heavy arm fell across her stomach and a face covered in day-old stubble nuzzled her neck. Avery sighed loudly. It was time for Josh to leave.

"What's your exit strategy?" she asked.

The man kissed her neck and traced his fingers across her hip. "I was hoping for seconds," he mumbled into her ear.

Avery wrapped the scratchy comforter she'd bought at Target over her chest. "Well, that's too bad," she said. "Because I was hoping for breakfast."

She kissed him on the cheek, then turned to put her feet on the floor. The air mattress had partially deflated overnight, making it awkward for her to stand. Fighting the headache already building behind her eyes, Avery slipped into a robe and then walked out the door into the hallway, where she let out a silent scream and stamped her feet.

She couldn't believe Josh was still in her bed! It was Sunday, for Christ's sake. At the beginning of their relationship—if you could even call it a relationship—they'd agreed to one rule. *One rule!* No one stays over; no one gets caught. How hard was that for him to understand?

When she'd moved into her Army quarters four weeks ago, she hadn't considered that living across the street from another second lieutenant could make life so painfully awkward. Living on post meant that she was close to work, and could wake up at 0550 and still be at PT by 0600 every morning. But now, Avery deeply regretted her choice to live among her coworkers. As a part of the Signal Corps, she planned wartime communication strategies with her neighbor Lieutenant Erik Jenkins during the day, and waved to his twenty-three-year-old wife from the opposite kitchen window at night. There was no way Josh would leave undetected. Did he realize that her reputation was on the line? If someone saw her, an officer, with him, a first sergeant, it could mean the end of her career.

*People get court-martialed for this shit,* Avery thought. But did they? Really? With all that was going on in the world, would the Army really prosecute her for a little fraternization? Surely not. Avery felt painfully stupid, but not just because her head was pounding. Two days ago, she'd been sitting across from a female soldier having a conversation about this exact same subject.

On Friday afternoon, a girl with dark brown hair had appeared in Avery's office, having just arrived at Fort Bragg from Advanced Individual Training. The girl wore tight jeans and an even tighter white T-shirt. Thick eyeliner encircled her blue eyes; a slick of gloss accentuated her lips. With curves and a slight tan, this new private had all the flair you're supposed to have when you've just graduated from high school: dewy skin, bright teeth. She looked nothing like a soldier. Sitting in front of a woman in civilian clothes, Avery couldn't help but think how unfeminine and ridiculous she must have looked in her Army combat uniform. Loose at the thighs and tapered at the ankles, her ACUs looked like a better fit for MC Hammer, and the jacket was a size too big, with a black nameplate on her right breast pocket. Instinctively, Avery had touched the patch of acne that had appeared on her jawline. Wasn't she too old for zits?

"Welcome to Fort Bragg, Private Bradley," Avery had said, replacing the beginnings of jealousy with the voice of authority. "I'll be your direct superior from this point forward. If you need anything at all, if you have any questions, you can bring them to me."

"Yes, sir." The girl blushed. "Ma'am. Sorry."

As Avery thumbed through the girl's file, the new soldier chewed her fingernails. Eyes wide and anxious, she appeared dazed and jittery, just like Avery had been back at West Point on those first days. Cleavage threatened to spill out of the private's shirt, like she'd dressed for a job interview at a strip club, not the

U.S. Army. Had this kid looked in the mirror before walking in here?

"How old are you, Private Bradley?" asked Avery.

"Eighteen. Nineteen next month."

*Eighteen.* The number flashed before Avery's eyes. When Avery was eighteen, her civilian life had ended, too. Four years had passed since then, but somehow, seated at her own desk with West Point behind her, twenty-two felt ancient. In minutes, this new recruit would head back to the barracks, where an onslaught of twenty-something males would see her as their newest opportunity for conquest. Unfortunately, it was Avery's job to keep that kind of drama to a minimum. Her boss had sent out a memo the week before, reminding his lieutenants that certain STDs disqualified soldiers from readiness for deployment. Apparently chlamydia was making a comeback.

The girl had been sitting on her hands. Something about her oozing sexuality and ignorance had felt deeply embarrassing to Avery, like interacting with her former self. She refused to make eye contact, but instead kept looking at the items on Avery's desk: a half-eaten paper pint of oatmeal, a green juice in a clear plastic container, a framed photo of three girls standing in the middle of New York City. Watching the private's eyes widen with anxiety, Avery felt a sudden wave of compassion—a desire to keep this girl from making all the mistakes she'd made at eighteen, nineteen, and twenty. She wanted to tell her that even the nicest, most innocent-looking men could stab you in the back. In the heart.

"You just finished high school?"

"Yes, ma'am. Last spring."

"First time away from Mom and Dad?"

The girl nodded, smiled.

"There's no easy way for me to say this." She tapped the papers together into a stack, trying a firm and strict tone on for size. "It's very important that you carry yourself *professionally* here. I can't have you getting involved with anything that might distract you or your fellow soldiers from training. Because, to be completely honest, that training could save your life one day."

The girl sat up straight. Her eyes had a vacant and subtly terrified expression, like a deer on the verge of being flattened by an SUV.

"I'm just saying, be on your guard," Avery continued, trying a softer approach. "As far as any of these men are concerned, there's only one woman in uniform . . . and it's you."

"I'm not sure what you mean," she'd said.

"What you do reflects on all of us, Private Bradley."

Avery had known, seated there on Friday afternoon, that she was engaging in a losing battle. But she had to try.

DOWNSTAIRS IN THE kitchen, Avery pulled a carton of eggs from the refrigerator and a skillet from the cabinet. As a single second lieutenant, she had plenty of storage space that she didn't need and didn't use. Most of the cabinets were hollow and empty. She hadn't had the luxury of registering for everyday china after graduation like Hannah and Tim. Shouldn't girls have an *I'm single but I still want to cook registry*? Or an *I may never get married so someone buy me sheets shower*? Avery thought so.

And yet, all the Pottery Barn linens that Hannah and Tim had received as wedding presents were still in boxes. Avery knew, because she was the one tasked with collecting any delivered packages while Hannah was at Sapper School in Missouri and Tim was at Ranger School in Georgia. Three sets of perfectly good five-hundred-thread-count sheets sat in boxes in the Nes-miths' house, while Avery suffered under itchy cotton bedding that deserved to be in a Motel 6 Dumpster. It would have been easy to steal—no, borrow—the newlyweds' new goose-down comforter, but Avery hadn't resorted to theft. At least not yet.

She still couldn't believe one of her friends was *married*. Even the word sounded odd when it came out of her mouth. *Marriage.* Total commitment to one person, for the rest of your life, until you died or they did—whichever came sooner. It seemed like the worst possible contract you could ever sign. And Avery still couldn't believe that Hannah and Tim had decided to do it. They were only twenty-two years old, and both facing long-term de-ployments. Avery couldn't understand the rush.

But then again, Avery didn't understand any of their relation-ship. The summer after their sophomore year of college, while Hannah and Dani attended Airborne School, Avery had stayed at West Point to complete Air Assault training. She'd been grateful to learn that Tim Nesmith was in her company, but for some reason, he'd avoided her all summer. And when she heard that he'd kissed another girl in their training class, Avery went ballistic.

"Is it true?" she'd snapped at him one night, pushing him hard with both of her hands. She had tracked him down in a small tunnel that ran underneath Washington Road. The Beat Navy tunnel featured placards from the years Army had defeated Navy in football, and was echoey, a place where people shouted and cheered for their team. It was odd to stand in that tunnel and remain so silent. Tim stepped away from her, and though she didn't want to see his emotion, it was plastered all over his face: shame, fear, regret. The rims of his eyes turned red.

"It was a huge mistake," he'd said. "I'm going to tell her, Avery. Please. Just let me tell her first."

Avery had spent the better part of junior year telling Hannah not to take Tim back. Not after what he'd done. Not even after his apology. By the time they were Firsties, Dani had to stage an intervention of her own.

"You realize he's going to propose, don't you?" she'd said to Avery one night their senior year. It was after Tim's accident. After his radical conversion and Hannah's unconvincing speech to Avery that he'd *changed*. "You've got to forgive him, Avery," Dani had told her. "He's one of us now. He's in the cult."

After that, Avery had tried her best to swallow her pride. She'd even helped Dani coordinate Tim's ridiculous proposal—Avery was the one who'd scattered rose petals across the floor of Cullum Hall. She'd lit the candles. She'd sketched the ring: a full-carat diamond, princess cut, perched on a delicate gold band—the style Hannah had let drop to her friends in casual conversation, knowing Tim would ask for their input.

In June, three hundred guests had gathered at Hannah's grandfather's ranch in Austin, Texas, under Chinese lanterns hanging from trees, cows lowing in the distance. A dance floor and a ten-piece band set up outside, under the stars, and played loud into the night for Hannah, Tim, and all of their friends. Instead of cake, they'd served ten different types of pie—Hannah's grandmother had baked them all from scratch. Hannah wore a lace dress and her mother's old veil, and when she'd walked down the grassy aisle between the guests, Tim had cried. Hell, everyone had cried. It was all so soul-crushingly *meaningful*.

"I don't know if it'll ever happen for me," Avery had said to Dani, seated on the Speer's porch swing.

"Of course it will."

"Not like that," Avery had retorted, pointing her beer toward the outdoor dance floor. Hannah and Tim were swaying in each other's arms.

"Well of course not like that."

"There won't be pies," said Avery.

"Tequila shots, maybe."

"Yes." Avery had pointed her beer at Dani. "Tequila shots and maybe a man dressed in an Elvis costume, officiating. And my mother, sobbing in the corner because she finally has proof that I'm not Catholic."

"Just don't make me wear yellow," Dani had demanded. "On second thought, I'll do the Elvis thing."

They'd laughed their way back to the dance floor, arms wrapped around one another's backs.

While the memory simmered in Avery's mind, two eggs sizzled in a lightweight pan, whites oozing around the edges like spilled paint. As breakfast cooked, high-quality coffee beans filled Avery's kitchen with the bittersweet smell of oak and butter. If she was honest, it was kind of nice to have a man upstairs, waiting on breakfast. It felt good to have a chance to share her house with someone other than the cast of *Grey's Anatomy* on Thursday nights. She could get used to this new arrangement.

Just then, the dark-haired man from her bed snuck up behind her and cupped his hands over her hips. Turning, Avery admired Josh's eyes, deep brown, like the earth. And his hands, so warm against her skin.

"I should go," he said.

"What do you mean? I'm making breakfast." She pointed at the eggs with her spatula.

He yawned and raised his arms up over his head, revealing a thick torso rippled with muscles.

"Stay," Avery ordered, reaching for his pants seductively. "And that's an order."

The heel of his hand rubbed against one eye, as if he had a migraine. "Avery, I don't get you. It's yes, it's no. It's 'Don't drive to my house,' then 'Who cares about the neighbors.' I never know which version of you I'm going to wake up with."

He stared into Avery's eyes so unflinchingly that she burst into a nervous laugh. "Come on, Josh," she said. "You know we have to be careful. That's not fair."

"Yeah? Well, now you know how I feel."

"So go," she snapped. "Leave then."

"I can't."

Avery stared at him and he stared back in silence. The eggs hissed and whined in the pan, turning brown and then black at the edges.

"I need a ride back to my car," he finally explained. "You drove last night, remember?"

In one motion, Avery grabbed the skillet handle and slammed the eggs into the sink. As she climbed the stairs to change and get her keys, yellow trails of yolk inched toward the drain.

THE DRIVE BACK to the bar where they'd met up the night before only took them a few miles off post. They didn't speak, and soon Fort Bragg's gate filled the rearview mirror. The silence was a horrible sound. Avery knew that if Dani were here, she'd know exactly what to say—a joke to throw out and defuse the ticking time bomb. But anger had momentarily paralyzed Avery's vocal cords.

When she pulled her car into the bar's gravel parking lot, Josh coughed, as if he too needed to shake an emotion out of his throat.

Avery fully expected him to apologize for staying so late and violating the one boundary they'd established for their pseudo-relationship. She thought he'd kiss her and get out of the car, and they'd be back to their odd version of normal. Instead, he turned toward her and took in a breath.

"Can I say something?" he asked.

"I think you have that ability, yes."

"What is this?"

"This is me, dropping you at your car."

"No. I mean, *this*." Josh swung his hand back and forth between them. "Us."

Avery rolled her eyes. "You can't be serious."

"I want to hear you say it."

She tugged on her blond ponytail. "What? We're screwing around. Being kids. Is that what you want me to say?"

Josh shook his head. His voice barely exceeded a whisper. "You're incredible. Really, fucking incredible. You do whatever the hell you want, whenever you want. No matter who gets hurt—"

"Hurt?" Avery reared her head back in anger. Her voice was low and mean.

"I should have known—"

"I put my entire career on the line—"

"*Your* career?" he laughed. "You truly think you're the only one in this equation, don't you? It's the *Avery Adams Show*, twenty-four-fucking-seven."

"Get out of my car."

"Gladly." Josh opened his door and climbed out, then looked back at her again. "Do yourself a favor, Avery. Stop fucking around with people that love you."

With that, he slammed the door and walked toward his truck, a silver Toyota Tacoma—the only vehicle left in the parking lot. Avery stepped on the gas, spewing rocks and dust into the air behind her.

*LOVE,* AVERY THOUGHT with a laugh as she pulled back into her driveway. That was a joke. They'd only known each other a few months. When they'd met, she was recovering from a year of involuntary chastity at West Point, and Josh had the body of an English soccer player. The sex was good. Hell, at times it was great. But if this guy thought he was in love, well then Avery had fooled him. And she didn't feel bad about it either. If she felt bad about anything at all, it was being a hypocrite. She'd told Private

Bradley to be careful on Friday, just to return to her own reckless life on Saturday.

Avery was glad Josh had ended it. As with so many other relationships, she was convinced that this one should have never even started.

ON MONDAY, AVERY arrived at work before the sun came up and completed a freezing-cold PT run with her platoon, finishing the two-mile course in 12:07. Not her best time by any means, but she crossed the finish line a full minute before anyone else. She'd seen it time and time again: once her soldiers tasted her dust on a PT run, their skepticism softened into respect. She would have hated their conditional admiration if she didn't savor it so much. But she often wondered if without her physical edge, she would have remained invisible. What if she was slower? Would such weakness merit scorn? These were the questions that rolled in her mind while she savored her post run endorphins.

After a shower and a microwaved bowl of oatmeal at her desk, Avery noticed an e-mail in her inbox from her boss's boss, Major Philip Gaines.

*"LT Adams, please report to my office this morning. I need to see you as soon as possible."*

Avery's blue eyes scanned the screen again, while her heart raced in her chest. It was unusual for someone to jump the chain of command—up or down—but even more disconcerting, Gaines had carbon-copied her direct superior, Captain Morris. The subtext screamed that something was wrong. He'd sent the e-mail Sunday afternoon, meaning he'd heard something during off hours that he wanted to discuss. Did he know about Josh? Had someone, somehow, turned her in?

*Erik fucking Jenkins,* Avery swore internally. She closed her eyes and tried to remember her neighbor's porch, Sunday morning when she and Josh had rushed out in anger. Erik's wife—Melinda? Melissa?—whatever her name was, Avery distinctly recalled her red hair piled in a messy bun as she stared out the window onto the street, a hand resting on her hip. *Shit,* Avery thought. *We should have been more careful.*

The Army, at times, infuriated Avery. All of its rules. Its demands. Its ladders of authority. The Army was a lot like her dad, actually—constantly providing new bars to reach, moving each bar higher every time Avery got close. It wasn't that she needed to be coddled, but to hear that she was doing a good job every once in a while wouldn't have hurt. She could handle being read the riot act for leaving a job unfinished or not meeting the standards. But was she really about to be counseled about who she *dated* on the weekends?

She always chose the wrong people to date on the weekends.

As Avery took a deep breath, her eyes veered to the framed photo on her desk, and she felt longing mixed with regret. It wasn't like she wanted to go back to her dysfunctional family in Pittsburgh, or to West Point—her friends had left that place behind, too. And yet she couldn't shake the feeling that she wanted to go home. But where would that be?

How could she be homesick for a place that didn't exist?

In the photo, she and Dani stood on either side of Hannah, their smiling faces surrounded by the madness of Times Square.

The photo sent a kaleidoscope of memories spinning through Avery's mind. Hannah's short red dress, stretching as she pulled it down her thighs in the firefighters' limousine. Dani's commanding moves, dominating dance floors. The limousine's tinted windows, distorting city lights into a blur. A firefighter's callused hands rubbing Avery's lower back. Avery had been so committed to staying out all night—so convinced that it was their only chance to be young and free.

In some ways she was right. Only a few weeks later, she'd been blindsided. Knocked out cold. Avery would never forget walking into her dorm room and seeing photos of her own nakedness splayed out in Dani's shaking hands. Nausea had swelled into her throat, like the earth was falling out from beneath her. She'd collapsed into Hannah's arms, overcome with anger, sadness, and shame.

Wiping her eyes, Avery forced the memory back into the recesses of her heart where it belonged, like a collection of junk stuffed into a dark basement. There was no reason to unpack that box. It was in the past. Dealt with. Over. And reliving that time—that trauma—wouldn't help her now.

Steeling herself, Avery breathed in deeply, rolled her shoulders back, and stood from her desk. There was nothing to feel ashamed of. She hadn't done anything to deserve what Collins had done to her, and she definitely didn't deserve to lose her career over a momentary misstep—a relationship with Josh that no longer existed. She imagined facing Major Gaines and denying everything. After all, the Army took everything she had during the day. Couldn't they leave her nights alone?

"YOU WANTED TO see me, sir?"

Major Gaines was in his early thirties with thinning hair and a large, mostly bald head. Turning from his computer, he gathered a few papers off his desk and tapped them into a neat stack, without looking Avery in the eye.

"Yes, take a seat. I've got a few things to finish up, then we can chat."

Typing at his keyboard, he composed an e-mail, added an event to his calendar, then closed down all the tabs on his desktop. He worked quickly, Avery noticed, like a squirrel gathering nuts in the last few days before winter.

"All right," he sighed, finally turning to look at her. "Thanks for coming to see me."

"Of course." Sweat seeped out of the pores in her hands, her armpits, her neck. "How can I help, sir?" She forced a smile.

"I have a job that I need to assign. It starts in a few months. It's a big job, actually, and it's going to require someone that can remain focused and work really fast."

All of her pent-up anxiety deflated like a balloon. So he *didn't* know about Josh. *Thank God.* She shifted in her seat, listening closely.

"One of the new Special Forces facilities needs wiring. Phones, Internet. The works. It all needs to be wired and encrypted. Captain Morris says you're one of his best lieutenants. We'd like you to lead the job."

Avery nodded with confidence, though she simply felt relieved that this meeting had nothing to do with her romantic indiscretions.

"Wow, sir. Thank you. I'd be honored to do it."

"Those SF guys are always in and out, so the important thing is that you don't get in their way. You'll need a team of ten or twelve I'd say, and the same rules apply to everyone." He stared at her intently. "You don't talk. You don't ask questions. You don't make friends. You get in, keep your heads down, and get out. Understood?"

"Yes, sir. I'm honored that you'd choose me to lead the job."

"Is there a reason I shouldn't?"

A beat passed before Avery answered, "Absolutely not, sir."

"Good. Let's put a few more meetings on the books. You've got a few months to get all of your ducks in a row, choose your team, order all your equipment. And let's keep Captain Morris carbon-copied on all our communication on this. Keep him in the loop."

"Yes, sir," Avery said. It was rare for a second lieutenant to be given such a huge responsibility. *Special Forces. Just wait until the Nesmiths hear about my job.* Tim was hoping to join the Army's most elite unit as soon as he got the chance. He'd be green with envy.

**From:** Avery Adams <averyadams13@yahoo.com>

**Subject:** Re: Re: Re: **Update

**Date:** August 27, 2004 12:03:15 PM GMT +01:00

**To:** Dani McNalley <danimcnalley@yahoo.com>, Hannah
  Nesmith <hannah_nesmith@yahoo.com>


HEY HEY HEY.

How is everyone?! Dani . . . any news on the job front? Hannah—how is Sapper School treating you? I'm dying to hear an update from the cult.

Things here are fine—nothing major to report. Although, Hannah, you've received about 6.5 million presents in the last few weeks. I'm probably going to start opening them and picking out the things I want to take for my cut. It's only fair that your favorite bridesmaid get a little slush on the side.

In other news . . . I got a really crazy assignment today from my boss's boss. It's going to start in the spring, and I can't really e-mail about it because it's classified (what?! Who am I??)—but the good news is, it's here in Fort Bragg, so I'm still not going overseas for a while.

What about you, Hannah? Have you heard anything about deployment dates for your unit?

ALL HAIL THE CULT,

Avery

*Summer 2004 // Fort Leonard Wood, Missouri*

A fist slammed into Hannah's face, hard. An African-American soldier named Private Daniel Stanton stood in front of her, his red boxing gloves drooping at his sides. Her vision blurred and suddenly, all of the sounds in the gymnasium were submerged in water. She swayed.

The next thing Hannah knew, she awoke on the ground, staring at a ceiling of fluorescent light. The scent of old wrestling mats and sweat assaulted her nose, and she tasted metal in her mouth. When she touched her fingers to her nostril they were covered in blood.

Things were not going as planned.

When she'd arrived at Fort Leonard Wood for Sapper School, Hannah knew the odds would be stacked against her. In the history of the Army, only twenty-three females had ever attempted the highest training school available for combat engineers—and of those, only nine had graduated. Hannah wanted desperately to be number ten. In the past eight weeks, she'd built helipads, jumped from a moving helicopter into open water, and, just the day before, scored full points rappelling from a cliff with a 220-pound soldier strapped to her back. All of it without a single complaint. Not even a groan.

There was only one test left. If Hannah could just wrap Private Stanton's hands behind his back—if she could just achieve the clinch—she would graduate, the tenth female Sapper in history. All she had to do was step to her six-foot-three attacker, drive her head into his neck, push his arms out to the sides, and pin his arms around his back. But so far, every time Hannah stepped closer to him, all she got was Stanton's fists in the face.

"All right, boys, I think I found our weakest link." A shadowy figure leaned over Hannah's body until his face was just inches from hers. The barrel-chested NCO, Master Sergeant Moretti, had yellow teeth and breath that smelled of weak coffee. He flapped his clipboard over Hannah's face. "Come on, get up, Nesmith."

Stilted laughter pounded against Hannah's ears as Moretti offered her his hand.

"I'm all right," she said, forcing herself to stand without his help.

Moretti rolled his eyes and inspected her face. "It's broken."

"I've had a broken nose before," Hannah said. When she was six years old, her sister, Emily, had accidentally thrown an elbow in her face while they were playing freeze tag. "I'll be fine."

"Stanton, hold her head still," Moretti yelled to Hannah's opponent.

Stanton's palms pressed against her sweaty hair while Moretti placed both of his hands on either side of the bridge of her nose, like he was praying. He paused. "This is going to hurt."

"Just get it over with," Hannah muttered. She closed her eyes and braced for the pain.

With one swift motion, Sergeant Moretti slammed his fingers against the right side of her nose, snapping it back into alignment. A shock of blue light flashed through Hannah's brain. An involuntary shout emerged from her lungs. Hannah chewed on her lips to keep from crying, then walked a few paces to regain her breath.

"None of us enjoy watching you get the shit beat out of you," Moretti said. He'd followed her to the side of the gymnasium and placed a hand on her shoulder. "I'm thinking it may be time to call it quits. Come back next cycle. Try again."

Hannah forced herself to breathe. She didn't want his sympathy. She hadn't stumbled into Sapper School by mistake. Couldn't he check his clipboard? Wasn't it just that morning that she'd smoked them all on the six-mile run? But there was no way around the fact that Stanton's fists flew faster and harder than she'd expected. He was denser than she could ever be. And the way he looked at her, with some kind of perverse hunger, it was like he wanted to break not just her nose but something deeper. Hannah had been one of the highest-ranking cadets at West Point—guy or girl. Now her ovaries were a flashing neon sign to everyone in the room that she couldn't keep up. All around, men crossed their arms over their chests, waiting. Some looked bored. Some looked concerned. Most looked amazed that Hannah was still standing.

With a fresh wave of nausea, an echo of words swirled in Hannah's mind, a phrase she hadn't considered in some time. *It's not a matter of capability.*

What if her grandfather had been wrong? What if she really couldn't keep up? What if he'd been right, that she shouldn't be here?

Tim had warned her of this. That summer, after graduation and their wedding, Hannah, Tim, and a dozen other class of '04 grads had flown to Rome and boarded a cruise ship that had transported them between six different Mediterranean cities. While their friends drank themselves silly, Tim and Hannah had secluded themselves as much as possible, knowing it was the closest thing they'd get to a honeymoon. They were lounging on the deck of a ship, a few hours before it docked in Florence, when Hannah told Tim that she'd been given a slot at Sapper School, starting in the middle of August. He'd raised his aviator sunglasses and his eyebrows.

"Sapper School?" he'd said. "Really?"

"I think I can do it," replied Hannah.

"I *know* you can do it," he'd said. "I just don't see why you'd want to. Those guys will hurt you on purpose, just to prove a point."

"No they won't. And even if they did, should that stop me from trying? Why do you want to get a Ranger tab?" Hannah had added defiantly. "It's the same thing."

Tim leaned back in his chair, sighed, and put his glasses back on his face. Ranger School was the Army's most intense, brutal training. It was a rite of passage, a symbol of capability, an immediate indicator that an officer could be trusted, and the most direct path to the Special Forces, which had been Tim's dream since childhood. Sapper School wasn't nearly that extreme, but it held a similar cachet, and when Hannah arrived in Fort Bragg to lead her first platoon, she wanted her soldiers to know that she was a serious leader, serious about the Army. If anyone could understand that, she knew Tim would.

"Well then I guess we have to get you ready, Rocky," Tim had said, looking around the deck of the ship. "They got any stairs we can run around here?"

True to form, they'd spent their last few weeks together preparing. They went on long, fast runs through the hills of Santorini. He held her feet while she did sit-ups in the ship's fitness center. At night, they'd drink an entire bottle of Italian wine before walking back to their room, where Tim would undress his wife slowly and lay her down against the bed. He'd made her work hard, but he'd rewarded her for it, too.

In the three years since they'd gone dancing at Cullum Hall, Tim Nesmith had completely transformed her life, and she his. The entire corps of cadets was shocked to learn that they'd paired off—Tim was known for his wild escapades on the skydiving team, while Hannah's nickname was *Miss Congeniality*. At school, she and Tim would stay up late, having long conversations about religion and God and family. They'd dream about their future.

"Is that what you want?" he'd asked early on in their dating relationship, after Hannah had described her grandparents. "To grow up and be like Barbara? House. Kids. Ranch."

"I don't know," Hannah had said. "It's not a bad life."

"But what about a career? Do you want to work or stay at home?"

"Do I have to have an answer right this second?"

"No, of course not. You can change your mind a million times. I just wonder what you picture. That's all."

At the time, Hannah didn't exactly have a vision of what she wanted. She imagined getting married. Having children. But she'd been successful at West Point, far more successful than she'd even expected. At the time, her junior year, she'd ranked in the top one hundred of their class, even higher than Tim. Uncertain, she'd shrugged. "What do you picture?"

"My parents have such a traditional marriage," Tim had said. "Mom stayed home. Dad worked. She packs his lunch, even to this day. And at night, she fixes his dinner plate, like he's a child. I don't think I could do that. I don't want some wife that just sees herself as my servant or something. I want an equal. A teammate."

From that point forward, that's how they'd built their relationship. As a team. They always supported one another, always encouraged one another. In the summer, when West Point offered them different assignments or schools, they went, without talking about the distance. It wasn't always easy. They'd broken up for an entire semester junior year, after Tim had admitted to kissing another girl while he was at Air Assault School. That all felt so silly now. So long ago. His accident had brought them back together, and now, Hannah couldn't imagine a life without him.

A lesser man might have told Hannah to slow down—to choose a low-key Army career that could more easily follow his path. But Tim told her to live out loud. To take on the challenge of Sapper School. To chase greatness while they still had the chance.

"We're going to be married for our entire lives," he'd said to her when they parted ways after the cruise. He kissed her forehead. "These few months apart are nothing in the scheme of things. I know it's going to be hard. I know this isn't normal. But we're stronger together. And I'd rather have you and be apart than not get to call you my wife."

Just before Grad Week at West Point, Dani had jotted down the dates like a mathematician on a scrap piece of paper. Two weeks on the cruise. Then Hannah would spend a month at Sapper School, while Tim went to Ranger School. Three months at Officer Basic Courses in different states—Hannah to become an engineer, Tim to join the infantry. After that, they'd take turns at the National Training Center with their units. Then back-to-back deployments, twelve months if they were lucky, fifteen months if they were like everyone else. Staring at the list, Hannah had felt the onset of vertigo.

"Hannah," Dani had said. "Do you realize that you guys will have, like, five weekends together . . . in the next two years? No." She'd tapped on the paper quickly, as though arriving at the correct answer to some equation. "Four. Four weekends!"

Hannah knew. Tim knew, too. But as if ignoring the calendar would make the days pass more swiftly, they'd never spoken of it. So far, any time Hannah had ever taken a step of faith, God had provided her the strength to get through it. Fingering the cross necklace she wore, Hannah said a prayer and shook off all the uncertainty she'd felt moments ago, when Moretti adjusted her nose.

She could do this. If she could survive four years at West

Point—if she and Tim were going to survive the next two years apart—then she could survive a little hand-to-hand combat.

At least she hoped she could.

"I'LL GIVE YOU one more go. But after that, we've got to call it. Understood?"

"Yes, sir," she said to Moretti. "Just give me a second."

Stepping outside, Hannah placed one finger against her right nostril and blew air through the left. A rocket of blood and mucus flew to the ground. She did the same for the other nostril, and then wiped the rest of the blood on her shirttail, exposing a strong, toned stomach. It wasn't very ladylike, but at this point, Hannah didn't care. She didn't care whether or not these men thought she should be here. She just wanted to achieve the clinch with Private Stanton and get the hell out of this place.

"All right then." Moretti turned to the men waiting in the gymnasium once Hannah had returned. "Set it up, Stanton. She's coming back for more. Don't let him make you his bitch, Nesmith. Get in low and punch up."

Hannah knew what she had to do. This was her last chance to prove she was worth the investment the Army had already made. That four years at West Point were not in vain. That everything she'd already survived wasn't a fluke, and everything she was about to face she was capable of overcoming. That Tim wouldn't have to worry about her in Afghanistan, and that nothing could hold her back from coming home to him. Stanton's face blurred into nothingness. The walls of the gymnasium fell away and she focused on his chest. Then Hannah lurched forward, one last time.

THREE DAYS LATER, Hannah sat among three rows of men, all of whom were wearing desert-colored fatigues. A general delivered a speech. Someone projected a video onto a large screen with clips from their weeks of training overdubbed by heavy metal music. The video elicited plenty of oohs and ahhs from family and friends who'd made the trek to Missouri for the ceremony. But when Hannah's parents, Bill and Lynn Speer, had asked if she wanted them to fly up for the graduation, Hannah had insisted they save their time and money. In the Army, goodbyes were far more important than congratulations.

These days, when Hannah mentioned going to the field or breaking her nose in hand-to-hand combat, her mother barely flinched. Injuries, deployment, weaponry—it was as if she were talking about what she was making for dinner. Hannah looked around the room and had a depressing thought. All these parents would have to say goodbye soon enough. Then they'd know what all this was really about.

"Second Lieutenant Hannah Nesmith!"

Master Sergeant Moretti called her to the podium, where he reached out, shook her hand, and then saluted her.

The Army was organized into two distinct hierarchies. Officers, like Hannah, held college degrees, and could climb in the ranks from second lieutenant all the way to general. Soldiers, like most of Hannah's cohort at Sapper School, could enlist right out of high school and hoped to advance from the Army's lowest rank, private, to sergeant, first sergeant, or, like Moretti, master sergeant status. Because Moretti was a noncommissioned officer, it didn't matter that he had been in the Army for nearly as long as Hannah had been alive. Simply because she held a college degree—simply because she was an officer—she outranked him. For the weeks of Sapper School, Moretti had been her instructor, but now that was over, and protocol pushed Hannah immediately back into her rightful position as his superior. After his salute, she returned the gesture.

The small green patch in his hand looked like something her mother could have sewn onto her Girl Scout uniform when she was a kid, only this one was lined with rough Velcro. Hannah turned to the side and stood at attention.

"Sappers lead the way," Moretti said proudly. He attached the tab to the fuzzy patch on Hannah's left uniform sleeve. Then he saluted her again. Hannah saluted back.

"Sappers lead the way."

WHEN THE CEREMONY ended, Hannah lingered by the table of refreshments and twirled her wedding ring around her finger. She smiled and shook hands as people passed and introduced them-selves, but on the inside, she felt like she'd swallowed poison. She tried to tell herself she shouldn't feel depressed. She'd just accom-plished something incredible! Only nine other women in the his-tory of the universe had graduated from Sapper School! Certainly they hadn't felt this crummy afterward. Hannah shook her head and took a swig of weak lemonade. Was it that she was alone? Or was it that having the patch didn't make her feel any more ready for what was ahead?

"You know, the Army doesn't love you back," Wendy Bennett had said to Hannah one night at her house.

It must have been Firstie year—around the time that Hannah was trying to decide which branch of the Army to choose. She'd been on a run around campus when she found herself surrounded by the trees and redbrick homes in Lusk Area. The Bennett's house was lit up, and despite her sweaty appearance, she decided to drop in to say hello. Maybe deep down, she'd known she needed a cup of coffee and some advice more than she'd needed the run.

"You and Tim are both really ambitious," Wendy had said knowingly. "But the Army will take everything you have to give. Uncle Sam rarely says thanks."

Just then, Hannah felt a tap on her shoulder. When she turned around, it took her a moment to place Private Stanton. He smiled so wide and so kindly that he hardly looked like the same menacing force that just three days ago had broken her nose. He stood next to a stout woman with dark braided hair and a large bosom.

"Ma," Private Stanton said, "this is the one I told you about. Lieutenant Nesmith."

Hannah smiled. The woman opened her arms wide, then squeezed Hannah in a tight embrace against her ample chest. Hannah couldn't help but feel relieved to have the human contact. Stanton's mother smelled earthy and fresh, and Hannah breathed her in greedily. The scent of cocoa butter reminded her of Dani, and made her suddenly homesick, not for a place, but for her people.

"Daniel tells me you're goin' to Fort Bragg, too," the woman said. She gripped a silver cross in her well-manicured hand— much larger and more intricate than the one hidden beneath

Hannah's uniform collar. "I just thank God someone's gonna be lookin' after my son."

Hannah stared at Stanton with wide eyes. Even though Hannah was combat trained, the Army had regulations against women leading combat platoons. Hannah would *not* be looking after him at Fort Bragg. She was headed to a headquarters unit, tasked with building combat outposts, not living or fighting in them.

"Please tell me your mother doesn't think I'm your platoon leader?"

"That's exactly what she thinks because that's exactly what he told me." Stanton's mother reared her head back. "You wanna explain, Dan?"

Private Stanton passed his mother a cup of lemonade. "No, Ma. I said I *wished* she was my platoon leader. You ought to get your ears checked."

Hannah was shocked. The fact that Private Stanton wanted her as his platoon leader spoke volumes about his respect for her—but then she laughed. "He's only saying that because he feels bad for breaking my nose. Let me guess. He didn't tell you that either."

"No, he told me that." The woman nodded, eyebrows raised. "I hear he messed you up good."

AS SHE WALKED out of the Army building, past a flapping American flag and into the dusk, Hannah pulled her cell phone out of her pocket. Indulging her sadness, she dialed Tim's number, knowing that because he was still at Ranger School, he wouldn't answer. But the sound of his voice on his outgoing voicemail message would be enough to soothe her loneliness. The phone rang once. Twice. And then she heard his voice.

"Hannah?"

"Wait." Hannah stopped in the middle of the parking lot, stunned that he'd answered. "Tim?!"

"Yes!" he laughed. "It's me! How are you? God, I miss you."

"I miss you too!"

"Am I talking to a Sapper?"

"*You are!* I'm literally walking out of the graduation ceremony right now. I did it!"

"I knew you would," he said with pride. "You deserve it."

"But I didn't expect for you to answer," she said. "What's going on? Did you finish?"

A sigh resounded across the miles, touching them both with its audible breeze.

"I recycled," Tim admitted. He'd been cut from the training, offered a chance to try again.

Hannah's eyes closed; she felt the pain in his voice. "Oh, babe, I'm so sorry."

"I'll start again in a week."

Hannah felt her heart sink. More time apart.

"I only have one more phase to pass," he continued. "The mountain phase. I think I can do it. I was just so sleep deprived and hungry, I just lost my cool. You should see me. I look like a skeleton."

"I wish I were there to nurse you back to health."

"Soon enough."

"I don't want to hang up," Hannah said as she approached her rental car. It was stuffed with her gear, ready for her drive to the airport.

"Then don't," Tim said.

With that, Hannah pulled out of the parking lot with a smile on her face, a phone on her ear, and the assurance that everything would be okay. Every risk had its reward, and hers was Tim's deep, smooth voice over the phone. Sure, their marriage wasn't traditional, but they were a team. Stronger together, even if they were apart.

"Tell me everything," he said. "You kicked ass, I assume."

"Well, I'll start with this. A private broke my nose."

**From:** Hannah Nesmith <hannah_nesmith@yahoo.com>
**Subject:** Update from Sapper School
**Date:** August 30, 2004 12:03:15 PM GMT +01:00
**To:** Dani McNalley <danimcnalley@yahoo.com>, Avery
    Adams <averyadams13@yahoo.com>

Check out this picture, ladies. You're looking at America's tenth-EVER female Sapper. Not bad for a day's work. (Actually more like a month, but who's counting?)

Tim is still at Fort Benning at Ranger School. We're hoping he'll finish up before too long, so we can finally have a minute together. Looks like Christmas will be our best bet. Seriously, our life gives new meaning to "ships passing in the night." To be honest, this is far harder than I ever expected. When I get back to Bragg, I'm going to need some serious hang time with my people.

Dani, can you come to Bragg to see us? Avery—hope your new job won't keep you too busy to hang when I get back!!

Can't wait to be home.

Hannah

*Summer 2004 // New York, New York*

D on't forget your swag bag!"

A man standing at the ballroom entrance offered a neon green tote to the woman standing in front of him. The banner above the door read, *Service Academy Career Conference,* and his name tag said, *Hello. My name is BRAD!* in dark marker.

"There's a lot of great stuff in there," he said, tipping a shock of white hair toward the ballroom of potential employers. He extended the bag a few inches closer.

Dani took the bag reluctantly. The truth was, she didn't want any "swag." The thought of being at a career fair had humiliated her enough before *BRAD!* had entered the picture. Since graduating in June, she'd collected three flimsy bags from three separate career fairs, sixteen brand-emblazoned pens, several empty promises, and not a single paycheck. Every swag bag was a rude reminder that she was broke, living with her parents, and on the verge of coaching middle school basketball, just to get health insurance. Couldn't *BRAD!* see that?

People back in Ohio kept saying inane things to try to draw a silver lining around her disappointment. "Everything happens for a reason," they promised her.

"When God closes a door, he opens a window!"

But that line of thinking wasn't logical, let alone biblical. Who was to say the room only had one door? And how did you know it was even a room? What if the room you were supposedly stuck in was really just a prison of your own making? Dani wasn't about to sit around waiting for some theoretical window to open in her life. She was going to pick up a hammer and make her own way out.

"What company?" *BRAD!* asked.

"E & G," answered Dani. "I'm supposed to meet Jim Webb."

He laughed. "No, I mean at West Point. What company were you in at West Point?"

"Oh, right," Dani said, trying to hide her surprise. Over the summer, she'd grown her hair into a short and twisted Afro, a modern version of what her mother's had been like in the 1970s. No one in the civilian world would ever have guessed that six months ago she'd been on track to be an officer in the U.S. Army. The way Dani dressed, with her new leather jacket and big hoop earrings, made most people assume she was an artist or a poet, and she didn't mind the mistake. She was impressed that Brad could cut through her appearance that quickly and see the truth. People saw what they wanted to see. She'd half-expected him to ask if she'd wandered into the service academy career fair by mistake.

"H-4," Dani answered.

"I was class of '66." He looked away for a moment, then looked back. "I should probably keep my mouth shut. But I'll say this. Perseverance. This whole transition thing can be a long road. Just keep on moving. Persevere."

A sudden rush of emotion swelled in Dani's throat. The constant pain in her pelvis, unaffected by the Advil she popped every few hours, didn't help. Hot tears filled her eyes and she fought valiantly to keep them from falling on her cheeks. Her lack of emotional vulnerability had made her successful at West Point and it was going to help her to succeed in the business world, too. But somehow, this man, with a class ring that matched her own, had spoken to a part of her heart that needed to be touched.

*Persevere.* She knew he was right, but she didn't want this to be a long road. She wanted a job. She wanted to feel that, like her friends' lives, her life was actually going somewhere.

"Thank you," she said, clearing her throat. "I appreciate that."

After shaking his hand, Dani limped past the entrance and into the hotel ballroom. But before she was out of his line of sight, two other veterans approached Brad and received swag bags. One had a prosthetic right arm, while the other looked completely normal—uninjured, unmarred by the journey he had taken to get here. Compared to the amputee, who'd clearly given a limb for his country, Dani's "disability" was a joke. The naked eye couldn't see why the Army had given her a medical release, setting her free from the five-year service commitment cadets had to complete after West Point. The men at this career fair couldn't understand how weird it felt to be here, in this ballroom, instead of preparing for war. Then again, Dani didn't know why the man standing next to the amputee had gotten out of the Army either.

Some wounds are invisible. It doesn't mean they're not real.

The room was larger than she'd expected, with several dozen rows of six-foot tables. Music thumped from speakers in the front. A host of young veterans in brand-new suits wandered through the room like lost, overdressed children. An NBC news crew held court in the center of the room, where a blond reporter interviewed men about their service. She kept asking banal questions that showed just how little she understood about the military: *What kind of job are you looking for today? Oh, and what exactly is civil engineering?*

When Dani had learned she wasn't going to receive a commission from the Army, Colonel Bennett had made several phone calls on her behalf, trying to help her scrounge together gainful employment. Surprisingly, his Rolodex didn't only include other Army colonels. He'd called several business owners in New York, three congressmen, and even one Supreme Court justice. All of those leads had turned into dead ends. Jim Webb was her last shot.

Dani rarely felt this nervous. If Avery were here, she'd march up to every table with a smile and her natural sex appeal and have three job offers before noon, Dani knew. But thanks to an undisciplined summer, Dani had gained more than a few pounds, thickening her middle, where her six-pack abs used to be. Even if the Nordstrom employee had been right—even if her black pants and brown leather jacket produced a natural slimming effect—sex

appeal wasn't her strongest weapon anymore. And if her relationship with Locke was any indication, it probably never had been.

On the cruise they'd all taken through the Mediterranean that
summer, Dani was convinced their relationship would finally
cross into new territory. Tim and Hannah couldn't keep their
hands off of each other. Avery was constantly flirting with the
waitstaff, in particular a Syrian bartender named Ludo. Meanwhile, Dani and Locke continued their practiced dance, constantly stepping closer and stepping back. Days upon days of
spreading suntan lotion over each other's bodies had driven Dani
nearly mad. And just when she thought that it was all in her head,
the ship had docked in Florence and Locke had disappeared with
his football buddies for a few hours, only to reappear holding a
brown package wrapped in twine.

"Open it," he'd said, with his signature gap-toothed grin.

Unwrapping the package, Dani found a saddle-colored leather
jacket, supple and worn, just her size. She'd taken one look at the
price tag and told him there was no way she could accept it, but
he'd ignored her protests and placed it around her shoulders.

"Your new uniform," he'd said. "Trust me. It's perfect."

That night, he'd found his way to her room, into her bed, next
to her body. They'd interlocked fingers and fallen asleep. That was
it. Four years. One leather jacket. And then, nothing.

"Not even a kiss?" Avery had asked at breakfast the next day.

Dani shook her head. "Nada."

"Do you think he's gay?" she'd whispered.

Dani had rolled her eyes in response, as if that were the dumb-
est question she'd ever heard—though the possibility had crossed

her mind, too. In the years since she'd arrived at West Point, her little brother, Dominic, had come out of the closet—and Locke knew that she'd supported him. If Locke was gay, she was certain he would have told her by now. As it was, Avery couldn't understand how two people could *not* fornicate when left alone.

"He's not gay," Dani had answered finally.

Her friend raised an eyebrow and took a bite of eggs. It was unspoken but understood that Avery should drop the subject, and she did. Over the years, Dani and Locke had had plenty of deep conversations—much deeper than the conversations Avery had probably had with her latest fling. Dani still held out hope that Locke would eventually realize the truth: they were best friends. And what else did you need in a soul mate than for them to be your best friend?

Standing to the side of the ballroom, she pulled a brand-new Motorola cell phone out of her purse and flipped it open. Her fingers flew fast across the Razr's thin keypad, toggling through each number to get to the right letters. Phones needed to be equipped with keyboards, she thought. It would save so much time.

*Made it to NYC,* she wrote in a text to Locke. *I'm the best dressed in this place. San Lorenzo 4 tha win!*

*Atta girl,* he sent back in a flash. *Tell New York hello for me. Just don't go getting lost with the FDNY this time, K?*

Dani chuckled, then replied: *No promises.*

PULLING A MAP from her neon sack, Dani quickly decoded the madness around her. E & G, the company she'd come to meet, was tucked between FedEx and a cable company on the opposite side of the ballroom. Google had a table on the far north side, Microsoft had set up to the south, and a host of Fortune 500 companies floated in between. There weren't any creative companies here, Dani noted. No television studios or music labels. As if America's veterans didn't have stories to tell. Shaking off that thought, she stepped into the maze, walking between booths like she was avoiding dirty carnies.

"Good morning!" chirped a woman with slightly bouffant hair. "Enter our raffle for a Bluetooth?" She pointed to a roachlike clip on her ear. "They're the next big thing."

Dani respectfully declined, turned a corner, and spotted a booth filled with two leather couches facing one another on a Persian rug. All the other booths looked sterile and boring, but the scene ahead looked like it had been ripped from one of Hannah's home decor magazines. An older man sat on the left couch, one leg crossed over the other. He wore round tortoiseshell glasses and a black half-zip sweater. A blue collar peeked out from beneath the sweater and his salt-and-pepper hair was trimmed close on the sides—handsome, Dani thought. Lean, like he woke up every morning to run. Like a West Pointer. Dani wasn't one to bet. But she would have put her life savings on the fact that this was the man she was supposed to meet. This was Jim Webb.

Suddenly, he stood from the couch and smiled in her direction. Dani limped forward and her heart began to pound.

"Now, I'll be damned if you're not Dani McNalley," he said. He had a Southern accent and a warm handshake, broken only by the cold platinum mass of his West Point class ring.

"Damnation avoided, sir," Dani said.

Jim Webb laughed out loud.

"Here, Dani," Jim said, "there's someone I want you to meet. Laura Klein, this is the kid I was telling you about. Dani McNalley."

Suddenly, a woman with short blond hair and a tight black dress appeared in front of her, fingering a pearl necklace and smiling, like she'd just been told some hilarious joke. Wrinkles fanned out from the sides of her eyes like spiderwebs. Red polish shined brightly on her fingernails.

"Oh, *you're* Dani," Laura said with an air of laughter. Her words were elevated by an aristocratic British accent. "I was expecting a man! You know. *D-a-n-n-y*," she spelled. "No offense, but you don't exactly look like you went to West Point."

"I don't usually bring my guns to interviews," Dani said. Laura Klein stared back blankly—apparently the British didn't follow American sarcasm. "I'm kidding. They took the guns away."

"What'd I tell you?" Jim said, addressing his colleague. "She's quick."

With a confused chuckle, Laura took a seat on one of the sofas.

"When did they start letting in your kind, Dani?" Jim asked.

Dani clenched her teeth to keep her jaw from dropping open. *Her kind?* "West Point admitted females in 1976, sir," she replied evenly. "Its first African-American in 1870."

"Well aren't you the double threat?" Laura remarked, taking a sip from her Evian water bottle.

"Triple," Dani said. "I'm also handicapped."

Jim laughed again. "Mark said I'd like you. Here, take a seat!"

Dani smiled and tried to hit her internal reset button. Jim Webb had made some strange comments—so had Laura—but Dani had heard worse. One awkward moment shouldn't ruin her chances at a great job opportunity.

"About that handicap. Now that you've brought it up," Jim continued, "I can legally ask. You just graduated this spring, right?"

"Yes, sir."

"So why aren't you out there fighting the Taliban?"

He said it like a Southerner—*Tally-ban*. As if they were an Afghan tribe that prohibited taking a count of anything. But it was a valid question. One that divided people into two clear groups: the people who genuinely cared about Dani's condition, and the people who secretly thought she'd invented an ailment to avoid the war. She couldn't tell which camp Jim fell into, but if nothing else, she appreciated his candor.

For a moment, she wondered how much of the story she should tell. Should she start at Beast, when she felt a twinge in her hip while trying to qualify with her rifle? Or fast-forward to Buckner, when her hip had snapped brutally while she carried Locke uphill? Should she recount the surgery? Or the moment the doctor had presented an X-ray showing the ligaments in her pelvis frayed like rope, white and fuzzy against the light? She could tell him she'd led the women's basketball team to a winning season her junior year—scoring more points than any female player in academy history. But that was a rabbit trail. Most important was the crack she'd heard while leading plebes on the thirteen-mile ruck march back to campus from basic training, when she was a Firstie. Once again, the X-ray blurred white, telling her everything she needed to know. Another surgery. Another round of rehab. Wendy sat next to Dani in April of her senior year, eight weeks before graduation, when a look of dismay appeared on her doctor's face. He shook his head, presented Dani with a form. *Medical Release.*

It was the longest story she'd ever lived, but the shortest way to tell it was to speak the truth.

"I'd always had aches and pains while at West Point. But, as you can imagine, I thought that came with the territory. I was running sprints and lifting weights with the basketball team. I did all the rucks. All the training. I had a few back spasms, here and there. But my health devolved.

"The doctors kept thinking I was tearing ligaments. There were surgeries. Two actually, one my sophomore year, and one my senior year. I thought I'd recover in time for graduation, but after that second surgery, I ended up getting a second opinion, and the civilian doctor said I shouldn't have had the surgeries in the first place. It was never a torn ligament—it was chronic arthritis."

"Arthritis? Isn't that something grannies have?" Laura Klein asked.

"Grannies and me," Dani said with more kindness than this Klein lady deserved. "The long and short of it is, I probably should never have been admitted to West Point. After that, my fate was sealed. I appealed it. But there was no way I was going to receive a commission. I was medically discharged the day after graduation."

"Well." Jim sighed. "That's quite a story. Although, you may have dodged a bullet. I'm not sure women should really be on the front lines anyway."

"Unfortunately, I'm not sure there are 'front lines' anymore, sir," said Dani.

"True enough. The good news is, in the corporate world, women have been my best assets. In my experience, women have more integrity. They're better listeners. Better multitaskers. Women don't let their ego drive decisions. Do you know what I mean?"

"Yes, sir, I think I do," said Dani.

Laura smiled, looking content with Jim's shower of compliments on their gender.

"A man earns a little money," Jim continued, "he makes a few good decisions, and he kicks back, thinks he's infallible. Like it's going to come easy. When a woman gets some success, it's never enough. She's already looking for the next challenge. All I'm saying is if I see two equally qualified people, I'd choose the woman every time."

Dani nodded. In some ways she agreed with him. She'd seen more than enough male ego at West Point to last her a lifetime. And sure enough, she was hungry for the next challenge. If her time at West Point had taught her anything, it was that she wanted to do something with her life that *mattered*.

"Your credentials are quite impressive," Laura said, picking up where Jim had left off. She looked down her narrow nose at a piece of paper Dani assumed was her résumé. "NCAA athlete, ranked in the top fifteen percent of your class. Somehow, you maintained high physical performance scores despite your condition, so I know you have a high pain tolerance. That counts in this profession, believe it or not. You have to have thick skin."

Laura paused, and in that moment, Dani assessed that everything she said seemed rehearsed, like she was playing a part for Jim's benefit. The smart, authoritative businesswoman. Dani wanted to reach over and tell her it was okay to take off the mask. To relax and be herself. Instead, she just listened to Laura's tight intonation and overconfident up-speak.

"I just want to make sure you have the math brain for what we'll be asking you to do here," Laura continued. "It's research. Statistics, data mining. Dry stuff."

The news stories Dani had scanned the night before had informed her that E & G was trying to land a five-hundred-million-dollar client, a men's product line based in France called Gelhomme. She'd already read the job description online, and every line she'd checked off in her mind—she had exactly what they needed.

"Behavioral psychology isn't dry to me. And, at the risk of sounding overconfident, I'm light-years ahead of any other applicant in terms of understanding the male psyche, simply because of my time at West Point. Honestly, if you want to get Gelhomme's business, you're going to need me."

After a long pause, Jim said, "You understand it will require you to watch men shower?"

"Well, they'll have on trousers," Laura said, to clarify. "Swim trousers."

"Of course," Dani added. "That doesn't bother me. The trousers or the showers." Just wait until Avery heard her job description. The research would have its perks.

Jim grabbed his chin and looked her straight in the eye. "You'll be based out of Boston," he said, suddenly shifting the tone of his voice. "It's going to require sixty, maybe seventy hours a week. And travel—a hundred global interviews in the first ninety days."

"I understand," Dani explained. "I'm not afraid of hard work."

"All right," he said. "Well in that case, welcome to the team."

WITHIN THE NEXT half hour, Dani had signed a contract. There was a hefty signing bonus, and somehow, the sight of those zeroes helped Dani breathe a little easier. Earlier in the day, she'd refused to hail a taxi, simply to save a few bucks. But now, exiting the hotel lobby onto the muggy streets of Manhattan, Dani smiled broadly, stepped to the curb, and raised her arm into the air.

*"Taxi!"*

**From:** Dani McNalley <danimcnalley@yahoo.com>

**Subject:** Re: Update

**Date:** September 1, 2004 17:56:41 PM GMT +01:00

**To:** Avery Adams <averyadams13@yahoo.com>, Hannah
  Nesmith <hannah_nesmith@yahoo.com>

GUESS WHAT?!

  I got a JOB!!! Finally. Everyone exhale!

Now get this. I'm moving to Boston. Who's coming to visit? We can go to Martha's Vineyard, or whatever yuppie people do around here. I'm so stoked.

PRAISE JESUS, I'm not homeless anymore!

Now . . . you girls give me an update! Are you both feeling settled at Fort Bragg? Still don't know how you managed to get stationed at the same Army post. I'd be happy for you two if I weren't so jealous.

Much Love to the Cult:)

Dani

14

*Spring 2005 // Fort Bragg, North Carolina*

A wire snapped, shooting sparks into the air.

"Shit!" Avery spat. She sucked her finger for a moment, then shook the pain out of her hand. A soldier cutting a large hole in the wall lifted his safety goggles.

"You all right, Adams?" he asked, but replaced his glasses and revved the saw before she could answer.

Looking at the mess of wires in front of her, Avery knew she had to start over. *At least with that one,* she thought, tracing the cable back to the wall.

"Do we have another five-gauge?" Avery yelled over the noise. No one answered. The team was dispersed around the room, focused fully on their own tasks—breaking through walls, running wires, testing circuits. White dust filled the room like puffs of baby powder.

If Avery had known that joining the Signal Corps would mean managing an electrical construction team, she would have branched engineering, like Hannah. As it was, she could barely program her own television remote, let alone rewire and encrypt an entire building's communications system. But who wouldn't jump at the chance to work with the most elite unit in the entire Armed Forces?

"As in black ops, D," Avery had told Dani over the phone several months earlier. "Special Forces."

"Aren't they out somewhere hunting Bin Laden?" Dani had asked.

"Yeah, well, I guess the hunt's on hold," Avery replied, spooning cereal into her mouth. "They're home and I'm the cable guy."

Dani had burst into laughter and Avery had followed suit. It was completely absurd. But Avery lived for the kind of life-changing events that morphed into great stories. Plus, she had a simple philosophy on life: Say yes. Figure the rest out later.

When Avery stepped outside, she took a deep breath of fresh air. New York's false springs were really just extended winters—snow rarely melted at West Point until mid-April. But spring in North Carolina was proving to be a different experience altogether. The sun warmed her skin. Fresh grass, verdant green, emerged all over post. A cool breeze wafted across her face surprising her with its kindness. *Soon, everyone will be discussing their summer plans,* Avery thought before she realized that wasn't true anymore. All of her friends were professionals now. There was no such thing as summer break anymore.

In that way, Major Gaines's top-secret project had come at the exact right time. She needed a distraction from normalcy because normal—in the real world—sucked. Josh hadn't called. He hadn't written. Not even an e-mail. Not even a text message. But for months, she'd checked the mailbox extra carefully, imagining he might drop a love note in the mail in some grand romantic gesture to win her back. As if guys did shit like that anymore.

Every time, the stack of mail looked exactly the same—coupons, advertisements, *People* magazine. Her life had become like that pile of junk mail. Perfectly, absolutely unremarkable. It made her itch. And it made her run.

In addition to the PT workouts she did with her soldiers on post, Avery had taken up running again, nearly as intensely as she'd trained in high school. She logged fifteen, twenty, sometimes thirty miles a week, at night and on the weekends. She needed to sign up for a race, because at least then she could justify the amount of time she was spending in her running shoes. It was better to have a goal than to run with no destination. And that's how it had felt to Avery lately—like she was running fast with nowhere to go.

IN THEIR LAST meeting, Major Gaines had looked over Avery's final binder of plans with a surprised nod of approval and handed it back to her.

"The fact that I'm entrusting this to someone so junior should feel really good, Lieutenant Adams," he'd said. "This could be big for your career."

She knew he was probably full of shit—just trying to psych her up for a job that was going to dominate her life. But she'd taken his words to heart. Achievement in the Army was about all she could take home to impress her parents at the moment. When she'd explained how she'd be spending the New Year at Christmas, her father had grunted.

"As long as you're not deploying for Bush's ridiculous personal vendetta in Iraq," he'd said. "Fine by me."

"It's not a vendetta, Dad," Avery had said, surprised that she was taking up for a president who'd never earned her vote. "Saddam Hussein is a horrible guy."

"The world is full of horrible guys, Avery," her father had replied.

She hated to admit it, but every day, as men came home from deployments with combat patches stuck to their uniforms, Avery had started to worry that her empty sleeve looked weak in the hallways of their offices. More than a year had passed since she'd graduated from West Point, and most of her classmates had deployed to Iraq or Afghanistan, or, like Hannah and Tim, at least had a date on the calendar. With every passing month, the fuzzy square on Avery's uniform sleeve felt more and more like a barren garden plot: no fruit to show for her labor.

Shaking that thought from her mind, Avery marched diagonally across a field of grass, toward the tool shed.

"One, two, three, *one!*"

"One, two, three, *two!*"

Her eyes roamed from the ground in front of her to the bearded men finishing a training workout to her right. Eight men in a semicircle had dropped to the ground to complete a round of push-ups.

Gaines had been pretty clear with his instructions: get in, get out, and don't let anyone know you were there. It had taken Avery about 3.4 seconds to break those rules.

The lean, blond-haired man leading the workout wasn't tall—five foot nine at best. But he was barrel chested, with a gold beard and calf muscles that looked like steaks. Sweat glistened on his bare shoulders as he pressed into the ground, like someone had oiled him up for a photo shoot. He had a sleeve of tattoos on his right arm that spilled onto his chest. His face attracted the sun and shadows in a way that accentuated his beard, his straight nose, his gray eyes. Avery felt her insides go weak as he stood, hands on hips, and locked his eyes on hers.

They'd been doing this every day now for a week.

Avery quickly ducked into the tool shed, closed the door behind her, and tried to catch her breath. *Holy shit*, she laughed to herself. She stared at a wall of wrenches, wires, and cables. *What was it she needed, again?*

The one thing she *didn't* need was another failed attraction. Heartbreak always pushed Avery into a cave of isolation, and after the whole debacle with Josh had imploded, she'd vowed to be single forever. Relationships didn't work for her the way they did for everyone else. She was either too trusting and got burned, or too suspicious and exhausted the guy's patience. She either acted too serious and scared the guy away, or acted too cool, leaving the guy confused about her commitment.

At times, the psychologist in Avery wondered if her issues

stemmed back to high school. She'd been just fourteen years old when Matt Maloney, a senior, had spotted her in the high school cafeteria. After a few weeks of flirtation, he'd invited her to his house, where he'd carefully and patiently taught her how their bodies were designed to fit together. And then, two months later, Avery had crawled broken into her bed, the physical pain of his betrayal and disregard too heavy for her to stand up straight. Days later, her mother sat on the edge of her bed, stroking her daughter's cheek until she'd finally stopped crying.

"Don't you ever let a little shit do that to you again," her mother had said.

It was the most profound profanity her mother had ever spoken. And it was what Avery had repeated to Hannah when Tim cheated—only Hannah ended up marrying the little shit. Hannah may have forgiven Tim for his unfaithfulness, but Avery never would.

They were all little shits, really. Her high school boyfriend. The one at West Point, *he-who-would-not-be-named*. She knew it wasn't healthy, thinking about John Collins. But for some reason, lately, she couldn't get his green eyes out of her mind. Her memory played tricks on her, reminding her of all the mistakes she'd made—showing up to his room, breaking it off so abruptly. She wanted to find a wrinkle in time, a place to jump back and do something different that would change what he'd done.

Avery remembered walking into her dorm room at the end of their sophomore year, clueless that e-mails were transporting images of her naked body around campus.

"What's going on?" Avery had asked. Dani and Hannah were there, waiting for her, their eyes puffy from crying. Dani held a stack of papers in her hands.

And then her world had fallen apart.

"He won't stop unless he's caught," Dani had said after showing Avery the photos.

Avery didn't cry. She simply stared at the white cinder-block wall, feeling cold and numb. "Everyone will know that I slept with him. They'll know I ratted him out."

"He didn't just do it to you," Hannah had said. "He did it to all of us."

The world seemed to conspire to teach her the same lesson over and over again. You couldn't trust anyone.

In the tool shed, wire-cutters, stacks of batteries, and cables littered the walls, sorted on shelves and hanging from hooks. Avery's eyes scanned the equipment until they landed on the wire she needed, and she reached for it, feeling its weight in the palm of her hand. *If only there were tools like this to rewire her heart,* she thought.

Avery took a moment to remind herself of the facts. There were rules to follow. And this one, this gold-bearded, perfect-bodied Special Ops little shit, was extra shitty because he *lied for a living*! No matter how perfect he might have looked from the outside, he spent his entire Army career paid—no, trained—to manipulate other people for information. Road. Closed.

A sigh of relief exited her lungs. The responsible part of her brain had won the argument. She prayed that when she stepped back outside, he would be gone. She didn't want to see his face because ultimately, she didn't trust herself to walk through the mental gymnastics of "no" again.

Before she could leave, Avery heard the door behind her open and close. She turned, and there he was, standing between her and the door.

"Excuse me," Avery said, lowering her eyes and trying to walk around him.

He placed a single hand on her shoulder, stopping her from moving any farther. He'd put on a beige Army undershirt, but the tattoos on his right arm were visible from under the sleeve—a bird? A skull?—the colors were vivid, black and blue. His beard was tidy and combed. He stood several inches taller than she'd originally assumed. Avery lifted her chin and looked him right in the eye.

"Please move," she said.

"Are you married?" he asked.

Avery cocked her head to the side. "Excuse me?"

"I said, are you married." His voice didn't waver. His eyes were pale gray, two round clouds, about to storm.

"No," she huffed, while simultaneously eyeing his unadorned left hand. "Now, if you don't mind . . ." She tried to push around him, but this time, he grabbed her wrist. A folded note pressed into the palm of her hand under the weight of his thumb. And then he left.

Once the door closed, Avery found herself quickly unfolding the yellow Post-it note in trembling hands. Her whole body shook with desire and confusion.

8 PM *Friday. I'll pick you up.* —Noah

So that was his name. Noah. Staring up at the single hanging bulb in the tool shed, Avery shook her head and groaned. How arrogant was this guy to think she didn't have any plans Friday night? And how would he know where to pick her up? She found herself staring at his dark handwriting—a message written in the tiniest letters. She studied his name.

Was he the kind of man that would build a vessel to bring her to a new world? Or the kind of man that would shut her out and let her drown?

"JUST TELL HIM you're sick," Hannah said a few days later.

She sat cross-legged on Avery's bed, holding a cell phone between her hands. She was waiting for a call from Tim, who was finishing his Infantry Basic Officer Leader Course.

"How would I do that?" Avery replied, stepping out from her bathroom. "I don't even have his phone number. And what—like they're going to kick me out of the Army for having dinner with the guy?"

She wore nothing but black underwear and a matching bra, her hair held up in hot rollers.

Things had progressed so quickly in that tool shed, she'd completely forgotten that she and Hannah had made plans to hang out tonight. But it wasn't like they had tickets to a concert or reservations at a restaurant. When Hannah had arrived a half hour earlier, holding a pint of Ben & Jerry's Phish Food and a rented DVD of *Pride & Prejudice,* Avery had thrown her head back and slapped her forehead. Hannah's face had fallen in disappointment.

"I promise I'll make it up to you." Avery said, stepping out from the bathroom.

"It's fine. I'll watch Keira Knightley fall in love by myself. In my sad, empty house, by myself. Eating ice cream. *By myself.*"

Avery walked over and sat on the side of the bed. "You hate me."

"I don't hate you. I'm just annoyed."

"You'll understand when you see him."

"Isn't it weird that the very first question he asked was whether or not you were married?"

"So the guy doesn't want to get involved with someone else's wife," Avery scoffed, then stood and walked to her dresser. "I thought you'd like that."

"Just don't disappear, okay?"

"What, like he's going to kidnap me?"

"No," Hannah chuckled.

Avery began letting down her hair from the hot rollers at her dresser and turned to look at Hannah, who shrugged.

"I leave in March," Hannah said.

"That's still like, a year away."

"Eight months," Hannah said, correcting her. "It'll go faster than you think."

She sighed and placed her phone down on the bedside table.

"Just don't go fall in love with this guy and then vanish from my life."

In the silence that followed, anger and shame welled in Avery's chest in equal measure. The two emotions always seemed to travel as a pair. How could Hannah say something like that? It was Hannah who had gone off and gotten married. She was the one who had gone to Sapper School. *She* was the one who'd barely kept in touch. Avery didn't want to be ugly, but for some reason, she wanted to scream at her friend for not being more supportive. Couldn't Hannah just be happy for her, for once? Instead, she had to infuse the entire conversation with worry and judgment, like Avery was about to do something unethical. But there wasn't anything *wrong* with going on a date! And what would Hannah know about dating in the real world, anyway? She and Tim had coupled off so fast, she never had a chance to experience single life. She would never understand.

"There's plenty of time," Avery said finally. "Don't worry so much."

Hannah sighed. "You're right. I'm sorry. It's just starting to feel real."

Now it was Avery who exhaled. "I really do feel bad about bailing tonight."

"Don't," Hannah said, heading back toward Avery's closet to peruse her clothes. "What are you going to wear?"

At that moment, they both heard the low grumbling sound of an engine coming to a stop right outside Avery's window.

Hannah peeked out the curtain. "I think it's him," she said.

"Oh shit!" Avery went into hyperdrive.

"He's on a motorcycle," Hannah narrated. "He's taking off his helmet. Oh my gosh. You weren't kidding. He's . . ."

A black silk camisole with lace trim slipped over Avery's shoulders. She wore black jeans, and for a layer of warmth, she chose a gray cashmere sweater that hung open in the front and draped toward her knees. Her blond hair curled in big, loose waves to her collarbones, offset by a rose shade of lipstick. As Avery slipped on a pair of black high heels, Hannah shook her head.

"Wear the sneakers," she instructed. Avery quickly switched to a black pair of high-tops.

"Oh my god, I'm so nervous." She stood, opened her arms. "How do I look?"

"Amazing," Hannah affirmed. "Text me if he's a psycho and you need me to come get you."

Smiling, Avery gave her friend a hug and grabbed her purse.

"Just lock the door behind you when you go," Avery said. "See you later?"

Hannah nodded.

"Thank you, Hannah. And I promise I'll make it up to you."

Avery stepped outside and closed the door behind her.

"YOU READY?"

Noah stood on the sidewalk, dressed in dark blue jeans, a gray T-shirt, and a black leather jacket. If it was humanly possible, Noah looked even better fully clothed than he had shirtless. As Avery approached him, he held out a shiny black helmet for her to put on.

"Where are we going?" she asked, taking the helmet in two hands.

"You're going to have to trust me."

"I just met you," she replied. "Of course I don't trust you."

He reached over and helped secure the helmet, and the warmth of his fingers under her chin sent shivers down Avery's spine.

"And how do you know where I live anyway?" she asked.

"I'd be a pretty bad Special Forces officer if I couldn't figure out where someone lives," he answered. "Ever ridden on one of these?"

"Yes," she lied.

"Good," he said, and then placed two hands on either side of Avery's helmet. With a smile that broke Avery's resolve, Noah winked.

He got on the bike, looked at her, and shrugged. "So are you coming or what?"

**From:** Hannah Nesmith <hannah_nesmith@yahoo.com>
**Subject:** urrg.
**Date:** April 12, 2005 17:29:15 PM EST +01:00
**To:** Dani McNalley <danimcnalley@yahoo.com>

She did it again. We'd planned to do dinner and a movie for weeks, but when I showed up she said she'd forgotten. And had some date with a dude she met on her assignment.

At what point do I just give up trying?

**From:** Dani McNalley <danimcnalley@yahoo.com>
**Subject:** Re: re: urrg.
**Date:** April 12, 2005 17:31:20 PM GMT +01:00
**To:** Hannah Nesmith <hannah_nesmith@yahoo.com>

Don't give up. We just need a chance to all be together. I'm working on a plan. What are you doing for Thanksgiving?

**From:** Avery Adams <averyadams13@yahoo.com>
**Subject:** Re: Hey Hey
**Date:** June 15, 2005 09:03:15 AM EST +01:00
**To:** Dani McNalley <danimcnalley@yahoo.com>

WHOA.

Can't believe that it's been a month since you sent your last e-mail, D. My apologies. As Hannah can probably attest, the Army is a real bitch and I'm barely keeping my head above water. But I do have some good news.:-)

I met a guy.

I KNOW, I KNOW. SHOCKER.

But seriously, this guy is the real deal.

His name's Noah Candross. He's thirty, so a little older than us, which you know I love. You know that Special Ops job I told you about a few months back? Well, it's a long story, but he basically cornered me in a tool shed and told me that he was taking me on a date. How's that for assertive, right? (I'm begging him to give Locke some lessons in that whole making-a-move thing . . . but alas.)

Anyway, for our first date, he picked me up on his motorcycle and we took a long drive through the hills during the sunset. We stopped and had wine at this little café far outside of town, talked for hours. You know. The basics. I attached a picture of us, so you can see that he's gorgeous. It's insanity.

He's taking me to Napa Valley next weekend. NAPA VALLEY.

I'm smitten. EEEEK!!!:-):-):-):-)

How's Boston treating you? And work? Sometimes I feel like keeping up with you is like a game of Where in the World is Carmen Sandiego. Hannah said something about you going to Paris soon? You're so badass.

Any guys up there I should know about?:-)

LOVE YOU. (Duh.)

Avery

## 15

*Summer 2005 // Fort Bragg, North Carolina*

I t would just be three days, Tim," Hannah said into her cell phone. "Fly up Wednesday, fly back Friday. Dani said she'd pay for our tickets and we can stay at her place. It's totally free."

Hannah felt anxiety crawl up the back of her neck. Logistics were the last thing she wanted to talk about in the few short minutes they had to speak. And yet, when else were they going to figure out their plans? Thanksgiving was just a few months away. Christmas would be here before they knew it. And then it would be 2006, the year they were both scheduled to deploy.

Her unit had already begun the predeployment protocol— cleaning equipment, writing supply packing lists, setting up home-front meetings for the wives her soldiers would leave behind. Training had ramped up. They'd received orders to pack their trunks. In less than two months, everything Hannah needed for a year would be put on the back of a cargo ship and sent to the

Middle East. At the moment, she was standing in a bare building in a far corner of Fort Bragg, waiting her turn to start Soldier Readiness Processing. March still felt so far away, but every day, it sped closer.

"I think my parents really wanted to spend Thanksgiving with us since I'll be gone next Thanksgiving," Tim replied. He sounded tired, like he was rubbing his eyes. "But we can figure it out. I know you want to see Dani before you go."

A week ago, they were supposed to have two overlapping days at home in Fort Bragg—the first time they'd been in their house together since they'd exchanged vows more than a year earlier. After a cycle in the laundry room, all of their uniforms exploded into the bedroom until it looked like the inside of an Army surplus store, the items mixed up and unidentifiable. They shared the same nameplate and rank, and they'd spent an hour sorting through their items, ensuring they ended up with the right things in their separate trunks. *So all that laundry duty plebe year really did have a purpose,* Hannah had thought dismally as she held up each T-shirt, inspecting it for size. She was a small. He was a medium.

Their first night at home, Hannah had burned a chicken. Saving the evening, Tim defrosted and seared two filets mignons in butter, roasted a head of broccoli, and opened a bottle of wine at their dining room table, an oval-shaped hand-me-down that Tim's parents had forced them to take after the wedding. It felt strange to eat at a table so big, Hannah thought, just the two of them. But they'd relished the chance to play house and had spent the evening talking about their favorite childhood television shows, the books they were reading, the vacations they wanted to take after their deployments were over. They'd grown expert at avoiding the massive gray animal that had taken up residence in every room—an elephant named *March*.

And then his phone rang, cutting the dinner short.

Hurricane Katrina had made landfall in New Orleans, displacing millions of people in its path. A storm of that strength hadn't hit the U.S. since Hugo, and the Army's swiftest infantry unit, the Eighty-Second Airborne Division, had been called to help in search and rescue efforts. Tim had only been home for twenty-four hours when he walked back out the door in uniform.

Now, listening to his voice over the line, Hannah remembered watching the news. Last night, video footage had shown a helicopter hovering over a house in New Orleans's Ninth Ward. A soldier descended on a ladder, then reached out his hand to save a family stranded on a roof. The camera angle was too far away. But Hannah had sat on her sofa, alone, wondering if the man in uniform might be Tim.

"We don't have to decide about Thanksgiving right now," Hannah said. "We'll figure it out."

"When?"

"Later."

He sighed.

"You sound tired," said Hannah. "How are you, really?"

"Well, I'm standing downwind of the rankest floodwaters you can imagine, and thousands of people still need to be evacuated from the city. So, you know. Basically the definition of awesome."

Hannah laughed. "Basically."

"I miss you," he said. "It's hot here. But at least we're doing something real, you know? Something that matters."

A woman at the desk waved at Hannah to come forward. She'd grown to hate goodbyes. Especially abrupt ones. "Hey, Tim, I have to go. I'm sorry."

"It's okay," Tim said. "I love you. And hey, happy birthday."

"Thanks. I love you too," Hannah said, feeling the tears well in her eyes. "Bye."

"NAME?"

"Lieutenant Hannah Nesmith."

"Date of birth?"

"Eight, thirty, eighty-two."

"Hey," the woman said. "That's today."

"Sure is."

"Any current medication?"

"No," Hannah said, then lowered her voice. "Actually, I'm on birth control. I don't know the name . . ."

"Sexually active?"

"Somewhat," Hannah joked, but the nurse stopped pumping the blood pressure monitor she'd wrapped around Hannah's arm and waited for a direct answer. "Yes," Hannah clarified. "I'm married."

The nurse raised her eyebrows. "Honey, that don't mean the answer is yes." She released the pressure that had built and made a mark on a clipboard. "Any sexually transmitted diseases?"

"No."

"Date of your last period?"

Hannah tried to remember. "Uh . . . I think about three weeks ago?"

The nurse handed Hannah an empty plastic cup. "We need a sample. Pregnancy screening." She pointed to a partition behind her. "You can go behind the curtain."

"Oh, I'm not pregnant."

"Let's just be sure. You'd be surprised how many women get knocked up so they don't have to ship out. We can't send a fetus to Fallujah, now, can we?"

The audacity with which the nurse spoke made Hannah's neck grow hot with anger. Not once had Hannah heard of a woman intentionally getting pregnant to avoid deployment, and yet, it was a trope that constantly passed through the ranks, as if it were a mark of weakness to conceive a child.

"Afghanistan," Hannah said, correcting her, now taking on the same short and snippy tone that the nurse had used. "I'm not going to Iraq. I'm going to Afghanistan."

"Same rules apply," the woman said, though her tight expression had softened ever so slightly. She pulled back a curtain and pointed for Hannah to go behind a three-paneled screen situated in a half-moon in front of the cinder-block wall. Squatting, Hannah held the cup between her legs and sighed as it filled with warm urine. There was nothing like the Army to humiliate you before sending you to war.

Next, a nurse checked Hannah's hearing and lung capacity. She moved down the hall for an eye exam. Then a male nurse wearing blue scrubs ordered her into a room, where she sat on a cold medical cot and lifted the sleeve of her gray PT shirt.

"Hepatitis A," he announced as he jammed the first needle into the fleshy part of her upper arm. He reloaded. "Polio." Hannah winced. "And, last but not least . . ." The needle looked like a small saber. Hannah closed her eyes.

"Typhoid."

The small tube of toxins released into her upper arm. The only way to fight a contaminated world was to contaminate yourself, too, Hannah thought dismally. He rubbed a cotton swab over the area he'd attacked and then taped a cotton ball over the wound.

"Drink plenty of water. And don't worry about your arm. It'll only be sore for a few days."

IN A SMALL office on the other side of post, an elderly man wearing a black cardigan sweater and a "Vietnam Vet" hat welcomed Hannah inside. She could tell, walking into his office, that this man wasn't in any hurry. With a single outstretched hand, he directed her to take a seat in front of his desk, and the calm with which he ambled to his own chair forced Hannah to take a deep breath. He pulled a large folder from beneath the desk and set it before them carefully.

"All right, Lieutenant Nesmith," he said, rubbing his hands together. "Now for the important stuff. This here is called a D—D—nine—three." He spoke slowly, as if Hannah needed to absorb each letter and digit individually. "Are you married?"

"Yes."

"Any children?"

Hannah shook her head. "No."

"Okay." He paused. "Sometime in the next few weeks, you'll need to fill out the name and address of your spouse . . . skip this line for dependents, and then down below, list your parents and any other family members that you would like to be notified in the event that you become a casualty."

He took his glasses off his face and watched her look over the blank form. Hannah swallowed and nodded.

"You'll need to keep a copy of this form in your possession. So pack one in your trunk and give a copy to someone at home—preferably a spouse or relative." He paused again, looking to Hannah for some kind of recognition or understanding. "Am I going too fast?"

"Nope," Hannah said. She felt herself detaching from the room. Detaching from the possibilities. The sooner he could breeze through the paperwork, the better.

"Good. Last few forms here and we'll get you on your way. This here is your S—G—L—V form eight—two—eight—six. Life insurance. You'll need to list your assets. Anything of value or debt. Your car, mortgage, any outstanding loans. That kind of thing. And this here? This is a power of attorney. You'll need to have this one notarized."

Hannah listened dutifully as he flipped through the rest of the paperwork, but her mind wandered. In contrast to the chaos of her life, the SRP documents all seemed so organized. As if paperwork had power over tragedy. As if all this preparation would help if the worst really happened.

She wasn't exactly sure what she'd expected life to feel like as an adult, but she hadn't expected this. She was married but hadn't seen her husband in months. She had friends, but they were spread out all over the country, or worse, they lived down the street but might as well have been light-years away. Avery had disappeared—again—like she always did when she started dating someone new. It would have been annoying if it weren't entirely predictable.

Hannah had assumed that after the trial, Avery would change the way she related to men. Of course, she'd never blamed Avery for what John Collins had done. He deserved what he'd received, and then some. But he was one in a long line of Avery's poor dating decisions, and Hannah worried that the streak wasn't over.

Instead of changing her patterns with men, Avery's relationship roller coaster had only grown more extreme. The highs got higher. The lows got lower. She and this new guy—Noah Candross—had only known each other for a few short months, and already, he'd basically moved into Avery's house. Hannah grew annoyed when her text messages to Avery went unanswered, even though she could see Noah's motorcycle parked outside of her house at night. And despite the fact that he seemed to always be around, Hannah had only met him once. They'd met at Noah's favorite vegetarian restaurant, because apparently he didn't eat meat—and though the things he said were nice enough, he kept looking around the restaurant, as if someone more interesting were going to arrive any minute. Meanwhile, Avery had never looked more in love, gripping his arm. Hannah had smiled and tried to act happy for her friend, but she couldn't shake the feeling that something about that guy was off. Hannah wanted to like him—after all, she remembered all too well how it felt when your best friend hated your boyfriend.

Ever since the summer after their sophomore year at West Point, Avery had held Tim at arm's length.

Tim had mailed Hannah a handwritten letter explaining the whole thing: How he'd made a mistake, allowing a flirtation to build with another girl. They'd kissed, he admitted. But as soon as it was over, he'd regretted every second. The letter was full of remorse and shame and scattered with round blots where his tears had fallen on the page. Hannah had read it in her bunk at Airborne School and cried, wondering what to do. She still loved him so much.

"You *cannot* take him back," Avery had insisted after they'd returned to school that fall. She'd read the note, and Hannah had to pull it out of her hands, for fear that Avery might rip it apart. "If he loved you as much as he's claiming, he never would have done this. It has to be over. You can't let people mess with you, Hannah."

Those months of junior year watching Tim from afar were some of the worst of Hannah's life. And while grudges seemed to give Avery something powerful to hold on to, they only weighed Hannah down.

Now, staring at all the forms assembled in front of her, Hannah wondered if their friendship would survive this deployment. They were so different. And if they couldn't make it work living on the same street, how would they do it living on separate continents?

"So that's that," the man in front of her said. He tapped all of the papers into a neat stack and slid them into a black folder with her name on it. "Do you have any questions? I've got all the time in the world."

From the look of the wrinkles on his face, the nearly imperceptible shake in his hands, Hannah wasn't sure that was true.

"I don't think so," she replied. "Seems pretty straightforward."

"Nothing is straightforward about war," he said, though not condescendingly. "Oh!" He snapped his fingers. "Last thing. Do you need assistance writing a legal will?"

"Actually, no," Hannah said. She remembered writing a will as a Firstie at West Point. A strange final assignment that she'd updated after the wedding. "I already have one."

"Then you, my dear, are all through." He stood and shook her hand firmly, passing her the black folder. "By the way. I noticed your necklace."

Hannah reached for the silver cross and wrapped her palm around it tight. It felt smaller, somehow, under the gaze of his eyes. "Yes, sir."

"You're lucky to have it," he said sagely. "Not the necklace. The faith." He smiled, took his seat, and put his glasses back on his face.

PULLING INTO HER driveway that evening, Hannah grabbed all of her gear out of her car and hauled it toward the front door—purse, PT bag, two empty plastic water bottles, accumulated over the last few days. It was always sad to come home to an empty house, lights off and eerily quiet. She'd started turning on the television as soon as she got home, just to have the sound of other people's voices to keep her company. But tonight felt particularly lonely. Last year, she'd been at Sapper School on her birthday, and Sergeant Moretti had led the entire mess hall in singing. He'd even procured a grocery store cupcake that he'd marked with a sloppy 22, in blue icing.

Tonight, Hannah's plans included eating the rubbery leftover salmon that she'd overcooked the night before, drinking a glass of wine, and tucking in early. After all, she had to be back at work at 0600 for PT in the morning. Her sister, Emily, had sent a bouquet of tulips to work. A card from Wendy Bennett had arrived in the mail the day before, stuffed with a $50 gift card to J.Crew—and her parents had sent exactly what she'd asked for: a small digital camera that she could take with her to Afghanistan. Other than Tim's phone call from New Orleans, she hadn't received anything from him in the mail. But that was okay. She couldn't expect him to send her a present for her birthday when he was busy saving lives.

Opening the door, she shuffled into the dark and put her bags on the ground. Flipping the light switch Hannah looked up toward the kitchen and gasped. A mass of people, standing beneath a silver banner, shouted, "*Surprise!*"

The crowd of familiar faces made Hannah laugh, even though they'd scared her half to death. Avery stood front and center, holding a cake. There were a few couples from church, all hooting and clapping. One of Tim's friends from West Point, Erik Jenkins, stood on the stairs with his pregnant wife, Michelle, who was holding a laptop computer face-out toward Hannah. On the screen, she saw Tim, alight with glee. The picture blurred as he laughed, leaning back in a chair.

"What in the world!" Hannah said. "You scared the crap out of me!"

"Are you surprised?" Avery asked.

"I nearly peed my pants! Was this your idea?"

Avery shook her head and pointed toward the computer screen.

"Happy birthday, babe," Tim said. The image was grainy and imperfect, his voice choppy from a bad connection, but she could still see the deep dimple imprinted in his right cheek. "I love you so much. We all do."

**From:** Dani McNalley <danimcnalley@yahoo.com>
**Subject:** Re: Re: Re: Update
**Date:** September 2, 2005 06:32:15 PM GMT +01:00
**To:** Avery Adams <averyadams13@yahoo.com>

(1) How was Napa? Tell me everything.

(2) We really need to see each other.

I've been trying to figure out a way to get us all together. Would you want to come up to Boston for Thanksgiving? I have a bunch of frequent flyer miles, so I'm flying my mom, dad, and brother up here. I asked Hannah and Tim, too. And Locke, of course.

I'll have a big turkey and some desserts. It will be amazing. I feel like we need a reunion so bad!! Apparently Thanksgiving up here is a big deal, too. If we want, we can drive up to Plymouth Rock or something equally American. Or we can all just stay here and eat until we're sick. Which is also American.

I really want you to come. Like I said, flight's on me. Will you think about it??

Also, I just talked to Sarah Goodrich. She's deploying to Iraq tomorrow. Thought you'd want to know.

Love you,

D


**From:** Avery Adams <averyadams13@yahoo.com>
**Subject:** Re: Re: Re: **Update
**Date:** September 3, 2005 13:27 PM EST +01:00
**To:** Dani McNalley <danimcnalley@yahoo.com>

FINALLY! A cult reunion! It's about time.

I'm totally in. And . . . feel free to say no . . . but would it be okay if I invited Noah?

A

**16**

*Fall 2005 // Jamaica Plain, Boston, Massachusetts*

A man stood under the drizzle of a warm shower in his apartment, wearing a pair of navy swim trunks. Coarse hair formed the shape of a heart on his chest and narrowed into a thin trail down his stomach. With broad shoulders and large arms, he was bulky and strong, Dani assessed, with hair cut short and an accent that proved he was definitely a local. *Boston* became *Bwaston*. *Coffee* became *cwahfee*. Shampoo bubbled around the edges of his temple, threatening to spill over the edge of his raised eyebrow.

"Am I doing okay?" he asked.

"Just pretend I'm not here," Dani instructed. She pulled the shower curtain open a little more.

The guy laughed. "You going to take me out to dinner, at least?"

"If you play your cards right."

"Well at least tell me something about you, so I don't feel so . . . exposed."

"Unfortunately that's not how this works. I get to ask the questions, and right now I don't have any. So just . . . keep on showering."

Since she'd been hired at E & G, Dani McNalley had completed sixty consumer interviews like this in twenty U.S. cities; she'd logged thirty-five interviews in Europe. The research was fascinating. Men would complete their morning routines and, without even knowing it, provide Dani with little nuggets of insight to take back to the office. Most men kept their shampoo bottles upside down in the shower, to more efficiently squeeze a dollop into their hand. In Europe, men still used a soft-bristled brush to apply shaving cream. In America, men slapped it on with their bare hands, and if they used after shave, they put it on like Macaulay Culkin in *Home Alone*. While washing their bodies, two-thirds of men faced the showerhead; the other third faced away. She hadn't figured out why that was significant, but it felt meaningful. Perhaps the ones facing away from the water had some psychological reason to avoid the heat.

There were other interesting trends too. She'd learned that most men hadn't seen the back of their heads in years. While women had mastered the physics of double mirrors to check that their hair looked perfect, men never took the time. They simply combed their hair until they liked the view from the front, then went on with their morning routine. Once, Dani's subject had noticed her playing back video footage. He grabbed her camera and pulled it in close to stare at his own bald spot.

"Wait, is that me?" he'd asked, touching the back of his head, as if to confirm the truth.

"Aw," Dani had said, patting his shoulder. "Maybe it's time to get into hats."

Dani had gotten pretty good at consoling men about hair loss. She'd gotten pretty good at a lot of things actually. Packing a carry-on bag that could pass through security with ease. Walking through airport terminals with a BlackBerry in one hand and a latte in the other, without losing the dexterity to push her four-wheeled suitcase in front of her. She'd grown used to ignoring the stares of men who found the presence of a young black woman in first class so disconcerting. With the amount of miles she'd racked up, she'd earned her position at the front of the cabin.

Sadly, the list of cities she'd traveled to in the last year didn't include the two places she'd hoped to visit: Fort Bragg, to see Hannah and Avery, and Fort Hood, to see Locke. Apparently E & G didn't believe it was necessary to interview America's military population, which made little sense to Dani, since men in the military were *required* to shave. It was just another way that her life felt separate from that of her college friends.

Dani had assumed that after college, her bonds of friendship would remain the same. But things were shifting. She could feel the seismic waves, like emotional plate tectonics. It had been weeks since any of them had replied to their dwindling e-mail chain, and a few months earlier, when Dani had made a conscious effort to call Hannah on her birthday, the conversation centered on the one thing that they couldn't seem to avoid. Schedules.

"Well, I was supposed to be with Tim this weekend," Hannah had said. "But you've seen the news."

"Sure," Dani had replied, though she wasn't sure what Hurricane Katrina had to do with Hannah's weekend plans. "It's awful."

"They sent Tim's unit," Hannah had explained. "He's literally there, fishing people out of their houses."

"Like a true disciple," Dani had said, trying to crack a joke. "A fisher of men."

Hannah had laughed, but had chased that with a sigh. Dani couldn't imagine surviving a long-distance relationship, let alone a long-distance marriage, but Hannah had a way of smiling through pain that put even Dani's endurance to shame. Of course, most of Dani's pain was physical. Maybe it was easier to tolerate pain if it only existed in your heart.

"It wouldn't matter that much if I had any friends around here," Hannah had said.

"What about Avery?"

"What about her? We had a plan to meet up for lunch last week and I sat there for an hour waiting."

"She never showed up?" Dani had asked, incredulous. "Did you call her?"

"I texted. She never texted me back. I have a weird feeling about this new guy she's dating."

"Something must be going on," Dani had said, trying to knock some sense into Hannah. "That's not normal."

"Ha! Normal? What's that word mean again?"

Dani had felt utterly helpless over the line. At one time, she was the glue that held their group together, but they were loosening and she had no control over it. In a way, that fact made Dani more uncomfortable than the arthritis in her hips. In college, they'd tackled countless challenges together. But with all this distance between them, nothing felt right.

Things with Locke had changed, too. They still talked on the phone every few weeks, exchanging stories about their jobs, laughing about old times, and swapping workout regimens, which Dani couldn't bring herself to admit she wasn't actually completing. As she walked around the streets of Boston, her limp only slightly hidden, Dani thought of Locke. If he ever came to visit, he'd like the open-mic poetry night she'd found in the Back Bay. And she'd take him to Copp's Hill Burying Ground, where they would plant their feet on soil where more than a thousand slaves were buried, discussing the confusing history of this misguided, imperfect nation that they both loved and he still served.

But those dreams had died when Locke let it slip that he'd taken a local girl out on a date.

"*Amanda*," Dani had reported to Wendy Bennett over the phone. Lately, it seemed Wendy was the only person who reliably called her back. "Apparently she's a kindergarten teacher."

"Oh, Dani," Wendy had said. "I'm so sorry."

"It's fine. I doubt it's anything serious. Just took me by surprise, is all."

"Life has a way of doing that, doesn't it?"

AS DANI TOOK notes on her clipboard, she noticed the date and felt accosted by shock. For her entire life, the rhythms of the academic year had marked the passing of time, like posts upon which you could hang the fabric of life. October used to come with football games and full notebooks and midterms. Breaking time into manageable academic chunks must have slowed it down, Dani thought, because out of college, the calendar had become a ruthless conveyor belt ushering her onward, crushing months like cans. In the real world, fall was no longer a beginning. It was just the middle, like everything else.

The pen in Dani's hand suddenly ran out of ink. She scratched invisible lines on the page, frantically trying to get it to come back to life.

"Damn it," Dani whispered under her breath.

"You okay?" her subject, James O'Leary, asked. He'd turned off the water and was toweling off outside the shower.

Digging a new pen out of her overstuffed purse, Dani stopped her stopwatch and jotted down the time. *7 min. 32 secs.* It was a relatively long shower. Most guys limited their showers to five minutes, tops. Ignoring the inquisitive smile on his face, she started in on her list of questions.

"So, James, when you're in the shower, what do you think about?" she asked. "What's going on in your brain?"

"I'd say I'm mostly going through my schedule. Or thinking about what I'm going to eat next. Don't write that down. That was a joke."

Dani wrote it down, mostly because she knew it was true.

The clipboard in her hands listed his name and demographic stats, and though she'd already read it over a half dozen times, she found herself studying his details again.

*JAMES O'LEARY. White 28-yr-old male, $38K. Educator/coach.*

It seemed impossible for someone to live on that kind of salary in a city like Boston. Sure, he lived in Jamaica Plain, and his apartment was nothing like the four-bedroom, three-bathroom pent-house with a view of the Charles River Dani had secured. But how did James O'Leary buy groceries on $38,000? No wonder he worried about what he was going to eat next.

Her yellow legal pad had filled with notes about everything from the type of shampoo he used to the order in which he washed his body. Observation was the only way to find insight—and that's what Dani needed to find. A lightbulb. A general psy-chological truth, baked into an aha moment, that E & G could use to inspire Gelhomme's next commercial campaign.

"What are you doing now?" she asked as he approached the sink.

"Now, I shave," he said, opening his arms to present the long counter in front of him. "If you must know."

"I must. It's why I'm here."

He spread a smear of shaving cream across his jawline—a square and impressive jawline, Dani noted. He rinsed his hands, then reached for a silver razor on the counter. Running it under warm water, James slid it down his face, cheek to chin, cheek to chin, in perfect vertical lines.

"Do you enjoy shaving?" asked Dani.

"Of course not. It's a chore. Does anyone like chores?"

"So why do you do it?"

He rinsed the blade under the faucet. Little black hairs had gathered like confetti along the counter.

"What do you mean, why do I do it?" he said. "I have to."

"Says who?"

He splashed his face with warm water and retrieved a hand

towel from the floor. Dingy and damp, it looked like it hadn't seen the inside of a washing machine in weeks. Dani made a note of the moldy smell in the bathroom and the water splotches on the mirror.

"I guess there's something to be said for a good habit," he said. "Like making your bed every day. There's a ritual to it. You may not love doing it, but it gives you something in return."

"What does it give you?"

He sighed, placing the razor back in a dirty cup on the counter.

"Control, I guess. Maybe that's all we want anyway."

Without waiting to see if his interviewer was satisfied with that answer, James disappeared into his bedroom.

"I'm just changing," he said through the crack in the closet door. "Help yourself to coffee in the kitchen. I'll be out in a sec."

TAKING HER SUBJECT up on his offer of coffee, Dani held a steaming cup in one hand and flipped through the set of notes she'd taken that morning, leaning over the island in his kitchen. Something about his answers had struck her as meaningful. Perhaps even essential. *Control. Ritual.*

There was something to what he'd said, but she couldn't put her finger on it at the moment, so instead packed away her notepad in her bag and prepared to leave.

Her subject emerged from his bedroom dressed in khaki pants and a slim fit collared shirt, in what Dani assessed must be his school's colors—burgundy and white. He picked up the remote control and pointed to the television screen, swapping the *Today* show for ESPN.

"You a Red Sox fan?" asked Dani, lifting her mug, which had the team's classic logo on the side.

"Unfortunately yes. Last year was incredible. But I doubt they'll win a World Series again in our lifetime."

"How can you say that? That's the beauty of sports—every new season is a fresh slate."

"Nothing's a fresh slate."

"Ah, so you're a pessimist."

"Sure, the Red Sox won a World Series. But that cursed mentality still persists. You got guys with those old mind-sets, old habits. Old injuries. You're always fighting the past. And the Red Sox. They've got a hell of a past. And I'm a realist, not pessimist."

He paused, then pointed his thumb back toward the bathroom.

"It's not like if I shave *really really* well one day, the hair won't grow back. No matter how good a job I do today, I know I'll look in the mirror tomorrow and have to shave again. Coaching is like that. It's just grooming. Every day I show up, and I have to remove the bad little insecurities and old habits that have cropped back up overnight in my boys. I can't change who they are or what they bring with them every day. Best I can do is groom it."

"That's actually quite poetic," Dani said, wishing she still had her pen and paper to write it down. She lifted her bag to her shoulder and started toward the door. "You know, I used to want to be a coach."

"Used to?" The guy laughed. "You don't look old enough to have a dream that died. How old are you, anyway?"

"Twenty-three."

"Ah, a geezer," he said. "So why aren't you coaching?"

Dani remembered the salary that had been listed under his name. "I don't really know," she said. "For one, my basketball career didn't really go as planned."

"Well, that's a dumb reason not to do what you love. Nothing *ever* goes as planned."

They stood there looking at one another for a moment before Dani shrugged and headed toward the door. "It's been good talking," she said, reaching her hand out to shake his. "Thanks for the interview."

"Hey, before you go, can I ask you something?"

"Shoot."

"Are you single?" he ventured, putting his hands on his hips. "I don't mean to pry, but I was thinking I could set you up. There's this girl—my sister actually. She's a few years older than you. But smart. Quick-witted. I think you two would really hit it off."

"Oh," Dani said. "I'm not . . . I'm straight."

"Oh shit. Well now I really feel like an asshole. I just thought . . . the short hair . . . the . . . Right? God. My bad. Forget it. Forget I said anything."

"Don't worry about it. Honest mistake. And hey, thanks again. You gave me a lot of good stuff to work with here. They'll send you a check in a few weeks for your time."

ONCE SHE'D MADE it into the back of a cab, Dani leaned her head against the window and groaned deeply. Shaking her head, she reached for the bottle of Advil in her purse, swallowed three pills dry, and carefully pulled the emotional dagger out of her chest.

At every turn, people got it wrong. Black people thought she acted too white; white people saw her as black. People knew she was an athlete, but any time she tried to succeed, they thought she was cocky. For years, she'd fallen more and more in love with Locke, but he simply saw her as a friend. And now, James O'Leary had tried to set her up with *his sister.* Clearly, the energy she was putting off was completely different than the energy she *wanted* to put into the world.

Was she too masculine? Too intense?

What was it going to take for someone to finally see her for who she really was? And like what they saw?

In her reflection in the window, wet tears glittered on Dani's cheeks, mingling with her freckles. Wiping the wetness with the palm of her hand, Dani blew air out of her lips and pulled herself together. There was no use in getting upset.

"Where to?" the cab driver asked.

She wasn't expected back at the office for a few more hours. And while there was plenty of work to do unpacking this interview with James, both professionally and personally, Dani knew she couldn't do it yet. Not when her frustration was this raw. In just a few weeks, everyone she loved would arrive for Thanksgiving. Her parents were driving from Ohio; her brother, Dominic, and his partner, Charles, were flying in from Chicago. And despite their crazy schedules, Locke, Avery, and Hannah had all found a way to travel to Boston, too—significant others in tow.

She'd be the only person at the table alone. The odd one out, who'd invited everyone in.

She thought about the fresh money in her bank account and the winter displays that had appeared in the windows of her favorite boutiques downtown. The idea of brand-new clothes with fresh tags, perfectly folded in a thick shopping bag, soothed her, and she hadn't even spent a dollar yet. Retail therapy. It was cheaper than real therapy, she told herself.

"Back Bay," she answered. "Anywhere on Newbury Street."

A FEW WEEKS later, the office buzzed with the chaos of a deadline. Phones rang loudly. The graphic design team moved their mouses briskly over multiple screens, deftly adding color and pizzazz to the research Dani had painstakingly compiled in the past year, hoping the numbers would tell a story. The first *deliverable*—another stupid marketing term that Dani loved to hate—was due to Gelhomme, and unfortunately, the French didn't celebrate Thanksgiving. No one was going home until the report was complete.

"Pete," said Dani, rolling her chair out of her cubicle to peer into his. The lead graphic designer was an overweight thirty-two-year-old with a muss of brown hair and a patchy beard. He wore a black hoodie to work every day and was so good at his job, no one even mentioned the fact that he smelled of cottage cheese. "For the final slide, we need *length of shave time, number of shaves a week,* and *number of razor brands purchased* in a year— all averages. Got it?"

"On it," he said, without lifting his eyes from the screen.

Dani nodded, closed a few windows on her browser, and breathed. *Wait 'til Gelhomme sees this,* she thought brightly.

She'd never been so proud of a project in her life. A year had passed since she'd joined E & G's research team, and she relished sifting through all those dry figures spread out across Excel spreadsheets. Survey answers coded and entered as numbers, each in its perfect little cell. Human motivations measured and analyzed. She could get lost in the matrix for hours, like a pirate searching for treasure. It didn't even bother her that this report would go up the chain of E & G without her name on it. In her view, excellence was far more important than ownership.

While Pete finished the presentation, Dani took a moment to walk to the office kitchen and refill her coffee mug, ignoring the ache in her hips. The pain had increased rapidly in the last few weeks, as she'd spent more time in her office chair, staring at a computer screen. Her general practice doctor had referred her to an allergist—apparently changes in her diet might help with the pain—but the allergist didn't have a free appointment until after the holidays. Her GP had prescribed a narcotic to help with the pain, but Dani hadn't filled the prescription. She'd heard how addictive those pills could be and didn't need to add that to her list of problems. Pain was nothing new. The only new thing was the word *chronic*.

Thankfully, there were more important things for Dani to focus on than her body. Though her town house in Boston's North End had been in various states of disarray since she'd moved in last fall, she'd used her incoming houseguests as an excuse to finish decorating. In a rush of hard work and expense, an interior designer had arrived with a team of handymen that helped finish positioning the furniture, hanging the art, mounting the television, and styling the tables. Yolanda, her cleaning lady, would do a deep clean Wednesday morning, and a local chef she'd found on Craigslist would come that afternoon to get a head start on the feast. The chef would arrive again Thursday promptly at six A.M. to finish off the preparations, filling her kitchen with aromas of thyme, sage, and cinnamon. It would be worth the cost.

Dani wanted this Thanksgiving to be perfect, but preparing the house hadn't done a single thing to prepare her heart for her guests—Locke in particular. *I'm thinking I might invite Amanda to come to Boston,* he'd written. *What do you think?* While changing the sheets on the guest beds, Dani couldn't stop thinking about what he would look like with a different girl standing beside him. The thought made her sick. But how could she say no? As soon as he arrived and saw her house, he would know that there *was* plenty of space at the table.

Tightening the sheets on the guest bed, Dani had tried not to think about who would soon be sleeping side by side on the mattress. She was going to have to meet Amanda. Worse, she was going to have to pretend to like her.

Dani sipped her coffee and stared out the office kitchen windows at the brilliant city below. The Charles River, a choppy dark navy, split the city into two sections: Cambridge to the left and North Boston to the right. If she squinted, she could nearly see her apartment, tucked near the harbor, surrounded in orange foliage. If they were lucky, the weather would stay like this all week: brisk but golden.

"Boston's skyline," said a familiar voice behind her, "compared to New York City. It's just so . . . quaint."

Turning from the windows, Dani found Jim Webb standing behind her. He wore a navy suit with a gray and burgundy striped tie, as dapper as the day they'd met. Dani suddenly felt like a foreign dignitary had come to visit.

"Surprised?" he said.

"Completely! What brings you here?"

"My wife's family does Thanksgiving in Nantucket. Thought I'd pop in. I had a few things I wanted to run past you about Gelhomme anyway. You have a minute?"

"Yep. Actually, Pete's about to finish up the report." Dani started toward Pete's desk. "Let me show you."

They walked through the numbers and figures, Dani pointing to each perfectly designed chart and graph, as Pete sat with his arms crossed, listening to the vice president of the company interrogate Dani about the work. From the questions Webb asked and the smile on his face—Dani could tell that their boss was impressed.

"You did this?" he asked the graphic designer once they'd finished.

"Yes, sir," said Pete, wiping a bead of sweat from his brow. It wasn't every day that someone as senior as Jim Webb showed up to your cube. "Dani's been feeding me the numbers. But I did the design work."

"Not bad," Jim said. "Not bad at all. Has Laura Klein seen this?"

Laura Klein, the woman who had helped Webb interview Dani last year, led E & G's London office. It was Laura's team that would create a commercial campaign informed by the insights Dani and the other junior research fellows had compiled into this report. Dani secretly wished she could follow the report through to completion—help with the creative side. But her job was nearly finished. Soon, Jim Webb would assign her a new research project for the next E & G client and the process would start over again.

"Not yet," answered Dani. "We're going to send it to her as soon as Pete finishes the design."

"Incredible. She'll be thrilled." Jim Webb straightened his tie. "Hey, let's step into your cube for a moment, Dani. I wanted to have a little chat."

Seated in Dani's nook, Webb looked like a giant—long legs crossed, mind deep in thought. Her desk was orderly, bare except for a coffee mug and a silver framed photo next to her keyboard. In the photo, she, Avery, and Hannah stood in the middle of Times Square, laughing. To this day, the thought of that crazy twenty-four-hour trip made Dani smile. Twenty years old, alone in the city. Dani was between injuries. Avery's world had yet to be rocked by scandal. And Hannah had just fallen in love with the man of her dreams. The shine on their faces said it all. They were unencumbered. They were free. It was hard to imagine that at the time their biggest grievance was Coach Jankovich. Now that woman was long gone from West Point. But then again, so were they.

"I'm thinking you should let the other researchers take the reins this next go-round," Mr. Webb finally said. "No need to waste your talent on the grunt work."

"I like the grunt work," Dani said. "I like the research."

"Well, unfortunately, I don't see you here much longer."

Dani furrowed her brow in an expression of utter confusion. What did he mean, he didn't see her here much longer? And why in the world was he smiling if he was about to fire her?

"Let me be straight with you, Dani," he said, then paused. "I'm here to offer you a promotion. How would you feel about moving to London?"

Dani stared at him and then laughed, thinking this surely was some kind of mistake. Twenty minutes ago, she was staring at Boston, excited about her Thanksgiving plans. And now Jim Webb was sending her to live in a different country?

"You want me to work on Laura Klein's team?" Dani asked. Her memory was fuzzy. She remembered the woman's British accent. The posh black dress. At that career fair, Laura had made some joke about expecting Dani to be a man. The few e-mails they'd exchanged in the last year had all been short. Terse, even. "Wait. Does she know about this?"

"It's less about what she wants, and more about what the company needs. We need someone like you on the creative side. Someone who can bring all that"—he pointed toward Pete's desk, indicating the research—"to the actual creative product. I think someone who knows the target consumer as intimately as you do needs to be on the marketing team."

Dani's mind raced. When she considered all the logistics of an overseas move—the housing and the packing and living so far away from family—it seemed like such a hassle. She'd only just finished decorating her apartment here! And she'd be even farther removed from her friends. But then again, Hannah was deploying to Afghanistan and Avery lived in North Carolina, which required a plane trip anyway. Why limit herself to the States?

"When?" Dani asked.

"January. That gives you a couple of months to move and get situated. Oh, and I forgot the most important part," Webb added. "It's a change in salary, too."

He wrote a number on a piece of paper and pushed it toward her. Despite the shock she felt at seeing the number, she kept her face neutral. She'd learned at West Point, the first rule of negotiation was to never to show your cards too quickly.

"That's great, but you and I both know the cost of moving will be steep. The cost of living in London, I imagine, is pretty different than Boston," said Dani.

"We can include a corporate travel account with Delta, so you won't have to pay for your flights to and from the U.S. And you'll be eligible for bonuses at this level. So that will sweeten the deal a good bit. You're good at your job, McNalley. You deserve this."

On the outside, Dani nodded and acted as though she were considering it all very soberly. On the inside, her mind was racing. To turn down this job would be stupid. So what if she was only selling razors? Razors made people's lives better. This was a blessing, Dani decided. A gift. Staring at the number on the page in front of her, she wondered what she would even do with that kind of money.

"Okay," Dani said, nodding as if she were trying to convince herself that this conversation was real. "Okay."

## 17

*Fall 2005 // Boston, Massachusetts*

C *link, clink, clink!*

"A toast."

Dani's brother, Dominic, stood at the center of the table, holding a glass of champagne. He looked almost exactly like Dani, Avery thought, only tall and bald, with thick Buddy Holly–style glasses and the same glowing McNalley aura. Dominic's partner, Charles, a Canadian-born physics professor, sat beside him, surreptitiously feeding their pug, Daisy, scraps of food under the table.

A half-carved turkey rested in front of Avery, surrounded by empty dishes, where an hour earlier had been the most beautiful assortment of delicacies: sweet potatoes, roasted corn, fresh broccoli, creamed spinach, acorn squash stuffed with mushrooms and rice. Tim stretched his arm over the back of Hannah's chair. Locke Coleman cut his girlfriend, Amanda, another slice of pumpkin pie. Dani's parents had retired to the living room to watch football, leaving two empty chairs beside Dani, who sat at the head of the table, rolling her eyes at her brother's theatrical toast. Noah's hand warmly massaged the back of Avery's neck, and a thimbleful of red wine sat in her glass. She was surprised to see the glass so empty. It had been full at least twice during dinner.

Everyone was leaning back in their seats, bellies full, smiles wide, though in all honesty, Avery was still hungry. Noah had convinced her of the benefits of vegetarianism, but staring at that leftover turkey on the table, Avery's mouth watered with desire. She'd never *not* eaten turkey at Thanksgiving. She found herself growing jealous of Dominic's pug.

"I drink to the general joy of the whole table," Dominic began, raising his glass.

"That's Shakespeare," interjected Charles. "How about something original, Dom?"

"Pipe down, Charles. I'm talking."

Noah reached for the open bottle of wine and refilled Avery's glass.

"Like I said," Dani's little brother continued, "I drink to your joy. But most of all, I drink to my sister, whose greatest joy in life is to share it with others."

"Here, here," said Locke.

"Here, here," said Hannah.

The table clinked glasses.

Avery took a big swallow of wine. Dominic was right: Dani did love to share her joy with others. And her wealth, too, now that she had it to share. Dani had purchased plane tickets for Avery and Hannah with her frequent-flier miles. She'd even offered to put Avery and Noah up in a hotel nearby, but Noah didn't feel comfortable accepting that much charity, so instead of staying at the Hilton with Hannah and Tim, they were stuck at a Holiday Inn.

It was strange to think that this soon after college, the world had already pushed Dani into such a different tax bracket. In the Army, everyone of the same rank made exactly the same amount of money—Avery could look at Hannah, Locke, and Tim, and know exactly what their bank accounts likely said. You had to hand it to communism. At least with forced equality, you didn't have to deal with your feelings of inferiority.

Avery hated that she felt—what was it? Envious of? *Surprised by?*—her friend's success, but it was hard not to. When Avery and Noah had arrived in Dani's cobblestoned North End neighborhood earlier that morning, they'd speculated how much rent she must have been paying to have such a stunning view of the river. The historic three-story town house must have been at least three thousand square feet. Her fully renovated chef's kitchen had black onyx countertops, a shiny marble backsplash, and stainless steel appliances. A man dressed in white was busy chopping onions on a butcher block—he turned out to be a private chef Dani had hired for the occasion. As if she couldn't be bothered with stuffing a stick of butter in the ass of a turkey. As if, all of a sudden, that was below her.

Across the room, an industrial dining table had been set for a crowd, with silver place settings and crystal water goblets next to delicate wine glasses, like in a restaurant. A brown leather sofa in the living room was flanked on either side by low-slung modern chairs. And Dani's apartment walls weren't bare, like Avery's quarters. Colorful African art had been hung professionally in every corner, like Dani had hired an interior designer. And the final touch was Tim and Hannah—Tim with his high and tight haircut and classic blue collared shirt, standing next to Hannah, whose long dirty blond hair fell in loose waves down her shoulders. When Avery and Noah had arrived, the Nesmiths had stood in Dani's kitchen sipping a beer, like the entire scene had been staged for an open house. Avery's mouth had hung open, in awe.

"Insane, right?" Tim had said, noticing Avery's surprise. "Not exactly Fort Bragg. But it'll do."

Hannah had given Avery a stiff hug and mentioned how ironic it was that Noah and Tim would meet for the first time in Boston, rather than at Fort Bragg, where they all lived.

"Where have you been, stranger?" said Hannah.

Avery had tried not to take that dig personally, but there was an edge in Hannah's voice that was hard to ignore.

Just after three o'clock, Locke Coleman had arrived, walking through the door with his arms up over his head, like a heavyweight wrestler who had just won a match. He looked exactly as he had in college: shining face, gap-toothed grin. Hugs abounded. And Dani looked the same as she always had whenever Locke was around: dazzled. But before Avery could leave the kitchen to welcome Locke, a petite girl with rich brunette hair came up the stairs behind him, holding a pie. For the second time in one day, Avery's jaw had dropped.

"I'm fine," Dani had said later, when she, Avery, and Hannah were alone together in the kitchen. "Why wouldn't I be? Locke and I are just friends. We were always just friends."

Avery and Hannah had exchanged a look, their agreement over Dani's denial momentarily bridging the distance that existed between them. They stood in silence until Dani poured herself a generous glass of wine and took a long guzzle.

"Let's talk about something else," Dani had said, changing the subject. "Tell me about tool shed guy."

Avery started with the long rides on his motorcycle that he'd taken her on throughout the spring, rides that ended in lakeside picnics or hikes to waterfalls. She'd described his vintage two-door BMW—*so sleek*—and the trip they'd taken to California that summer, which he'd paid for entirely. She'd complained about his schedule: Noah constantly left on deployments that were sporadic and unpredictable in their length and location. And since his work was classified, she'd had to learn to be comfortable not knowing where he was going or when he might return. She told her friends what she and Noah shared in common—a love of fitness, good wine, and music—and avoided any subjects that might raise their concern. As it turned out, Noah wasn't thirty, like he'd originally said. He was actually thirty-six, a fact Avery only discovered when she'd asked to look at the picture on his driver's license and noticed the year he was born. He said he'd never lied—he promised that on their first date, he'd told her he was in his *thirties,* but Avery remembered it differently. Not that it mattered. It was only a thirteen-year difference.

She knew his age would matter to her friends, though. So she avoided admitting the truth about his age, because she didn't want to spend Thanksgiving justifying their relationship. Instead, she was going to spend it feeling his warm hand against her neck.

As Dominic took his seat, the table quieted and candlelight flickered across all of their faces. In particular, Avery focused on Tim and Hannah, who were seated across from her. All night, they'd been leaning into one another. Touching. Kissing. Nothing inappropriate, of course—it was Hannah after all—but even from the outside, you could sense an urgency in their faces. Time was running out before they deployed. And while Avery still wasn't a huge fan of Tim, she appreciated how quickly he'd welcomed Noah into their fold, offering him a beer and talking to him about the Army all afternoon.

Avery tapped her spoon against her glass. "Okay, my turn." She stood, straightened her black silk top, and tucked her hair behind her ears. She was horrible at improvising, especially when she was a little bit drunk. But if she couldn't get sentimental *now*, then when?

"To West Point. The place that brought us all together," Avery said. "West Point took a lot from us, but it gave us each other. And for that, I'm grateful."

"Here, here!" Dani said, looking shocked by the softness of Avery's toast.

Locke picked up where Avery had left off: "And to all the eighteen-year-old assholes who are finishing their applications and have no idea what they're signing up for."

"Here, here!" said Tim, raising his glass.

The toast ended and Dominic sighed heavily. "Well, I'm stuffed," he said.

"Amanda, your pie was incredible," offered Hannah. "I wish I could make pie from scratch. Believe me, I've tried."

"I can show you how to do it," said Amanda. "It's actually pretty simple. Nothing compared to all this. I still can't get over the meal, Dani. The sweet potatoes! That acorn squash was divine. What was that cream sauce on top? Did you make that?"

"Didn't you see the guy in there earlier?" said Locke. "Dani hired a chef."

Dani laughed. "Life's too short to chop onions."

"Locke has told me so many stories from West Point," Amanda continued, looking up and down the table. "You guys are in all of them. Especially you, Dani."

Avery fought the urge to cringe. *This chick is so completely oblivious.*

"He told me one recently. What was it, Locke? Something about New York City and a tongue ring?"

Locke pointed his fork in Hannah's direction. "Didn't Coach Jankovich make you rip it out when you got back?"

"She did," affirmed Dani. "It bled all over the court at practice."

Tim leaned forward to look at Hannah, whose face was nearly as red as the wine in Avery's glass. "Wait a second," he said. "How do I not know this story? My wife had a tongue ring and I didn't know it?"

Hannah shook her head in embarrassment. "It was when we were on our little *break*," she explained. "Junior year. Locke and some of the other football guys went with us to the city for a twenty-four-hour pass. And you kept telling people . . . what was it?"

"That I was—" Locke started.

"That he'd just been recruited by the *Ravens*," finished Dani.

"The Ravens!" exclaimed Avery, bubbling over with laughter. "All the other guys with us were acting like Locke's bodyguards. Which was annoying, because no guys would come near us."

Dani picked up where Avery had left off. "So, everywhere we go, doors are opening. Drinks are flowing. And suddenly, we look around and Avery and Hannah are gone—"

"We were there to meet men, not to be protected from them," added Avery.

Dani continued. "—and no one can find them. And when we finally get back to Grand Central to catch the last train back to West Point, there they are—"

"—and Hannah is holding an ice pack to her mouth," Avery squeaked, barely able to contain her laughter. "You were, like, drooling and couldn't speak in full sentences, because your tongue was so swollen."

"You sanctioned this piercing, Adams?" said Tim, looking at Avery.

"Of course I did!" Avery said, holding up her hands. "I was trying to help her get over *you*! I guess I failed at that job. She needed help. Before that, she was begging to go to the *Today* show, all right? I wanted her to live a little."

Hannah's mouth opened, like she'd just been stabbed in the back. She pointed across the table at Avery. "You know Katie Couric is my idol!"

They were all laughing hysterically now. But when Avery turned to look at Noah, to ensure that he was having as much fun as the rest of them, he'd vanished from the table.

"HEY, WHY'D YOU leave?"

She found Noah on the balcony outside, talking on his cell phone and smoking a cigarette. The river was black, like the sky. Once she stepped outside to join him, he quickly ended the call with a brief, "*Yep, love you too.*" Stuffing his cell phone in his pocket with one hand, Noah put out his cigarette on the railing with the other, then pulled Avery in for a kiss.

"You know I hate it when you do that," she said.

Smoking was a disgusting, carcinogenic habit. But then again, his bad-boy persona was part of the ethos that had suckered her in. "Who were you talking to?" she asked, trying to sound nonchalant.

"My mom," he said. "I was wishing her a happy Thanksgiving."

Avery checked her watch. "Aren't they still on a plane?"

Noah nodded, looked down at his feet, and rubbed out an imaginary cigarette on the ground with his toe. "Yeah, it was delayed."

"Oh. That sucks. I bet your brother's pissed."

"Yeah. They'll be all right." Noah reached for her waist and pulled her close to his body. "You ready to head out of here?"

"It's only eight o'clock. Dani has a whole game night planned or something."

Noah rolled his eyes. "Game night? What are we, five?"

"Come on," Avery said, cajoling him. "It'll be fun."

While he nibbled on the edge of her ear, Avery looked over his shoulder through the window at Dani, Hannah, and Amanda, who were busy cleaning the kitchen.

"I should go help them," Avery said.

"Okay," he said. "I gotta make one more call. I'll be right in."

Avery paused and looked at him quizzically. Who else would he need to call on Thanksgiving?

"It's a work thing," he said. "It'll be quick."

AVERY LEFT THE balcony and walked around a corner toward the kitchen. But when she heard her friends talking in hushed voices, she paused, standing behind a column.

"He's been on his phone the whole night," Hannah said.

"Avery seems happy," added Dani. Avery felt a sudden surge of gratitude. At least *someone* was taking up for her. "But I keep wondering how old he is. He seems older, right?"

"Here's what I don't understand," Amanda said. Locke's girl-friend wore a black crewneck sweater with a white Peter Pan collar. Avery could see her from around the corner, with her little ballet flats and little ballet voice. Who did she think *she* was to weigh in on Avery's relationship? She didn't even belong here! "He doesn't eat meat, but he *does* smoke cigarettes? In what world does that make sense?"

Clearing her throat, Avery stepped into the kitchen. They all froze.

"You know, you guys can say these things to my face," Avery said.

The silence persisted until Dani cleared her throat. "We're just curious, Ave," she said. "That's all."

"About what?" Avery was suddenly overcome with a readiness to defend herself. Like she'd stepped into battle. "Speak now, or forever hold your peace."

"Okay," said Hannah. "So, nicotine aside . . . you like him? He's treating you okay?"

Avery groaned and poured herself another glass of red wine. "He came all the way up here." She paused, taking in the sight of Hannah's concerned eyes and Dani, who was staring straight at her, wiping her hands on a kitchen towel. "Yes, he *treats me okay*. He treats me great. What is the problem?"

Hannah looked at Dani pleadingly, which sent heat rushing to Avery's face. "Stop," she said, no longer trying to keep her voice down. "Stop silently communicating with each other right in front of my face. Just say it. You don't like him."

"I didn't say that," Hannah said.

Amanda stepped gingerly off the step stool she'd been using to put away dishes in cabinets she couldn't reach. "I'm going to . . . let you ladies talk." She tiptoed out of the room.

"He's been looking at his phone all night," said Dani. "It just seems odd, that's all. We just want to make sure we're seeing it clearly. Maybe there's something we don't know."

"There's a lot you don't know," said Avery. "He's been on his phone because his parents have been stuck in an airport all day, trying to get to see his brother in Kansas City. He's been trying to rebook their flights. I promise you guys, once you get to know him, he's great."

At this they seemed to soften, and Avery felt a mix of relief and shame—relief that she'd won them over, and shame that she'd

had to try so hard. She didn't know for certain that he'd been trying to rebook their flights. But that helped his case, so the white
lie felt justified.

"So how serious is it?" Dani asked.

Avery shrugged. "I don't know. Noah . . . he's different. He
seems committed to things. To us."

"Good," Hannah said. Stepping forward, she placed her hands
on Avery's shoulders. "He's extremely lucky. Do you know that?
You deserve for someone to completely cherish you. That's what
we want."

For some reason, Avery cringed at Hannah's shower of compliments, her touch. Was it because she'd questioned Noah behind
her back? Or because Avery didn't believe the things Hannah had
said were actually true? Ever since Noah had shown up in that
tool shed, it was Avery who had felt like the lucky one.

"And you," said Avery, stepping out of Hannah's embrace, toward Dani at the sink. She picked up a dry dish towel and snapped
it against Dani's leg. "You did so much to make this happen today.
I don't think I've had a chance to say thank you."

To Avery's surprise, thick tears formed in Dani's eyes. She
turned off the water and turned to look at Avery and Hannah.

"What's wrong?" said Hannah.

"I have to tell you guys something," Dani said. "Don't worry.
It's good news."

"Then why are you crying?" Avery asked, then whispered,
"Did you poison Amanda's drink?"

Dani coughed a laugh. "No. I got a promotion. At work."

"That's great!" Hannah sang.

"Yeah." Dani scrunched her nose. "There's just one catch."

THE REST OF Dani's guests hurried into the kitchen when they heard Hannah scream.

"Dani's moving to London!" Hannah announced.

"London?" Locke repeated. "Like, England? Dude, I'm coming to visit."

Amanda looked at him as if this international visit was news to her but smiled and grabbed his hand, as if to say she was fine with it.

"That's crazy!" Tim said. "I'm not surprised. You were always the smartest one of all of us. Way to go, D."

Dominic started laughing. "You're gonna do it, right? You've got to do it. Charles, tell her she has to do it."

While Dani rapidly described all of her moving plans, Avery tried not to let her jealousy show on her face. She wanted to be happy for Dani—she really did. But how could you celebrate someone else's successes when your life felt completely stalled? In just a few short months, Hannah would be in Afghanistan, Dani would be in London, and Avery would still be stuck in Fort fucking Bragg. Her friends were moving on to bigger and better things: marriage, deployments, promotions. And she was . . . what? Here? In love? She looked outside at Noah, who had finished his second cigarette but was still on the phone.

"You all better come visit," said Dani. "Oh, Avery, why are you crying?"

"I don't know," she lied. The truth was, she felt like she was being left behind. And unfortunately, all the questions they'd brought up about Noah hadn't rolled off her shoulders like she'd hoped, but were sinking into the pit of her stomach. Everything suddenly felt very out of control. She had no idea how to express any of that except to say, "I'm going to miss you guys. That's all."

Hands damp from washing dishes, they stood in the kitchen in a small semicircle with their arms wrapped around each other's backs. If time could stop, Avery would have pressed pause right then and there. Before Hannah packed her trunk and put it on the back of a cargo ship headed to the Middle East. Before the movers arrived in Boston to pull down all the art from Dani's walls and wrap it in paper. Before Avery put her purse over her shoulder, said goodbye to her friends, and walked out the door under Noah's heavy arm, smelling the stale odor of cigarette smoke, masked by mint gum.

They say hindsight is twenty-twenty. But what good is hindsight when all you want to do is look through the glass and shout at your old self to not take one more step?

"Stop that," said Dani. "We'll be together again before you know it."

## 18

*March 2006 // Camp Buehring, Kuwait*

Prayer flags waved at the front of the bus, flapping against the air-conditioning vents. The driver, a bearded man wearing a tunic, turned up the volume on a recorded track of Arabic prayers, loud enough to drown out the sound of the engine. To Hannah, who sat in the third row behind the driver, staring out the window to the right, the prayers sounded ghostly, more like chants than prayers. Tim was the one who'd taken Arabic at West Point. When they'd said goodbye a few weeks earlier, he'd given her a phrasebook that he'd marked up and tagged, sticking little pink Post-it notes on the pages he thought would be most helpful. Now, staring out the window at an entirely new world, Hannah wished she'd memorized some of the phrases. At least then, the prayers coming from the speakers wouldn't sound so foreign. She imagined that Muslims asked God for the same things she wanted: Help. Protection. Peace. They said there was nothing more genuine than the prayer of a man in a foxhole. And this whole country was one big foxhole.

Hannah's parents and her sister, Emily, all understood that this deployment wasn't a disruption to her life. It wasn't something that scared her or made her feel anxious. The night before she left Fort Bragg for the airport, Hannah didn't worry any more than a child frets knowing they're leaving in the morning for Disney World. To say she was excited would be wrong—because this was a war zone—but she felt ready. After years of anticipation, Hannah wanted to get started and get it over with. She kept a pocket calendar and had already marked off two days. Four hundred and forty-eight to go.

The bus barreled down an unpaved road toward the entrance to Camp Buehring, where her unit would spend two weeks acclimating to the heat and recovering from jet lag, before their final flight into Afghanistan. Her silver cross rested between Hannah's thumb and forefinger and she slid the charm right and left on the delicate chain, before hiding it away again under her uniform. The air inside the bus smelled stale and brimmed with the quiet tension of fifty soldiers on board, each one staring out their own window at the same merciless view. Sand stretched for miles in every direction. A woman in a long black cloak with only slits for eyes—a burqa—walked along the road in the dust. Where she was going, Hannah had no idea. And for the first time, she felt a jolt of fear. From this point forward, it was going to be nearly impossible to tell friend from enemy.

Soon, the line of buses reached a security checkpoint and

a crew of Army soldiers dressed in desert fatigues checked the buses for explosives, then waved them through.

That was all it took to get to war. Five years of training and a wave.

OVER THE NEXT few weeks, Hannah's unit conducted a series of training events. They were instructed to drink a gallon of water a day to hydrate, and at night, Hannah fought to stay awake until it was time to go to sleep in Kuwaiti time. Each morning, she woke up before the sun, not because she was forced to, but because her mind hadn't caught up to her body's geography. Despite her surroundings, everything in her heart and mind believed she was still in North Carolina. One morning, she woke up in the darkness of her tent completely confused about where she was and why the air smelled like burning trash.

She adjusted soon enough. They completed medical simulations and vehicle rollover simulations, and for two consecutive days near the end of their time in Kuwait, her unit practiced counter-IED training, to help them detect and disable roadside bombs. Every time Hannah stepped outside, sand whipped up from the ground, into her ears, eyes, and mouth, as if it were trying to bury her alive. And everyone had the same complaint: it was so *hot*. In an e-mail to Dani, she'd tried her best to explain how it felt: like someone was blowing a hair dryer in your face. Temperatures stayed in the hundreds and regularly hit 125 by the afternoon. Breath stifled, pores full of dirt, Hannah learned to drink water before she was thirsty, to walk in the shade, and to stay inside between the hours of twelve and three P.M. The climate was as much of an enemy as the Taliban.

By the time her unit reached Forward Operating Base Sharana in southeastern Afghanistan, thirty kilometers from the border of Pakistan, Hannah had marked thick black Xs through seventeen days on her pocket calendar.

She carved out a routine, which Sarah Goodrich, who'd completed her first deployment, had promised would help pass the time. An alarm went off every day at 0530. She ran around the perimeter of the forward operating base, showered, and read a few pages in her Bible. Then she'd make it to the cafeteria for breakfast, before heading to the tactical operations center to meet with her superior officers and discuss tasks for the day.

At times, it was easy to forget she was even in Afghanistan—that is, until she would walk outside, feel the dry heat attack her sinuses, and see dusty mountains in every direction. Afghanistan had a barren beauty that Hannah grew to appreciate and even admire. At night, the sky was so lit up with stars, it looked like a laser-light show and far outperformed the view from her grandfather's porch. There, she could see constellations. Here, she saw galaxies.

In an area this remote, snail mail was still the most reliable and consistent form of communication. Tim's handwriting—dark, all-caps—became the thing Hannah most longed to see on the outside of a white envelope. They wrote often, filling the pages with minutiae like what they'd eaten the day before or their most recent workout. But every now and then, Tim would surprise

Hannah by sending a poem or a long passage from a book he'd been reading, if he felt it applied to their situation.

She kept his letters in her pillowcase until the stack became too thick. By the time her unit took their first convoy away from FOB Sharana to build an outpost for a crew of NATO troops, the collection was three inches tall. She wrapped the letters with a spare shoestring and locked it in the trunk at the foot of her cot. When they returned a week later, she riffled through them again, laughing at the little drawings he'd put in the margins. The most recent one featured a sketch of Hannah and Tim on opposite sides of the world, arms wrapping around the globe like Stretch Armstrong, reaching across the oceans. He'd never been much of an artist.

*It's only 15 months,* she told herself. *That's nothing.*

Once at West Point, Hannah's computer had crashed, destroying a sixteen-page term paper in the process. Tim had shown up at her room with a carafe of coffee and a calculator.

"Look," he'd said, crunching the numbers of her GPA. "You can literally turn in nothing, and you'll be okay." She was crying. The numbers hadn't convinced her that the world wasn't ending. He'd put his hands around her face, wiped her tears with his thumbs, and then kissed her softly on the mouth.

"I dare you to believe me."

After that, Hannah had spent the entire night drinking coffee and listening to Tim tell stories instead of rewriting her paper. It was a risk, and not once during the night had she felt comfortable taking it. But in the end, he'd been right. She'd turned in five pages of nonsense—something she'd written quickly the following morning. And even though she received an F, the world didn't end. Her GPA only changed by a tenth of a point. She believed he was right about this deployment, too, that spending all this time apart would be worth it in the end. Like one failed paper didn't impact her GPA, one year apart wouldn't change the totality of their relationship together.

It was just fifteen months. Basically, a year.

A year is nothing in light of a life.

"HE SAYS A U.S. mortar round landed on his land, killing his prized cow."

An interpreter spoke quickly in Pashto to a dark-skinned Afghan man, the plaintiff, who spat back something angry and defiant, pointing once again at the photo on the table in front of them.

Three months into her deployment, Hannah had been called into a JAG meeting. The translator, Amjad Ebrahim, was something of a minor celebrity around FOB Sharana. When their unit had first arrived, the translator had collected a few dollars from every officer and showed up the next day with a freshly slain lamb. Skinned, bled, and roasted over a fire, the lamb accompanied an assortment of sauces, spices, tandoori bread, yogurt sauce, chopped mint, preserved lemon, falafel, rice, and steamed greens. It was still the best meal Hannah had ever had—and that included all the meals Wendy Bennett had made at her home at West Point.

Twenty-seven, with a wife and three children at home, Ebrahim had long hair that curled slightly under his ears, dark eyebrows, and a ready smile that defied his circumstances. Every day, he wore a uniform that matched Hannah's, only his had a patch on the left that read "U.S. Interpreter" where hers said "U.S. Army."

But today, Ebrahim's face was all business. The man across from him wore a white shalwar kameez, frayed and dirtied on the edges from his long trek into the Army compound.

"Does he have documentation?" the JAG officer asked. "A receipt? Any kind of evidence?"

The interpreter repeated the question in Pashto, and the offended Afghan man answered vehemently in the affirmative, pushing his photo and a piece of paper across the table. The paper was covered in writing, but Hannah couldn't help but think the ink looked fresh. She'd only been asked to attend this meeting because the finance officer attached to their unit was down with some kind of stomach bug, but she suddenly felt way out of her league. The room felt tense, like the man was about to explode with rage.

"He says it's a receipt," said Ebrahim.

"What does it say?" the JAG officer asked. "Is it a receipt?"

Shrugging his shoulders, Ebrahim continued, "It says he purchased the cow this year for two hundred U.S. dollars."

Without thinking, Hannah laughed out loud, forcing the JAG officer to scowl. She felt mortified at her accidental lapse in decorum, but there was no way this man had paid that much money for a cow. For many Afghans, two hundred U.S. dollars was enough to feed a family for a year! She looked at Ebrahim for some sign of recognition. Some mutual understanding that they were being swindled.

"Pay him," the JAG officer instructed Hannah after looking over the paper. Then, looking at Ebrahim, he said, "Thank him for coming. Tell him we hope this makes up for his loss."

A bead of sweat ran down Hannah's temple as she passed an orange envelope of cash to the man across from her. He accepted the envelope haltingly, as if a woman's hands had soiled the funds. When he pulled the cash from the envelope, he began to argue with the translator again. Ebrahim shouted in return, his face reddening, as if he were scolding a child. Hannah noticed he pointed toward the door, but the Afghan man refused to leave.

"What's he saying?" Hannah asked.

"He says without the cow, they've missed out on income," Ebrahim answered, exasperated. "He demands another two hundred dollars."

Wide-eyed, Hannah turned to the JAG officer, stunned. Surely the U.S. Army wouldn't be extorted by a petty thief. He probably didn't even own a cow in the first place! And even if he had, $400 amounted to a half year's salary in Afghanistan. Would the JAG officer really enable this man to quit his day job? Military Intelligence was clear on what unemployed men spent their days doing—and it wasn't milking cows. It was fighting alongside the Taliban.

"Do it," the JAG officer ordered.

And Hannah followed orders, sliding another $200 across the table. But this time she didn't laugh.


"BAD DAY?"

Hannah looked up from her plate of gray meatloaf topped with red sauce to see Private Murphy staring at her. He kept shoveling food into his mouth, but she knew from the tone of his voice that he actually cared. He tapped his fork on the table and went back to his plate, stacked high with mystery meat.

"Suit yourself. But it's got to go somewhere, ma'am."

Pushing her food around her plate, she realized her eyes must have looked as heavy on the outside as they felt in her head.

"We paid a local guy four hundred dollars today for a cow that probably never existed."

Private Murphy grunted.

"I feel like I'm just wasting my time here," Hannah said.

"You could always come to the clinic," he said. "We could use an extra set of hands."

The week before, at the exact same table, Private Murphy had told Hannah about the medical center outside of FOB Sharana. The battalion that had lived at the FOB the year before had set up an old containerized housing unit, or CHU, a few hundred yards beyond the base to act as an emergency room for locals. Afghans traveled, sometimes for days, to get there. The rectangular clinic was outfitted with medical equipment—old stretchers, IVs, first aid gauze, and a dwindling stash of Medihoney, a medical-grade honey product for the management of wounds and burns. They weren't doctors, but with the training they'd received in the military, they knew more than most. The battalion commander, Colonel Markham, allowed them to go out on Saturdays between building assignments.

"So you treat mostly burns?" Hannah said.

"Yeah. I guess it's common here for parents to burn their children as a punishment," Private Murphy said with cold indifference. "Last week, a father brought in his seven-year-old son. He'd disobeyed somehow, and as punishment, he'd dipped his son's arm in kerosene and then lit a match."

"Oh my God."

"It's pretty messed up. But they won't take the children to an Afghan hospital."

"Why not?"

"Well, for one, the closest hospital is in Kabul. It would take about a week to get there. Plus, Afghan doctors would amputate. We're not equipped to do all that. So we do the best we can. Try to save the limbs. The parents like that."

"I want to go," Hannah said.

"No you don't. It ain't pretty."

Hannah stared him down until he relented.

"Don't say I didn't warn you."

THE FOLLOWING SATURDAY, Hannah woke at 0530, slung her weapon over her shoulder, and slipped out of her room into the rising sun. Colonel Markham, Private Murphy, and three other soldiers waited at the FOB gate, and once Hannah had joined them, Markham waved to the soldier on guard. A heavy concrete door clicked loudly and swung open, then closed behind them.

The scene from beyond the wall unfolded before Hannah, shocking her with its beauty. The rising sun cast an eerie red light across the desert. Heat waves swirled through the air like the ones she used to stare at when her father grilled steaks on the back deck, only this was natural heat—terrifying, since it was still so early in the morning. She could hear the short, fast *pop-pop-pop* of magazine fire in the distance, and as they crested a small sand hill, the makeshift CHU she'd been told about came into view, next to an open-air wooden structure, built as a waiting room for patients. Under the structure, a crowd of families waited in utter silence as the medical team arrived.

Mothers wearing hijabs fanned their children, who'd been carried on quilts or doors. Red and burgundy burns slashed and splotched the children's faces, arms, and legs. Some of the burns oozed, others bled. Dark skin flapped in charred masses and fresh white splotches of exposed epidermis screamed with pain, though the children refused to cry. Fathers stood, stoic and dark eyed, watching as Colonel Markham passed the patients, evaluating each case by sight. He didn't waste any time choosing the most severe cases. *It's triage,* Hannah realized. Worst cases first.

"One," Markham said, and pointed to a child stretched out on a quilt. "Two." He pointed to another child, on the opposite side of the shelter. "Three . . ."

Hannah, breathless and sick to her stomach, waited for him to finish creating an impromptu appointment list.

"Just like every other day, don't go crowding the gate," he said. "We will get to everyone eventually."

Once they were inside the CHU, Markham closed the door behind them. The structure was long and thin, with three stretchers for patients lined up diagonally down the middle of the trailer. Shelves on every wall held equipment: thermometers, Medihoney, steroids, bandages. Two rotary fans and a small AC unit churned stale air. A radio filled the room with the sounds of old Beatles songs. As Hannah moved about the room, trying to find the right place to stand, Private Murphy and the rest of the soldiers took off their uniform overcoats.

"Lieutenant Nesmith," Murphy said, "time to scrub in."

Hannah mimicked Murphy's every move: she secured her M16 in a locker, removed her helmet and Kevlar, hung up her jacket, rolled up the sleeves of her tan T-shirt. Standing next to Murphy at the center of the CHU, they both snapped a pair of purple rubber gloves over their hands.

"This is the real fight. A chance to show mercy," Markham said as he propped the door open with a rock. "Number one!"

Two soldiers at the entrance waved metal detector wands over the patient, who was covered by a white blanket, then checked the patient's parents as well. And before Hannah could prepare, Markham had directed the patient's parents to stand in the back corner and began to slowly lift the quilt off the small body underneath.

A young girl lay naked, shaking, watching as her skin peeled back off her arms, stomach, legs, and feet, still attached to the blanket. Without thinking, Hannah squatted down beside the patient, stroking her dark black hair. The child opened and closed her eyes with pain, the sounds of her small cries drowned out by the music coming from the radio.

"Shh . . . shh . . . ," Hannah said, holding all of her emotion in her belly. "It's okay. It's going to be okay."

The girls' father looked on, blank and expressionless, as his daughter's skin peeled off like brown paper, attached to the fibers of the blanket. Hannah found herself praying. *Please, God, save this child.*

Private Murphy started in, cutting dead skin away from the girl's body with a pair of sterilized scissors.

"If you leave it, infections will set in," he said. "She needs an IV. Morphine. Nesmith. Can you do it?"

Hannah suddenly remembered the training she'd done at Buckner, when she'd shoved a needle into Avery's arm.

"It's been a long time," she answered.

"It's okay. Just do what I say."

Following his instructions, Hannah placed a long needle through a vein in the young girl's forearm, trying carefully not to cause more pain. And as she did, Hannah did everything she could to keep herself from crying.

LATER THAT EVENING, as the sun was setting, Hannah sat in her room stewing. She had propped her bed on stilts in order to fit a trunk underneath, and had built a set of bookshelves so she could have a place for books—most of which had been chosen by Tim. As little as he'd liked to complete assigned reading in college, he was a voracious reader now. He said books tasted better when you were hungry for them. At the moment, she was one hundred pages into *East of Eden*. And he was right. She couldn't get enough of Steinbeck's words. The more she consumed, the more she desired.

On her desk, a stack of supply requisition forms waited for her signature, necessary for the upcoming site build her platoon was scheduled to complete. But she didn't feel like reading or doing paperwork. She didn't feel like doing anything.

She was still trying to understand what she'd witnessed that

morning at the burn unit. It seemed utterly evil, what those parents had done to their children, but culturally speaking, it was
completely acceptable—around here, it was discipline. Sitting in
her CHU, Hannah remembered Colonel Bennett's philosophy
class her plebe year, and the conversation he'd led about justice.
Was it injustice, what these people were doing? Or was it cultural
difference? Was it up for debate, or was there truth, with a capital
T? Did God care about those children? Did he see?

Shaking the thought from her mind, she changed into a pair of
black shorts and a gray T-shirt, and pulled her hair into a ponytail. Being in an engineering platoon had its perks—one of which
was that they could build just about anything if they had the right
materials.

A week earlier, she'd joined a group of soldiers in building a
makeshift basketball court on the tarmac. Since then, they had an
unspoken standing pickup game every night at seven P.M. Even
the translator, Ebrahim, had started playing, though admittedly,
he wasn't very good. Hannah always picked him for her team, just
as a show of good faith.

When she arrived at the court, the interpreter was already
there, stretching. He wore a pair of white Air Jordans that Private
Murphy had given him.

"Hydration is the key to longevity," he said philosophically. He
offered Hannah a plastic water bottle and she took it.

"I swear, Ebrahim, your English is better than mine," Hannah
said, taking a sip of the cold water.

In the months since she'd arrived at FOB Sharana, he'd become
the closest thing Hannah had to a friend. His English was im-

peccable, his sense of humor approachable, and his addiction to outdated American romantic comedies common knowledge. He'd told Hannah that he'd learned most of his English by watching Julia Roberts in *My Best Friend's Wedding*. He would often stop and shout "Kimmi!" for no reason, as though he had Tourette's syndrome. It always made Hannah laugh.

"Hey, can I ask you something?" she said.

He nodded. "Shoot." He put his hands up. "Don't shoot!" They laughed at his silly joke, and then he said, "Of course. Ask me anything."

"The other day. That guy with the cow. What are the chances he was telling the truth?"

After a pause, Ebrahim shrugged. "Who's to say?"

Shaking her head, Hannah sat on the tarmac to tighten her shoelaces. "How can you be so calm about it?" she asked. "Doesn't that kind of thing keep you up at night?"

"I don't lose sleep over things I can't control."

Hannah focused on the sky while her mind reeled. Her interpreter worked with her nearly every day, having conversations, not offended that her hair was uncovered or that she spoke to him without first being addressed. But she was well aware that his wife at home wasn't allowed to speak out of turn, or leave the house without his permission.

"For the life of me I don't understand," Hannah said, finally letting her arms drop to her sides.

"Don't understand what?"

"With any other woman, you wouldn't dare sit and have a conversation like this. Out in the open."

"No."

"So what's the difference?"

"You're American."

Hannah sighed. "But what about your wife? Your daughter? Don't you want them to have an education? Don't you want them to have opportunities?"

"And what has your education gotten you? A trip to a war zone?" Ebrahim laughed, still trying to keep the tone light. "I imagine your father wishes you were at home."

Hannah raised her eyebrows. He had a point.

"Sometimes I just wonder if being here is really going to make any difference," she said. "It just seems impossible."

Ebrahim let Hannah's question linger between them. Then he cleared his throat.

"When I was a boy, my father would get up every morning and call around to his brothers, to see who was still alive after the bombing through the night.

"The bombing was constant. After the Russians left, this area was controlled by warlords that constantly fought for territory. Then the Taliban came in and kicked out all of the warlords. And the rules they put in place—they were crazy, sure. It seemed a small price to pay for safety. To sleep and know that you would wake up in the morning.

"I was fifteen when things changed. First, they said that women couldn't go to school, which wasn't hard because my family was too poor to send my sisters to school anyway. Then they destroyed the cinemas. We couldn't listen to music. There was no art. No industry. No festivals or feasts, like there had been when I was a boy. My wedding day was one of the bitterest days of my life. I went to pick up my wife from the salon—there were salons then, if you can imagine that. We drove together to my parents' home for the celebration. But on the way, they stopped us. Pulled me out of the car. Beat me. Cut my hair. They said I shouldn't have been with her, like that, alone, because we were unmarried.

"And things just kept getting worse. They killed people and hung them from streetlights. They'd leave the bodies there for weeks, until they rotted and fell to the ground for the dogs to eat."

He paused, although Hannah couldn't be sure if it was to collect his thoughts or contain his emotion.

"We can never go back to that. Never," he said, looking straight at her. "We were dead under the Taliban. There was no life. No reason to live. No traditions. No beauty.

"But now, we feel again. We hope again. I can listen to music and dance." He snapped his fingers, wiggled his hips. "I'm here, playing basketball with my American friends. That's something. Right? That's a . . . what did you say? Lasting change? Yes."

He unscrewed the cap of his water bottle, took a long sip, then twisted the cap back in place and wiped his mouth.

"Maybe hope is the only lasting change one human can give to another. And for the first time in my life, I have hope. You gave that to me."

## 19

*Spring 2006 // London, England*

D ani!"
Laura Klein had the annoying, completely unnecessary habit of shouting across the office to get Dani's attention, when, in reality, all she had to do was stand up and look outside her office door and kindly say, at a normal decibel level, that she needed something.

That woman always needed something. But at the moment, Dani didn't want to move. She'd just read an e-mail that had stunned her into paralysis.

**From:** Locke Coleman <lockestockand@hotmail.com>
**Subject:** booked!
**Date:** April 6, 2006 9:13:15 AM CST +01:00
**To:** Dani McNalley <danimcnalley@yahoo.com>

Booked my ticket! Coming to London May 14–21. Call me and let's start to make some plans.

—Locke

*"Dani!"*

Pushing away from her desk, Dani limped from her chair to her boss's door frame. The London office was aesthetically disappointing—dark carpet, clusters of cubicles, a tiny kitchen with a refrigerator full of other people's forgotten lunches, stinking and spoiled. Laura Klein, it turned out, was as short and brittle as a boss as she'd been in that first interview a few years earlier. She had platinum blond hair, and wore the same dark maroon lipstick and black three-quarter-length dress, as if it were easier to wear the same thing every day than to make fashion decisions. In nearly every conversation, she found a way to mention her current separation from her husband of twenty-two years, and Dani wondered if he'd grown bored with her clothes or simply annoyed by the sound of her nagging voice. Either way, she couldn't really blame the guy.

Dani poked her head into Laura's office. "Yes?"

"What's this I hear from Webb about new slides?"

"I cc'd you on that."

"Cc," she repeated, lowering her glasses down her nose.

"Carbon copy."

"Right. Well I didn't see that. And I need to see them before my presentation."

Dani wondered if she'd heard Laura correctly—if her boss had actually put emphasis on the word *my*. As if Dani would forget who was giving the most important presentation in E & G history. After more than a year and a half of global research, they were finally presenting their research findings and marketing recommendations to Gelhomme. Dani had been assigned the task of building the PowerPoint deck that Laura would use to deliver the presentation, which meant that nearly every other moment, the woman was calling Dani to her side.

"I'll send them again," Dani promised. "But the gist of it is that I think we should add digital advertising to our recommendations."

"Digital," Laura repeated, as if it were a foreign word. "As in ..."

"As in the Internet."

Her boss laughed. "You must be joking. Everyone knows banner ads are a colossal waste. Gelhomme doesn't need that. They have a thirteen-million-dollar budget, Dani."

"I'm just saying that it may be worth using some of that budget to start playing online."

"Our clients don't want to *play*. They want to make a *profit*."

"Sure. But you should take a look at the numbers. There's this new website called the Facebook that's really taking off with college kids—"

"What is it, porn?" Laura laughed at her own joke and went back to work at her computer.

"It's a place you can chat with your friends, see what they're up to. Share pictures. There are like, thirteen thousand new users every day and—"

"We are not advising our biggest client to throw money away at some online fad. They'll laugh us out of the room. They hired us to create TV commercials. Not reinvent the wheel."

"The wheel is about to be made obsolete," Dani said with conviction.

Laura stared up at Dani, her fingers perched on the keyboard of her computer.

"I don't think you appreciate the opportunity you've been given here," Laura said, putting her glasses on her desk. "When I got my start in this industry, women were seen as secretaries, not future executives. I had to keep my head down. Learn the rules. Play the game. I suggest you do the same." Laura picked her glasses up again and said under her breath, "Of course, you wouldn't understand."

Dani stared at the side of Laura's face, which was now trained on the computer screen. "I'm sorry. Why wouldn't I understand?"

"Well, you know. There's such a push for diversity these days. It's easier for you. Things didn't get handed to us, back in the day."

Dani's head reared back, as if Laura's words had hit her in the face with force.

"Easier," Dani repeated. "You think it's easier. For *me*?"

She wanted to show Laura pictures of her grandmother, picking cotton as a sharecropper on a white man's land in North Carolina. She wanted to recite the statistics: How unemployment among black women was nearly twice as high as among white women. How even though white women earned eighty cents for every dollar white men earned, women of color earned just sixty-three cents. Dani wanted to take Laura back and show her how hard she'd worked at West Point, earning the respect of her peers and professors, only to get tossed to the curb when her body couldn't keep up with her mind.

*Easy?* she wanted to say, and show her the pharmacy of medication in her purse. *Nothing about this is easy.*

"You know what I mean," said Laura, with an added layer of kindness. To Dani, it seemed like her boss was trying to say something sincere, but it was coming across so desperately insulting. "You're good at your job, and it looks good for the company to have you at the table. It's a win-win. Comparatively, I just look like the old hag that refuses to retire. That's all I'm saying."

Dani sighed and chose to push forward with the marketing, rather than the debate over who had it easier in the workplace. "Let me just tell you a few more things about this online strategy."

Laura leaned back and nodded.

"With TV ads, you can get certain data from a consumer: age, zip code, gender, race," Dani conceded. "But with the Internet, we can drill down to the minutiae—what kind of music they listen to. How they lean politically. Where they spend their time online. It's data on a whole different level."

"I hear you. But unfortunately, we don't have the benefit of time," Laura replied. "The presentation is next week. It's too late. What we have will do."

Laura looked Dani up and down, taking in the sight of her black trousers and blue button-up shirt.

"Oh, and Dani, don't take this the wrong way, but you'll need to wear a dress and heels to the presentation," she added. "It's Paris, after all."

THE MORNING OF the Gelhomme presentation, Dani showered in an expansive hotel suite in the Seventh Arrondissement of Paris, then toweled off while taking in the view of the Eiffel Tower. The rain outside her window tempted her to get back in bed, but thankfully, a shot of pre-presentation adrenaline pumped through her veins, which acted like speed to get her moving.

The last weeks had been moving at a breakneck pace, as E & G prepared to present its final recommendations to Gelhomme's CEO, Paul Duval. The London team had fleshed out six different marketing campaigns, which, thanks to a focus group of consumers, had been narrowed down to the final one. Somehow, through it all, Dani's concept had survived. She had a football coach in Jamaica Plain to thank for that.

When the pressures of work mounted, Dani found herself staying up late at night to either revise Laura's PowerPoint presentation, plan the itinerary for Locke's upcoming trip, or shop online. The clothes and shoes she purchased only made her happy for a few days before they found their way to the bottom of her closet, a pile of unfulfilled promises. But she had no time to travel. And her doctor had put her on an extremely restrictive diet, hoping it would help with the arthritis pain. So she couldn't eat out at fancy restaurants or drink alcohol. So what if clothes had become her guilty pleasure? What else was she supposed to do with all that money?

Wrapped in a Burberry trench coat and lavender cashmere scarf, Dani stopped to check her reflection. It had been nearly impossible to find a barber in her Notting Hill neighborhood who could do black hair—but she'd finally found someone, and he'd relaxed her hair and added a weave. It was straight and silky, parted on the side, with extensions that reached her collarbone. But no matter how she styled it, she still didn't feel like herself when she looked in the mirror. Even her freckles seemed to have faded in England's rainy climate. Her skin glowed thanks to the high-end products she could afford with her new salary. She looked expensive. But she felt cheap.

Yesterday, she'd received an e-mail from Hannah detailing life in Afghanistan. In the photos her friend had attached to her e-mail, Hannah stood in the midst of a desertscape, wearing ACUs and her Kevlar vest, smiling widely. Her platoon had convoyed out to a remote location, where they were building an outpost for incoming NATO troops. The photo looked like the set of M*A*S*H. There were six GP medium tents, Army green against sand. In another photo, Hannah posed outside of a wide aluminum shipping container with three young girls whose hands were wrapped in white bandages. The burn unit Hannah had described in the e-mail sent chills down Dani's spine. In the photo, Dani saw dark shadows under Hannah's eyes, pain hidden within her smile. By comparison, Dani's life was completely self-serving—a picture of comfort and luxury. How could she complain to her friends about the existence of Laura Klein, or the loss of a man she'd never had, when by comparison, their chief complaint was the existence of Afghanistan?

WHEN SHE ARRIVED at Gelhomme's Paris office, Dani made her way directly to the conference room to set up the audiovisual equipment. A simple spread of pastries, fruit, and coffee waited at the center of the table. The rest of the room looked like it had been prepped for a visit from the queen: wood floors waxed, windows washed, oriental carpet steamed, table shined, all twelve leather chairs placed in a perfect oval around the table. The buttery scent of croissants tempted Dani, teasing her senses with the memory of bread, but she refrained. The allergist's proposed diet—no dairy, gluten, sugar, or inflammatory vegetables—had decreased her pain significantly. Hanging her jacket on a hook outside the door, Dani felt immediately powerful in the dress she'd chosen to fulfill Laura's demand. White, with cap sleeves and a conservative neckline, the dress fit tight around her curves and stopped just below her knees. "Showstopper," was the word the shopkeep had used when Dani had walked out of the dressing room. When he rang it up at the register, Dani hadn't even listened when he said the total cost. She'd just handed over her credit card.

Jim Webb had flown in from New York, with three other E & G executives. They lingered outside of the conference room, in crisp suits of different shades of gray. The tension in the atrium became palpable as the minutes drew closer to nine o'clock. Hundreds of thousands of dollars spent—on the building, the research, the insights, the art, the preparation—and if the deal happened, another few million dollars would change hands in an instant. All of this just to sell disposable razors, Dani mused, eyeing her superiors' glittering watches and shined shoes. Four little blades on a plastic stick.

Just then, Laura Klein came through the door, a flurry of energy and anxiety. She wore the exact same black dress she wore every other day, only this time, the blond-haired woman had chosen a pair of red high heels and red-rimmed glasses to match. Giving Dani a once-over, her boss winked, the closest thing to approval Dani had received from her to date.

"Is it ready?" Laura asked.

"Yep." Dani picked up the remote from the table and clicked through a few slides, then back to the beginning. "It's all ready to go."

"Audio, too," said her colleague Philip, who was standing behind the computer, testing the speakers.

"Good," Laura breathed. "No surprises. This has to be perfect."

"You'll do great," Dani said, hoping to sound encouraging. But from the look on Laura's face, Dani knew it came across as condescending.

As the crowd of white men migrated into the conference room, Dani stood back in wonder. It felt like a dream, really, to be this female, this black, in this room. Jim Webb made the introductions, taking time to properly flatter the man of the hour, Gelhomme's CEO, Paul Duval. Dressed in a three-piece suit, with a swooping hairstyle, Duval held the seat at the head of the table, looking unimpressed. He checked his watch.

"Over the last year and a half or so, our researchers have conducted nearly one thousand in-home interviews in more than one hundred target countries," Jim Webb began. "This is the largest consumer study E & G has conducted for a single client."

"I can assure you," Laura said, interrupting Webb, "we've watched more men shower in the last six months than you'd care to know."

The CEO didn't laugh.

"Laura, why don't you go ahead and share what we've come up with for Gelhomme's new razor launch," Jim said.

Laura smoothed her black dress. She stood, took her place at the end of the table, and switched the computer screen to the presentation Dani had painstakingly written and designed for this very moment.

"As you well know, Gelhomme is the standard bearer for men's products," Laura said. "In interview after interview, we found that subjects mentioned Gelhomme with reverence, by name. You have a brand that is trusted and respected, Mr. Duval. That is no small feat.

"But . . ." Laura pressed a button, but the slide didn't change. She shook the remote, pressed the button again. "Well. Sorry. This was supposed to go to the next slide."

Philip quickly moved to the computer and tried to manually move the presentation forward. Nothing. You could feel the energy in the room shift, and Dani exchanged a worried glance with Jim Webb across the table. It was doubtful Laura had the order of the presentation memorized, Dani knew. She and Philip were the ones who'd written it and rewritten it time and time again. When they'd run through it last night, Laura had stumbled over the taglines—to get it right, Dani had noticed her boss had to read them off the screen.

"Sorry," Philip said. "I think we're frozen for a moment. I have to restart the computer."

"That's fine," said Duval from the head of the table. "Just continue. It'll eventually catch up."

"Certainly, certainly," said Laura, but by this point, she was visibly flustered. She cleared her throat, shuffled some papers in front of her, and adjusted her glasses. Buying time. "Well, as I was saying . . . uh . . . Gelhomme is a household name. A trusted brand. But. Er . . . There's no denying that the market is changing."

Quietness fell on the room. The CEO of their biggest client checked his watch again and looked at the door. Dani felt her stomach twist. Laura was fumbling. *She was ruining all the work they'd done for nearly two years.* Jim Webb shot Dani a look of desperation. He lifted his chin, as if to say . . . *You. Now. Take it away.*

"Laura's right," said Dani, still seated at the table. Paul Duval turned to look at her. "The women's beauty market is a massive thirty-billion-dollar industry. By contrast, the male beauty market figures in the single-digit millions. Minuscule in comparison. Obviously, the two pies will never be the same size. We won't argue that point. Women are too vain to let men look better than they do."

The CEO grinned. Laura adjusted her weight on her high heels and smiled, as if this were all part of the plan.

"But clearly, there's an opportunity up for grabs in the male sector," Dani continued. "Our research shows that in the next ten years, men's grooming will grow from a ten-billion-dollar industry to something closer to twenty billion. Unfortunately, if you continue with the messaging of yesterday, Gelhomme won't capitalize on that growth."

"Go on," Duval said, spinning his chair toward Dani.

"For decades, your brand has dominated the market by making one promise: your razors provide the closest shave. Period. It was a functional claim, and that worked for a while. But what happens when every razor gives a close shave? What happens when your consumer stands in front of the mirror, day after day, knowing that no matter how close the shave is today, he'll be back again tomorrow doing it all over again?"

Laura leaned her hands against the table, and Dani felt the energy in the room shift in her direction. She wasn't bold enough to stand up, but she sat up straight and began using her hands demonstratively, the way she'd been taught in her West Point public speaking classes.

The computer finally came back to life, and Philip quickly advanced the slides until the photo on the screen showed an image of John F. Kennedy, Marilyn Monroe, and his wife, Jackie Onassis.

"What happens is, he cheats on you. He shops around. Tries different products. And why wouldn't he?! If every razor does the same thing, with the same results, why not try a different model?"

The men chuckled and leaned back in their seats.

"You are not in a monogamous relationship with your customers," Dani said. "If you want them back, you have to win them back. You have to make them love you again."

She paused, thankful that the joke had worked. Jim Webb looked relieved, Laura Klein looked furious, but all that mattered was that Paul Duval was still listening.

"I met a guy six months ago named James O'Leary," she continued, the screen showing a silent video of their morning in Boston. He leaned toward the mirror, making one long strip with his razor from cheek to chin.

"He's a football coach. An all-American, middle-class guy, smack-dab in the center of your target market. You wouldn't think he's a sensitive guy. But he is. He cares about the athletes he coaches. He cares about the kind of men they become. For him, shaving is just another ritual. Like running. Like lifting weights. You don't do it once. You do it day in, day out, to fight off decay. You do it to prove to the world that you're still in the fight.

"Rituals give us a routine. They give us a grounding. Rituals give us hope.

"It's our belief that male consumers are ready to be engaged on a level beyond function," Dani said. "It's not about how close the razor shaves, but about how that ritual prepares them for the day ahead. About how that ritual makes them *feel*. Not here." She touched her cheek. "But here." She pointed to her heart.

Images played on the screen in front of them, flashing everyday scenes: A man burning a piece of toast while his child screams in a high chair. A man stuck in traffic. A football coach on a green field, helping a player up off the ground. A soldier in BDUs, staring in a mirror, his face covered in shaving cream. Then the words they'd worked on for months came up on the screen—white letters against a field of black. Dani read the words aloud.

"Gelhomme Quattro. Your first weapon in the fight."

THREE HOURS AFTER the presentation, Laura Klein, Jim Webb, and Dani were still seated at the conference table.

"Calm down, Laura," Jim was saying, pressing his hands down on the table in front of him. His voice was quiet but insistent. "Dani was just trying to redeem the presentation."

"It didn't need saving," Laura said, her voice several octaves higher than normal. Someone had shut the door. "My authority was completely undermined. As far as Paul Duval knows, I didn't even touch that presentation."

*You didn't,* Dani wanted to say. But she knew better than to open her mouth; she'd already done enough of that today.

"They seemed pleased," Webb said. "That's all that matters. We're moving forward."

Laura grabbed her things and left in a hurry. Jim put his hands on his temples and shook his head.

"She didn't know the slides," Dani said, by way of explanation. "The way you looked at me, I thought you wanted—"

"You overstepped, Dani. It makes us all look like a bunch of bumbling idiots to Gelhomme. You don't think they know you're Laura Klein's junior? You gambled with nearly thirty million dollars, Dani. Our biggest client. For most people, a move like that would get them fired. Of all people, I thought you would understand respecting the hierarchy."

They sat in silence. Webb stared at the conference table, while Dani stared straight ahead, holding her emotions in check.

"Laura is going to expect an apology from you tomorrow. And it needs to be a good one," he said, gathering his things. "You took a big gamble today, Dani. And you better hope it worked."

IN THE MIDDLE of May, three weeks after the Gelhomme presentation, Locke Coleman emerged from the international terminal at Heathrow Airport, followed in close succession by two friends who had decided to join him on his trip to London.

"Holy shit, McNalley!" Locke yelled. "Since when do you drive a Land Rover?"

They filled the SUV with their suitcases, then pulled out of the airport parking lot, with Dani perched in the right-side driver's seat. Locke sat beside her, running his hands across the beige leather interior.

"I got us tickets to *Wicked* for tonight," Dani said. "It just debuted in the West End, so people are going crazy for it. And tomorrow, Portobello Road Market sets up right outside my house."

"I'm just glad to be out of Fort Hood," one of Locke's friends said from the back seat. Will Chapman had strawberry-blond hair, strawberry-blond eyebrows, and a reddish face, trained toward the Thames River out the window to his left. Locke's other friend, Joel Truman, had light brown skin and deep brown eyes that kept closing, pulled down by jet lag. Will punched Joel in the arm.

"Dude, don't give in. You've got to push through."

After dropping their bags at Dani's flat, Will and Joel took off for Buckingham Palace, while Locke and Dani walked to the pub next door for lunch. Locke ordered a pint of beer and a basket of fish and chips, while Dani ordered her usual, an undressed Caesar salad with chicken. Her doctor would have been proud.

Sitting across from him, Dani couldn't help but notice how little he'd changed in the two years since they'd left West Point. He'd lost the football weight, so his body looked thinner, but his smile was still just as mischievous.

In the weeks since the Gelhomme presentation, life at work

had become even more unbearable for Dani. This visit was the only thing that had pulled her through the rainy days of spring, days in which Laura Klein had continued to act cold and distant, sending most of her communication via e-mail, even though Dani's desk was mere feet from her own. Luckily, Paul Duval hadn't just bought E & G's commercial campaign recommendations—he'd decided to expand the advertising budget by 10 percent. Laura Klein had accepted Dani's apology, but they both knew she had no choice.

In preparation for Locke's arrival, Dani had outfitted the guest bedroom in her apartment with a king mattress positioned to best appreciate the impressive view of Notting Hill's pastel row houses. His friends were a surprise, but Locke had promised Dani that Will and Joel would be happy crashing on air mattresses. Taking a personal day, Dani had spent the morning cleaning and blowing up two twin air mattresses in the home office. At half past ten, she'd jumped in her SUV and headed to the airport.

Scarfing down the fried fish, Locke told stories about Fort Hood, his soldiers, his unit, his family. She noticed that he hadn't mentioned Amanda—and wondered then if they were even together anymore. Locke paused and washed down the food with half his beer.

"What?" he said. "Do I have something in my teeth?"

In truth, Dani was enjoying the feeling of sitting across from someone that she knew so well. She hadn't realized how lonely she'd been in London until Locke was seated across from her, picking his teeth with a toothpick.

"Just thinking," she said finally. "Do you ever wonder how your life would have gone if you'd done something different?"

Locke focused his brown eyes on Dani's, and after a pause, said, "Different than the Army?"

"Yeah. Like, what if you'd played football for USC instead of West Point. Or . . ."

"Of course. Sometimes I wonder if I would have made it to the NFL or something. But you can't think that way."

"Why not?"

"It's easy to imagine an alternate reality better than the one you're in. No one ever imagines an alternate reality that's worse. I can't question all the decisions I've made. I'd drive myself nuts. Where's this coming from?"

Dani put her fork down. "Sometimes I wonder why I even went to West Point. I look at all of you, going off to war, and I think, what was all that for? Why did I go through all that pain, just to abandon ship?"

"You didn't abandon ship."

"Well, I didn't get on it."

"That's not your fault," he said. "Let me ask you this. If you could go back, what would you do differently?"

At this, Dani grew quiet. The truth was, when it came to choosing where to go to college, she wouldn't have done anything differently. She'd been so confident in her decision, so convinced that West Point was her destiny. Only now, her destiny was beginning to feel like a dead end. Locke's skin shined under the dim pub lights. The clear whites of his eyes glimmered around his brown pupils as he waited for her answer. The only thing that she would change was sitting right in front of her.

"Do you ever wonder what would have happened if we . . . ," she started.

He looked down, picked up his fork, and took a bite of fried fish.

"If we'd what?" he said, his mouth full.

"If we'd given it a shot. You and me."

The silence stretched on for what felt like an eternity. Locke sighed and finished off his beer.

She'd splurged on a shiny manicure the day before, and it reflected the pub's sconces as her fingers danced around the edge of her water glass. She wanted to tell him that it was all for him. The hair, the nails, the new outfit she'd bought to wear when she picked him up from the airport. She wanted to tell him that she'd been dreaming of his visit for months, and wanted every day to be perfect so he'd come back again and again and again until he never left. Instead, she just shrugged. He reached for her hand and squeezed it on top of the table warmly.

"D," he said. "I have something to tell you."

20

*Spring 2006 // Pittsburgh, Pennsylvania*

You know, it'll be the *whole* family," Avery stated over the sound of the Foo Fighters on the radio. Her manicured toes tapped the beat on the dashboard of Noah's 1986 BMW. A black M3 coupe, it had charm, dignity, and a plug-in air freshener to mask the scent of his cigarette smoke.

"You mentioned that," Noah said between drags.

She smacked his arm. Like usual, Noah looked calm, confident, and unfazed by the fact that his car was barreling down the highway toward certain disaster. And yet, Avery felt extremely concerned. She knew how critical her father could be. And worst of all, her brothers would be home. That, in and of itself, would prove to be a challenge. But Noah had promised he'd rather be celebrating Avery's father's sixtieth birthday than be at Fort Bragg alone. No amount of warning had deterred him.

She had to admit, she was grateful that he'd come. These days, his socks intermingled with hers in the laundry. Little golden hairs from his beard trimmings were scattered across her bathroom counter. Their lives were intertwined, and since Avery was no longer working on the Special Forces compound, they didn't even have to keep their relationship much of a secret. She still hadn't met any of his friends—simply a matter of bad timing, Noah had assured her. In truth, the fact that he'd had a chance to meet Dani and Hannah last Thanksgiving was a miracle, considering that Avery's closest friends were both now out of the country. And plus, she didn't care that much about meeting his friends. When Noah was home, she wanted him all to herself.

He flicked the lit cigarette through his window onto the road, then rolled the window up, sealing the car from the sounds of the highway. "Don't worry. I'm good with parents." He paused and looked her in the eye. "They're going to love me. Because you love me."

Avery shifted in her seat. "Is that some kind of Special Ops trick?" she said. "Force me to confirm or deny?"

"Well you do, don't you?" He smiled, took her hand.

Staring at his profile—sharp jawline, eyes gray like stone—she wondered what he'd seen in the last three years of his life. She imagined him in a war zone, under the cover of night, jumping from a helicopter into unknown territory. Busting down doors. Waving his weapon in the faces of terrified women. He'd said terrorists always sent their wives out first. Using women as a shield gave the men time to escape.

"I do love you," she said. "I do."

Noah looked back at the road as if what she'd just said wasn't the biggest deal in the entire world. A determined black column of asphalt rushed underneath them at eighty miles per hour. Avery's mind raced just as fast. Was that all? He was going to make her say it, and then not say it in return?

"Every time we're apart, I think about you constantly. God. I wish . . . I wish so many things," he said, breaking the silence. He stared at her evenly, his eyes heavy.

"What do you wish?"

"I wish I wasn't gone so much, for one," he said. "And I wish . . . I wish you weren't so damn young. You were not in my plans, Avery. But here you are. And yeah. I love you, too."

He spoke as if all of his feelings of love existed against his better judgment. But Avery chose not to hear the sadness in his voice. She refused to see the clouds in his eyes, any more than she paid attention to the storm brewing outside. Instead, she began imagining their wedding. They'd have to wait until Hannah got back from Afghanistan, of course. The bridesmaids would wear blue, or maybe hunter green. Green looked good on everyone, Avery thought, and Dani would just have to get over the fact that she was going to have to wear a dress . . .

"Oh shit," Avery said, suddenly throwing her hand to her forehead.

"Not exactly the response I thought I'd get, but I can take it."

"No, yesterday was Dani's birthday. I just remembered."

"Dani?"

"Dani McNalley. We stayed with her in Boston," Avery said, annoyed that Noah had forgotten her friend. Her cell phone was lodged in the bottom of her purse, uncharged. "Great. My phone's dead. Can I use yours?"

In a snap movement, he quickly put his hand over his phone, like a protective shield. She furrowed her brow in his direction— what was that about?

"Of course," he said, releasing the phone into her hand. "But we just had a moment. I thought we could, you know. Enjoy it."

Avery sighed. Noah was right. Dani would understand. Plus, it was the middle of the night in London. What was one more day?

While they'd been talking, thick clouds had rolled in, filling the sky with a dark gray blanket. A crack of lightning followed a low rumble of thunder, and soon, thick drops of rain gathered on Noah's windshield. The wipers turned on, swishing water out of the way, so Noah could see the road ahead. It was all red lights.

"There must have been an accident," he said. "Everyone's slowing down."

Avery put her head on his shoulder, closed her eyes, and believed the future was opening up before them like an empty four-lane highway. They were in love and they were happy.

That's how it's done. You can deceive yourself into believing almost anything, if you want it badly enough.

"TOOK YOU LONG enough."

Hank Adams came down the stairs, staring at the watch on his wrist, as if he'd been timing his daughter since she'd left North Carolina that morning.

The Adamses' home hadn't changed one bit. Beige carpet, dusty oversized light fixtures, a dining room painted red. The phone with its accordion-style stretchy cord was still attached to the wall next to the fridge, right where it had been for more than twenty years. The place looked like it had frozen in time, and it immediately transported Avery back to her childhood. For some reason, she felt like she needed a shower.

"You stop to pee every two hours?" Hank wrapped his arms around his daughter tight, then pulled back to stare at her. "You nearly missed dinner."

Ignoring his comments, Avery leaned into Noah's side and wrapped her arm around his waist.

"Dad, this is Noah," she said, looking between the man that raised her and the man she loved. They couldn't have looked more different. Noah's muscles were bulging under the sleeves of his light gray T-shirt, and as he reached his arm out, she watched her father's eyebrows lift at the sight of so much black ink.

"Thanks for having me, sir." Noah shook Hank's hand firmly.

"Well, she refused to come if we didn't invite you, so we really didn't have a choice," Hank said jokingly. "Can I get you a beer? We've got Yuengling."

They moved into the kitchen, where Avery introduced Noah to her brothers. Caleb, now twenty-one years old, had the same sheet of blond hair covering his eyes that he'd had since he was sixteen. The tongue of his Rolling Stones T-shirt looked as if it was trying to lick Avery's chest as Caleb reached out to hug his big sister, who now was several inches shorter than him. No longer in his awkward phase, he'd stretched nearly six feet tall and was considering applying for film school in California.

Blake looked exactly as he always had—thick brown hair,

with a square jaw and clean-shaven face. He'd just finished his residency and had moved back to Pittsburgh to practice family medicine. The most boring kind of doctor, in Avery's opinion: he'd be treating colds and hemorrhoids the rest of his life.

"Hey." Avery's older brother shook her boyfriend's hand. "Heard a lot about you, man. This is my wife, Carolyn."

"Carolyn." Avery smiled, reaching to hug her sister-in-law. "How are you?"

From the looks of it, Carolyn had either gained thirty pounds or was three months pregnant—Avery couldn't be sure and wasn't about to ask. They hadn't spoken since Christmas, when Carolyn had given Avery an extremely ugly sweater from Ann Taylor Loft that still hadn't come out of the box.

"I'm good," she said, reaching for a Yuengling from the counter. *Not pregnant, then,* Avery assessed. Carolyn lifted her beer toward her husband. "Blake's been forcing me to go to the gym with him. Me! In the gym! Can you imagine it?"

*No,* Avery wanted to say. *I'd rather not.*

"Where's Mom?" Avery asked Caleb.

"In the back. Sweet sleeve," Caleb said, noticing Noah's arm of tattoos. "How long did that take?"

While Noah showed off his body art, Avery walked toward her parents' bedroom, where she could hear the low hum of her mother's hair dryer.

It was strange to watch your parents age, Avery realized, inspecting her mother's reflection in the master bathroom mirror. She finished drying her hair, then applied lotion to the sagging skin on her neck. In your twenties, time was measured in milestones: marriages, new jobs, promotions. But later, time marked itself with wrinkles, like scars. Her mother looked great for her age—her skin glowed and her hair was an enviable shade of gold—but something in her eyes betrayed a quiet sadness. Like she was embarrassed by what she saw in the mirror.

"Mom."

"Oh, Avery!" Lonnie jumped. "You scared me!"

They embraced tightly, rocking back and forth, before Lonnie pulled back and got a bright glint in her eye. "Is he here?"

"Yes," Avery answered, rolling her eyes. "Don't make a big deal out of it, okay?" No questions about her job. Not even a question about the drive. Her mother had jumped straight to the one thing she cared about: Avery's relationship status. "We're taking it slow," Avery added.

"Well, it *is* a big deal." Her mother fished a pair of pearl earrings from a jewelry dish on the bathroom counter and slipped them into her sagging lobes. "Meeting the family."

"Just be cool."

"I'm cool!" Lonnie said. "Oh, before I forget, something came in the mail for you."

Her mother led the way across the hall to Avery's childhood bedroom, which Avery expected to have remained untouched, like the rest of the house. But when the door opened, rather than her pink-painted walls and queen-sized bed, she saw the room had been transformed into a home office, complete with a large desktop computer and a rolling ergonomic chair. Gone were her AAU basketball trophies and the bouquets of dried flowers, hung upside down on the wall like trophies of their own—artifacts of relationships long past.

Avery's mind tried to quickly catch up to what her eyes were seeing. Everything of hers had been removed. A stack of cardboard boxes waited in the corner, with her name written on them in Sharpie marker.

"What happened to my room?"

Her mother looked amused by Avery's surprise. "You've been gone for six years, Ave. I needed an office."

"For what?" Avery said cruelly. Her mother didn't work. "And what about Blake's room?"

Her mother's face stiffened. "Blake still comes home, believe it or not." She walked to the desk, picked up a white envelope, and handed it to Avery. "It's from West Point. I didn't know if it was important. You'd think they'd have your current address."

Lonnie walked out the door toward the kitchen, muttering something about checking on the pot roast. When they entered the kitchen, Avery mindlessly ran a finger under the envelope's sealed flap. While Noah traded workouts with Blake, a single sheet of paper unfolded in Avery's hands.

*Our records show that you were listed as a plaintiff in the Department of Defense Case #03–2754, Department of the Army vs. Jonathan T. Collins.*

Avery closed the letter quickly. The warmth disappeared from her face.

"What was it?" her mother asked from the other side of the kitchen.

"They're just, uh, asking for an alumni donation."

"God. As if you haven't given that place enough already." She pulled the pot roast out of the oven, its juices oozing into the bottom of the pan. "Who's ready for dinner?"

"Oh, we're . . ." Noah looked to Avery. "You didn't tell her?"

After slipping the envelope in her purse, Avery furrowed her brow, unsure of what Noah meant, until she realized the hunk of meat steaming in the dish didn't fall within Noah's restrictive vegetarian standards. "Right. Sorry, Mom. He's . . . Actually, we're both vegetarians."

Avery faked a smile to Noah, ignored the silent derision in her father's eyes, and then helped set the table. But as a bowl of salad passed from one set of hands to the next, Avery filled her plate, without a second glance toward the main dish. Somehow the news delivered in that thin envelope had ruined her appetite.

THAT NIGHT, IN Blake's childhood bedroom, Avery couldn't sleep. Noah was in the living room, on the pullout couch. She'd tried to convince him that her parents wouldn't notice if he slipped into her bed after they'd all gone to sleep, but he'd refused.

"It's one night," he'd said. "I'll see you in the morning." Then he'd pointed her down the hall.

Flipping on a light, Avery reached for her purse, dug out the envelope, then buried herself under the covers, holding it between her hands. Back then, Dani had been so certain that going to the authorities was the right thing to do. But she didn't know what it was going to cost.

None of them did.

They'd traversed campus in silence, until they stood inside the Criminal Investigation Command office, staring at a man behind a reception desk, whose eyes bulged when they explained why they were there. He'd moved them to a windowless office, offered water. The investigator, a short woman in her midforties, had thanked them for coming forward and had started with simple questions. Dani had turned over the photos. Hannah had made a statement about what she'd seen the year before: Collins, coming out of the girls' locker room, with a thin excuse and a guilty look in his eyes. After Avery admitted that it was her body in the photos, she'd answered the investigator's questions honestly and directly, encouraged by the presence of Dani on her left and Hannah on her right.

"We're going to need more evidence to pursue charges. We'll use your statements to get a warrant to search his room."

Avery had turned her eyes pleadingly to Hannah. The truth was, if John Collins was arrested out of the blue, people would want to know who'd turned him in. Locke was trustworthy enough, but Avery knew how rumors at West Point worked.

"Is there any way to do this without relying on our statements?" Hannah had asked. "At least for now?"

The female detective had exhaled heavily. "It's hard to protect victims and witnesses on college campuses," she said. "Rumors spread so fast. A story like this is hard to contain."

"His computer," Dani announced suddenly. "Cadet computers are government property, right? And the academy does sweeps every six months or so to check for viruses and porn and whatever. Can't you do a sweep? I mean, get the warrant. But search everyone. That way, it can seem random."

The detective had exchanged a glance with her colleague, who looked simultaneously annoyed and impressed by Dani's suggestion.

"It's not a bad idea."

The detective had nodded, then looked back at Avery.

"This kid. This . . . Collins. It seems like the risk of getting caught was part of the thrill for him. We can charge him with criminal trespassing. Criminal video voyeurism. Distribution of pornography. Misuse of government property. Maybe more. He could go away for a long time. But, Miss Adams, since the majority of these photos are of you, you'll still have to be the one to press charges in the end."

She'd paused, rubbed her forehead.

"It'll take at least twenty-four hours to do the sweep. And for this to work, the three of you have to stay silent. You can't tell anyone that you came here tonight."

Avery breathed a sigh of relief and looked to Hannah and Dani as if to check that this was the right plan. Dani nodded.

"So that's a yes?" the detective asked. "As you can imagine, I haven't had great success with nineteen-year-olds keeping secrets."

Dani spoke with certainty. "We're not your normal nineteen-year-olds, ma'am. We're like a cult. You can be certain, nothing will leave this room."

Now, staring at the letter in her hands, Avery's eyes began to water. So much time had passed since that moment, and yet, she still felt the same sickness in her stomach that she'd had forty-eight hours later, when military police had escorted John Collins out of the barracks in handcuffs. The Corps of Cadets had turned into a cacophony of gossip as the students guessed at the cause of his arrest. No one understood why someone so close to graduation would be taken away. They'd grasped at straws, wondering who had turned him in—was it a member of the football team who'd seen the photos, or the girl—*who was that girl?*—on display in them?

Putting those memories out of her mind, Avery unfolded the letter and read it quickly, as if the faster she read, the sooner it could all be behind her again.

*March 15, 2006*

*Dear Ms. Adams,*

*Our records show that you were listed as a plaintiff in the Department of Defense Case #03–2754, Department of the Army vs. Jonathan T. Collins.*

*On behalf of the Department of Defense and the Criminal Investigation Command of West Point, it is our responsibility to inform you that the defendant in this case is to be released on parole on March 17, 2006. A restraining order remains in place and the defendant will be listed on the National Sex Offender Public Registry for the remainder of his probationary period, which ends on 05–13–2015.*

*We have included in this letter a one-page copy of the sum-mary case record. We apologize for any disturbance this may cause and are available to address any concerns you may have about your case.*

*Respectfully,*

*Capt. Peter Irving*

*Judge Advocate General Corps*

*Criminal Investigation Command, West Point, New York*

On Sunday, Avery pretended to sleep as Noah navigated south. He'd won over Avery's parents and brothers far more quickly than she'd anticipated. He'd complimented her mother's cook-ing, helped with the dishes, and even put the foldout couch back together before they'd left that morning.

"I think this one might be a keeper," her mother had said before they'd hit the road that morning. Avery wanted to believe that was true. But something about receiving notice that John Collins was out in the world again, free to live and do as he pleased, had set Avery's instincts on high alert. Suddenly, all of the old red flags she'd ignored were flapping wildly again.

"What?" Noah said. Avery had pulled her head off the pillow against the passenger window to look at him.

"Can I ask you something?" she asked.

"Shoot."

"Why were you so weird about your phone the other day?"

He reached for his pack of cigarettes. "What are you talking about?"

Wrapping the pillow in her arms, Avery looked to the side mirror, where she saw her reflection. Her blond hair had grown long, past her shoulders. Eating like Noah, as a vegetarian, meant she'd resorted to eating a lot of pasta, which had made her face puffy and bloated. She didn't feel like herself. But she couldn't blame her irritability on her diet or the man sitting next to her.

"I feel like something has been up with you this whole weekend," Noah said, deftly turning the conversation back to Avery. She didn't force him to answer the question he'd avoided. Instead, she sighed.

"You know that letter I got from West Point?"

He nodded.

"It wasn't about making a donation."

"What was it?" he asked.

And then she told him everything. When she was finished, she held her breath, waiting for Noah to say something to soothe the gaping emotional wound she'd just undressed before his eyes. Vulnerability can bring two people closer together, or it can expose a distance that can't be overcome. Avery closed her eyes and waited for him to speak.

"Well," Noah said with a smirk. "Can I see the pictures?"

Avery felt herself shrink, like she was Alice in Wonderland. Falling down that rabbit hole. Swallowing that pill. Suddenly, she was three inches tall.

He reached for her hand. She pulled it away.

"Oh come on. I'm only kidding," he said. "What do you want me to say?"

"I don't know," Avery replied. "But not that."

## 21

*Summer 2006 // Jekyll Island, Georgia*

In the middle of her war, Hannah flew home for two weeks of paid leave. It was strange really, the thought that she could fly out of the Middle East, while her men and her mission stayed put. Rest and recuperation, better known as R & R, was a benefit that every soldier and officer received when they were deployed. Two weeks to regroup and be with your family, followed by several more months overseas, finishing the deployment. It was an odd pause. A whiplash of change, from one part of the world to another. From fear to safety and back again.

It was the middle of August. And thankfully, this year, there were no hurricanes on the horizon. After picking Hannah up from the airport in Savannah, Georgia, Tim drove her to Jekyll Island, where he'd rented a place for them to pass the time.

The cottage smelled as though salt water had seeped into the clapboard siding, giving the entire place the odd feeling that it had been built by the tides themselves. Canopied by gnarled oak trees, the white bungalow was perched at the tip of a peninsula, where a creek ended and the ocean began. A dock jutted into the creek, outfitted with kayaks, fishing rods, and a hammock. There was another hammock on the front porch, and a third out by the wooden steps that led to the beach. Humidity wafted through the air and snuck through the cracks in the old windows, but they hadn't let the heat defeat their plans. Summer in south Georgia had nothing on Afghanistan. Here, even 100 percent humidity felt like a reprieve to Hannah. They had two weeks alone together, with no plans, nowhere to be—just the two of them and the ocean.

It felt like a dream world. Every morning when they woke up, Hannah would hold his face in her hands and say, "Can you believe it? We don't have to say goodbye!"

They'd start the day with coffee, watching the sun rise over the ocean, and end the day with wine, watching it set into the marsh.

On their seventh morning together, Hannah lay in bed beside her husband, in no rush to start the day. When they'd first arrived at the house, she'd felt nervous to undress, aware that he hadn't seen her naked in months. Would he still like what he saw? But that initial hesitation was immediately replaced by an overwhelming sense of urgency and desire. They only had fourteen days. There was no time for modesty.

The clock on the bedside table read 4:58 A.M., but Hannah knew she wouldn't be able to go back to sleep. Instead, she admired Tim's chest, rising and falling with each breath. His hair had grown back since Ranger School and was dark on the white pillow. The tattoo of an Irish cross on the inside of his left bicep had faded slightly, as tattoos do. Hannah wanted to wake him—to shake him until he opened those bright hazel eyes and looked at her with that same sense of childish adventure she'd grown to love. But he looked too peaceful to disturb.

Hannah ran a finger along the jagged scar on his right shoulder. Unlike the tattoo, it hadn't yet faded.

The accident had happened about this time, four years ago. During the season-opening football game their junior year, Hannah had stood in the stands with the rest of the Corps of Cadets staring at the sky. The crowd had erupted in shouts as six tiny black specks emerged into view, and all of a sudden, all six parachutes spread out like small yellow blooms over their heads. Hannah scanned the sky for Tim. After what he'd done that summer during Air Assault training, they weren't speaking. But she still loved to watch him fly. She saw the red and white stripes of the American flag waving behind him and breathed a sigh of relief.

What happened next would forever remain in Hannah's memory. A strap snapped off his shoulder, sending the yellow parachute vertical. He spun out of control, falling like a bird shot out of the sky. The entire crowd gasped and Hannah went silent, covering her mouth with her hands.

When she'd arrived at the hospital, Hannah immediately knew that she was no longer angry. Tim had been propped up in a bed, his right arm and shoulder stabilized in a metal contraption that looked like a vise. When he noticed her in the doorway,

Tim shook his head, his chin quivering and face reddening with emotion.

"I didn't think you'd come," he said. "I'm so sorry . . . I—"

"Shh." Hannah had placed a hand on his uninjured arm, squeezing it tight. "I forgive you."

He'd started laughing through his tears. "When I was hanging in that tree, all I could think of was how mad I would have been if I had died and we hadn't made up. We have to make up. I still love you."

Hannah had laughed through her tears, too. Six months later, they were engaged.

Tim's accident hadn't just resurrected their relationship. It also resurrected his belief in God. Even the doctors couldn't understand how he hadn't died, simply from the height of the fall. Had he not been scarred, Hannah wondered if she would even be sitting here, in his bed, married. So she loved his scar. It symbolized everything that had brought them back together. And even though Tim wasn't perfect—he was flawed and cocky and at times a bit too charming for his own good—Hannah knew he was perfect for her.

Slipping from the sheets, Hannah grabbed her copy of *East of Eden* from the bedside table and stepped outside onto the porch, where she could watch the sun rise over the Atlantic. Two months earlier, on Hannah and Tim's second wedding anniversary, Dani had sent her a sweet e-mail, full of memories and photos of their wedding day. Even her sister, Emily, remembered the anniversary—sending Hannah a bouquet of flowers all the way to FOB Sharana in Afghanistan. But not Avery. That girl had fallen off the face of the planet.

Hannah only heard from her in group e-mails that Dani addressed to all of them, and even then, Avery's responses were shallow and short. Hannah couldn't understand how you could be so close with someone for so long only to let the friendship fade. After everything they'd been through, Hannah had been certain that Dani and Avery would be her best friends until they were old and gray. But things had changed. She was married now. Maybe her best friend wasn't supposed to be a girl from her college basketball team—maybe her best friend was supposed to be the man still sleeping in the other room.

Just then, Tim emerged onto the porch with two steaming mugs of coffee. Passing one to Hannah, he stretched and yawned.

"How many people our age do you think wake up this early?" he asked.

Tim took a seat in the rocking chair next to hers and began rubbing her neck slowly with his warm hand. Hannah involuntarily closed her eyes. His touch was like a drug.

"I guess we get more out of life than they do," he said.

"Maybe. But they get more sleep than we do."

Tim sipped coffee, then said, "Eh. Sleep's overrated. I'll sleep when I die."

Hannah bristled. She didn't like hearing that word. Not when they were counting down the days. Her flight back to Afghanistan left in less than a week. Tim left for Iraq a few weeks after that. It would be late 2007 before they were together again.

"What?" Tim asked, feeling her tense up. "Die?"

"Yes. Don't say it."

Tim laughed. "Okay," he said. "I won't roll the die, or discuss your hair dye, or remember Princess Di. There are so many conversations we'll miss out on now. But whatever you need."

Hannah punched him in the arm. "Don't be an ass," she laughed.

"But I'm so good at it." Tim looked up at the sky. "I think it's supposed to storm today," he said.

Indeed, the sun hadn't yet come up, or if it had, it was covered by a mass of dark gray clouds. In the distance, a roll of thunder pealed loudly. Hannah's sister used to tell her during intense thunderstorms that it was just God bowling. Thunder was the roll of the ball, the lightning a signal that he'd hit a strike. Apparently, God always hit a strike.

"Oh, that's too bad," Hannah said ironically. "What in the world will we do all day?"

HOURS LATER, THEIR bodies feeling light and connected by invisible strands of energy, Hannah shook her head and slid the cross charm on her necklace from side to side. They dressed, ate lunch, and then watched a cheesy movie on the Hallmark Channel before scrounging through the kitchen to put together dinner.

Tim had found an old game of Scrabble in a closet, and opening a bottle of wine, they sat near the windows overlooking the rain and the ocean, smiling at each other and placing individual letters in a row.

"No." Hannah pointed at the word Tim had just played on the board. "*Quid* is not a word." Taking a sip of wine from her glass, she remarked, "*Squid*, maybe. Not *quid*."

"It's a word," argued Tim. "I'm telling you."

"Use it in a sentence."

"Easy . . ." Tim squinted his eyes and a little wrinkle appeared between his eyebrows, like it always did when he was thinking hard. "I bet you a hundred quid that *quid* is a word."

"Look it up," said Hannah. "You think you're so smart."

And he did, running a finger down the page of the dictionary they'd found on the shelf next to a stack of John Grisham books. Tim sat back, smiling, as he read out the definition.

"It says here, 'Quid: One pound sterling. Or, a lump of tobacco for chewing.'" He replaced the tiles where they were meant to go. "Triple word score. That's forty-two points."

"This is the worst game ever invented," Hannah said. "You're destroying me."

"You're not too far behind," he lied. "Just, a couple . . . hundred points."

Hannah set down her glass and looked out the window. "I wish it weren't raining. I feel like we deserve perfect weather, every single day we get together. Don't you think?"

Tim inspected her face, put his glass down on the table, and then stood up and took his shirt off.

"What are you doing?" laughed Hannah. "You're not done beating me."

"Come with me," he said, offering her his hand.

"Out there? It's pouring!"

"We can do this the hard way or the easy way," said Tim as the dimple appeared in his right cheek.

Hannah crossed her arms over her chest and shook her head. Her husband—it still felt so funny to say that, to think it!—her *husband* was crazy. And accordingly, he grabbed her waist, hoisted her over his shoulder, and carried her out the door into the rain.

"*Tim!* Put me down!"

He did, and in moments, they were both soaked through, the water piling up on their eyelashes. He grabbed her hand, and together they ran down to the shoreline.

"Take off your clothes!" Tim shouted as he pulled off his own.

"*Tim!*" Hannah instinctively looked around, even though she knew for a fact there was no one else on this beach. "We're going to get struck by lightning!"

"Don't be scared!" he shouted, running toward the water. She could see his outline through the rain—round shoulders, thin waist, and white butt—all in perfect contrast to the gray water and sky. As she hesitated, the rain began to slow, and the sun's heavy rays began peering through the clouds from behind the house.

"I married an idiot," Hannah said to herself and the rain. But as she was saying it, she was pulling off her clothes, tentatively at first, and then quickly.

"Come on!" shouted Tim from the choppy surf.

And soon, she reached him, their bodies touching under the surface, their mouths touching above. All she tasted was salt.

SIX DAYS LATER, they stood outside of the security line at Jacksonville International Airport, trying to say goodbye. Like he'd done so many times before, Tim held Hannah's face in his hands and wiped the tears from her cheeks with his thumbs. He was wearing board shorts, flip-flops, and a gray T-shirt, while Hannah, on the first leg of her flight back to war, was wearing her full combat uniform. Her hair twisted in a bun, rucksack full and snug on her shoulders, she felt encumbered by the weight of it all. Of this moment. Of the future. For once, Tim didn't try to put it in perspective.

He pulled her into his chest. "I'll leave you a perfectly clean house. When you get home, it'll be spic-and-span."

"Leave Avery a key," said Hannah, angry that she was using their last few moments together to discuss logistics. "Just in case."

"Okay." He squeezed tighter. "I love you."

"I love you, too," Hannah said, her voice small and choked.

"I'll see you soon," Tim offered. "Write me. Call me. We'll figure it out."

"Okay."

And with that, Hannah forced herself to step away.

Sometimes the greatest wars we fight are in our own minds. And for the next three days, Hannah battled hard. She tried to remember why they said this would all be worth it. She prayed for strength, and whether God provided it or not, she wasn't certain, but she arrived back at FOB Sharana, back at her CHU. Back to Ebrahim and her soldiers and the heat. This time, it took longer for her heart to catch up to her body. Without a doubt, she'd left half of it behind.

**From:** Hannah Nesmith <hannah_nesmith@yahoo.com>
**Subject:** made it back
**Date:** September 2, 2006 03:19:02 PM GMT +01:00
**To:** Dani McNalley <danimcnalley@yahoo.com>

Hi:)

I'm sorry I missed your Skype call. Internet here is spotty at best, but I have a little time now and the signal seems good so I figured I'd send you an update.

The last two weeks with Tim were . . . perfect. There's really no other way to say it. We literally put Nicholas Sparks to shame. Every day I woke up and had to remind myself that I wasn't dreaming. The weather sucked the last half of the trip, but we watched movies and cooked meals together and drank tons of wine. I just can't believe how much time is going to pass before we can be together again. If I think about it, I get overwhelmed with sadness so I'm just trying not to count the days.

How did Locke's visit go? I think of you often and hope that you're finding friends there in London. Have you met anyone?

Much love to you, Dani. Miss you.

                                                                H

## 22

Dressed in jeans, wellies, and her slick new Barbour rain-coat, Dani grabbed a large black umbrella from beside the door and walked down the steps of her flat and into the gray. Despite the impending rain, Portobello Road Market had assembled itself into a beautiful stretch of life. Clanging garage doors opened to reveal storefronts. Colorful tents popped up for miles. The voices of people haggling filled the air, while the rain sprinkled the pavement. Customers shielded under umbrellas inspected tables full of antiques and curios. They perused stalls of hot bread, sniffed at fresh-cut cheese, watched as young women spilled batter in large circles at the creperies. Three German tourists loitered outside Dani's apartment entrance, wrapped in scarves and holding a map. Humidity increased the pain in her joints, but she couldn't stay inside. Out here, she could be anonymous. Part of the scene, not the leading actress. She could roam for miles, looking. Thinking. Hidden by the crowd.

In the last three weeks, so much had changed.

The Gelhomme advertisements had hit the airwaves and though it was too early to measure, preliminary benchmarks indicated that the campaign would increase sales by more than 12 percent. Though she still acted suspicious of Dani's instincts, Laura Klein had grown to rely on them more than ever. Every additional assignment found its way to Dani's desk, and one draft was never enough. Laura required four, sometimes five drafts of the same presentation. And worst of all, in their most recent meeting with Paul Duval, Laura had presented a groundbreaking new strategy: digital marketing on the Internet, with a keen eye on a new social media platform called the Facebook.

Dani had sat at the table, dumbfounded that Laura had so blatantly stolen her idea and claimed it as her own. But aware of Jim Webb's eyes on her every action, Dani had stayed silent. After all, what would she do? Stamp her foot and say, *That was my idea*? She was proud, but she wasn't an idiot.

The next day, Laura had called her into her office.

"I saw your surprise yesterday," her boss had said in an uncharacteristically kind tone. "When I gave them your idea for the digital push."

"I wasn't surprised you presented the idea. I was surprised you said it was yours."

Laura had paused, then sighed and put her reading glasses down on her desk. "The divorce was finalized last week."

"I'm sorry to hear that," said Dani.

"I shouldn't have done that. I shouldn't have presented your idea as my own. I think I've just been realizing how high the stakes are for me. For ten years, I've enjoyed this job, but now I *need* it. To support myself. My children. I think I acted out of fear. I hope you'll forgive me."

Dani had nodded, shocked by her boss's candor. It didn't justify her actions—but at least it provided context.

Work wasn't the only place her life felt unmoored. Hannah was back in Afghanistan after her two weeks of R & R, and soon, Tim would follow his wife overseas for his own fifteen-month deployment to Iraq.

*We put Nicholas Sparks to shame,* Hannah had written in her latest e-mail. Dani didn't know if it was a blessing or a curse that Tim and Hannah would be deployed at the same time. On one hand, they would complete all their time apart faster that way. On the other, Dani couldn't imagine knowing that you *and* the person you love were in constant danger. Hannah had more faith than any person she'd ever met.

But the hardest change of all?

That was the news Locke Coleman had dropped when he'd come to visit in the spring, and the trip to South Carolina that awaited Dani at the end of the week.

Choking on her Caesar salad in the pub that day, Dani didn't have to feign surprise, but she'd had to strain to hide her emotion. She didn't sob. She didn't wail. That came later, once he and his friends had left the continent and Dani had found herself alone in her apartment shower, where the heat and the water washed away her internal pain. But at the table, she simply coughed and wiped her mouth with a napkin. Locke had gazed at her with sympathy in his eyes, as if he'd known all along how much the news would hurt.

"I didn't know how to tell you," he'd said. "I thought in person would be best."

"You could have just called."

The rest of his trip had passed in awkwardness, until Dani had hugged him at the airport, promising that she'd do what he'd asked and book her ticket.

"I wouldn't miss it," she'd said, aching. "I'm happy for you guys."

Now, walking among the chaos of the market, Dani allowed herself to feel everything she'd been avoiding. Sadness and anger, of course. But the emotion that seemed to rise without warning was an all-pervasive fear—that somehow, somewhere, she'd made a terribly wrong turn.

THE WEEKEND OF Locke and Amanda's wedding, a United Airlines flight attendant brought Dani an extra hot towel to her seat in first class. The flight from London passed in a haze of mediocre movies and fitful sleep. In Atlanta, she burned a two-hour layover with a venti Starbucks vanilla latte that tasted like heaven but made her body feel like hell. During the final flight to Charleston, pain crept from her hip into her back. It was her own fault, she knew. Airplane seats offered little relief for her joints, and if she veered from doctor's orders and drank caffeine and dairy, all bets were off.

At first, things weren't as hard as she'd anticipated. Locke had

been kind enough to include her in all the wedding weekend activities: a brunch on Friday morning, the rehearsal Friday
night. They'd even asked her to read scripture at the wedding.

"What passage?" Dani had asked when the happy couple had
cornered her at the brunch. Amanda looked positively radiant,
dressed in a baby-blue strapless dress.

"Surprise us," Amanda had answered.

Late Friday night, alone in her hotel room, Dani picked up her
cell phone and tried Avery. After Locke's visit to London, they'd
been playing a never-ending game of phone tag. The time difference had made catching up nearly impossible, and so Dani had
finally decided to drop the bomb in a two-word text message.
*Locke's engaged.* Avery had called her back immediately. But that
was weeks ago. Since then, they'd gone back to their normal routine of missed calls and unreturned messages, and all of Dani's
attempts to add a stop at Fort Bragg to her itinerary had come up
empty. The phone rang three times, and then Dani heard Avery's
serious outgoing voicemail message.

*"This is First Lieutenant Avery Adams. Please leave a message.
If this is an emergency, please call the Fort Bragg . . ."*

*This* is *an emergency,* Dani seethed as she ended the call. Staring
at the BlackBerry in her hand, she dialed a different number—
one of the few she remembered by heart.

"Bennett residence," said a familiar voice, "Wendy speaking."

"Wendy. It's Dani."

"Dani! How are you?" she said. "What time is it there?"

"Well, I'm actually not in London. I'm in South Carolina."

"South Carolina? Why?"

"It's kind of a long story," said Dani. "Do you have a minute? And a Bible? I think I might need some help."

THE NEXT DAY, the wedding quartet began with Vivaldi at six P.M. sharp. Dani had slept in that morning, then walked the streets of Charleston alone. A technician filed and painted her nails in the afternoon, and once the sun had set into the Atlantic, she emerged from the hotel dressed in a black silk gown that draped gracefully across one shoulder, ready to join a group of guests in a shuttle to the chapel. Dani was grateful that she'd splurged on the thousand-dollar dress, with its modest slit up the left side. There was no price too high for feeling beautiful at the wedding of someone you loved, especially when that person was marrying someone else. A thousand wasn't too much, Dani decided, especially because she'd saved on the shoes—a pair of simple snakeskin flats with pointed toes. Amanda's father was a retired army colonel who now served as athletic director at the Citadel, and the crowd of guests looked fit for a royal ball— ladies shimmered in long jewel-lustered gowns; men tugged on their ties, tuxes, and tails. When she crossed the church to ascend the podium for the reading, Dani hoped no one could tell she was wearing flats underneath the designer dress. With her hip in this much pain, she couldn't have risked wearing heels.

"A reading from the Old Testament."

The congregation of more than three hundred sat in their seats, silent, a diverse crowd of black and white, military and civilian.

They stared up at Dani with expectation as Locke and Amanda stood hand in hand at the altar, waiting. Wendy had helped Dani pick out her selections, the first for fun, the second for sentiment.

"Deuteronomy chapter twenty-four, verse five," Dani began slowly. "'If a man has recently married, he must not be sent to war or have any other duty laid on him. For one year he is to be free to stay at home and bring happiness to the wife he has married.'"

When she looked up from the Bible with a smirk, Locke's groomsmen, many of whom were his football teammates from West Point, began laughing and clapping. One of them shouted *hooah*. Amanda laughed and shook her head, looking supremely happy that she'd chosen Dani for this job. All of the gathered guests snickered as they realized what she'd read was a joke.

"Now, seriously," Dani said. "A reading from the New Testament." She flipped the pages toward the back half of the Bible. "A reading from First John. *'Dear friends, let us love one another, because love is from God . . . The one who does not love does not know God, because God is love. . . .*

"'Love consists in this: not that we loved God, but that He loved us and sent His Son to be the atoning sacrifice for our sins. Dear friends'—Locke and Amanda—'if God loved you in this way, you also must love one another . . . There is no fear in love; instead, perfect love drives out fear. . . .

"'*We love because He first loved us.*'"

She paused and looked at Locke, whose face was still and serious. In his dress blues, dark jacket and blue pants with gold stripes on the side, Locke looked devastatingly handsome, just as he had the day she'd met him, on the back of that truck at Camp Buckner. So handsome, in fact, Dani found it difficult to look him in the eye. But she did anyway, wiping a tear from her cheek, knowing that this was the most loving thing she could do for a friend.

At the reception, Locke's saber sliced through the first layer of a three-tiered cake. Twinkle lights hung around the white reception tent, millions of little gold orbs. And while Amanda swayed with her ring bearer on the dance floor, Locke pulled Dani in for a hug near the open bar. For a moment, Dani thought he might ask her to waltz, like they'd learned to do so many years ago. But then, in a pang of deep sadness, she realized those days were over.

"You got a little emotional up there, McNalley," he said, pinching her elbow.

Dani took a breath and held it, wondering if it was too late. What would it matter now if she told the truth? What would it change?

"Of course I did," she said, turning her eyes to meet his.

They stared at one another, and in that moment, Dani saw recognition. A slight nod of his head. A longing in his eyes and hers that spoke clearly, even as they said nothing at all. *I thought it would be you,* her eyes told him. And he squeezed her hand. *I did too,* he didn't say. Dani looked down, satisfied that it was over.

She sighed. "You better get out there." Amanda was waving him toward the dance floor as the band struck up the next song.

Later, Dani stood underneath that white reception tent, among the twinkle lights and candles, watching. With every turn of Amanda's gown, the life Dani had written for herself unraveled. The person she thought she would marry had married someone else. The friendships she thought would survive anything now felt as thin as smoke. The future, once a destination, had become a cloud of confusion. Nothing was clear. Nothing was certain. And yet, she'd still put on that dress. That was something. And when the song changed and Amanda reached her open arms toward Dani, she still found the power within her to dance.

"DO YOU HAVE anything a bit more feminine?"

A week after Locke's wedding, Dani stood in the dressing room at her favorite store in London, inspecting her reflection in the mirror. The retail associate waiting outside the velvet dressing room curtain was a slender brunette with blunt bangs and thick-rimmed glasses. She looked young, Dani thought—younger than Dani, which felt strange, since she still felt like she'd only just graduated from college. Could there actually be people working in the world that had graduated from college after her? Nonsense.

"Have you seen the new gray lot we got in?" the girl asked, her accent posh and British. "It just arrived this week. I'll grab one. You're a U.K. size twelve, right?"

Dani hated to think she shopped here so often that this woman knew her size.

"Right. Bring a ten too, just in case." That was the other resolution Dani had made, after eating a Nutella crepe that morning at the market. She needed to get back to clean eating like the doctors told her to, to keep her arthritis from flaring. And she needed to join a gym. It was time to revive the athlete inside. It was a thin plan, full of vanity, she knew. But sometimes, when the future looks foggy, you have to draw your own map.

An hour later, Dani left AllSaints with a slate-colored leather jacket that draped open in the front. No zippers. No buckles. Just the perfect cut in the perfect color, with all the promise she'd desired. As she made her way back to her apartment, the sun teased London, dropping little specks of gold onto the ground. It was the perfect temperature for an afternoon coffee—decaf, of course. After the wedding, she'd been following doctor's orders—but before she could duck into the coffee shop on the corner, Dani heard a familiar sound.

They say sound and smell are the senses that connect most to our memory. The hollow bounce was like a laugh, a clarion call from the past. So full of meaning and regret and nostalgia and promise. She felt transported in her spirit to her driveway as a kid, then to the gym at West Point. The game she'd so wanted to leave behind, she couldn't fully abandon. It was knitted into her skin, into her senses. The sound made her heart beat faster.

A chain-link fence encircled a court to her right. The five-on-five pickup game looked like it had been raging for quite a while, based on the amount of sweat that had gathered on the boys' faces. They looked to be teenagers—thirteen or fourteen, Dani guessed. There was one black kid among the white boys, all equally lost in the game. They shouted and shuffled, playing shirts against skins, as the boy with the curly hair dribbled, shoulder down, and pushed into his defender. The defender fell and the game stopped. No ref blew a whistle. No one yelled or started cursing. The offending player offered his hand, and the defender stood up and took the ball to start the game again.

Mesmerized by their ungraceful steps, botched passes, and poor shots, Dani had to keep herself from laughing out loud. They were terrible. But they didn't care. They kept right on playing. Dani wondered if they were even keeping score. She wondered if the score even mattered.

Her senior year, after the second surgery, Dani had planted herself on the sidelines, leaning on her crutches, forced into silence. Two plebes had quit midseason, and after they lost four games in a row, West Point's athletic director had called Coach Jankovich into his office. Avery reported that she'd seen the coach walking in, wringing her hands. But when the season ended and Jankovich still hadn't been fired, Dani, Hannah, and Avery had started scheming. They couldn't leave West Point without telling someone the truth.

"You gotta pump a fake!" Dani shouted instinctively after one of the kids on the skins team threw up another blocked shot.

The game stopped. All ten kids turned to look at the woman behind the gate. The black kid put his hands on his hips and laughed, lighting up the court with his smile. He reminded Dani of Locke, all confidence and swagger.

"Oh yeah?" the kid shouted, his smart British accent calling out across the court. "Care to demonstrate?"

The boys all groaned, using the spontaneous break to grab water and wipe their faces on their oversized shirts. Taking the dare, Dani walked around the chain-link fence and dropped her shopping bag by the entrance.

"Oh rubbish!" one boy shouted, shocked. "She's going to play!"

"What?" Dani laughed. "You don't think I can hack it?"

"American! Go figure. Cheeky bastards," someone shouted.

"Here." The boy passed her the ball. "Let's see what you've got."

Dani bounced the ball a few times, just to appreciate the sensation. It had been nearly two years since she'd touched the leathery plastic of a basketball. The tiny bumps massaged her hand as it fell to the court and bounced back to her palm. Knowing she was showing off, but without a care, Dani picked up the ball and spun it on one finger.

"Okay, okay," the kid answered. "But can you shoot?"

With that, Dani took off, dribbling first to the left and then to the right, unaware of the pain in her hip. Her opponent matched her steps, lifting his arms up and mimicking her every move. Dani took a step back to the three-point line and pretended to shoot. In that moment, the boy lurched up and toward her with one hand high in the sky, and as he landed on the ground, Dani took her shot, the ball soaring from her fingertips straight through the net.

Swoosh.

"OHHHHHH!"

"DAMN! SHE SCHOOLED YOU!"

Dani spent the next hour teaching them things she'd nearly forgotten she knew. A set of streetlights went on. The sun fell, spilling cans of purple and red paint across the sky. She lost all sense of time, just like a little kid. On the court, something changed in her, like a key had been placed into a lock. The boys looked at her to learn. There was no ego. No disdain that they were hearing from a woman. Just the honest hope that they would improve their game. Respect and gratitude appeared in their eyes. And it didn't matter that Dani's body ached.

Her soul soared.

*Fall 2006 // Fort Bragg, North Carolina*

The first Sunday in November, Noah left for a monthlong deployment to an unknown destination. Saturday, he'd packed his rucksack, thrown the rest of his gear into his car, and told Avery not to worry. Like usual, he'd kissed her goodbye in the middle of the night, and then he was gone.

In the morning, she found an empty water glass, an open jar of peanut butter, and a plate full of crumbs on the kitchen counter—remnants of Noah's midnight snack. She put the peanut butter jar away, wiped the counters of the trail of ants that had invaded, and then stared out the kitchen window onto the street outside. Throughout the neighborhood, fathers with military haircuts were mowing their grass. Pairs of mothers pushed strollers down the road and waved with gloved hands. Yellow ribbons wrapped around trees where wives sat alone inside, wrangling children without the aid of their husbands. The Nesmiths' house was all dark, with two blue-star flags hung side by side in the front window. At the beginning of October, Tim had arrived at Avery's door with a spare key to their house and a zip-lock bag full of morning glory muffins.

"Since when did you become Betty Crocker?" Avery had said, receiving the bag from his hand.

"Just cleaning out the freezer," he'd said. "Thought you might enjoy a snack. Microwave them in the morning, thirty seconds."

"You all packed up?"

"Yep," he'd said, rocking back on his heels. "Tomorrow."

"You ready?"

"As I'll ever be."

A moment passed between them, and Avery considered inviting him inside, but before she could, Tim clapped his hands together and smiled. "Guess that's it."

Avery reached for him and hugged him hard, if not for herself, then for Hannah.

"Geez, Adams," Tim had said with a laugh. "It's not like I have cancer."

"Just be safe," she'd replied.

"Will do." He'd offered a small salute. "Hey. When Hannah gets back—watch out for her, all right? I think when she gets home, it'll be harder than when she's over there."

"I will." Even as she made the promise, Avery wondered if she could keep it, or if Hannah would care.

Then he'd walked back to his house, three doors down.

OPENING THE GATE to her neighbor's backyard across the street, Avery found the dog leash underneath the grill. She and Eric Jenkins had struck a deal—Avery would take his dog, Bosco, on long runs, and in exchange, he shoveled her driveway in the winter and mowed her lawn during the summer. It was a good deal because Bosco helped Avery feel safe when she ran alone in the woods. But unfortunately, Eric's wife had a permanent scowl on her face every time she saw Avery leashing up their dog in the backyard, as if Avery were purposefully trying to point out that she was out of shape. Michelle *was* out of shape. But Avery wasn't trying to rub it in.

Seeing her, in the kitchen window, Avery gave a little wave and a false smile.

*Bitch.*

The word came into Avery's head before she could stop it. When had she become so hard? Had she always been that bitter? Who cared if Michelle stared at her and Noah, judging them, when he left in the mornings? Who cared if she hadn't *once* invited Avery to any of their barbecues that they had in their backyard? She still shouldn't call the woman a bitch.

At that moment, Michelle opened the back door and smiled at Avery.

"You sure you want to take him?" she asked kindly, bobbing a baby on her hip. *When did she have that baby?* "I know he's a lot to handle."

Just then, a black Labrador came barreling out of the house. He darted around Michelle's legs, through the yard, and jumped straight at Avery's knees.

"Whoa, Bosco! You want to go running?" Avery looked back at Michelle. "No, it's fine. Really."

"Eric and I are heading to Oklahoma next week for Thanksgiving," Michelle said happily. "We leave Tuesday."

"Oh great," Avery said. "To see your family?"

Michelle gave a slight shake of the head. "Eric's." She stepped outside and looked at the sky, as if to assess the day's temperate weather for the first time. "I wish I liked running. I've never understood it. It's like . . . what are you running from?"

"Yeah," Avery said. She felt so tired of holding up the neighborly charade. "Well, I'll bring him back soon. Maybe in an hour?"

Michelle raised her eyebrows like she'd never heard something so insane. "Knock yourself out," she said with a laugh, then looked at the baby. "We'll be here."

The dog panted, stretched, and flipped his black tail back and forth with force. Avery felt a surge of gratitude toward the dog—*At least you want to hang out with me,* she thought, staring at his happy brown eyes. *There it was again.* That little, bitter voice. The only thing she could do to shut it up was to run. And so, turning out their gate, she ran.

THE TRAIL WAS eight miles long, hidden by the woods. The entrance, an inconspicuous path marked only by a small wooden post, was Avery's confidential cardio treasure. It weaved an oblong loop and passed over a creek twice, ascending and descending gradually across varied terrain. There were roots to dodge, rocks to kick, and spiderwebs to pull off her face along the way.

Avery pushed herself faster than she'd ever run before. Off his leash, Bosco sniffed grass, marked his territory, and trotted far ahead, a black spot among the rotting brown leaves on the ground. Avery breathed in perfect rhythm—inhale, four steps; exhale, four steps. Her hair collected sweat and her legs turned over, warm on the inside even as a cold breeze passed over her thighs. This was perfect running weather—cool enough to keep her going for hours. And at least when she was running, she was supposed to be alone.

As she ran, she did the math. She and Noah had been together more than a year now—several months longer than Avery's longest relationship, and that was back in high school. But the truth was, Noah had become like a ghost, coming in and out of her life as he wanted, never giving much explanation for where he was going, how long he'd be gone, or why he couldn't answer his phone. When his job took him away, it was like he didn't even exist. Avery didn't want to be demanding—she couldn't imagine stooping to the level of a girl who stamped her foot and asked for a ring. But some kind of assurance that their relationship was moving *forward* would have been nice. It didn't even have to be moving forward! Just moving . . . somewhere.

Instead, Noah left her alone in her kitchen to watch her neighbor's children grow up before her eyes. Dani was living in London and gallivanting all around Europe on the weekends. While Avery was sure deployment sucked at times, at least Hannah had a chance to put her training to work. And what about Avery? She had a shadow boyfriend, a messy house, and not much to show

for her two years out of college, other than a few pieces of furniture she'd bought at IKEA.

Then there was the letter. Ever since she'd received notice from
West Point that John Collins had been paroled, nothing had felt
right. The first thing she should have done was call Dani and
Hannah. But that night, sitting on the guest bed in her parents'
house, she couldn't bring herself to pick up the phone. It was the
middle of the night in London, and Hannah was tucked away in
some far corner of Afghanistan, unreachable. It had been a year
since they'd been together at Dani's apartment in Boston for
Thanksgiving, and even then, they'd seemed so suspicious of her
new boyfriend. She couldn't call them with the news about John
Collins or her worries about Noah. She didn't want to hear *I told
you so.*

As she ran, Avery tried to untangle the web of her own shame.
Who was she to feel bad about her life, when Dani had just
watched the person she loved most tie the knot with someone
else? And Hannah—she wouldn't see Tim for another *year.* Compared to them, Avery had no right to feel anything but fine.

At that moment and without warning, Bosco halted in the
middle of the trail. Stumbling over his body, an eighty-pound
obstacle, Avery caught herself, her hands planted in a puddle of
fresh mud.

"Bosco!" she cried. "What the . . ."

Standing up, Avery brushed her soiled hands across her pants,
leaving trails of dirt behind. The dog crept into the woods next to
the trail, sniffing at something in earnest. Stepping closer, Avery

caught her breath and peered into the pile of leaves. A small rabbit lay on its side, its brown pelt punctured in two places at the neck. A small trickle of red blood seeped from its mouth. Bosco pushed it with one careless paw.

"Hey, leave it," she ordered. Bosco whined, then stepped away.

The rabbit's mouth opened and closed once.

Avery crouched closer. It was still alive—barely. Its eyes were open wide, as though it was experiencing terror in its last moments. The woods were very quiet now, her loud thoughts halted by death. And for a moment, Avery felt scared and alone.

"Leave it, Bosco," she said. "Let's go."

The dog bolted up the trail. Then, with a sigh, she started running again.

LATER THAT NIGHT, a pot of water boiled on her kitchen stove, jumping in eager anticipation for the box of fettuccine sitting on her counter. She'd recorded Thursday's *Grey's Anatomy,* and the episode opened with Derek and Meredith making out in a bathtub, which, Avery knew, was one of the most uncomfortable things a couple could do. She and Noah had tried once, with some success, but at times, she wished television shows would include the *actual* awkward moments in a relationship: the moment you realize you can't step *out* of the tub without his seeing you from all the wrong angles; the strange, uncomfortable clean-up that happens after the main event. Sex wasn't nearly as seamless as television led everyone to believe. But with Noah, it came close.

Whenever he arrived at her house, he could barely drop his

bags by the door before filling his hands with her breasts, her hips. He looked at her like he wanted to devour her—and his hunger made Avery feel sexy and powerful and in control, even as the voice in the recesses of her spirit warned that he was taking rather than giving. Whenever he prepared to leave again, he'd grow agitated and uncomfortable, like he was sitting on pins. He blamed his anxiety on the impending deployment—and Avery would try to rub his shoulders, but eventually he'd push her off. After his last trip, Avery had found a pile of Pakistani rupees on the nightstand next to a receipt for two foot-long Subway sandwiches that he'd purchased at Fort Bragg. Looking at the date on the receipt, Avery's eyes had narrowed. October 12. How could he have purchased two turkey club sandwiches at the Fort Bragg post exchange if he was supposedly in Pakistan? And why did he need two? Avery had willed her eyes away from the receipt, refusing to follow those questions to the root. Surely there was an explanation.

But now, as the pasta water began to boil over, Avery reached to turn down the heat and began wondering again about that little piece of paper. Perhaps there was an error in the computer system that had misprinted the date. Or maybe she was forgetting what dates he'd been gone in the first place. Maybe she was going crazy. Or maybe she was just too paranoid for her own good, always looking for evidence that he was like every other guy she'd ever dated. She didn't want to be distrusting. But then again, some quiet voice in the back of her head that sounded a lot like Hannah wouldn't shut up about that stupid receipt.

Avery took a seat on her couch, placing her cell phone on the coffee table and holding the bowl of pasta in her hands. For a moment, her body looked at the noodles, covered in butter, and craved meat—it had been nearly a year since she'd eaten beef, simply because Noah had convinced her to be a vegetarian. Now she remembered the look on Dani's face when Avery had passed on the turkey last Thanksgiving. It wasn't a look of disapproval. It was a look of confusion.

"*Is he treating you well?*" Hannah had asked.

In a flash of certainty, Avery set her dinner down and grabbed her cell phone. The phone would likely go straight to Noah's voicemail like it always did when he was gone. But she couldn't stand it. She had to ask him. About the receipt. About those fucking foot-long sub sandwiches. Turning the television on mute, she waited, listening to the sound of three distinct rings.

"Hello?"

Avery pulled the phone away from her ear. The voice on the other end of the line wasn't Noah. It was a woman. Something in the woman's voice had trembled. Or maybe the cell service had cut out. Avery wasn't sure. She stared at the phone, verifying that it was Noah's name on her screen, then placed it back to her ear. Her hands began to sweat.

"Hello?" the woman repeated. "Avery? I know you're there."

So this woman knew her name. A long pause passed, while on the silent television screen in the living room, a doctor lifted her bloodied gloves in the air.

"I'm sorry, who is this?" Avery said, her voice angry and defiant.

The woman on the other end of the line sighed. "This is Noah's fiancée."

# 24

Hannah's platoon swung their arms up and down like they were playing timpani in slow motion, hammering raw wood boards together to create a platform for the GP medium tent that would house the TOC, or tactical operations center. The crevice between Hannah's thumb and forefinger was red and bleeding. She sucked it, then shook her hand. Sweat spilled over Hannah's eyebrows and into her eyes. She breathed, tilting her head toward the sky, letting the salt water roll into the hair above her ears.

Had she known what the day would entail, would she have smiled at the sun? Had she known, would she have laughed?

In the eight months since they'd arrived in Afghanistan, Hannah's platoon had built six infantry outposts like this for incoming troops. From their headquarters in Sharana—where Ebrahim's family lived—her platoon would convoy out far into the desert into hotly contested areas and get to work building, so that a surge of troops could arrive and retake the territory from the Taliban. Everything they built was temporary. An infantry team would secure the area while Hannah's platoon built tents, dug trenches, and assembled plumbing for a future bathroom trailer. It took two days to get the first tents erected, so her engineers would have a place to sleep. Then they built a simple sand wall for defense, which took about four days. Then they'd move on to digging trenches for bathroom facilities.

They'd arrived in mid-October. By the time they left a month later, the outpost would be ready to house NATO troops for a short-term deployment, fighting in the hills no more than five minutes from where they stood. Hannah's soldiers worked round the clock in 120-degree heat, always aware that they were sitting ducks. After three weeks in this remote location, her hands were showing evidence of all her hard work, and her body ached. Dirt caked under her fingernails; calluses formed on her palms. And every morning, she found handfuls of her hair on her pillow—it had started to fall out because of the stress.

Two days ago, her platoon had returned from dropping supplies and soccer balls at a nearby school. Since then, the little boy's angry face had haunted Hannah's dreams. But the physical exhaustion helped her sleep at night, even when she knew that Tim had arrived in Kuwait, hundreds of miles away, and was preparing to fight his own war. If she'd been at home, Hannah was certain she wouldn't have been able to function knowing he was in harm's way. But if Tim was going to be deployed, at least she was here, distracted by her own mission. It felt good to do work that mattered. And the harder she worked, the faster the time seemed to pass.

It hadn't crossed Hannah's mind that she might want time to slow down.

ONCE THE TARIN Kot tactical operations center was up and running, Hannah had spent several hours connecting a secure cable to the post's sole computer. Technically, the line was only supposed to be used for military communications and since there were so many people around, there wasn't much privacy. But with the few spare moments Hannah had alone with the only secure Internet connection, she decided to take a risk.

iCasualties.org, a rudely named website, logged all military casualties in both Iraq and Afghanistan since 2001. Hannah checked it at least once a week when she was at FOB Sharana. It wasn't a fancy website. No graphics. No photos. Just a crude table of data. Each row described a tragedy. Every column defined the details. Date, name, rank. Age, cause of death, place of death. Military branch, hometown, unit. The final column listed the soldier or officer's current duty station. Most newspapers could, from one line of text, write an entire obituary.

Hannah scanned the most recent additions. She looked at the dates first—in October, 107 U.S. soldiers had been killed in Iraq. Thirty-four more had been added to the list since the first of November. After scanning the dates, Hannah skimmed the names for any she recognized. It was a morbid ritual—a sacrament

Hannah knew every soldier and officer and wife and mother had completed more than once over the last four years. But by reading the list, searching for names she knew, Hannah inadvertently honored the names she didn't.

*Martinez, Misael*, a staff sergeant from North Carolina.

*Powell, Kyle W.*, twenty-one years old.

Hannah had read the names so many times that she'd learned to do it unemotionally. But every now and then, a name would stop her from scrolling, and the weight of anonymous loss would hit her all at once.

*Seymour, David S. "Scotty." Specialist. 24. Hostile—hostile fire—small-arms fire.*

Hannah wondered who'd given him the nickname and whether he liked it or hated it, smiled or sulked when guys called him "Scotty." He and Hannah were the same age. Twenty-four. This year, her birthday had passed without much fanfare. Tim had mailed her a care package, but as of last week, it still hadn't arrived.

After she scanned iCasualties.org, she opened an e-mail that had arrived from Tim. Two sentences, short and to the point, like all his e-mails. But for some reason, this one left Hannah with a heavy feeling in her chest, like her lungs were filling with water.

*Heading out for a ten-day mission. I'll be in touch when we get back. RILY.*

*RILY* had become their secret code. Their shorthand for all the emotions wrapped up in these months apart. *Remember I love you.* She remembered. It was forgetting so she could focus on anything other than her fear that was the hard part.

"LIEUTENANT NESMITH!"

Private Murphy called to her from across the build site, holding a two-way radio in his hands. An eighteen-year-old kid from Arkansas with a girlfriend at home and an unhealthy obsession with NASCAR racing, Murphy was a great soldier. Tough as nails, and always the last one to put away his tools. Hannah had grown to respect him.

"Yeah, Murph," she yelled. "What's up?"

"They're saying we've got a big one coming. Twenty miles out."

"Shit," Hannah cursed, shocked at the profanity that came out of her own mouth. But there honestly couldn't have been any worse news. It was sandstorm season in Afghanistan, and though they'd prepared for this possibility, Hannah had never expected it would come so soon. Twenty minutes wasn't long enough. But it was all she had left.

Looking at the nearly finished construction site, Hannah put her forefinger and thumb in her mouth and whistled hard and loud, gathering the rest of the platoon together.

"Listen," she ordered, commanding their attention. "We can't afford to waste a single second. Murph, you and Willis join me and finish platform one. Johnson, Kiggler—stop digging the trench and help finish the plumbing so that's not ruined by the sand. And then the rest of you, get moving securing the anchors and any other equipment. We've got less than half an hour. Any questions?"

Without hesitation, her platoon moved into overdrive. For the next fifteen minutes, Hannah forgot that she was thirsty and hot and tired. She simply pushed through the pain until her heart took over and the sky turned dark. Soon, they were all sitting in the shade of the tent, drenched in sweat, laughing at the feat it had required to finish the work in such a short amount of time. As they chugged water and tried to regain their breath, Hannah spied the rumbling darkness in the distance and felt her eyes narrow.

An ocean wave would terrify an ant. That's how Hannah felt, standing several thousand yards away from the edge of a sandstorm. Every second the wall grew, massive and brown, with arms and fingers rolling more dust into its belly, stretching wider and higher into the sky. The majesty of it struck Hannah so immediately, she didn't even have time to register that it was coming right toward them.

Where did it get the energy to move?

Was God himself in the storm?

Tiny particles of sand flew into her hair, her neck, her cheeks, like a thousand shards of glass.

"Get inside," she ordered. "Everyone get inside."

The platoon moved underneath the cover of the canvas, zipped closed the door, and checked that all the window panels were securely attached—so they could watch it go by, without the sand destroying every weapon and tool in the tent. If you think you're important, if you feel that your life matters, all you need to do is spend some time in nature, Hannah thought. Stand before an ocean. Climb a mountain. Stare out over a canyon. Creation—wild and untamed—reminded her of her size in this universe. But feeling small did not send her into despair. She was like a child, trusting her Father when he said the storm would pass.

As the storm rolled over their heads, Private Murphy held a camera up to one of the clear plastic tent windows, recording video. "Holy shit. It's a fucking monster . . ."

The entire world turned from day to night as the cloud passed over, pummeling the tent with twenty-five-mile-per-hour winds.

"Looks like we might be in Tarin Kot a little bit longer than we thought, Lieutenant Nesmith," Murphy said.

"It'll pass," Hannah answered. "It may take some time. But it'll pass."

THE STORM DIDN'T pass.

For twenty-four hours, they were stuck inside that tent, smelling of sweat and dirt. They ate MREs, read books, and slept. They only ventured outside to relieve themselves, and even then, came back in the tent coughing, and covered in dust. Hannah filled her time with paperwork, and stopped every so often to listen to the sound of the wind. The Taliban were unlikely to fire rockets or mortar in the midst of a storm—their equipment was just as susceptible to sand as the U.S. Army's—but Hannah still felt on edge. She'd rather have heard the constant, sporadic accompaniment of gunshots outside the camp than the sound of the wind swirling around her. Rapid fire, popping in the distance, reassured her. It meant the enemy was being defeated. But in silence like this—quiet like this—there was a real temptation to forget she was in danger. Hannah found herself straining to listen so she wouldn't be caught off guard if an explosion disrupted her imagined peace. To die in the midst of a firefight or while on convoy was one thing. But what Hannah feared most was death arriving, when it was completely unexpected.

ONCE THE SANDSTORM passed, Hannah's platoon finished construction. On Wednesday, they began the long, winding convoy back to FOB Sharana, stopping overnight in Kandahar. On Thursday, their six-vehicle convoy bumped along the unpaved roads, churning up dust under their tires. Buckled into the front passenger seat of the second Humvee, Hannah watched the walls of the FOB come into view and breathed a sigh of relief. Their work was done, and the storm had done limited damage. As they passed through the gates, she made a mental list of the things she wanted: a shower and a chance to check her e-mail. She needed to see if she'd received an update from Tim.

Murphy put the Humvee in park. Hannah stepped out.

But as soon as Hannah closed the vehicle's door, she knew something was wrong. The unit's commanding officer, Lieutenant Colonel Markham, stood a few feet away from the vehicle, looking directly at her, as if he'd been waiting for her to arrive. His eyes spoke of sadness. His shoulders slumped under an invisible weight.

Before he even said a word, Hannah knew what he was going to say. Her jaw went numb. The sky above and the views around her blurred as her eyes focused on only his face.

"Hannah," he said, using her name and not her rank. "I need you to come with me."

In his office, he told her to sit, but Hannah refused. It was the first time she'd ever disobeyed a direct order. A blue tissue box sat on the colonel's desk. The Army chaplain sat in a chair, leaning forward with his hands intertwined. Hannah couldn't breathe. She couldn't remember if it was night or day or if it mattered.

For years, she would replay this moment in her mind, wishing to erase it from her life. It was a doorway. And as soon as she walked through it, the door behind her would shut and disappear, closing her off from everything before. Including the girl who could look up at an Afghanistan sky and smile.

Bracing for impact didn't help at all. Even if every muscle in her body had tightened, there were no muscles strong enough to protect a heart from breaking.

"No," she said. "Please."

"I'm so sorry, Hannah," the colonel said. "I'm so very sorry."

# THE CORPS

*The Corps bareheaded, salute it, with eyes up thanking our God*
*That we of the Corps are treading,*
*where they of the Corps have trod*
*They are here in ghostly assemblage*
*The men of the Corps long dead*
*And our hearts are standing attention*
*While we wait for their passing tread*
*We sons of today, we salute you, you sons of an earlier day*
*We follow close order behind you, where you have pointed the way*
*The long gray line of us stretches*
*Through the years of a century told*
*And the last man feels to his marrow*
*The grip of your far-off hold*
*Grip hands with us now, though we see not*
*Grip hands with us strengthen our hearts*
*As the long line stiffens and straightens*
*With the thrill that your presence imparts*
*Grip hands, though it be from the shadows*
*While we swear as you did of yore*
*Or living or dying to honor*
*The Corps, and the Corps, and the Corps*

# BEYOND

*November 2006*

## 25

*November 16, 2006 // London, England*

T he limp was worse than it had ever been.

With every step, a searing knife shot through Dani Mc-Nalley's right side, forcing her to put more weight on her left leg while dragging her right. And yet she moved forward, her feet bobbling over the cobblestones. She had to get back to her apartment, and then she had to go home.

The pregnant sky released its first few drops of rain onto her head. Dani watched them fall and die on the sidewalk. In her haste to leave work, she'd forgotten her umbrella on the hook by her office door. Paralyzed with indecision, she couldn't decide whether to go back to the office for the umbrella or keep walking forward toward Notting Hill. People maneuvered around her with their chins down, hands stuffed deep into their pockets, like Dani was a lamppost or trash can—simply an obstacle to avoid. Life was moving on as if nothing had happened. Cars and taxis barreled down the road, kicking up water under their tires. The tube underground rumbled, moving people from one stop to the next. It was hard to believe all this activity. All this life. A couple of toddlers on the other side of the road dressed in yellow raincoats had the audacity to laugh, turning their faces toward the sky to catch the rain on their cheeks.

Dani felt her chest tighten and for a moment, she thought she might lose control right in the middle of the street. Gripping her BlackBerry tight in her hand, Dani looked up to the sky and blinked back the tears in her eyes, swallowing the emotion. She'd done it plenty of times before. At some point, she would need to let her tears flow freely. But now was not the time.

An hour ago, she'd been sitting in a meeting with Laura Klein and the rest of the E & G marketing team discussing their next round of commercial shoots when her phone buzzed on the table. Laura's eyes had bored into the side of Dani's face as she reached for the phone. She hadn't planned on answering it. She thought she would look at the caller ID and send the call straight to voice-mail. But the name on the caller ID sent ice into Dani's veins.

*Bill Speer.*

Hannah's father. She imagined him on the other end of the line somewhere in Texas, waiting for Dani to answer. And without thinking—without explanation—she took the phone in her hand and walked out of the meeting.

"Mr. Speer?" Dani had said, her voice already shaking. "Is everything okay?"

She heard him clear his throat.

"Dani, I'm sorry," he'd said. "I have some very bad news."

Dani sat down in the office kitchen, a windowless room with bright fluorescent light. Her breath went shallow and she clenched her eyes shut. Bill's voice was steady as it traversed an ocean to speak the truth.

"Tim was killed in Iraq, Dani. I'm so sorry."

Since then, the BlackBerry in her hand hadn't stopped buzzing. Messages arrived often. E-mails, texts, and phone calls, all of which went unanswered.

From Sarah Goodrich: *I just heard that Tim Nesmith was KIA. Tell me that's not true?*

She knew she wouldn't sleep tonight. Most people didn't even know that she was living in London—a full six hours ahead of Eastern Time. The phone would ring, buzz, and beep through all hours of the night, with messages from people who had questions—the same ones she'd asked Hannah's father.

*Have you talked to her? How is she? I can't believe this. How did it happen? When is the funeral? What can we do?*

She had no answers. Neither had Bill Speer. A sandstorm had rolled into the southeastern region of Afghanistan, stalling all transportation and communication. Hannah was stuck waiting for the air to clear so she could go home. But Dani had no such obstacles. She'd grabbed her purse and computer from her cubicle and left the office, without telling Laura a single thing. She was getting on the first plane to North Carolina. And until her feet were on American soil—until she saw Hannah face-to-face—everything else could wait.

A stream of tourists emerged from the train station and walked east along the sidewalk, smiling and chatting under their hats and umbrellas, anticipating the pleasures that awaited them down the road. Dani moved between them, parting them as if they were the Red Sea. As she stuffed the phone back into her pocket, she descended into the bowels of the tube. And somewhere along the way, without even noticing it, she forgot about the pain in her hip.

THAT NIGHT, AS Dani packed a bag and searched for flights online, she tried to call Avery, without success. She would keep trying. But in the meantime, she needed to pack a bag—if nothing else, just to have something to do.

Her suitcase opened up like a black mouth on her bed, while the heavy square phone vibrated against her nightstand. The name *Wendy Bennett* flashed at the center of the screen. Dani could picture her in the living room of their home at West Point, waiting for Dani to answer. At the thought of hearing Wendy's voice, Dani's eyes flooded. She pressed the green button and answered.

"Hi, Wendy." Dani moved slowly to the side of her bedroom, leaned her back against a wall, and sank into the floor, listening to Wendy's sobs on the other end of the line. After some time had passed, Wendy finally spoke.

"Has anyone heard from her?" Wendy asked, her words interrupted with a hiccupping cry. "At all?"

"I don't know," Dani said, wiping her eyes. "I haven't. She won't answer her phone."

"What are you doing right now?"

"Packing," Dani said, though the word felt weak as it came out of her mouth. "I don't know what else to do. I found a flight that leaves tomorrow, first thing. I haven't bought it yet." She sighed. "I just have to get there."

"I understand," Wendy said. "Did you tell your boss you're leaving?"

"No," Dani replied. "It doesn't matter." And it didn't. Laura Klein would be angry that Dani had walked out of the meeting without an explanation. But there was no way she was going to stay at the office waiting for her boss's permission to leave. Laura could get over it, or she could fire her. It didn't matter anymore.

"Have you talked to Avery?" Wendy asked.

"No," Dani said finally, her voice cracking with emotion. "I . . . I'm sorry, Wendy . . . I need to go."

"Okay. I love you. I'm praying. I'm praying so hard."

*If only I'd kept my nose out of Hannah's business, maybe Hannah and Tim would never have dated in the first place,* Dani thought. *Maybe then things would be different. If only I'd been commissioned into the Army. Then I would understand. If I'd lived through the war, maybe I would be less shocked.*

In the place of combat boots, Dani's bedroom floor was covered in designer shoes and limited-edition sneakers. A cream-colored cashmere scarf hung from the hook on the door, and her latest extravagance, a Cartier watch, mocked her with every click of the second hand. She ripped it off and threw it against the wall, then screamed, her face buried in the carpet on the floor.

Eventually, Dani moved to her bed and tried to close her eyes. Perhaps a few short minutes of sleep would help her to breathe easier. To calm down. As much as her soul ached, it soothed her to lie in one place and cry.

With her eyes closed, a memory appeared bright and clear in her mind. A crowd of children playing soccer in a schoolyard. They were laughing, all chasing around the ball. Rather than fight the memory, she let it come back to her. She focused on the little black girl sprinting down a green field, her braids flopping in the air as she ran. She was always so happy when she ran.

Back then, she had no limp. No pain. For this invitational soccer tournament, the coach had decided to move Dani, just twelve years old, up to the team of fourteen-year-olds. Her team wore bright yellow jerseys, and Dani stood a head shorter than the rest. She'd been so excited to play that day, Dani remembered. Eager to prove that she deserved the spot she'd been given.

The little brown-skinned girl tore up and down the field, sweating under the heat of the sun. Smiling. Her freckles jumping like little flecks of dark chocolate as she cut left and right, dribbling the ball deftly between defenders. She kicked a ball as hard as she could and it soared past the goalie into the top right corner of the net. Her teammates ran toward her, wrapping their arms around her in excitement. It was her first moment of athletic success. Her first taste of glory.

But as she'd walked off the field, a sound carried over the wind. The adults behind the opponent's bench were laughing. A tan man with a swoop of brown hair had wrapped his hands around his mouth, shouting in Dani's direction. She remembered looking at him, wondering if he was yelling at her or the referee.

"Bahh!" he'd shouted, his voice shaking like a sheep's. "Bahhh!" he'd yelled, letting his arms drop to his sides. The other parents, dressed in red, all joined in laughing and bleating, some loudly, and some out of the corners of their mouths. They were bleating at her, the black sheep.

That night, still dressed in her yellow uniform, Dani had cried, sitting on the closed toilet in the bathroom. Her mother wiped her tears.

"Those people are ignorant," Harper McNalley had said.

"They said I was a black sheep," Dani cried. "Like I didn't belong out there."

"So what?" her mother had snapped defiantly. "So they say you're different? Guess what. They're *right*. You *are* different. You're better."

Dani couldn't remember how many soccer games she'd played after that. Five? Ten? The following year, she'd told her parents she didn't want to play soccer anymore. She'd explained she wanted to try basketball instead.

The ceiling of Dani's apartment in Notting Hill blurred, distorted by the hot tears in her eyes. At first, she didn't know why that memory had come to her mind. But now, she knew.

Had those parents not singled her out—had they not shouted their hate—she would never have played basketball. And if she hadn't played basketball, she would never have attended West Point.

The dominoes that put her on her back, grieving for Tim and for Hannah, had been put into play far before she'd ever signed some document for Coach Jankovich. For some people, that lack of control might have made them angry with God. But for Dani, she finally felt like she saw her life with clarity for the very first time.

What if the only reason she'd attended West Point was to be available for Hannah, when she needed a friend like Dani most? What if it took all the injuries and the pain and the sacrifices they'd made simply to forge a friendship that could withstand even this?

Dani had earned more frequent-flier miles in the last two years than she would ever know what to do with. But now, without thinking, Dani pulled up an airline website on her computer and cashed several thousand in.

She was going home.

**26**

*November 16, 2006 // Fort Bragg, North Carolina*

A week after she spoke to Noah's fiancée, Avery still hadn't gotten out of bed. A stomach bug was going around the unit, which had made it easier to call in sick, stay in bed, and throw up occasionally. It wasn't a total lie; Noah was a virus and she had to get him out of her system.

Her room was a disaster area, covered in tissues and water glasses filled to varying levels—most of the contents dusty and undrinkable from sitting on the nightstand for three days' time. Her cell phone sat in the corner, turned off, so she wouldn't be tempted to call him. Laundry grew in piles around the room, stinking with dried sweat from the punishing ruck march she'd made her platoon complete for no other reason than she could. She had no energy left for running. No desire to take Bosco on a backwoods trail. All she could bring herself to do was sleep, wake up, remember that she'd wasted more than a year of her life on a liar, and then turn over and go back to sleep.

The puzzle pieces fell into place in Avery's mind, each one a crude reminder that she was an idiot, unfit for love. Red flag number one: the first question out of his mouth had been whether or not she was married. Red flag number two: he rarely explained where he was going, or for how long, or why. Red flag number three: she'd never been to his apartment, never met his parents. Red flag number four: at Thanksgiving, she'd known he was lying about talking to his mother, and had looked up their flight online and seen it was not, in fact, delayed. Red flag number five: Did she need five red flags? Really?

If she was honest with herself, really honest—if she listened to her *actual* heart and not the heart that she *wished* existed—if she got in touch at *that* level, then she'd known all along he was lying, or at least that something was wrong. But even now, she preferred to live in a world where he *wasn't* lying and did love her. That was her first question. *Did he ever really love her?*

Maybe he did. It was possible to love two people at the same time, Avery knew. But from the beginning, he had kept a part of himself hidden from her. For that reason, they'd never had a real chance. And the worst part about it, the part that made Avery pull the sheets up over her head and cry so hard she thought her eyes might fall out, was that he hadn't really wanted them to have a chance. He'd just wanted . . . what?

That was her second question. *How did he think it was going to end?*

Noah's fiancée hadn't sounded angry or bitter on the phone. She hadn't cussed or threatened. She'd just stated the facts.

"I know about you and Noah," she'd said. "And it needs to stop."

"I didn't know," Avery had said, her voice trembling. "I truly—truly—didn't know."

Avery wondered how Noah's fiancée had found out. Was it the receipt for their hotel room in Napa last summer? Or the smell of her perfume on his clothes? The calmness of her voice, the reservation, had set Avery on edge. Had Noah done this before? Was this the cyclical pattern of their relationship—their *engagement*—with him constantly running, and her constantly bringing him home?

She got up from her bed and went to the toilet to throw up once more. *Why did this keep happening to her?* That was her third and final question.

Avery became her own judge and jury, and the conviction came swift. All the things John Collins's lawyer had said during the court-martial came back to her mind. She'd worn her dress gray uniform for her testimony, as she'd been told to do, and tried to keep her eyes away from John Collins's expressionless face as he sat next to his team of lawyers—four in total. His hair was cut short and tidy. And his eyes, bright green, followed the lead defense lawyer as he paced in front of the witness stand.

"Ms. Adams, you had a consensual sexual relationship with my client, isn't that correct?" the lawyer began.

"Yes."

"And you enjoyed these sexual liaisons?"

Avery felt her throat constrict, but she refused to be unsettled. "To be honest, the sex was mediocre, at best."

The judge cleared his throat. "Get to your point, counsel."

"Isn't it true that you initiated these sexual encounters, arriving of your own volition to Mr. Collins's dorm room repeatedly throughout the 2000–2001 school year?"

"I . . ." Avery looked to the prosecutor's table, and the lawyer there nodded. "Yes. But we both—"

"And he asked you to keep the relationship a secret, isn't that right?"

"Yes. We both chose to—"

"He was ashamed of you. Wanted to hide you away from his friends. That must have been hard to hear."

"No . . . like I said—"

"It must have hurt to think he didn't want his friends to know about you."

Avery steeled her jaw. She knew where Collins's lawyer was going with this, and she wasn't going to let him get away with it.

"What hurt was knowing that he violated an entire group of women by filming us in the privacy of our locker room and then distributing those images across campus."

"You've already testified that the images that were distributed were of you. And only you. Isn't it possible that you were angry that he'd cut off the relationship? And, feeling rejected, sent pictures of yourself to him to try and seduce him? Just like you'd done the first time?"

"No," Avery said. Hot tears had gathered in her eyes. "I . . . that's not—"

"No further questions, Your Honor," he'd said. Then he sat back down next to his client, whose green eyes twinkled in smug satisfaction.

Avery wondered now how she'd been so blind. Steadying herself against the bathroom sink—another disaster area, covered with jewelry, toothpaste splatter, and a mildewing hand towel—she stared at herself in the mirror and read the verdict aloud. *It's your fault,* she said to herself in the mirror. *This is what you keep getting, because it's what you deserve.*

Turning on the shower, she twisted the knob until the hot water covered the mirror with steam. The pressure pounded her naked body, turning the front of her stomach, arms, and legs red. As soap crossed over her body, she realized that she'd never get clean enough. Something was wrong with a person who only chose men who abused her, or abused the men that she chose.

AN HOUR LATER, Avery made her way downstairs, dressed in sweatpants and an oversized T-shirt. The window over the kitchen sink framed the Jenkins house, across the street. She filled a glass of water, and at that moment, Eric and Michelle Jenkins walked out of their front door. They were supposed to be gone by now, Avery thought—hadn't Michelle said they were visiting Eric's family for Thanksgiving?

But the couple both looked pale, like they'd caught that stomach bug everyone kept complaining about. Eric slid his hand back and forth across the top of his head and wiped his nose. Michelle's eyes were bright red, like she'd been crying. It seemed odd that they would come outside looking so disheveled, odder still that they were crossing the street toward Avery's house. *Did something happen to Bosco?* she wondered. *Or the baby?*

Avery left the kitchen to meet them at the front door. She opened it before they could even knock. They were standing on her stoop, shivering, both of them with their arms crossed over their chests.

"We came over as soon as we heard," Michelle said.

Avery felt her heart drop several inches in her chest as she stared at them with confusion all over her face. "Heard what?"

Eric and his wife exchanged a worried glance.

"We thought you knew," Eric said. "Y'all were so close."

Avery couldn't breathe. She wanted to reach out and strangle them until whatever they were talking about came exploding out of their mouths. "Who? What's going on?"

"Avery," Eric said, looking her straight in the eye. "Tim Nesmith was killed in Iraq three days ago. I'm so sorry. We thought you knew."

SEVERAL HOURS LATER, Avery had no tears left. She'd turned on her phone and it had blown up with messages—from their classmates, and from Dani, who'd left several voicemails. She was now midair, on a flight to Fayetteville.

"I don't know what's going on with you, Avery. But I'm going to need you to pull yourself out of whatever hole you're in and come get me at the airport," Dani had said in her last voicemail message. "I land tomorrow at three."

Michelle had sent Eric home and stayed with Avery for a long time, sitting next to her while she sobbed on her bed. For two years, they'd stared at one another from across the street. Avery had always assumed that Michelle hated her, but now, everything she'd ever believed was being called into question. While Avery returned phone calls and e-mails, Michelle had pulled her red hair into a bun on top of her head and busied herself picking up dirty clothes in Avery's room. She started a load of laundry, filled the sink with dirty dishes, wiped the counters, swept the floors. Emptied of all emotion, Avery didn't even have the energy to tell Michelle to stop. By the time her neighbor finally left, it was well past ten P.M., and the house was cleaner than it had been since Avery moved in two years earlier.

Michelle's kindness reminded Avery of something Wendy Bennett had said a long time ago, while they sat in that hospital waiting room. *People remember who showed up for the shitty moments far more than they remember who showed up for the party.* And for some inexplicable reason, Michelle Jenkins had shown up.

In light of everything, it became painfully clear to Avery that she'd *not* been that kind of friend. Not in years. She'd grown envious of Dani's travels and her wealth. She'd grown cold toward Hannah, too. God—she'd treated Hannah horribly. Her friend had been deployed for more than a year and Avery had done little more than send her an e-mail on her birthday. Kind, loyal, dependable Hannah. For years, Avery had taken advantage of her loyalty. She'd taken her for granted.

The clearest sign of her failure was that somehow, Dani had become the point person for every friend, acquaintance, and distant relative who wanted to express their condolences and find out how they could help. Avery lived down the street from the Nesmiths, and still, a girl who lived five time zones away had become the hub of all communication. It hurt to know that in the years since they'd graduated from West Point, she'd let her relationship with Hannah deteriorate that much. But the more Avery asked Dani what she could do, the less it seemed her friend had any answers. *Just pray,* Dani had typed in her last e-mail, sent from thirty thousand feet above the Atlantic.

*Pray.* For what? To whom?

Avery crawled into her freshly made bed with her cell phone and laptop, and tried to stop shivering. It was too horrible to imagine. From what Eric had heard through the Eighty-Second Airborne Division newswire, Tim was killed by small-arms fire in a skirmish in Samarra. Two of his soldiers had been shot, and running to their aid, Tim found himself in the midst of the cross-fire. The soldiers both survived. Tim bled out before the medical evacuation team could arrive.

Clenching her eyes closed, she tried to put those images out of her mind. The Tim she wanted to remember was the one at Thanksgiving—sitting at the table, rubbing his wife's neck. Laughing. Clinking his glass against hers. Or the one senior year, getting on one knee in front of Hannah, surrounded by rose petals and candlelight. Or the one four weeks ago, who'd dropped a key in her hand and smiled, giving her one final salute. She couldn't just sit here, thinking about him and worrying about Hannah. And so, in a rush of movement, Avery flipped open her laptop and began clicking quickly.

Flights from Austin, Texas, to Fayetteville, North Carolina, weren't cheap at the last minute. Avery clicked through a list of options on several different screens. Hannah's family would need to be here when Hannah finally got home. Then, scrolling through her phone contacts, Avery landed on Hannah's sister's name. *Emily Speer Daniels.*

Married with a two-year-old son named Jack, Emily was living in Austin with her husband. Avery had met them several times over the years: a few times at West Point, most recently at Hannah's wedding. She didn't know Emily all that well and it was possible that she was overstepping. But Avery couldn't spend another moment without doing something for her friend.

Holding the phone up to her ear, Avery heard a few voices in the background before Emily answered.

"Avery. I'm so glad you called."

"I just heard," Avery said weakly. She paused, aware that the conversation might need to move slowly.

"Yeah." Emily sighed heavily. "We're all still in shock."

"Have any of you heard from Hannah?"

"She's still in Afghanistan. They still haven't found a way to get her out of the FOB. Apparently, a sandstorm has shut everything down."

"Have you guys decided when you might come to Fort Bragg?"

"No," Emily replied. "We thought we'd wait to hear from Hannah. See when she wants us to come."

Avery knew she needed to tread lightly here. It wasn't her place to make plans for anyone else, but then again, she knew the Army well enough to know that it could be several more days before Hannah's plans were finalized.

"I've been thinking," Avery said. "I really think you need to be here as soon as possible. Things with the Army can move slow. And I don't know when Hannah will get home, but I do know she'll want you to be here when she does. I'm just a few streets down, and I've got a spare key. I'm not sure how Tim left things. So we can go get the house ready for her."

Emily was silent for a while, considering what Avery had said.

"I took the liberty of looking up some flights," Avery said. "I hope that's okay."

Emily gave a light laugh. "You're amazing, Avery. Really."

"It looks like there's one leaving Austin on Sunday morning. I've shopped a bit, and it looks like a pretty good deal." It was silent on the line, then Avery sat up in bed. The words that followed bubbled up from a place within her that she didn't know existed. "Emily, I know this may sound crazy, but I want to pay for your flights. For you, your husband, and Jack. And for your parents, too."

Avery tried to ignore the dollar signs adding up in her mind. She wasn't even sure she had that much in her savings account.

"Oh, Avery," Emily said, voice trembling. "You don't have—"

"It's not about the money. I want to."

"We couldn't possibly—"

"Please let me. I just need to do something. I'm sitting here going crazy by myself and it's the least I can do."

"Gosh," Emily said. "I don't know . . ."

"You don't even have to tell your parents. Just tell them the Army paid for it," Avery said, then chuckled. "It's not a total lie. And it's one less thing you have to do right now. Check it off your list."

Avery waited a moment while Emily blew her nose.

"Ugh, I'm such a mess," Emily said. "Okay. I think Sunday sounds good. Let's do Sunday. But that's *five* plane tickets. Are you sure?"

"I've never been more sure of anything in my life." Avery clicked "purchase" on the computer screen, then pinched the cell phone between her ear and shoulder to type with both hands. "Okay, tell me your full name . . ."

# 27

*November 19, 2006 // Camp Buehring, Kuwait*

No one ever tells you that when someone you love dies, you still have to eat.

You still have to brush your teeth and pack a bag and look at the clock and watch it ticking. No one tells you that grief feels like fear—it amps you up, making you want to run for your life, even though there's nowhere to go, no place where death will be unreal. Grief chokes you and paralyzes you, making the most menial decisions feel impossibly huge.

"Who do you want to call?" the chaplain had asked.

She'd stared at him in utter confusion. Tim. *She wanted to call Tim.*

Who do you call when your husband dies and you're twenty-four years old, alone in Afghanistan?

Who do you call when the only voice you want to hear no longer exists?

AS IF IT had chased Hannah all the way across Afghanistan, a sandstorm had arrived at FOB Sharana, hours after LTC Markham broke the news. Once again, everyone was shut up in their rooms, unable to move or operate. Trucks were halted. Helicopters grounded. Alone with her grief, Hannah waited. Two days later, the storm lifted. The chaplain told her to pack, which she'd already done, and a convoy transported Hannah eight hours from FOB Sharana to Bagram Airfield. From there, a helicopter flew her to Camp Buehring, Kuwait, where a silver-haired transportation officer told her to find a bunk in any female tent—that they'd get her on the first flight out with an available seat. Forty women slept in each tent, and for all those women knew, Hannah was going home on R & R, just like the rest of them. For all they knew, she just stayed in bed because she was lazy.

The next morning was a Sunday—the only reason Hannah knew this was because as she walked across Camp Buehring to the Mess Hall, she heard hymns coming from a tent nearby. Strong and harmonious, the voices sang a familiar song, but she didn't let them draw her in. Instead, Hannah forced herself to eat a full breakfast—though now, stretched out on a bottom cot near the door of the bunkhouse, she couldn't remember what she'd put on her plate. Everything tasted bitter. Everything tasted like nothing at all.

The mess hall tent had been decorated with orange accordion-style pumpkins and brown streamers. Fake ivy hung from the rafters and twisted down tent poles. She hadn't tasted a single thing as the meal slid down her throat. *Is food really the only thing that keeps us alive?* Hannah asked herself. If that was true, why couldn't they revive Tim with a piece of bread and a cup of wine?

She couldn't understand how a person could just end. The more her mind circled around that drain, the more she felt the beginning of a battle she would someday have to fight with God. But for now, she couldn't sleep unless she held on to her cross necklace and prayed—begged—for a moment of rest, for a moment to forget. She took Tylenol PM in the highest possible dose. When it finally came, sleep was relief, but when she woke up, the nightmare began all over again.

Hannah cried through much of the second night at Camp Buehring, grateful for the girl in the bunk above her, whose snores muffled her sobs. She envied army wives who got to hear the worst news of their lives in the comfort of their own homes. There were three parts of her heart: One that wanted to get on a plane and run away from this place. Another part that wanted to dig a hole in the ground, get inside, and never get out. And the third, loudest part of her heart wanted a bomb to drop right on top of her—because that was the only thing that made sense. If he was gone, she wanted to be gone too.

IN THE MORNING, her cell phone rang.

Hannah stared at it for a long time, reading her sister's name on the caller ID. If she didn't answer, she could go on pretending for a few minutes that Tim was still alive, that there had been a mistake, that some other young soldier with the same name had been killed. That some other girl was about to hear news that would shatter her life. That Hannah could piece hers together again.

But the phone kept ringing.

She'd ignored every single call that she possibly could. She'd spoken to Tim's parents from the satellite phone on FOB Sharana, and the ache in Margaret Nesmith's voice sank Hannah's heart so deeply, she already feared seeing them once she made it back to the States. Hannah was completely submerged in the grief of losing a husband; she couldn't carry the weight of their loss, too. Tim was a husband. A son. A friend. He was a different person to everyone he knew—filling a thousand different roles. But Hannah could only grieve one Tim at a time.

Text messages from Dani and others kept pouring in, but Hannah couldn't respond. She didn't know what she would possibly say. But Emily had called three times in a row now. So finally, with a heavy arm, Hannah reached for the phone and spent the energy it took to open it and place it on her ear.

"Hey." Her sister's voice was so slow and soft. So unlike her normal voice. "Did you make it to Kuwait?"

"Yes."

"What are you doing now?"

"Sitting on my bunk."

"Have you opened the letter?"

Hannah peered at the stack of books at the foot of her bunk. A Bible. *East of Eden,* with the corner of page three hundred dog-eared to hold her spot. Neither of which she had opened. In the middle of the Bible she could see the small white edge of a letter, acting like a bookmark. The chaplain had handed Hannah the letter just before she'd boarded the helicopter at Bagram Airfield. Covered in Tim's signature all-caps handwriting, it was postmarked November 12. The day he'd left on a ten-day mission into Samarra. One day before insurgents opened fire, sending three bullets into the chest of a soldier in Tim's platoon. Before her husband ran to stop the bleeding and sixteen shots ripped through his chest, ending his life. The day before her husband died, he'd written her a letter.

Every moment, it felt like an elephant was stepping on her chest. She couldn't breathe. *This isn't your life,* she told herself as she stared at the edge of the letter. *This can't be happening.* She hadn't had a moment alone since the chaplain had handed her the letter and she didn't want to open it until she could scream and wail as loud as she wanted.

"Hannah?"

"No. I haven't."

"Okay."

Hannah placed the phone beside her head and listened to her sister breathing. Hot tears created a warm wet circle where her cheek met the pillow.

After some time had passed, Emily said, "Any update on when you'll be back?"

The words made whatever was in Hannah's stomach start to swirl. Like something was in the back of her throat, pushing on all sides of her esophagus. "No," she said.

Silence.

"Okay. Well we're trying to decide if we should stay at the house with you or get a hotel. Either way. Whatever you want."

"It doesn't matter," Hannah said. But even as the words came out of her mouth, she knew it did. She had an opinion. She just didn't know what it was. She couldn't find it in her head. But it was there.

"Okay. We'll be here waiting for you when you get home."

LIKE EVERY OTHER building, the transportation office was a series of small offices, all inside a large tent. Fans whirred and buzzed in every corner, and men passed Hannah in beige camouflage uniforms, unconcerned about her presence. They didn't know what she was doing or why she was here, which made no sense. She felt like a part of her body had been ripped off. The fact that everyone didn't stare seemed absolutely impossible. How could a loss that big be that invisible?

By the afternoon, no one had come to retrieve Hannah and send her home. She wondered if they'd forgotten about her, the war widow, in the back of the bunkhouse. Days could pass before they remembered. Weeks.

So pulling herself up, Hannah had walked across Camp Buehring, to the office of the man in charge of outgoing flight manifestos. After she'd waited for more than an hour outside of his office, Lieutenant Colonel Williams stepped out of his door and waved her inside.

"Sorry about the wait, Lieutenant Nesmith," he said. "What can I do for you?"

The colonel leaned forward in his desk chair, brown eyes full of a sickeningly sweet emotion that Hannah realized she'd have to get used to: pity. He had three combat patches on his uniform, dark eyebrows, and steely eyes that seemed to look both at Hannah and beyond her.

"I understand you're trying to get home," he said. "Emergency leave."

"Yes, sir. I don't mean to bother you. I just want to know if there are any updates. I heard there's a flight leaving tomorrow."

"Unfortunately, there's not an open seat." He spoke so quickly, it felt like he'd slapped her across the face. "The R & R schedule has been set for months. You understand. These soldiers have plans with their families. I can't schedule your flight without bumping someone else."

Hannah felt her throat tighten, like she was being strangled by an invisible hand.

"But, sir, I really . . . I need to go home. Doesn't emergency leave give me any precedence?"

Cruelty was staring grief in the face and pointing to a spreadsheet.

Hannah didn't try to stop herself from crying. She let the tears fall onto her uniform, right in front of him. He could say no. But she couldn't shield him from the pain of that denial. She was done following the rules. She wondered why she'd ever followed them in the first place.

"Please don't make me beg for this. I've done everything you've asked of me. I voluntarily put my life on hold. I left my family and friends behind. I dug the trenches and built the tents and led my soldiers. I haven't complained. Not once. But now? Now that I actually have to grieve the war you asked me to wage? You say I have to wait? How can America ask me to sacrifice everything I have to give . . . *everything* . . ." Her voice broke. "And now to deny my request when I'm begging, begging to go home? Sir. It's been a week. Please let me go home."

"I wish there were something I could do," he said, his eyes softening.

"There is, sir," Hannah said. "You can put me on that plane."

He sighed, looked at his computer, and began rubbing his temples.

"All right," he said finally. "Let me see what I can do."

28

*November 20, 2006 // Fort Bragg, North Carolina*

Dani had arrived at Fayetteville Regional Airport late in the afternoon on Friday, feeling jet-lagged and exhausted. Inside the terminal, countless men in uniform had moved in and out with purpose—though it had been hard for Dani to tell who was coming and who was going. The men leaving held their wives close while their children cried. The men arriving did the same thing.

Avery had pulled up to the arrivals pickup lane in her rusty old Honda Civic, dressed in jeans and a gray hoodie. It had been more than a year since they'd seen one another, but Avery's massive CD case of angry alternative nineties music still rested on the passenger seat. The sight of it had given Dani a sense of nostalgia and comfort. Cheekbones high, ankles exposed, Avery looked thinner than Dani had ever seen her, with her bright blond hair piled on top of her head. But even if their bodies had changed,

Dani hoped their hearts would be found in the same place. It was time for the cult to make good on its promises.

"Thank God you're here," Avery had said, wrapping her arms around Dani's neck. They didn't cry—it was too surreal for that. Instead, they'd loaded Dani's luggage in the trunk and drove down the highway in silence.

AN HOUR LATER, they'd sat staring at the Nesmiths' front door, arguing about what to do. Two blue-star flags hung side by side in the window. The shrubs were slightly overgrown, the yard full of leaves. Inside, not a single light was on. It looked like it had been abandoned. Which, in a way, it had.

"I can't do this," Avery had said.

"We have to," Dani replied. "She can't go into the house with it like that. We have to turn on some lights. Turn on the heat."

"He was the last person in there." Avery held the key that Tim had given her in the palm of her hand. It was the color of her hair, Dani had noticed. Bright gold.

"He gave it to you in case something like this happened. Man up. We can do this. We don't have a choice."

With that, they'd walked to the front door. Avery carefully turned the key in the dead bolt, and then the door had opened, spilling sunlight all over the scene. Knowing that Hannah would come home from Afghanistan before he returned from Iraq, Tim had strung a banner across the stairwell with the words *WELCOME HOME* painted in big gold letters. There were multicolored balloons all over the floor.

"Oh God." Avery had put her hands to her face.

Dani had exhaled loudly and kicked a blue balloon out of her way. She hadn't expected this. Clearly, from the pained look on Avery's face, neither had she. Together, they had slumped onto the bottom stair and kicked the balloons in silence. Avery had been wearing a pair of brown leather boots, Dani a brand-new pair of hot pink sneakers.

It didn't seem fair that they were there, in Hannah's house, while she was still stuck in the Middle East, alone with her grief. At the time, Dani wasn't sure it was the right thing to do. But sometimes, when tragedy strikes, you just have to act. And if Dani were in Hannah's shoes, she wouldn't want to crush the last of her husband's breath out of the universe. There are some things a person just shouldn't have to do.

"What are you doing?" Avery had shouted when Dani jumped up and started stomping on the balloons with her foot. "Stop! Shouldn't we leave it?"

"I'm not leaving it like this." Dani had spat back. "She shouldn't"—*pop!*—"have to"—*pop!*—"do it." *Pop! Pop!*

Haltingly, Avery had stood from the stairs and joined her. Together, they'd slammed their heels into rubber, sending the sound of gunshots throughout the house.

ON SUNDAY, HANNAH'S family had arrived in a rental van from the airport, looking like the flight had gone through severe turbulence, although Hannah's sister, Emily, promised Dani the flight was fine. Dani knew that Hannah hated when people said she looked just like her mother, but the resemblance was striking. Lynn Speer had always looked young for her age, but as she'd approached the house, carrying her luggage, that no longer seemed true. The weight of grief had transformed her face. The skin underneath her eyes was thin and blue, like translucent paper. She had two deep wrinkles between her eyebrows. She looked like she hadn't slept in days. The sight of Lynn, like an aged version of Hannah, had made tears come to Dani's eyes. They'd held each other on the sidewalk for a very long time, neither of them daring to say a word.

She'd received a long, warm hug from each member of Hannah's family, ending with Hannah's father, Bill. He'd looked just as he had a few years earlier, when she'd seen him at West Point's graduation: tall, with a thick gray mustache and his signature University of Texas ballcap. He'd wrapped an arm around Dani's shoulders and kissed her cheek. And though his body had felt sturdy, his voice had wavered.

"It's going to be all right," he'd said, sounding unconvinced. "It's all going to be all right."

But nothing was right. Hannah still had not boarded a flight out of Kuwait. Dani left London in such a hurry, and now, all she could do was sit around in silence, aching for the fact that the one person who needed to be in the comfort of her own home wasn't.

Hannah's family moved their luggage into the house, but tried not to touch or disturb a single thing. Tim had left Post-it notes everywhere, little surprises for his wife to find when she returned from her deployment. His handwriting hovered around every corner. *You grow more beautiful every day*—stuck to the mirror in the hall bathroom. *RILY*—waiting on Hannah's bedside table. *I like the way you smell after PT*—a joke left on her sneakers in the closet. No one had dared move a single one, but Dani had begun to feel like she was avoiding a ghost.

That night, she'd slept at Avery's house, only to wake up and walk down the street to Hannah and Tim's, where everyone was keeping vigil, waiting in pained silence. Emily and her husband, Mark, were in the backyard chasing Jack, who didn't realize that this was not a time to be rambunctious. Inside, Bill Speer had claimed a seat in front of the TV, while Lynn sat at the dining room table, where she drank from a seemingly bottomless mug of coffee. Dani had joined Lynn at the table when Tim's parents finally arrived, their presence bringing with it an even heavier darkness. And even quieter silence.

It had struck Dani on her flight across the Atlantic that in losing their only son, Margaret and Charlie Nesmith had lost their entire family. Hannah had told Dani that after several miscarriages and years of waiting, they'd decided to put their savings into adoption, which brought Tim into their lives. For that reason, they'd put immeasurable pressure on themselves to be perfect parents. Where Tim was strong and vivacious, the Nesmiths were short, round about the middle, and awkward in large social settings. While Tim jumped out of airplanes and lived without fear, his parents seemed to be the worrying type, even before he'd left for war. And though the Nesmiths looked and acted nothing like their son, Dani remembered the thick laughter that came from their bellies at Hannah and Tim's wedding—the joy they found in their son's happiness. That much was never in question. They loved him unconditionally. And now they would grieve him unconditionally, too.

When Margaret and Charlie arrived at the house, there was

nothing to do except welcome the awkwardness with open arms. Dani stood in the kitchen while Margaret Nesmith spread her son's SRP paperwork out on the dining room table. All four adults sat down, staring at the papers, knowing there was nothing to decide. Two still had their child. Two had had theirs ripped away. There were moments you couldn't put into words, and seeing the Nesmiths stare at those papers was enough to send Dani back to bed in the middle of the day. Without making any announcement, she slipped out the front door and walked back to Avery's house.

THAT MORNING, AVERY had left a note for Dani on the kitchen counter.

*Headed to work. I'll be done around 6:30 tonight. Text me and let me know how things are going. Tell Wendy I can't wait to see her. —A*

Dani tried to answer a few work e-mails from Avery's living room couch, but the thought of discussing Gelhomme's latest commercials made her head spin. Her e-mails sounded garbled and confusing. She couldn't seem to focus or communicate with any clarity. And so, after an hour of effort with little to show for it, she shut her computer.

The clock seemed to move at a snail's pace. Outside, a breeze blew leaves up off the ground and back down again. Over the weekend, Eric Jenkins had raked and bagged all the leaves in the Nesmiths' yard, and Avery's as well. Seated at a round table in the kitchen, looking at the empty street outside Avery's window, Dani tried to think.

With their bullets, insurgents in Iraq hadn't just killed Tim. They'd sent aftershocks to Afghanistan, London, Texas, Maryland, Ohio, North Carolina . . . the list went on and on. One of their classmates stationed in Korea had just sent Dani an e-mail, asking where he could send flowers. People all over the world were dealing with the fact that enough evil existed on the planet to end the life of someone so young, with so much promise. That was the real cost of war, Dani thought. The aftermath.

It was difficult to grieve for Tim, because all Dani could do was think about Hannah. She'd tried to imagine her friend, alone in the desert, hearing the news. Convoying for eight hours with practical strangers. Knowing that somewhere in the world, her husband's body was broken in pieces. In every memory Dani could conjure of Tim, he was running, laughing, moving, sweating, or soaring through the air. How can someone that alive all of a sudden not be alive at all?

*And what for?*

Dani shut that line of thinking down quickly in her mind. She couldn't let politics cloud what needed to happen first, which was for Hannah to get home and be surrounded by the people who loved her most.

AT ONE O'CLOCK, a white Chrysler minivan pulled into Avery's driveway, saving Dani from her thoughts. Walking out into the cold, Dani waved at the driver and waited for her to unbuckle her seat belt and get out of the van.

Wendy didn't even shut the door behind her. Arms open wide, she fell into Dani's embrace, her body shaking from dry sobs. It was odd to Dani, to feel like the strong one. Wendy had always been the supporter, the cook, the listening ear, the shoulder to cry on. And now, it was Dani who held her up, keeping her from falling to the ground. After wiping her eyes, Wendy and Dani climbed back in her van.

On military installations, the commissary looked exactly like a civilian grocery store, but the products were tax free. That's why you had to have a military ID to get inside, and why Dani was so grateful that Wendy had arrived. Grabbing a grocery cart, Wendy showed her military ID to a security guard at the door and explained that Dani was her guest.

"What should we make?" Wendy asked, when they'd walked inside.

The plan was to stock Hannah's freezer with meals. Crowd pleasers. Things that their families could eat for days or weeks, if need be. They decided not to cook a traditional Thanksgiving, even though the day was fast approaching. Instead, Dani tried to remember which of Wendy's meals Hannah had loved the most.

When they were at West Point, every time they'd gone to the Bennetts' house—whether it was to simply have a break from the barracks or to have a full-on breakdown—Wendy had always had something delicious waiting on the kitchen counter. Lasagnas, spaghetti, fried chicken. Brownies, pies, and apple fritters. That woman only lived in New York because the Army had stationed her there, so even if there was snow outside, there was always warm Southern hospitality inside. "Oh, this old thing?" Wendy would always say when someone complimented her cooking.

She'd follow up with her favorite line from the movie *Steel Magnolias*: "'*It's in the "freezes beautifully" section of my cookbook.*'"

The memory made Dani smile.

If Dani wanted to cook, she had to grocery-shop from a hand-written list, but Wendy had so much experience in the kitchen, she knew what they needed by heart. Ingredients for lasagna and chili filled Wendy's cart, as they roamed the aisles mindlessly. As they walked side by side, Dani wondered how grief would affect Hannah's appetite. And not just for food. She wondered if Hannah would ever again have an appetite for life.

"So, what's it been like at the house?" Wendy asked. She pulled four cans of diced tomatoes off a shelf and put them in the cart.

Dani sighed. "Really quiet. Tim's parents got here this morning. But there's just nothing to do until Hannah gets back. So it's just..."

"Hurry up and wait," Wendy said, finishing Dani's sentence.

Dani nodded. "I can't stop thinking about her. Over there, still waiting. It's got to be excruciating."

"It's hard now. But she's still in shock. The hardest parts will come later. Six weeks from now. Six years."

"I just don't understand how this could happen," Dani said. "It still feels so surreal. It feels like a mistake. Like he's still out there."

"Mark said when Tim was in his class, he was late every single day. That he never completed the reading."

"I could see that," Dani said, and then smiled. She remembered sitting against the trees during Beast, helping him memorize passages from the plebe handbook. "He was so fun. I think that's what I'm worried about. Hannah can be so serious. Tim . . . he always made sure she had fun."

Wendy stopped, looked at her cart. "Oh shoot," she said. "What am I doing? I forgot the stuff for the soup."

"I've been doing that too!" Dani said. "I can't think straight. I feel like I'm walking through a cloud."

"I guess, in a way, you are," Wendy said.

And then they turned the cart around and walked back to the beginning.

A FEW HOURS later, Dani and Wendy unpacked the ingredients they'd purchased at the grocery store and got to work making lasagna in Avery's kitchen. Tomato sauce and cheese were off-limits for Dani's anti-inflammatory diet, but suddenly all those dietary rules didn't seem to matter anymore. They needed to eat. And if she had pain, she had pain. At least she was alive to feel it.

Her knife sliced through a raw onion, pulling sharp tears from her eyes. Meanwhile, Wendy smashed garlic cloves to release them from their paper skins. Dani cut fast and hard, letting the anger and her sadness come through the blade. Soon, the kitchen filled with the savory aroma of minced garlic and onions simmering in oil. Wendy stirred them together with a wooden spoon.

"You know," she said, looking at the little white pieces caramelizing in the heat, "when the girls were little, I used to hate it if Mark got home from work and I hadn't started on dinner. So I would just chop some onion and garlic real quick and sauté it in a pan. That way, when he got home, the house would smell like I was cooking, even if I had no idea what I was going to make yet."

"Nice trick," Dani said.

"I've always found it interesting that when you cook, everything has to be sliced, peeled, or smashed in order to be used. The best flavors come out when the ingredients are broken and exposed to heat."

Dani nodded.

"I think that's true for us, too. Faith isn't really faith until it's beat up and put through a fire. When you're crushed, you feel like you're dying. But you're actually coming to life. When you're broken, that's when the best of you comes out."

As good as that sounded—as true as it felt—it didn't make the sting of the onion in Dani's eyes any less painful.

Later, when the lasagna was baking in the oven, Wendy stood at the sink cleaning dishes.

"What ever happened to that guy Avery was dating?" Wendy asked. "The one that came to Boston?"

"Noah," Dani said. "To be honest, she hasn't said anything about him since I've been here. I don't know."

"And you?" Wendy didn't look up from her work. "Any guys in London I should know about?"

Dani shook her head.

"Well then. When are you going to tell me about the wedding?"

Dani sighed, handed Wendy the dirty cheese grater, and then sat down at Avery's kitchen table. "How much time do you have?"

29

*November 23, 2006 // Fort Bragg, North Carolina*

On Thanksgiving morning, Avery woke up fully clothed, sleeping next to Dani. It was still dark. The only light in the room came from an orange floodlight outside, cutting through the blinds. After two years of five A.M. wakeup calls for her job with the Army, Avery no longer had the ability to sleep in. She envied Dani's even breathing, the sure sign that she was deep in a REM cycle, and wondered how late she'd stayed up talking with Wendy Bennett, who'd driven down from West Point a few days earlier.

Wendy had rented a hotel room nearby, for her and Mark, who would fly in for the funeral and drive back with his wife. As time went on, more and more family and friends would arrive, Avery knew, filling hotel rooms and the Nesmiths' house. Avery worried that Hannah would feel overwhelmed by the sheer number of people. She worried too that Hannah wouldn't even want to see Avery. It was possible Avery had damaged their relationship beyond repair.

Fearing she might wake Dani with her tossing and turning, Avery rubbed her eyes and slipped out of the room without making a sound.

When the coffee finished brewing, Avery poured herself a cup and went to the living room, where she turned on the television, making sure to keep the volume on low. The *Today* show news team reported from the Upper West Side of New York City, waiting for the start of the Thanksgiving Day Parade. Avery's cell phone rested on the coffee table, conspicuously silent. It had been two weeks since Noah's fiancée had answered his phone. Since then, Avery had cradled her phone in her hands almost constantly, willing herself not to contact him, while simultaneously hoping he'd text or call. If they spoke again, would he try to justify what he'd done? Would he pretend it had never happened? Or would he simply disappear, free to proceed with his life, his marriage, his future, without feeling the consequences?

Over the last few days, as Avery had spent time in Hannah's house, it was impossible not to see the differences between her relationship to Noah and that between Hannah and Tim. Tim had left handwritten notes to Hannah all over their house. Everywhere Avery turned, there were photos of them together— including one on Hannah's bedside table of the couple in Rome. In it, Tim was smiling so wide. He held Hannah up off the ground, like a husband would carry his wife over the threshold of a new house. Avery had taken that picture. And even then, she remembered looking through the lens and feeling a sort of reverent melancholy. Not once had a guy looked at Avery the way Tim looked at Hannah: He was only smiles. Only pride. Only encouragement. And Noah? What was he?

Only absent. Only mystery. Only smoke.

No matter what people said, Avery knew they were wrong about the truth. The truth didn't set you free; it chased you down. It came at you from behind, gained speed, and then eventually overtook you until you could no longer deny its power. Lies might have been fast, but truth had endurance. And it would always outlast the competition.

Avery pulled her knees into her chest and let the tears fall on her cheeks. She held her phone in her hands and opened it and closed it, over and over again, wishing for a call to come through.

She hadn't told Dani about Noah, nor had she told her about the letter she'd received about John Collins's parole. With the money and resources in Collins's family, he would probably have a job on Wall Street in no time at all. It seemed completely unfair to Avery. Why did these men get to get away with their violence? Why did they get to move on from their crimes, while she felt so trapped by them?

"What time is it?"

Dani's groggy voice suddenly broke through Avery's thoughts. Avery turned and saw Dani standing in the dark hallway, rubbing her eyes.

"Six thirty," Avery said.

"My body is so confused. I never wake up this early. But it's like, noon in London."

"I made coffee," Avery said, lifting her mug. "Oh wait. You don't do caffeine anymore. I forgot."

Dani waved off Avery's concern, padded into the kitchen, and returned with a hot mug of her own. She sank into the other side of Avery's couch, under a thick blanket. "I'm not supposed to drink the stuff," she said, taking a long sip. "But I need it right now."

"Did you sleep okay?"

Dani shook her head. "I just keep thinking about her stuck over there."

"They can't keep her there forever." Avery shook her head as tears welled in her eyes. "I doubt she'll even want to see me when she gets back."

"That's not true."

"I flaked on her so many times last year. And for . . . such stupid reasons."

"Hindsight is an unfair standard to use against yourself," Dani replied.

Avery took a deep breath and another sip of coffee. It felt strange to be sitting so close to Dani and yet to feel so far away. A huge wall existed between them, built with bricks of time and distance and things left unsaid. But if Tim's death had taught her anything, it was that you couldn't waste a single moment with the people you love. As much as it was going to hurt, she had to muster the energy and scale that wall.

"I got a letter," Avery said finally, dispassionately. "I got it this summer, actually. I guess I just was trying to pretend it didn't matter."

Dani's eyes grew a few sizes larger. She put her coffee mug down and looked at Avery with concern.

"John Collins got paroled."

"Oh, Avery."

"I sure know how to pick 'em, don't I?" she continued, surprised by the sarcasm in her voice. "Every guy I've ever dated has ended up screwing me over. Or maybe I'm the one screwing myself over. God. Listen to me. Complaining about my life when Hannah—"

"Don't do that," Dani said, this time with force. "Do you hear yourself? Do you ever give yourself a break? A second to breathe? To feel what you're actually feeling before judging yourself so harshly?"

"That's the problem. I don't *feel* anything. I'm completely numb."

Avery felt hot tears form in the backs of her eyes, and soon, they were falling. How did Dani do it? She could always cut straight through the crap and directly to the heart of the matter.

"I don't feel like I deserve to feel upset about my life," Avery admitted. "I should be fine."

"You should *be* what you *are*," said Dani. "Sure. Your husband didn't just get killed. But your *friend* did. And all of this other stuff? The letter? That matters too. You don't have to be so strong all the time."

They sat in silence, letting their coffees go cold.

"You said every guy you've ever dated screwed you over," Dani said, disturbing the quiet. She let the statement linger in the air, without turning it into a question. But the subtext was clear.

Avery chewed on her cheeks. It was so complicated. Ever since she was a little girl, she'd learned that the only way to survive life was to suck it up. Hold it together. Get the grades. Earn the stripes. Go faster than anyone else, and never let them see you cry. She'd trained herself to be harder than she really was and couldn't fathom opening the box in which she'd carefully packed away her grief. Her weakness. If she opened it, she was pretty sure it would swallow her whole.

"He's engaged."

"You're joking."

"You and Hannah, last Thanksgiving . . . you tried to tell me. And I wouldn't listen. I didn't want to see what was right in front of me."

"We thought he was *aloof*," said Dani. "We didn't think he was *engaged*."

"He never took me to his place. Never introduced me to any of his friends. I was so blind." Avery shook her head and wiped her eyes with the sides of her forefingers. "And you know the worst part about it? That girl is going to *marry him*. I'm sure he's just groveling at her feet, telling her it was all some huge mistake. As if I was some seductress that pulled him into my web. But we were together for *a year*. He talked about buying us a *house*, Dani."

"He met your family!"

"He met my family!" Avery repeated, groaning at the thought of having to tell her mother.

"How did you find out?" asked Dani.

"I called him and his fiancée answered his phone," said Avery. "I think she found a way to unlock his phone. She said she'd read all of our texts. I haven't heard from him since." She laid her head in Dani's lap and let her friend stroke her hair. On the television, all the Macy's Thanksgiving Day Parade balloons floated above brownstones, ready for their march down Sixth Avenue.

"You know, you're not the only one that's made mistakes," Dani said after some time had passed. "I was so afraid of losing Locke as a friend, I never took the risk to tell him how I really felt, until it was too late."

"The wedding," Avery said, feeling herself cringe. She sat up and put her face in her hands. "Oh, Dani, I didn't even ask how it went."

"It's okay. It was hard, you know? Seeing him with her. And she's so nice," Dani said with a roll of her eyes. "Her dad works at the Citadel, so it was this whole big Southern wedding, which was just weird, seeing him marry someone so white, and all the things that come with that. I read scripture at the ceremony."

"No you didn't."

"I did," said Dani. "In a gorgeous gown, of course. I looked great. But I felt terrible. I just wished I could go back and do it all over again."

"What would you do differently?"

"I wouldn't be so afraid." Dani paused. "As a woman, you don't want to be the one that makes the first move. But now I realize if I had, I could have gotten it over with a long time ago. I could have saved myself a lot of pain."

"Is that the point?" Avery said. "Saving ourselves from pain?"

"I guess not."

"You did the best you could. Maybe deep down, you knew he wasn't the right one. And so you just let it play out. You can't fault yourself for that."

"And you can't fault yourself for believing Noah."

"Yes I can," Avery said. "I mean, thanks. But I'm realizing now, I can't keep blaming everyone else, like I'm some kind of victim. With Noah, I knew there were red flags; I just pretended they weren't there. I *wanted* to believe him. That was my choice. And I have to own that, or else I'm going to keep doing the same thing over and over again. I deserve better than to dupe myself into a relationship simply because I don't want to be alone."

Dani raised her eyebrows and nodded slowly, as if she was impressed.

"Dang, Avery," she said. "Did you just have a breakthough?"

"Yeah. Maybe I did."

"You know we can't talk about this stuff with Hannah," Dani added. "When she gets home."

"Oh my God, of course not," said Avery.

"We have to just put all this aside and focus on caring for her. She's going to be inundated with people. But you and me, we can be her buffer."

Avery sighed, picking up her coffee mug and feeling the cold porcelain in her hand. She needed a refill.

"I just can't believe she's still not home."

30

*November 27, 2006 // Fayetteville Regional Airport*

T welve days after learning that Tim had been killed, Hannah felt the lurch of the airplane as its wheels touched down in Fayetteville. After begging him for mercy, LTC Williams had finally put her on a flight from Kuwait to Germany. Then she'd taken three commercial flights—Germany to New York, New York to Atlanta, Atlanta to Fayetteville.

While the final plane taxied up to the gate, a stewardess reminded the passengers that the seat belt sign was still on and not to move from their seats. The man seated next to Hannah pulled out his cell phone and turned it on. A woman a few rows ahead reapplied her lipstick, blood red. The cabin grew hot and stuffy as passengers donned their jackets and scarves, preparing to battle the cold outside. Tim would never get another winter, Hannah realized. He wouldn't be there to celebrate another Christmas or his birthday or even go on that trip to Hawaii they'd planned to take when their deployments were over. Every realization was a new death. He died a million times a day in her mind.

Pulling her camouflage rucksack down from the overhead compartment, Hannah found her tiny flip phone inside, powered off. Normally, after a long flight, she would have immediately shot off a few text messages to tell her family that she'd arrived. But she had no desire to turn it on. It only brought bad news, thin apologies, and people's *thoughts and prayers,* which, to Hannah, felt like a really poor response to someone's life ending. She was grateful in some ways that people cared enough to reach out. But she couldn't text back, *I don't want your prayers. I want Tim back.* So she'd stopped looking at her phone altogether.

Finally, when the flight attendant at the front of the cabin opened the airplane door, the passengers filled the aisle, trapped in a long line of anticipation, eager to get off the plane and back to the people they loved. The cabin was airless and all the energy pushed forward, though people weren't moving at all. Hannah's body surrendered to a cold sweat.

"Thank you for your service," said the woman with red lips. "I'm sure you're glad to be home."

Hannah stared at the woman with grotesque horror and felt a surge of bile in her throat. She fought the urge to scream. The woman's words were like sandpaper over an open wound. Hannah's neck turned red, and she touched her forehead with her hand. It was clammy. She saw the people at the front of the plane shuffling out, but she still couldn't move.

She didn't know it was going to feel like this. Like every moment that passed was a step deeper into grief. She wanted to be walking straight. Instead, every step forward felt like a step down.

Eventually, the plane cleared and Hannah made her way through the terminal. It had been ten days of this. Ten days of moving, waiting, and remembering, with nowhere to go where Tim wasn't dead. *Dead.* The word had no meaning anymore; she'd thought it too many times.

Her soldiers had convoyed to the next building site in Afghanistan without her. She didn't care. Grief had filled her with a kind of numbness she'd never experienced before. She felt either far too much and wanted to hold back, or far too little and wondered why she couldn't muster any emotion. Most of all, she was tired and hungry and angry at herself for being tired and hungry. How could she eat when Tim would never get to taste ice cream or bite into a peach ever again? How could she sleep when Tim's eyes had been shut forever? She didn't want to live in a world he wasn't in. She didn't want to go to sleep and add another day to the days he'd been gone. Someday, Hannah thought, she would have more days without him than the days she'd had with him.

And just like that, he died again.

EVENTUALLY, SHE FOUND herself at the top of an escalator, with the sign for baggage claim pointing down. She took a deep breath, adjusted her backpack, and stepped on the moving staircase.

They waited at the bottom of the escalator. Her mother, wearing a gray turtleneck. Her father, standing tall with his silver mustache, wearing a black half-zip sweater. Emily and Mark, holding a squirming Jack in their arms. Dani and Avery, one in a leather jacket, the other in uniform. Hannah buried her face in her father's shoulder.

"You're home, sweetie," said Bill. "You're home."

They hugged quietly for a long time.

31

*November 28, 2006 // Fort Bragg, North Carolina*

The house was quiet early the next morning, when Dani heard the doorbell ring. She pulled on a pair of black sweatpants and stepped into the hallway, carefully tiptoeing around Hannah's father, who'd slept on a pile of blankets right outside Hannah's door. Hannah's neighbor, Michelle Jenkins, had brought over a spare air mattress, and Dani and Avery had blown it up in the upstairs office, sleeping next to unpacked boxes of books. Avery had already left for work, and even though it was ten A.M., no one had made the coffee. No one had dared wake Hannah up.

Dani was certain she would never forget the way Hannah had looked when she'd moved slowly down that escalator at the airport. Her face appeared ghost white. Her eyes bulged, her skin pulled taut with fear. Grief had aged her, and she looked sixty years old—even her hair looked tinged with gray. When they'd arrived back at the house, Hannah had walked straight to their bedroom, their closet, where she'd pulled a pile of his clothes to her face. Dani and Avery had waited outside the door, sitting in the hall. After hours of crying, Hannah had crawled into the bed, laid her head on his shirts, and finally fell asleep.

Downstairs, Dani opened Hannah's front door, just as a man in uniform reached to ring the doorbell again.

"Mrs. Nesmith?" the man asked. The man had brown eyes, dark brown hair, and a slightly Hispanic accent. He wore an Army combat uniform and held a stack of binders under his arm.

"She's upstairs," Dani explained. "Can I help you?"

"I'm Captain Huerta," he said, offering his hand to shake Dani's. "Mrs. Nesmith's casualty assistance officer." He checked his watch. "We had an appointment at ten. Do you mind if I come in?"

Ten minutes later, having rustled Hannah out of her bed, Dani sat next to her at the dining room table. Margaret Nesmith had arrived just after Captain Huerta, and seeing one another for the first time, she and Hannah embraced while the rest of them looked on in silence, willing themselves invisible. Dani knew she wasn't family—in some ways she didn't have a right to sit at this table. But Hannah had asked Dani to stay by her side, and now she was grateful she'd agreed. Seated on the same side of the table as Captain Huerta, Margaret Nesmith wore her dark hair in a low ponytail. Like Hannah's, her face and lips were the color of the third casket Captain Huerta had offered as an option: eggshell white.

Hannah held the binder full of pictures of caskets in her hands. One page displayed a cherrywood box, and the next page, black onyx. She flipped through the pages blankly, like she couldn't see anything at all.

Dani stared from the binder up to the face of Captain Huerta seated across from them. She was grateful that he hadn't tried to hurry Hannah along, although Dani could tell from the other binders in his bag that there were many other decisions to be made. Decisions no twenty-four-year-old should ever have to make. Choosing the coffin. Choosing the flowers. A location for the burial. Hannah looked at Dani, her eyes pleading for help.

"I think this one is beautiful," Dani said, pointing to an all-wood casket near the front.

Tim's mother lifted her chin to see. Dani turned the binder so she could see it more directly. "I like that," Margaret said. "It's classic. Like Tim."

Dani watched Hannah tense up at that statement, and knew exactly why. Tim wasn't *classic*. In Hannah's eyes, he was wild and willing to break the rules and so different from the parents who'd raised him. But Dani could see that all the fight had gone out of her.

"Okay." Hannah pushed the binder back to Captain Huerta. "We'll go with that one."

Dani watched her take a sip of water and place the glass back on the coaster. Every motion slow, purposeful, and pained.

"Can I ask a question?" Margaret Nesmith began, her voice a respectful whisper. Her eyes filled with tears and she wiped a tissue under her nose. "Where is he? Where have they taken him?"

The question hung in the air for several moments, awkward

and cumbersome, like a piece of furniture too large to fit through a door. Dani saw Hannah clench her jaw.

"Your son's remains are at the mortuary," Captain Huerta explained. "His remains are viewable for identification purposes only. That's something we'll need to schedule for you, Hannah. But more importantly, right now, we need to choose a date for the funeral. Do you have a day in mind?"

"December fifth." Hannah and her mother-in-law said it at the same time. He nodded at both of them, then wrote down the date.

"And location?"

"Springfield," Tim's mother answered. "Maryland. Our hometown."

A moment of silence passed, full of awkwardness and tension as thick as fog. Dani turned to Hannah. It was time for her friend to break this next piece of news. Last night, Hannah had told Dani that she didn't want Tim to be buried in Maryland. The only thing she'd decided about the funeral—the only thing Hannah seemed to care about at all—was that it took place where Tim would have wanted it to be.

"Actually, Margaret, we're waiting to hear back from Arlington National Cemetery," Dani explained, speaking on Hannah's behalf.

The elder Mrs. Nesmith looked confused and sad, her blue eyes swimming. "Hannah, we have a family plot in Maryland. We've already made arrangements."

Captain Huerta closed his binder. "Perhaps that's enough decision making for one day."

SEVERAL HOURS LATER, Dani sat in the living room, quietly listening to the terse conversation happening in the kitchen. She'd texted Wendy earlier that it wasn't a good time to come over, but that if she and Mark had any connections at Arlington National Cemetery, they'd appreciate their making some calls. Dani had asked Emily to write Tim's obituary and had called Eric to see if he could help make a list of the forms that Hannah would have to fill out for Tim's life insurance to kick in. The amount of bureaucracy that came after a death was enough to make your head spin. Dani wanted to shield Hannah from as much of that as possible.

"Maybe this isn't the best time to have this conversation," Hannah's mother was saying in the kitchen.

Tim's mother tried to whisper, but her voice came out louder than she'd likely intended. "Well, when *is* the best time? He's been gone for two weeks and I think—"

"Well, Margaret, Hannah . . . she just got home," said Lynn, trying to tread lightly.

When Dani opened her eyes, Avery had walked into the room, holding her keys. She'd taken the second half of the day off and had arrived back from work.

"I'm thinking we should take Hannah on a drive," Avery said quietly.

"I couldn't agree more," Dani replied. And with that, the two of them called Hannah out of the kitchen, and led her out the door, the banner still hanging from the ceiling behind them. *Welcome Home.*

THE WEATHER WAS unseasonably warm for late November. As they drove off post, the road shrank to two lanes and the scenery morphed from strip malls to cotton fields. The plants had dried into dark brown stalks, and some of them still held bright white bulbs of cotton, the ones the harvesting machines had missed. Dani looked out the passenger-side window. Every few minutes she heard Hannah sigh, as if she had to remember to keep breathing.

*It should have been me. I want it to be me.* Those were the words that Hannah had sobbed into her pillow the night before. And she was being serious. Dani had never sat with someone in so much pain for so many hours. And while she sat there, listening to her friend cry, all she could do was listen. Tim's life wasn't the only one that had ended. The life Hannah was going to have, the children she was going to raise—all of that had ended, too. Like they'd come to a fork in the road with God in the center. He'd pointed Tim and Hannah in separate directions, their momentary love lost forever.

Avery pulled the car off to the side of the road, under a canopy of large oak trees.

"Let's just stop here," Avery said, putting the Honda Civic in park. "I have no idea where I'm going anyway."

They all opened their doors and started walking along a gravel road, surrounded on both sides by fields of cotton. Hannah was wearing one of Tim's old sweatshirts. She looked so young, Dani thought. Her hair was bleached nearly as blond as Avery's from all the days she'd spent under the desert sun. Somewhere buried below the sadness, Dani knew, the old Hannah was still there.

Despite the sorrow, there was still a clearness in her eyes. Dani looked around and started to chuckle.

"What?" Avery said, turning to look at her.

"This is where you take me?" Dani laughed. Looking at Hannah, Dani whispered dramatically, "Did she bring me out here on purpose?"

Avery looked at Hannah with furrowed eyebrows. "What?" she asked. "What did I do?"

"You take us out of the house to cheer us up, and *this* is where you take me?" Dani said, putting a hand on her chest in disbelief. "Taking me on a walk through a cotton field? All you white people! Should have known all along."

Avery started laughing and so did Hannah. Dani, feeling the momentum of their release, frolicked through the cotton field, bending over and inspecting each plant for blooms. She stuck her butt up high into the air.

"Do you want me to start picking? Is that what you guys brought me out here to do?"

Deep in the brush of one plant, she found a white puff, covered over with leaves. She held it up in the air and then threw it at Avery, who ducked, unnecessarily. The cotton flew only a few inches from Dani's body. The laughter was real and deep, and seeing Hannah smile for the first time since she'd arrived back home touched a place inside Dani's heart that hadn't moved in a long time.

"Ahhhh, my gosh," Avery sighed, grabbing her cheeks. "I've missed you girls."

"Bringing me out here to pick cotton. As if that's gonna cheer me up," Dani said, but her words were cut short when the phone in Hannah's jean pocket started to ring.

Hannah held it in her hand as though she were trying to compute a difficult math problem. She walked over and handed it to Dani. It had been this way ever since Hannah had arrived home a few days earlier. She couldn't deal with people calling to offer their sympathy. She didn't know what to tell them when they asked how they could help. So, she either ignored the calls or passed the phone to someone else to answer.

Dani couldn't blame her. In the week since she'd left London, she'd received more than fifty work e-mails, none of which she'd had time or energy to answer. What did it matter now if Gelhomme sold thirty million or forty million razors? If life was this short, Dani wasn't sure that she could spend hers in an office with Laura Klein. How could she go back to London and care about a commercial or a digital banner ad ever again? How could she go back to making money but no impact in the world?

Standing in a field of cotton, thinking about how her ancestors had fought to free her from this place, she realized that she couldn't repay their sacrifices with a purposeless life. It was clear to Dani that God had sent her to West Point so that she could know these women. So she would be right here, right now. Beyond that, nothing was certain.

Dani took the phone from Hannah's hands and answered the call.

"Hello? Yes. . . . Okay. . . . Yes, sir. Thank you, sir."

After the call ended, Dani held the phone in her hand like she'd just spoken to a ghost.

"That was Arlington," she choked out. "They only have one opening in the next six months."

The whites of Hannah's eyes were whiter than the cotton in the field, her irises bluer than the sky. Dani couldn't bear to see her friend bracing for disappointment, but there, in that moment, she saw Hannah's shoulders fall.

Avery stepped closer and put her hand on Hannah's shoulder. "Oh, Hannah, I'm so sorry."

"No. The opening . . . ," Dani replied, her eyes welling with tears. "The opening they have is December fifth. He said we could have it."

## 32

*December 2, 2006 // Fort Bragg, North Carolina*

The Saturday before the funeral, Avery walked down to Hannah's house at noon with her fingers wrapped in the sleeves of the same sweater she'd worn the night Noah picked her up for their very first date. Could you call it a date if the person picking you up was engaged to someone else? Could you grieve a relationship that should never have even happened?

Her sadness about Noah paled in comparison to what Hannah was experiencing. And for that reason, Avery was grateful for her proximity to Hannah's sorrow. The sheer size of the mountain Hannah had to climb overshadowed the hills of Avery's life. When you allowed yourself to enter someone else's trauma, there were so many benefits: a righted perspective, a deeper sense of friendship, a holy devotion to the sacredness of now. Avery hadn't gone running once since Hannah had returned home. At the moment, nothing seemed more important than being present and available for her friend.

The temperature had fallen overnight to below freezing but was supposed to climb into the high forties by midday. Tree branches, bare and gray, sliced through the sky like witches' fingers. She shivered. Emily had agreed to go to the mall with Dani to find Hannah something to wear to the funeral, which left Avery to volunteer for a much different job. She didn't feel ready.

Hannah placed herself heavily in the passenger seat of Avery's beat-up Honda Civic. Tim's parents sat in the back, and the four of them drove across Fort Bragg to a redbrick building near the hospital. When they'd walked through that cotton field a few days ago, Hannah's face had momentarily regained its color— red cheeks, dimpled like God had touched her when her skin was soft as dough. But as they drove, Avery could tell that a tsunami of grief had wiped her out again. Margaret reached her hand around the headrest to rub Hannah's shoulder, but she pinched her shoulders up by her ears, refusing to accept the touch.

"Are you sure you want to do this, Hannah?" Margaret asked once they'd parked.

"I don't have a choice," she said dismally. "I have to see him. Otherwise . . . I—I just have to."

"I'm going to go in with Hannah first," Avery said, hoping she wasn't overstepping. But Hannah looked back at her with gratitude, like she'd just saved her life. "Captain Huerta said there's a waiting room. I'll send him to get you after."

"I hope it will give you some closure," Tim's father said. "Even just a little."

The night before, Avery and Dani had slept on the floor next to Hannah's bed. Every few hours, they would wake up and find Hannah in the bathroom, or on the floor, or in the closet. She kept saying the same thing over and over again, every time they helped her back into bed: *"If he's really gone, wouldn't I feel it? Why don't I feel it?"*

Avery felt her breath catch as they stared at the front doors of the mortuary. She couldn't imagine what Hannah was feeling, knowing that in just a few moments, she would walk inside that building and see the lifeless body of her husband.

Avery reached for Hannah's hand.

"Are you ready?" Avery said. Hannah's eyes welled with tears and she nodded, thankful and brave. In that moment, Avery was certain she'd never seen a more beautiful woman. Magazines air-brushed celebrities. Television romanticized relationships. They showed sex and flirtation and forbidden moments of passion. But they never showed this. This love without makeup and without pretense. This love that forgives. This broken gray bravery in the face of loss. And that was part of love too. To be willing to see it die.

Tim's parents found the waiting room, while Avery and Hannah walked down a hallway lit by fluorescent lights. With each step, Hannah's breathing grew more irregular, her grip on the silver cross around her neck more intense. At the front desk, a woman asked Hannah and Avery to show their military IDs, then pointed them to the elevator.

A momentary loss of gravity filled Avery's stomach as the elevator ascended. When the elevator doors opened, they walked down another hallway, to Captain Huerta's office. He navigated them through a maze of hallways to a heavy door that required his fingerprint to open. And then, he unlocked a smaller door with a key. Inside that room was a closed casket made of dark stained wood. *Classic.* Just like Hannah.

"Take your time," said Captain Huerta, closing the door behind them.

Now it was Avery's breathing that grew fast and shallow. Hannah took three steps forward. Several hot tears streamed down her cheeks, one after another, and her cries sounded like whimpers, caught far in the back of her throat. As Hannah lifted the casket lid, Avery tilted her chin down, wishing she could melt into the walls and disappear. But when Hannah collapsed on the side of the casket, sobbing loudly at her husband's side, Avery rushed over to hold her steady.

"It's okay," Avery said, though she wasn't sure she believed that was true.

Holding Hannah's broad shoulders, Avery let her eyes wander to the open casket. She held her breath, hoping to see what she'd always seen in the movies. A perfect Tim, quiet and at peace.

But the man in the casket was a shadow of the Tim she'd once known. His hair was the same dark brown; his nose held the same straight line. But his lips were a stiff shade of blue. His face was ashen, misshapen. The right ear seemed larger than it ought to be. And his eyes were closed and sewn shut—so shut, it almost seemed as if he were clenching his eyes closed. She found herself willing him to wake up, to shake and bring the color back to his face. But he stayed perfectly, tragically still. Avery fought her own breakdown so she could keep holding Hannah up. The green service uniform had his *NESMITH* nameplate above the right pocket, but aside from that, there was nothing left of the man she'd known. His spirit was gone. Only his body had been left behind.

Breathless, Avery walked Hannah toward the door, where there were two chairs waiting for them to sit.

"It's okay," Avery said, stroking Hannah's back. "It's over. You did it."

"It's not him," Hannah cried. "Tell me it's not him."

**33**

December 5, 2006 // Arlington National Cemetery,
Arlington, Virginia

Eight officers stepped up to a black hearse in two rows. They wore dress blue uniforms: dark jackets, light blue pants with a golden stripe down the side. The bills of their caps and the shine of their shoes reflected a gray sky. A carriage waited just ahead of the hearse, with seven dark horses standing perfectly still. This, Hannah knew, would go slowly.

And that was what she wanted. That was what Tim deserved. To have the slowest funeral procession ever recorded. For years to pass and the grieving to never end.

On the opposite side of the road, a full military band raised their instruments and seven riflemen raised their guns. The band began to play a hymn as one of the eight officers walked between the two rows toward the back of the hearse. Hannah looked through them, beyond them, feeling a cold gust of wind cross her cheek. She wore a brand-new dress—something Dani and Emily had picked out at a department store—but because the weather was threatening snow, she'd had to put on her down jacket and a scarf. She'd refused to wear sunglasses and hadn't put on mascara either. Her eyes were unadorned and looked tired, but at least they were still open.

Grief unimaginable coursed through her veins with every slow, painful step. They removed Tim's casket from the vehicle with exacting precision, as though they wanted to give his widow time to process each moment of the end. In unison, all eight officers stepped away from the hearse. They took another step away. Then another. And soon, the casket had turned several degrees, until it pointed toward the band. The American flag of the color guard waved in the breeze just behind the instruments.

There were no tears in Hannah's eyes, but she held a handkerchief in her hand just the same. Wendy Bennett had sewn a band of lace around a square of delicate white fabric and had given it to Hannah a few days ago, when she stopped by the house to see her for the first time. Knowing Hannah had been inundated with decisions and visitors, Wendy had waited in the wings, finishing the cooking that she and Dani had started, picking up people from the airport, and probably praying. It was an unselfish person that could arrive at a funeral and serve without expecting a single thing from the grieving widow. It was strange to see Wendy, just as it had been strange to see every other extended family member and old friend arrive in Virginia. Hannah still couldn't wrap her mind around the fact that they were really here for her—they were here because Tim had really died. But at least nothing hurtful had come out of Wendy's mouth. Hannah's grandparents and cousins felt they needed to comfort her with thin platitudes: *Everything happens for a reason; You're so brave; God has a plan.* Their words grated on Hannah. She was grateful they'd come but wished they would leave her alone. For some reason, it was different with Wendy. Wendy's service, with no strings attached, felt like real comfort. The dichotomy of her emotions was something she'd have to dissect another time. For now, she gripped the handkerchief, thankful for its presence in her hand.

The sound of the officers' shoes hitting pavement filled the air. When they reached the horse-drawn carriage, the men lifted the casket, then slowly moved it from their hands to the platform on four spoked wheels. With the casket secured, the horses began their steady, melodic walk to the grave, as if coaxed by the wind.

Hannah followed twenty-one paces behind the carriage, taking in the sights and the smells of the cemetery. She kept reminding herself that this wasn't a dream. That her husband was in that casket, being carried by those horses, to a grave that would bear his name. Hannah couldn't take it all in. The beauty of this place. The deliberate honor the officers were showing her family. The police escort that had shut down the Beltway for their procession to Arlington National Cemetery. The hundreds of souls that followed her up this hill. Mark and Wendy Bennett. Locke's new wife. Every basketball teammate she'd ever had—including Sarah Goodrich, who'd flown in all the way from Hawaii. There were old professors, Tim's parachuting team, and hundreds of others she hadn't had time to see or greet. Every step they took was sacred. *Tim would have wanted it this way,* she knew. *He deserved it this way.*

When they reached the graveside, Hannah lowered herself into a foldout chair, trembling. If it hadn't been for the birds, the hushed sniffles, and the phantom breeze, it would have been completely silent.

Seated in the cold, the image of that stretched, strange face in the casket resurfaced in Hannah's mind, and she clenched her eyes closed. She didn't want to remember Tim that way. Recalling a different memory, her mind expelled the image of Tim in the casket and replaced it with his smile as he stood at the center of Cullum Hall.

That night, their senior year at West Point, the doors had been propped open by two large lanterns, flickering against the darkness. When Hannah passed through the entrance, a glowing line of candles had directed her path through the darkened building to a wooden door. The ballroom was behind that door—the place where she and Tim had first danced, awkward, bumbling, and happy. Nervous, her hands shaking, Hannah had reached for the metal handle, pulled the door open, then burst into tears.

Tim stood at the center of the room, dressed in jeans and a white polo shirt, surrounded by hundreds of candles, dancing their golden light against the walls. Yellow rose petals had been strewn across the floor, lining a curved path between them. She walked across the petals slowly, her hands clasped over her mouth, in shock. She knew what this meant, and yet, she couldn't believe it was true. He wanted her. *Forever.*

He'd had tears in his eyes when she reached him. "Hannah," he said calmly. "You are beautiful, inside and out. You are smart and courageous and strong. You are forgiving and kind. And patient—Lord knows you're patient. You love your friends so deeply and I've been the grateful recipient of that love, even when I didn't deserve it. I've loved you for the last three years, but if you'll let me, I want to love you for the rest of my life."

He'd lowered down to one knee, pulled out a small box, and before he could even ask the question, Hannah was laughing and trembling, down on her knees right next to him.

"Yes," Hannah had said, wrapping her hands around his face. "Yes!"

He'd opened the box, slipped the platinum ring around her finger, just as the door to the ballroom opened again. Before she could turn to see what was happening, Dani and Avery had run up to scream and jump and hug her, as if they'd been listening with their ears pressed against the door. Then Hannah's family walked in— her parents, Emily and her husband, her grandparents. Mark and Wendy. All of Tim's friends from the parachuting team. Everyone filed in, and without hesitation, they all were dancing and hugging and celebrating. Unselfishly, Tim had known that she would want to share that moment with everyone she loved most. Turning back to look at him, she'd seen joy in his eyes, as he watched her relish her moment as the center of attention.

Now all those people were gathered here again, for such a different purpose. The memory ended and she stared ahead at the gray sky, surrounded by darkness, listening to the sound of her own breathing. He was gone. There was nothing she could do to undo what had been done. There was no rewind button, no do-overs. Overwhelmed and letting the tears fall quietly, she tried to picture his face as she'd dreamed it: lit by candles, full of joy. Instead of how she'd seen it in the morgue. It was a battle she knew she'd have to fight for the rest of her life.

Around her, hundreds of white tombstones snaked through the grass, rows and rows of lost sons and daughters. It struck her then that as soon as she walked away, Tim's tombstone would become anonymous to the visitors who walked these grounds every day. Her husband. Her philosopher. Her lover. Her friend. A striking visual. Another tomb of another unknown soldier.

A line of seven soldiers shattered the noiselessness, cocking their rifles. All seven pointed their guns at an angle, then fired, sending a violent burst of gunpowder and smoke into the sky.

A second round of shots was fired.

Then a third.

All three volleys from all seven guns emitted a sour, metallic odor. Then the smoke wafted away.

A lone officer under a canopy of red leaves raised his trumpet. He played taps. The song of a long, hard day of work, and a well-earned night of rest. Two sluggish and lonely stanzas, ending in one echoing note of finality. Then everything was quiet again.

She wanted to stop time and hold on to all of the memories, because the greatest injustice was that those memories would fade into sepia tones. Her brain wouldn't remember what her heart had seen. Not perfectly. Not in full color. He was gone, and soon time would rob her of what little she had left.

The men raised the American flag that had been draped over the casket, then began a choreographed and unhurried dance, passing hand over gloved hand, end over end, folding the flag thirteen times until it became a triangle of stars. Then the eight honor guards moved the triangle slowly through the air down the middle of the casket—it floated—until it was pressed firmly into the hands of an officer at the head of the grave.

Turning, he took four deliberate steps and bowed before Hannah with one knee on the grass. He raised the folded flag up, offering it to her as a gift.

How many days earlier had she been kneeling in the dirt, offering a soccer ball to a young boy, hoping he would believe the words that were coming out of her mouth? A year? A decade? The boy had spit on her shoulder. He didn't have the strength to accept a gift, knowing that gift had been tainted. Hannah looked at the flag and had the same dismal thought. She didn't want the flag. She wanted Tim.

"On behalf of the president of the United States, the United States Army, and a grateful nation, please accept this flag as a symbol of our appreciation for your loved one's honorable and faithful service," he said.

Placing one trembling hand on top of the flag and another on the bottom, Hannah received it from this man who wanted nothing more than to soothe her pain. Did he know he was making it worse?

Hannah didn't yell, holding her hands up to the sky, screaming at this injustice. She held the flag in her lap and did her duty to hold her emotions in check. Just a little bit longer. A single tear fell from her cheek as they lowered his casket into the ground.

He would never come back to her. And though she was surrounded by more than five hundred people who loved her, Hannah knew the truth.

She was alone.

*December 5, 2006 // Arlington, Virginia*

An hour after the reception started, the line to speak with Hannah hadn't shrunk at all. Dani went to the table of refreshments, picked up three water bottles, and walked them over to Hannah and Tim's parents, who accepted them with gratitude.

"The first time I met Tim . . ."

"God has a plan for all of this . . ."

"You're so strong . . ."

Hannah nodded, smiled when she could, and continually said the same words over and over again. "*Thank you. Thank you for coming.*"

Eventually, Dani made her way to a round table toward the middle of the reception hall. All of the tables were covered with white tablecloths and had a small flower arrangement at the center. Lilies and eucalyptus. One of the many choices Dani had made out of Captain Huerta's binders, when Hannah had lost the ability to make any more decisions. In the foyer, Dani could see Avery collecting coats from guests filing through the entrance. Dressed in a black coat and gray dress, Amanda Coleman had just arrived. It surprised Dani to see her; Locke had told her in an e-mail that he wasn't going to be able to make it to the funeral, because his unit was leaving for a two-week training in the field that he couldn't miss.

Spotting Dani across the room, Amanda waved. After handing her coat to Avery, she found her way to Dani's side. Her dark brunette hair fell in a single braid down her shoulder, and she hugged Dani tight.

"I only met him that one time, at your house," she said. "But still. I . . . I just can't believe it. You're such a good friend. To come here, all the way from England."

"What else was I going to do?" Dani said.

Amanda pursed her lips together and nodded in understanding.

For a moment, the two women stood in awkward silence. Then they sat down at the table beside them.

"Locke said they had a great time over there, last spring," she said. "That you have a great flat. Notting Hill, right?"

Dani nodded, feeling no desire for small talk.

Amanda looked around the room, then sighed, her eyes falling on Hannah. "How is she doing?"

Dani shook her head, angry that Amanda would ask such an obvious question. *How did Amanda think she was doing?* "She's devastated."

Amanda seemed to let Dani's harsh response sink in before gathering the courage to try again.

"I don't keep up with any of my friends from college anymore," she said. "When I see the way y'all are with each other, it makes me wonder if I had friendships or just . . . proximity."

Dani looked at her, surprised by the insight in her comment.

"I don't know," she said, shaking her head. She chuckled. "Push-ups aren't exactly my forte. But seeing you guys together makes me wonder if I could have done something like West Point. It kind of makes me wish I'd tried." She took a sip of water. "Locke tells so many stories about you. 'Did I tell you about that time Dani and I did this? Or the time that Dani did that?' If I'm honest, sometimes I'm jealous of all those memories you guys have together. I feel like I'll never catch up."

Dani felt a sudden surge of compassion. She'd never considered how it must feel to Amanda to constantly be on the outside. "You will. It'll take time, but you will."

"I guess I should get in line," Amanda said, looking over her shoulder at the long queue of people, waiting to speak to Hannah. She looked back at Dani and squeezed her hand again. "Hannah is really lucky to have a friend like you. So is Locke. And so am I."

AFTER AMANDA LEFT, Dani pulled the BlackBerry out of her pocket and clicked on the small envelope icon. It felt rude, but with the spare moment she had alone, she scanned through the subject lines of 112 unread e-mails. Most of them were junk, but several dozen were work-related. All had gone unread. Unanswered. Near the top of her most recent e-mails, a message from Laura Klein had been marked *urgent* by its sender. It had a little exclamation point at the end of the subject line. She opened it.

**From:** Laura Klein <laura.klein@egcorporation.com>
**Date:** December 5, 2006 06:39 AM GMT
**To:** Dani McNalley <danielle.mcnalley@egcorporation.com>
**CC:** jim.webb@egcorporation.com, sandra.myers@
egcorporation.com, legal@egcorporation.com
**Subject:** Re: *URGENT:* Bereavement Leave (!)

Ms. McNalley,

I've been in touch with Jim Webb, Sandra in HR, as well as our team of E & G lawyers, all cc'd here.

At this time you have overspent your allotted leave by six days. You no longer have any sick days, personal days, or bereavement leave available. However, as stated in my previous e-mail dated November 21, and confirmed by an e-mail sent to you from Sandra dated November 26, bereavement leave is a benefit to be reserved for immediate family only, with the presentation of a death certificate, for which, per your e-mail November 20, this current trip does not qualify. Your salary has been reduced for the missed workdays. Someone from Accounting will be in touch with the details.

Please respond immediately with your explanation of this extended absence, and your intended date of return. Please keep all parties above included on the correspondence.

Respectfully,

Laura Klein

Dani felt sick to her stomach. Of all people, Jim Webb would understand why she'd missed so much work. It would take one e-mail to explain to him why she'd left London in such a hurry and why she hadn't been in a rush to get back. Laura's e-mail was a thinly veiled threat and cc'ing Jim was only going to backfire on Laura—not Dani. Plus, in the days since she'd arrived at Fort Bragg, Dani had realized that all that pressure she'd put on herself with work was an illusion. Nothing was that urgent. Most things in life could get postponed, delayed, pushed back.

They were selling razors, for God's sake.

She put the phone on the table in front of her and rubbed her eyes. The thought of getting on a plane to go back to London, only to ride the train to the office every day while Hannah stayed at Fort Bragg, made Dani want to hit her phone with a sledge-hammer.

"Can we join you?"

Dani looked up to see Wendy Bennett standing next to her, followed by her husband, dressed in a gray suit. That was all it took for the tears to start flowing. The welcome scent of Wendy's perfume. The embrace of her arms around Dani's neck. Wendy wore a classic black crepe dress with white pearl earrings. After they'd all hugged and sat down, Wendy looked at the receiving line and shook her head.

"I've never seen so many people," she said. "This is going to go for a while."

Dani nodded, and watched as Wendy's eyes landed on Locke's new wife, who'd joined the end of the line.

"I just met Amanda," Wendy said, looking back on the little sandwiches on her plate. "She seems nice."

"Yep," Dani said. "She is."

"Hannah is going through something unimaginable," Wendy explained, "but that doesn't mean you can't grieve the ways your dreams have shattered, too."

It was difficult to swallow those words. *Your dreams.* What dreams did she even have anymore?

"I know your life hasn't exactly gone the way you'd expected," Wendy continued. "But Hannah is going to be experiencing a lot of loneliness now. A lot of loss. And you understand that pain, more than most people in this room. You know what it feels like for the future to implode. You know what it means to start over."

"That's true," Dani said, wiping her eyes. "I just... I don't know how to help her. She's so strong, Wendy. And I ... I don't know. Everything just feels wrong."

"Of course it feels wrong. That's called life."

"I'm earning all this money. And what for? I'm making all these connections, in a field I never wanted to be in in the first place."

"Your job in London afforded you the chance to be here now, for Hannah. Who else could drop everything for two weeks and set up camp for a friend? And you have to remember. God hasn't forgotten you. He hasn't forgotten Hannah, either. None of this makes sense. But the story isn't over."

A deep sigh came from the depths of Dani's lungs. Tim had touched so many people in his short twenty-four years. It was painfully clear to Dani now that if she died, far fewer people than this would attend her funeral. You only get one chance at life. And Dani was certain now that she couldn't live it behind a computer screen. Not anymore.

"You know what surprises me?" Wendy asked. She looked around the room, then back at Dani. "I don't see *her* here."

"Who?"

"Her," Wendy said, raising an eyebrow.

"Oh," Dani said, then sighed. "It doesn't surprise me at all. She never really knew us."

"I should have done more. I think about it so often. I should have tried to have her fired. But I thought if she found out that I was trying to get her fired she wouldn't let you girls come to our house anymore. I just . . . I didn't want to make things worse than they already were."

"You did plenty," Dani assured her.

After a pause, Wendy leaned across the table. "What happened? I mean, *really?*"

Dani took a sip of her water and smirked. She knew what Wendy was talking about, even if she hadn't said it outright. In the summer of 2004, just a few months after their graduation ceremony, West Point's athletic director had asked for Coach Jankovich's resignation. It made national news. But true to form, Coach Jankovich played it off like she'd received another coaching job and had chosen to leave. West Point didn't correct the error, but Wendy knew better.

"The cult happened," said Dani.

In April 2004, two months before their graduation, Avery, Hannah, and Dani were eating sub sandwiches in Grant Hall when their coach walked through the room, holding her head high like a crane. She'd passed them without saying a single word. Not a hello, not a goodbye. And after she'd gone, the girls had groaned and recounted all the ways she'd failed them over the years.

"Like I said," Avery had said, "if we'd all quit, they would have fired her. A player strike would have made a statement."

"Too bad it's too late for that," Hannah had added.

Dani had set her sandwich down. "What if it's not?"

That night, they'd gone back to Dani's room and written three separate letters, outlining every NCAA infraction, racial slur, personal attack, and poor coaching decision that woman had made. Dani had e-mailed upperclassmen who'd already graduated, requesting that they do the same, and by midnight, she'd received six more letters. It was disloyal, for sure. It even amounted to mutiny—but even Hannah had agreed to participate. They couldn't leave that woman behind to ruin the experience of any more athletes. Female cadets at West Point had it hard enough.

That night, Dani had slipped all nine letters into the mailbox of the commandant's house. Then she'd walked away.

"We didn't know what he'd do with the letters," said Dani, after recounting the tale to Wendy. "But when we heard they fired her over the summer, we knew that he'd listened. She'd always accused me of leading a cult to get her fired. And it turned out, I did."

Wendy sat, mouth agape, taking in the story.

"I think that's the best thing I've heard . . . maybe ever," she said, with a reverent shake of the head. "You girls. You know, it's not the same at West Point without you there. Mark's going to have to retire from the Army eventually. Maybe you can help him with his resume. Is E & G hiring?"

Dani laughed. Imagining Wendy's husband with his military-grade haircut discussing commercials seemed odd in Dani's mind. "I don't think he'd like the culture there all that much."

"Fair enough." Wendy took a sip of water. "You know, while we were talking to Amanda, she mentioned her father works at the Citadel."

"Yeah. I met her dad at their wedding. Nice guy."

"She also mentioned the Citadel is hiring."

"Oh, yeah? Think you guys would like Charleston?"

"Not for us, Dani," Wendy said slyly. She leaned forward and touched Dani's hand. "I hear they're looking for an assistant basketball coach."

## 35

*December 5, 2006 // Arlington, Virginia*

Avery stood at the front of the reception hall, smiling somberly at guests as they arrived to pay their respects. She and Emily had been standing in the foyer for an hour, taking people's coats, directing them toward the back of the reception line, which still stretched around three walls of the room. The closet had filled with peacoats, rain slickers, long down jackets, and even a few furs. Every time the door opened, a gust of cold air reminded Avery of the freezing temperature outside. But inside, she could barely breathe, the air was so thick with warmth.

She'd shed silent tears through the entire funeral. Arlington cemetery was a national monument, and watching the honor guard fulfill their duty with such painstaking precision felt like watching a movie of someone else's life. Throughout the procession, the burial, the twenty-one-gun salute, Hannah's face had remained serene. Avery didn't understand it. How could you stay so still in the middle of a hurricane?

While Emily took a few more coats into the closet, Avery turned to see a projector inside showing images of Tim's life. First came a photo of Tim, his cheeks flapping in the wind, mid-free-fall during a skydiving jump. He was giving the camera a big thumbs-up with both rows of teeth fully exposed. That photo faded out while the next faded in: Tim in a hospital bed, his right arm propped up by a sling, the same thumb still pointed in the air. There was a murmur of laughter from the people in the room. That was Tim—happy and fearless, whether flying through the sky or bound to a hospital bed. Over the loudspeaker, a song played that Avery didn't recognize, but she opened herself to absorb the music, though she couldn't make out the words.

Soon, the photo of Tim in the hospital dissolved and was replaced on the screen by a picture from Thanksgiving last year. The photo was crowded with people: Dani's family, Locke and Amanda, Hannah and Tim. Noah and Avery smiled from their position at the center of the photo. He had his arms around her waist. Like a fool, she stood there smiling, unaware of the future. Noah's steel gray eyes cut through the photo and stared straight at Avery across the room.

The sight of Noah sent Avery straight toward the coat closet. A cry came out of her throat, raw and guttural—a wail. Avery stumbled through the closet door, slammed it behind her, and then sobbed, loud and deep, like something in her gut was trying to crawl out of her throat and could only do so if she opened her mouth wide enough. Everyone out there could probably hear her, and so she shoved a row of beautiful coats off the rack and onto the floor, where she fell into the cloth and fur and wool, which muffled her cries. She couldn't begin to feel embarrassed when there was so much else to feel. Decorum didn't matter when compared to despair.

For the first time in many years, Avery thought about Wendy Bennett and a conversation they'd had in her living room. Something about Lazarus. And a prayer. What was it?

The words came to her as if from outside of herself. As if someone else had whispered them into her ear from the past. *Lord, if you had been here, none of this would have happened.* Suddenly, that felt like the most honest, heartfelt prayer she could possibly muster. She repeated those words over and over again until it became the cry of her heart. Where was God when she'd arrived at West Point, only to sit at John Collins's table? Where was God when he broke into their locker room and hid his camera? Where was God when she sat on the witness stand, being berated and called a liar? Where was he then?

And where the hell was he now?

Suddenly, the closet door opened, revealing a petite silhouette, a strand of pearls. Wendy must have seen Avery escape into the closet, because her hands were full of clean tissues that she handed to Avery after closing the door behind her. She was the last person Avery wanted to see, and yet, as Wendy took a seat on the floor beside Avery, she realized she didn't have the energy to pretend anymore.

"I don't really need a sermon right now," Avery said, letting her bitterness hit Wendy hard. She'd expected it to send Wendy out the door as quickly as she'd come in. But to her surprise, Wendy didn't budge.

"Keep screaming," Wendy coached. "You've got to let it out."

"I guess everyone heard me," Avery said, using the tissues Wendy had offered to wipe her eyes. The white fibers went black with smudged mascara.

"You're feeling what everyone is feeling. You're just brave enough to express it."

"How can Hannah be so calm? I just want to hit something. To tear something apart. I'm so angry."

"Hannah will get there. It might just take some time."

"I found out a few weeks ago that John Collins was paroled," Avery admitted. "And then, after that, I found out the guy that I'd been dating for a year was engaged to someone else the whole time.

"And, meanwhile, everyone keeps saying these are supposed to be the best years of our lives. College. Our twenties. But that can't be true! It just can't. And do you want to know the worst part?"

"Tell me the worst part," said Wendy.

"Hannah . . . Hannah has to stand out there smiling at her husband's funeral! And this whole time, I've been coming back into this closet and checking my phone because even though I know he's a liar and horrible, I miss Noah so much. And I just want him to call and tell me that he still loves me, even though I know that's never going to happen. What's wrong with me?"

She looked up at Wendy, waiting for her to give her some Bible lesson, some thinly veiled offer to pray. Avery wished that someone else had come into the closet, because Wendy's green eyes were just too intense. She wanted Wendy to say that *nothing* was wrong, and that it was all Noah's fault, and that Avery deserved better. Instead, Wendy sighed and clasped her hands together on her lap.

"You know, we're not all that different, you and me."

Avery laughed, looking at Wendy's short haircut and patent-leather shoes. "I don't mean to laugh, Wendy, but I highly doubt that."

Wendy raised an eyebrow. "You'd be surprised. I wasn't always married with kids."

Avery paused to consider that. It was odd to try to picture Wendy at twenty-four, but of course, at some point, she had been.

"When I was twenty-six, Mark and I—we were both really struggling. Our marriage was falling apart because I'd realized that he was never going to be enough for me. But I knew that if we got a divorce, I was going to be just as lonely—I'd been with enough men to know that the other guys didn't have what I wanted either."

"And what was it you wanted?"

"That's easy," said Wendy. "I wanted everything. I wanted great sex and movie-grade romance and love and electric connection, twenty-four/seven. I wanted perfection. But it turns out, here on earth, we don't get perfection; we get people."

"And people suck."

"And even the ones that don't suck let us down," said Wendy, her voice softening. "I know Noah hurt you. But you have to know that even the best relationship isn't going to fully give you what you're looking for. Look at Hannah. She had it. And now it's gone. The point of life isn't to quench our thirst, it's to realize we're thirsty for something that we can't find here."

Avery allowed her breathing to slow down. She imagined Hannah standing out there, still smiling, still forced to shake hands with every person who had ever known Tim. Hannah was so gracious and so beautiful in the midst of her pain. And here she was, throwing a tantrum. Like a child.

"How do I go back out there?" Avery said finally.

"With your chin up. You're the bravest one in this room, Avery, because you're actually being honest about how messed up things are. But you can't stay in here forever."

"I can't?" Avery laughed through tears.

"Don't think so."

There was no voice. No angel coming down on the clouds. But in that moment, a quiet peace washed over Avery's body. If Wendy was here, still loving her after that display of insanity, then maybe there really was hope. For the first time in two years, the knot in her stomach unraveled. The tears in her eyes dried up. And suddenly, she found she had the strength to grab Wendy's hand and stand up off the floor. The coats she'd pulled off their hangers were in a pile at their feet. Now she looked at them and laughed.

"Don't worry," Wendy said, pointing to the other side of the closet. "Mine's over there. You didn't ruin it."

One by one, she and Wendy put the coats on hangers and back on the rack.

*Maybe this is faith,* Avery decided as they worked in silence.

Maybe faith was having the humility to scream at God and the audacity to get up off the floor.

## 36

They'd been on the highway for several hours now, riding in silence. Hannah hadn't slept at all the night before. The funeral had completely exhausted her, but when she closed her eyes, all she could see was some imaginary slum in Samarra, Tim's body falling on the body of his soldier, and bullets ripping his insides apart. When Hannah was alone, the gagging set in. She forgot to swallow, and when she did swallow, even the saliva threatened to come back up. There was no place she could get comfortable. Not on the bed. Not on the floor. Not on the balcony overlooking Washington, DC. She'd imagined Lincoln's statue, staring over the reflecting pool, with his words from the Gettysburg Address engraved around him.

*We here highly resolve that these dead shall not have died in vain.*

What did that even mean?

And who got to decide?

"Do you want to listen to any music?" Avery asked, breaking through Hannah's thoughts. "My CDs are down there on the floor."

Hannah turned to look at Avery, whose voice sounded so distant, it was hard to believe they were in the same car. Avery was in the driver's seat, her hair loose and wavy, like she'd slept on it wet. She offered Hannah a closed-lipped smile. Adrenaline had pumped through Hannah's veins yesterday, enabling her to survive the three-hour receiving line. But now, she had no energy for false smiles. Somewhere in the recesses of her mind, she knew she was grateful for all that Avery had done—paying for her family's flights to Fayetteville, offering to drive to Virginia, taking off work. But those acts of service didn't make up for the ways she'd been a disappointing friend in the last few years. Hannah hated that she was angry, but she didn't have any other emotions to spare. So she looked back out the window.

"Avery, please tell me you've heard of an iPod," Dani said from the back seat. "Get with the times."

"It's not the same," Avery replied. "There's something therapeutic about looking through those CDs. It's the soundtrack to my life."

Mindlessly pulling the heavy leather CD case to her lap, Hannah began to flip through the sleeves, each one holding four CDs to a page. Foo Fighters, *The Colour and the Shape*. Dave Matthews, *Live at Luther College*. Alanis Morissette's *Jagged Little Pill*. Third Eye Blind. Avery had always been a nineties alternative junkie, Hannah knew. Tim loved hip hop and country. The two most polar-opposite music styles, which he claimed weren't opposites at all. "Rap and country artists sing about life how it is, not how they wish it would be," Tim had said once. "Pop music is shiny. Rap and country are real."

Her mind flashed back suddenly to his dorm room at West Point, when they'd pulled an all-nighter studying. At West Point finals were called "TEEs," short for "term end exams." He'd forced her to listen to the four-CD set of Garth Brooks's greatest hits and pulled her away from her computer to dance—terribly—to "Two of a Kind, Workin' on a Full House." Hannah stopped paging through the binder and put her head between her knees.

As she stared at the dirty floor of Avery's car, Hannah noticed the edge of a letter sticking out of the purse resting next to her feet. She knew she couldn't read it yet. Not in this car, with this little air to breathe. The phone at the bottom of her purse lit up. Someone was calling. She fought the urge to chuck it out the window and watch it get smashed by the tires of the car behind them.

"Sixty more miles," Avery said, placing her hand on Hannah's back. "It's okay. We're almost there."

THE REST OF the afternoon went by in slow motion. Her parents, sister, and nephew went back to a hotel. Hannah's brother-in-law said goodbye after the funeral and headed back to Texas, so he could return to work. Avery and Dani went to the kitchen to pull out another of Wendy's meals from the freezer to defrost. Exhausted from the drive, Hannah told them she needed some time to herself and retreated to her bedroom. *Her* bedroom. The pronouns of her life had changed. She was no longer a we. *Theirs* was now *hers*. *His* was now nothing at all.

After taking a shower, Hannah wrapped herself in a robe and got back in bed, holding Tim's clothes against her body and his letter in her hands. His scent was fading from the fibers of his shirts, she knew, and that made her angry. His words, tucked under the seal of the letter, called to her. Even clean, she felt tainted. Even warm, her body shivered. Even embracing the letter in her hands, her soul resisted.

Before the funeral, she'd walked through the house collecting every Post-it note Tim had left behind. Those he'd written months ago. But the letter he'd written days, maybe even hours before he'd died. It wasn't thick. But it was the last thing she had. For some reason, she felt empty and achy, holding it in her hands. Like if she read it, then he would be really, finally gone. If she left it unopened—even just for a few more minutes, a few more seconds—there would still be more that Tim could say.

She was crying when she slid the pocketknife Tim had left in his bedside table underneath the envelope flap. She didn't want to risk ripping what was inside. The paper unfolded in her hands, light and ethereal, and the date written in the corner crossed her eyes. November 12, 2006. And then she read slowly, trying to take each word in and make it last.

*Dear Hannah,*

*We're leaving tomorrow for what they say will be a ten-day mission, so I'm sitting down to write you this letter, to assure you that I love you. I miss you. And we will speak again soon.*

*I'm not naive. I believe fully in the training I've done and in my ability to do this job well, but I also know that what we are doing is dangerous and uncertain. But that's just life. There's no guarantee that anyone gets to see tomorrow, and I am no different. My only prayer is that I do well with the days God gives me. I pray the same for you.*

*If catastrophe strikes here, I will still feel so blessed because I have lived the equivalent of four men's lives in my short twenty-four years on this planet. I owe it all to God, who met me in that tree the day my parachute failed. And to you, Hannah, my best friend, who had patience with me as I learned to love you with everything I had, and not just a part.*

*I don't pretend to know what the future holds. I imagine us bringing children into the world, sipping wine, breaking bread, and growing old together, using our bodies up until they are sore and bruised and wrinkled and aching. But our joy does not depend on that dream coming true. No matter what happens, we of all people can afford to live fully unafraid because we know these breakable bodies house unbreakable souls.*

*I know our love can withstand everything that this year will bring. I know we can endure it. Here's a poem for you (I wrote it, don't laugh):*

*We are an oak tree, planted deep in the soil of love.*

*The heat comes to batter our branches,*

*The winter brings its icy burden,*

*But the oak will never fall.*

*Though it dies, it will rise to new life when the spring comes*
*    again.*

*Remember I love you.*

*Tim*

## 37

December 9, 2006 // Fort Bragg, North Carolina

Y ou've got to get her out of the house."

Emily stood in front of Dani, bobbing a screaming Jack on her hip. Outside, snow fell and stuck to the ground in thick flakes, adding to the sense that they were trapped. A red bird flew across the yard and landed on a bare tree branch. Dani watched it sit there, undisturbed by the cold.

"To do what?" Dani asked.

"Anything." Clipping Jack into his high chair, Emily placed a bowl of oatmeal on the tray and tested its temperature with her forefinger. "She's got to start experiencing the outside world. You've got to take control, D. Start calling some shots."

"What about a movie?" Avery suggested. She was standing at the stove trying and failing to make eggs over-easy. The yolks both broke.

"I think she'd feel claustrophobic in a movie," said Emily. "Maybe you should just ask her. See what she's up for."

Holding the plate of scrambled eggs, Avery walked upstairs, with Dani close behind. A large box fan whirred on the second-floor landing, which made enough noise so everyone could sleep at night—even if Hannah couldn't. A comforter was still crumpled on the floor beside Hannah's bed, where they'd taken turns sleeping night after night. Dani had finally purchased a one-way ticket back to London, scheduled to leave tomorrow. She hated to think of facing Laura Klein—but life was too precious to waste today worrying about tomorrow. And Emily was right. If this was Dani's last day with Hannah, she needed to make it count.

Stopping at Hannah's door, Dani placed her ear to it carefully. Hearing nothing, she turned the knob and went in. In the soft winter light coming through the window, Hannah looked angelic. She tossed a handful of used tissues into the air, and they fell on the bed like snot-laden snowflakes.

"Look at me," she said. "What a mess."

Dani smiled as she walked into the room. "Yep. You look like hell."

"Let's get you out of the house today," Avery said, handing over the badly prepared eggs. "Get some fresh air. Change of scenery."

Hannah blew her nose, loudly. "To do what?" she said through the tissue.

"One thing at a time," Dani said. "First, shower. I'll pick your outfit."

Dani pulled the covers off Hannah's legs and clapped her hands. "Rise and shine, soldier. We're burning daylight."

While Hannah trudged to the shower, Dani scanned Hannah's closet. Everything carried a memory. Nothing was void of emotion. Choose the wrong outfit, and the whole mission could be thwarted. She considered each piece carefully, then realized they hadn't even decided where they were going.

*Ice cream?* She considered. *No. It's too cold for that.*

*Shopping? No. Too many choices. Too many screaming kids.*

Then she thought of it. Grabbing Hannah a pair of stretchy jeans and a black T-shirt, Dani folded them perfectly and topped the stack with a bra and clean underwear.

Whether Hannah liked it or not, they were going to the spa.

HALF AN HOUR later, they arrived at a small strip mall outside of Fort Bragg, where an Asian woman invited them to come in from the cold. The walls inside were white and powder blue and somewhere an electronic fountain trickled water through stones. Dani could see several women with their hands lit by table lamps, getting manicures. All along the right wall, mirrors reflected women getting haircuts. And from the looks of the menu, there were waxing rooms, massage rooms, and a staff of hairdressers on site to cut, color, and style hair. In the back, a row of white chairs sat enthroned behind a row of water basins, where women could get pedicures. Dani pointed in that direction.

"Pedicures," she said to the woman at the front of the spa. "And can we sit together?"

"Sure. Pick color," the woman said, pointing toward a wall of nail polish.

As Avery walked toward the rainbow assortment of colors, Dani noticed Hannah's face contort with emotion.

"No, no, no . . . ," Dani said, grabbing Hannah's shoulders tenderly. "It's okay."

Without a response, Hannah pushed through the salon door, back out into the cold. A bell rang as she exited. Dani motioned to the staff to give them just one minute. Then she and Avery followed Hannah outside.

Dani shivered against the cold. Hannah unwrapped the scarf from her neck, as though it were suffocating her.

"Why did you bring me here?" she said, her eyes wet with tears.

"Maybe it will make you feel better, even just for a few minutes," said Avery.

"Feel better? Feel better?! Avery! I'm never going to feel *better*. TIM DIED. HE DIED."

Hannah collapsed onto a bench and put her head in her hands.

They sat next to her for a long time, watching their breath. Dani knew better than to touch Hannah or to respond too quickly. Sometimes you just needed the truth to linger between you, even if it felt awkward. Even if there were no silver linings.

Hannah finally looked up and locked her blue eyes on Dani's face. "Who do I have to look beautiful for?"

Dani sighed and Avery scooted closer.

"You're so young, Hannah, you have so much life ahead of you," Avery said.

"Oh my God, would you stop?" Hannah shouted, then shook

her head. "Don't talk to me about *my life*. You have no idea. You *weren't there*," she said, turning to Avery. "You were never there when I needed you. Tim was gone all last year, and you left me over and over again. And now what? You just want to pretend like nothing's changed? You know nothing about my life."

Dani was shocked at the anger in Hannah's voice, but in a way, she was also grateful. At least now she could speak her mind without having to tiptoe around everyone, being polite and charming. Death would do that, Dani realized. It would make you speak the truth, even if it was ugly.

Avery's face, rather than looking hurt and defensive, fell in shame and sorrow.

"You're right. Hannah, I'm so sorry. I fucked up. I really did. I let you down. I know that now." Avery turned to look at Dani, as though Hannah's anger confirmed her fear that their relationship was beyond repair. "I love you, Hannah. You know I love you."

"What are you feeling?" Dani said, putting a hand on Hannah's shoulder to calm her. "Explain it to us."

Hannah grabbed her cross necklace, pulled at it, digging a line in her skin that turned red, as if she wanted to rip it off.

"This wasn't how it was supposed to be," she said. "We did everything right. We . . . we did everything we were supposed to do. We waited to have sex until we were married. We went to church. And read the Bible and prayed together. We trusted . . . that . . . God would take care of us. And now . . . what was that even worth?" Looking up to Dani, Hannah's eyes were full of tears. "Take me home. Please. I don't want to do this. I don't have a reason to be beautiful anymore."

"Then do it for *you*," said Avery. Crouching down in front of Hannah, she put both hands on Hannah's knees. "Be beautiful just for you."

"You have millions of guys lining up for you all the time. I had *one*. *One*. And I lost him."

"You think that's it?" Avery sighed. "I just want to come here to look beautiful for all my thousands of boyfriends?"

"Millions," Dani corrected.

"Hannah." Avery sat down again on the bench. "I haven't told you this because I didn't think it was the right time. But Noah and I broke up. It turns out he was engaged."

That seemed to shock Hannah into sitting up straight. She wiped her nose with her gloved hand. "What? You're kidding. He met your parents!"

"I have never been in love like you and Tim. After everything that happened—I wanted to hate him, but the longer you two were together, the more I realized that I didn't hate him, I hated that I couldn't find what you had. You don't think that makes me want to crawl in a hole and never come out? What y'all had . . . it was . . ."

"Once in a lifetime," Dani said.

They sat outside for a few moments in silence. Hannah shivered and put her scarf back on.

"I'll wax my eyebrows off, okay?" Avery suggested. "Or . . . I'll shave my head. Do you want me to? You know I'll do it."

Hannah rolled her eyes.

"I'd pay to see that," Dani offered, digging in her purse for cash. "Here's a twenty for Avery going all GI Jane."

"Tell me what I can do. It won't make you feel better," Avery said to Hannah. "But maybe it will make you smile. Name it. I'll do it."

"You know she will," Dani said, laughing.

Hannah sat up straight. "Dye your hair."

"You want me to dye my hair?" Avery repeated.

Hannah nodded. "We should all do it."

"All right. You heard the girl," Dani said. Her voice was full of competitive excitement. "Let's move before she changes her mind. Hair dye it is."

DANI SWIVELED BACK and forth in a chair, wearing a black cape snapped around her neck. All three girls faced away from the mirror: Hannah and Avery's heads had been painted in wet, colored goop. Dani's head was covered in aluminum foil. Underneath the wrap, the dye had grown warm and itchy on her scalp. The hairdresser promised it wouldn't do too much permanent damage to Dani's already bone-dry hair, but she honestly didn't care. Hannah was smiling—she'd chosen the colors, keeping her choices a secret from Avery and Dani.

"Just tell me," Avery begged Hannah. "What color did you choose? Please say it's red. I've always wanted to be a redhead."

Hannah smirked, then nodded to the stylists standing in front of them. For the first time since Tim had died, Dani thought she saw a faint glimpse of something like joy in Hannah's eyes. She knew they were all at the end of their ropes, but at least they were hanging on together.

After washing and styling their hair, the stylists waited for their cue from Hannah.

"All right, turn us around," Hannah said. "On the count of three."

"Oh great," Avery moaned. "Here we go."

"One . . . two . . . three!"

HANNAH WALKED OUT of the salon with voluminous hair the color of roasted chestnuts. Dani followed with hair cropped short and bleached platinum. Trailing them, Avery hid behind black sunglasses and a mop of raven-black hair. She looked like a celebrity after a particularly rough night at the club, pulling a hoodie up over her head.

"My head is a white Brillo pad," Dani joked.

"At least you don't look like a witch," Avery shouted. "Sorry, Hannah. You know it's true. You screwed me on purpose."

When they reached Avery's car, Hannah turned around and looked at her friends.

"You guys look ridiculous." As her chin began to quiver, she laughed. "And I absolutely love you for it."

# BEGIN AGAIN

*One Month Later*

*January 2007*

*Winter 2007 // Fort Bragg, North Carolina*

Avery Adams was pretty sure that yoga was bullshit. But then again, if she'd learned anything in the last year of her life, it's that you can't judge a book by its cover—or by willowy women who stand in a doorway and welcome you with their soft voices, braided hair, and lavender scent.

After spending fifteen minutes on the floor of a closet with Wendy Bennett, Avery had decided that she couldn't simply go on with her life as if nothing had happened. As if Tim hadn't died and Noah hadn't cheated. Michelle Jenkins recommended Mona Anderson, a counselor who lived in Fayetteville and practiced out of her home—just a couch and a chair and several built-in bookcases, full of titles like *Inside Out, Shattered Dreams,* and *On the Road to Recovery.* The first time she'd walked in, claustrophobia had overtaken Avery, and it took everything inside her to stop herself from turning around and leaving. Mona had white hair cropped short, and was so petite, Avery thought she might crush the woman just by speaking. She'd tried to shock Mona, telling her every sexual escapade she'd had since age fourteen. But when she'd finished, Mona hadn't flinched. She'd simply looked at Avery and said, "That's all very interesting. But I'd rather start at the beginning. Tell me about your parents."

"My parents?" Avery had said, incredulous. "What do they have to do with this?"

"I'm not sure yet," Mona said. "But I'd like to find out."

With Mona's guidance, Avery realized that from a young age, her parents had taught her to run—both literally and figuratively. Her father, unable to connect with his sons, had begun to resent his daughter's success. Her mother, unable to receive the intimacy she'd needed from her husband, had detached, leaving Avery with a void that she'd filled with anything she could. She'd run to win everyone's approval. She'd run to find a place in the center of their eyes. But you can't outrun yourself. The emotions you've got, you've got. And ignoring her problems had only led to greater problems. Yoga had been Mona's idea, too—because it was a "*practice*," not a sport.

"Practice for what?" Avery had asked at her most recent session.

"Practice at being with yourself," Mona had answered. "Practice for standing still."

Though she was resistant to the idea, Avery prided herself on being the kind of person that would try just about anything once. What was the worst that could happen?

THE MORNING OF Avery's first yoga class, she stopped at the post exchange for a smoothie. Dani had mailed her a new iPod for her birthday, and she wanted to buy an adapter for her new car. The shiny black crossover SUV was the largest purchase she'd ever made, and she'd driven off the lot in tears. She hated saying goodbye to her rusty old Honda Civic but loved that she'd followed Mona's advice.

"You don't need permission to be an adult," Mona had said earlier that morning. "If you need a new car, you can buy yourself a car."

When Avery complained that she didn't have enough money, Mona waved her off.

"You have a stable job. You can finance the car and make payments, just like the rest of us." Mona had paused, seeing the look of surprise on Avery's face. "You can go today."

The post exchange, or PX, was like a military minimall, complete with name-brand clothing, a Clinique makeup counter, and an electronics section full of the latest gadgets, all tax-free, of course. Avery picked up the adapter, went through the checkout line, and was waiting at Smoothie King for her drink when the sliding glass doors of the PX entrance opened and Noah walked inside.

Avery's stomach sank. Her hands grew sweaty, her breath shallow. Had he seen her? Did she want him to?

He'd shaved his beard, but other than that, Noah Candross looked as he always had. He was dressed in a form-fitting gray T-shirt and jeans, since it was Saturday afternoon. He removed his sunglasses and looked right at her. She didn't have time to decide whether to run toward him or away, because as soon as he saw her, he began moving toward her.

Avery took her drink from the teenager behind the counter and tried to open a straw. The first buckled against the counter, breaking as it released from its paper skin. She grabbed another but fumbled again. Why was she shaking? How did his presence have such power over her body? Noah was standing there, beside her, but she didn't want to look at him. He reached for her trembling arm.

"Don't," Avery said, her voice even and sure. Her arm moved out from under his hand. "I don't have anything to say to you." Even as the words came out of her mouth, she knew they were a lie. She had so *many* things to say to him.

"Avery . . . ," he began, looking back at the interested teen behind the Smoothie King counter. "Lower your voice—"

"Does your fiancée know that we went to California? Does she know you met my friends? My *family*?"

"It's not what you—"

"It's not what I think? What is it then?"

Silence. Noah lowered his chin and shook his head—it was the first time she'd ever seen remorse on his face. "I told you, you weren't in the plans."

"Oh my God, you and your plans," Avery said, letting the tears come to her eyes. "You made me into a cheater. And a fool. But you know what? Those days are over. So thank you. Thank you for opening my eyes. I just pray that your fiancée sees the light before she marries you."

Noah held his hands up to his temples. "If you would just listen to me," he said, his voice suddenly loud and defiant. "I need . . . I need my uniforms back, okay? I think I left two of them at your house."

Avery blinked twice, and then started laughing the way you laugh when it's two in the morning and you're so ridiculously tired that everything sounds like the funniest thing you've ever heard. "No," said Avery. "You need help, okay? I don't have anything for you. Go home to your fiancée, Noah. And please don't talk to me again. If you see me, just keep walking."

With that, she turned to the teenager and pointed her Styrofoam cup toward Noah's shocked face. "He's gonna pay for this one."

SHE ARRIVED AT her yoga class fifteen minutes later, her limbs still shaking with adrenaline. A stream of lithe women walked through the door with rolled-up mats tucked under their arms. Avery watched from her car, slurping the cold smoothie into her mouth, shivering. Finally, she turned off the engine and walked inside. The instructor, a woman half Avery's height with a long brunette braid running down her back, pointed Avery to the center of the room.

"So you can see me," the teacher said.

*And so I can fall flat on my face in front of everyone,* Avery wanted to reply. But instead, she smiled, sat down with her legs crossed in front of her, and tried to breathe.

Much to her surprise, she felt an immediate resistance to the simple task of sitting. Her legs wanted to move. She wanted to bolt out the door and call Hannah and rehash everything she'd just said to Noah and the shocked expression she'd left on his face. She wanted to leave this place and go back to her office to accomplish the hundreds of tasks that she'd left undone over the holidays. Her unit had started SRP paperwork, in preparation for their upcoming deployment. Before Tim had died, Avery couldn't wait to get her turn overseas. But now, the prospect of getting on a C-130 for Iraq terrified her more than she wanted to admit. Noah's face interrupted her thoughts about work. She pushed that away, only to immediately feel overwhelmed by a deluge of things she needed to get done before her trip with Dani and Hannah. They'd decided to spend a week together in February, a last hurrah, before they all parted ways again. She'd thought about the trip, then realized all this yoga wasn't going to help her get the beach body she wanted.

"Breathe in, and breathe out," the instructor said. "Keep your eyes closed."

Avery opened one eye and peered around at the rest of the class. Most of her classmates were older women, sitting with their eyes closed, breathing, looking perfectly at peace. She had no idea how they were doing it. Maybe they were faking. Maybe inside their minds, they were fighting battles, too. After all, you don't have to be in the Army to be in the middle of a war. She had no combat patch to show for it, but she'd fought tooth and nail in the last few months to reclaim her life. Her sanity. Her dignity.

"The voice in your head will try and defeat you, before you've even started," the yoga instructor said. "If you feel an itch, instead of scratching it, try and welcome it and let it be there with you. It's just your body after all. The itch will eventually go away."

Avery took a breath and closed her eyes.

"In the same way, if you have a thought—even a negative thought—just let it come," the instructor continued. "Your work. Your relationships. All those demands you've put on yourself? Let those come to your mind. Welcome them, don't resist them. We spend so much of our lives in a state of *resistance*. Why don't you release your grip? Welcome the discomfort. Welcome the distraction. Thank it for reminding you that you are *alive*. And then let it go."

Avery tried welcoming the part of her body that wanted to run. The part of her that was hurting, and the part that was healing. The part that still wanted Noah to love her, and the part that had told him never to speak to her again. Both were real. Both mattered. The first was a girl with desires, the second was a girl content, even if those desires went unfulfilled.

This was the work her counselor wanted her to do. To stop running.

To breathe. Forgive. And live.

39

I don't understand."

Laura Klein sat behind her desk in the same black dress she'd worn every day since Dani had started working in her office. A clump of eyeliner had gathered in the corner of each of her eyes, making her look tired and unkempt. And for the first time since she'd made the decision to have this conversation, Dani felt guilty.

They'd never spoken about Dani's extended absence. But as soon as Dani had returned, Laura had come to rely on her more and more to carry her professional weight whenever an unforeseen personal obstacle arose. In the divorce, Laura had received full custody of her children, and a week earlier, her older son had come down with the flu. The week before that, she'd had parent-teacher conferences. Dani didn't mind holding down the fort in Laura's absence—she certainly didn't send any e-mails to HR about it. But now, the shock and awe on Laura's face betrayed an insecurity that Dani had always assumed was there but never expected to see this clearly.

"You take two weeks off for your friend's . . ."

"Funeral," Dani reminded her.

"Funeral. And Webb *still* gave you another two weeks off for Christmas." Laura Klein laughed nervously. "I mean really. What else do you want? If this is about the whole Gelhomme bonus . . . I don't know what—"

"What bonus?"

"That's not what this was about?" Laura continued. "I assumed Webb told you, seeing as you two are so . . . chummy."

"Told me what?"

"The online Gelhomme ads worked so well, they increased their digital advertising budget by ten percent. So there was a bonus. A commission. I'll split it with you, if that's what this is about."

"That's not what this is about," Dani said. In all honesty, she didn't care. Money didn't change the facts.

"Truly, I don't understand," her boss said again. She was beginning to sound like a plebe at West Point. "The sky is the limit for you here. You make more money than anyone at your level. We both know Webb is priming you to replace me someday. And you're . . . you're really good at your job. I don't understand why you would walk away from all of that."

It had been a long time since she'd heard Laura Klein's voice fill with such sincerity. It was a nice sound, but it wasn't going to change her mind.

"There are more important things than money. I might be good at advertising, but I could be good at a lot of things. I think I was made for this."

Laura looked over Dani's resignation letter, a single page that rested in front of her. "And you think you were *made* to be a . . . college basketball coach?"

"I don't know for sure," Dani answered honestly. "But I'm certain that if I never try, I'll always wonder. And that's enough for me."

Laura shook her head and laughed. "Are you sure that hair dye didn't go to your head?"

Dani touched her short hair, offering Laura a small grin. She liked her hair, just like she liked what she saw in her future.

"And, if you don't mind me asking," Laura continued, "what are you wearing?"

Dani looked down. She wore a tight athletic shirt, sweatpants, and Air Jordans on her feet. She hadn't felt this comfortable in years.

"I've got a game in an hour. Which is why I can't stay here and keep explaining my decision," Dani said. "I just wanted you to hear it straight from me."

"You know, we're going to be sunk without you."

"You'll be all right," Dani said as they shook hands. "You've got Pete and the crew. They're all great."

"Sometimes I think they hate me." Laura sighed.

"Give them a break every now and then," Dani said kindly. "We're all just doing the best we can."

With that, she turned and limped out the door, carrying a box of her belongings with her.

"*Dani!*" Laura shouted, one last time.

When Dani looked back, she noticed Laura's eyes had softened. Even the wrinkles on her face seemed to smooth out as she offered a nod of respect and mutual understanding.

"Good luck," Laura said. "And for what it's worth, I believe you'll be a very good coach."

WHEN DANI GOT home, she walked to the basketball court in Notting Hill where she'd spent the last three weeks coaching the boys and reveling in the sound she loved most. She still felt discomfort in her joints. They groaned more than ever, really.

But pain comes for you, body and soul, whether you're ready or not, Dani thought as she jogged onto the court. For some people, pain arrives in a phone call that shatters the once-perfect window through which you'd seen the world. For others, pain grows into a poisonous plant, buried so deep, the only way to uproot it is to dig it out slowly. For others—for people like Dani—pain was a constant companion, nagging and persistent. You could numb the pain. Bury it again. Ignore it forever. But you couldn't get rid of it. That was a war that would never be won.

A basketball flew through the air from a child to Dani and back again. She smiled, taking her first step toward the basket. It hurt. But she chose to enjoy the ache.

40

*Winter 2007 // Ali'i Beach Park, Oahu, Hawaii*

H annah lounged in a beach chair, reading the final few pages
of *East of Eden*. In the book, the main character, Adam, was
nearing his end while his son Caleb stood at his deathbed,
begging for forgiveness.

Picking her eyes up from the page, Hannah looked out at the
water, breathing in the scent of coconut and salt. The sun hovered
above the horizon, casting long golden rays across the sand. The
water looked like bright blue Kool-Aid, rolling and crashing with
waves. Nature, again, reminded her of her size in the universe.
But if humans were so small, why did they want life to matter so
much?

Sarah Goodrich had e-mailed Hannah after the funeral
with an offer. Their old basketball teammate was deployed to
Afghanistan—her second deployment since graduating from
West Point in 2001. But because she was deployed, her beach-

front home on the North Shore of Oahu was currently un-occupied. In that e-mail, Sarah told Hannah the house's lockbox code and said that she could go any time she wanted, no questions asked. And so, at the urging of Dani and Avery, the three of them had booked round-trip tickets using the last of Dani's frequent-flier miles. There were perks to having a network as wide as the Army and a friend as wealthy as Dani. And if she was going to wake up at four in the morning anyway, she might as well wake up in Hawaii.

The grief counselor said that sleeplessness was a common symptom of grief—that it might take more than a year before she could sleep normally again. But Hannah didn't want to be normal. If not sleeping was how she could keep Tim's memory alive, then she hoped she'd never sleep a full night again. That was why she was out there, alone. Digging her feet into the warm sand. Watching the surf come in. She wanted to remember him.

Out in the distance, three tanned surfers sat on boards, bobbing up and down in the water, waiting for the right wave to ride. Hannah caught herself watching them, wondering if they were teenagers, or if they were older. It was hard to tell. Soon, one paddled hard in front of a growing swell. He stood on his board and glided seam-lessly across the water until he crashed. When he emerged from the surf, he shook his long dark hair and gave his friends a wave of his pinky and thumb, the shaka. A girl throwing a Frisbee for her dog along the water's edge noticed Hannah and smiled, as if to say, *Isn't this morning amazing?*

It was amazing. And that was what made it so difficult. Tim had never been to Hawaii, and now he never would. Would every amazing moment she experienced now also feel like a loss? The grief counselor had said she would have to learn to hold grief and joy at the same time without minimizing either emotion. She wondered if she'd ever grow tired from the weight.

Tim would never learn to surf, although she could imagine his young body adapting to the waves with ease. And that was part of the sorrow, too: Tim would only ever have a young body. There would be no old Tim. No Tim the dad or Tim the grumpy Old Grad, visiting West Point for a class reunion, like her grandfather did when Hannah was young. Was her future already decided, even then? Would Tim the grandfather have told his granddaughter to choose a different school, just as Hannah's grandfather had tried to do? She wasn't sure. But despite it all, Hannah was still grateful she hadn't listened to her grandfather all those years ago. She just wished the story had a different ending.

In light of a life, four years together was far too few. Soon, the time she'd spent with Tim would pale in comparison to her time without him. Inevitably, her memories would fade. She feared the day she wouldn't be able to conjure his face in her mind. A flat, two-dimensional picture would never capture the sound of his laugh or the little wrinkle between his eyebrows when he was concentrating. Everything she had to remember him by was a shadow of the real thing. More than once, she'd let herself call his cell phone, just to hear the prerecorded voicemail message. At some point, that phone plan would be canceled. His voice would be deleted. It was more than she could handle.

She'd attended West Point, despite her grandfather's fears, because she felt God telling her it was the right move. She'd met and married Tim for the same reason. Every leap of faith had been worth the risk. Until now.

She looked down at the page in front of her. Caleb begged his father, Adam, for a blessing. Hannah had never had to beg for anything in her life. But she knew that if she didn't beg, her faith would grow cold and brittle, until it crumbled into dust.

Standing up from her chair, Hannah walked down the beach, letting the emotion well up inside her. For so many years, she'd followed a prescription that she'd trusted would result in a beautiful life. Girls don't fight back. They don't get angry. They don't demand things—especially not from men. They are loyal and faithful and quiet and trusting. But slowly, surely, all of those rules had unraveled. It was time to release. To let go. This was why she'd come here. To let the sound of the ocean drown out the sound of her cries.

Soon, the water lapped up against her bare ankles. She remembered the salty taste of Tim's mouth and the feel of his body next to hers in the water last summer. And then she screamed.

She screamed that it wasn't worth it.

That she hated God.

That she didn't trust him.

That if *this* was what having faith meant, then she wasn't sure she wanted it anymore.

She screamed of the betrayal and the fear and the loss. She screamed the same three words, over and over again, until her scream became a whisper.

*"How could you?"*

The wild waves pulled away from her feet and soon, quietness filled the space of her screaming. She left her shorts on the sand and dove under the water, feeling its cool, salty relief on her skin. When she emerged from under the water, the little cross necklace felt warm and wet in her hand.

EVENTUALLY, HANNAH CAME out of the water and walked back to her chair, dragging her feet through the sand. When she returned, Dani and Avery were sitting there, beside her things, holding an extra cup of coffee.

"You okay?" Avery asked.

"No," Hannah said. "But I'm still here."

"Good," Dani said. She patted a place on the towel next to her, and Hannah lay down, putting her head on Dani's lap. The sand was warm beneath her body.

THAT EVENING, BACK at Sarah's bungalow, Hannah sat under the twinkle lights on the lanai, sipping something fruity. Sarah had styled every corner of the patio as though someone from *HGTV* were arriving any moment with a camera crew. The guest room had a plush queen-sized bed, which, despite her sadness, Hannah had still managed to make like the Army would require, hospital corners and everything, every morning of their vacation. Some habits were hard to break.

On the floor next to the bed, Hannah's uniform sat pressed and ready. Her rucksack was fully packed with the same gear she'd brought home from Afghanistan two months earlier. It was time to go back.

Hannah was proud that Dani had decided to take the coaching job at the Citadel. The salary would force her to take a big step down in lifestyle, Hannah knew, but if anyone could adjust, Dani could. That girl was unstoppable, no matter where you put her. She wasn't a shooting star; she was a solar panel, always absorbing energy and putting it back out into the world again. And Avery had changed, too. They'd been talking daily since Hannah had returned from Afghanistan. She was softer, kinder—and for the first time since Hannah had known her, Avery didn't have a boyfriend. Baby steps. That was what had changed, Hannah realized. Avery had slowed down.

Tim's death had spurred on those changes. That much was obvious. But Hannah found herself constantly wondering how it would change her. Would it make her bitter? Would it make her angry? Would she lose her faith in God or gain more? She was afraid of the person she might become in a world without Tim.

And what about her war? Colonel Markham had given her permission to take on a rear-detachment job at Fort Bragg for the remainder of the deployment. She didn't have to go back. But she couldn't imagine working at a desk while Private Murphy and the rest of the guys sweltered in Afghanistan without her. What kind of message would that send? It was important to show her soldiers and her friends, and, to be honest, *herself,* that life could continue. That she could still have a role and a purpose. That her breakable body housed an unbreakable soul.

She looked down at the tattoo on her wrist—an oak tree, deep roots and high branches, with two dates scribbled into its limbs: 6.19.04., the date of their wedding, and 11.13.06., the date of Tim's death. The beginning and the end. Or the other way around, depending on how you looked at it. The tattoo was Avery's idea. A breaking from the Hannah of before. A new Hannah had been born.

"Dinner's ready."

Avery came out to the patio holding a bowl of ahi tuna poke that she'd purchased from a shop on the way home from the beach. She placed it at the center of the patio table. Dani emerged from the kitchen, her hair back to a large, natural Afro. She added a bowl of mango, corn tortillas, and her famous avocado salsa to the assortment. With her strange restrictive diet, Dani had become quite the chef. Avery put a pitcher of margaritas on the table, and suddenly, a memory came to Hannah's mind.

She'd made a pitcher for her grandmother back in high school, during an elective ceramics class. The first two pitchers she'd tried to make had fallen apart in the kiln. Both times, she hadn't scored the handle deep enough for it to attach to the body of the vase. But her third attempt came out just as she'd imagined. Staring at her friends at this table, she realized that their lives were like that pitcher. They all had rough edges, but those places were necessary to forge deep connections. All the things they'd survived. All the ways they'd laughed and limped and cried together. It was like a knife had cut into them so they could latch together and never break apart, even when they were put through the fire. She'd wanted to bond that way to Tim, but looking up at her friends' faces under the glow of the twinkle lights, Hannah knew she was equally lucky to be connected to them. Some people spent their whole lives avoiding pain. But by avoiding it, they avoided *this* too.

They'd all taken their seats when Dani placed her hands palms-up on the table, ready to pray. "Shall we?"

But just as they'd gripped hands and bowed their heads, Hannah's phone began to vibrate on the table. The phone number was long and unrecognizable, like a military call coming from overseas.

"Sorry," Hannah said, trying to turn it off. "It's not important..."

"No, get it," Avery replied. "We can wait."

Hannah looked at her phone. That little piece of metal that connected her to the world. She'd been so scared to answer it. She'd ignored it and turned it off, and at one point considered throwing it out the window of a moving car. The ringer sounded like a wind chime blowing in the breeze. She couldn't avoid it forever. She couldn't escape beauty or the passage of time, any more than she could escape breathing. Whoever was calling needed her. And it was a good thing to be needed.

She could do this. She wouldn't do it well. She wouldn't do it perfectly. There would be more tears, she was certain. There would be more death and more life. There would be more screaming at the sky and wondering if Someone was listening. But whatever came her way, she knew she was still of use in the world—not because of her own ability, but because like a pitcher, scored and scarred, put through the fire, she was ready to be poured out.

Hannah took a deep breath. She picked up the phone, flipped it open, and pressed it against her ear.

She said hello.

It was a small act, to answer that call. But it wasn't small to Hannah. In taking that breath—in saying hello—she told the world that she was still here. That she was still breathing. And in that way, it felt like a beginning.

# ACKNOWLEDGMENTS

The great thing about being a writer is that I'll never have a band threaten to play me off stage when I'm trying to say thanks.

First and foremost, this book would not exist if it weren't for my friend, mentor and creative consultant, Dionna McPhatter, who originally envisioned telling a story about the experiences of women at West Point, and entrusted me to do the job. From the beginning to end, she offered belief, encouragement, financial support, creative solutions, and a listening ear, and never failed to provide a hearty kick in the butt when I needed it. You inspire me in every way and I'm grateful God put you in my living room twenty years ago. The best is yet to come.

To my agent, Alison Fargis: I am forever grateful that you own a piece of real estate across the Hudson River from West Point. Thank you for pushing me to revise this manuscript into the novel it is today. Thanks also to Maria Ribas, who saw promise in my writing and introduced me to Stonesong.

I owe many thanks to my editor, Lucia Macro—your suggestions for this book helped tie up so many of my loose ends. And to the entire William Morrow team at HarperCollins—thank you for your kindness, enthusiasm, and prompt attention.

I am indebted to a long list of women who candidly shared their memories, feelings and experiences with me, without reservation. Jen Wardynski, Jackie Asis, Charlsey Mahle, Mandy Psiaki, Katie del Castillo Vail, Haley Dennison Uthlaut, Tiffany Allen Archuletta, Abby Moore, Mallory Fritz Wampler, Jenny Jo Hartney, Ariel Gibson, Kristin Gatti, Caroline "Annie" Pestel, Mary Tobin, Jenn Menn, Sarah Travaglio. Thank you for your vulnerability, courage, and patience as I asked so many invasive questions.

West Point is a small community with roots that extend deep and wide. Thank you to the many cadets and families who made an impact on my life during my most formative childhood years—especially Laura Walker (Class of '03), Tim Cunningham (Class of '06), Emily Perez (Class of '05), and John Ryan Dennison (Class of '04)—strong men and women of character who were killed in the wars in Iraq and Afghanistan.

To my parents, Bee and Laura. Mom, your wise counsel helped guide me during the years it took to write this book. Thank you for being one of my most early trusted readers, and for inspiring what I believe is the character at the heart of this book. Dad, your brilliance in engineering is the reason we lived at West Point in the first place. Thank you for your reflections on 9/11, for your selfless service to our country, and for always reminding me to "chip away at it."

To the community of writers, artists and encouragers in Nashville and beyond. Thanks to Lauren Ledbetter whose hand-drawn illustration resides in the first few pages of this book. To Russ Ramsey, I finally did what you told me to do; now go write your memoir. Katherine Carpenter, you read the first words of this thing, and managed not to laugh—bless you. And many more thanks are due to Holly Sharp, Sarah and Andrew Trammell, Shelley Ellis, Amelia Cornish, Jamie Lidell, Joe Johnson, Lisa Burzynski, Kim Green, and Susannah Felts. And a huge thanks to the ragtag community of homeless creatives that find shelter (and caffeine) at Ugly Mugs in East Nashville.

And finally, my deepest gratitude is and always will be reserved for my husband, Patrick, whose long-suffering patience, love, and kindness have sustained me in every way. Thank you for loving a broken vessel like me. RILY.

## About the author

## About the book

Insights,
Interviews
& More...

# Meet Claire Gibson

Lindsey Rome

An Army kid who grew up at the
U.S. Military Academy at West Point,
CLAIRE GIBSON is a writer and avid
reader whose work has been featured
in the *Washington Post* and the *Christian
Science Monitor*, among many other
publications. She lives in Nashville,
Tennessee, with her husband, Patrick,
and their son, Sam. Visit her website
at www.clairegibson.com. ❧

# How This Book Came to Be

As an Army brat, it's hard for me to remember all the houses I've lived in because I've lived in so many. But I'll never forget the house on Ruger Road. Like West Point itself, it was built in the 1800s and wasn't afraid to boast about its history. It was four stories, with a kitchen in the basement and a dumbwaiter that lifted things (like the neighbor's cat) to the dining room on the second floor. I think it's condemned now, and probably should have been when we moved in. But I didn't know the difference. I was only ten. My father, a lieutenant colonel in the U.S. Army with a PhD in systems engineering, had joined West Point's faculty. All I knew was that we were going to get to stay in one place for a while.

From 1997 to 2003, our lives focused almost completely on cadets. My father taught them. My mother hosted them. My sisters dated them. And I looked up to them (and, err . . . also dated some). Much like Wendy Bennett, my mom was the perpetual hostess, leading a Fellowship of Christian Athletes huddle, and turning our home into an unofficial bed and breakfast for West Point's busiest events, like R-Day and graduation.

Needless to say, we had cadets over constantly. They filled our living room with the smell of sweat and grass. They ate all of the food. And best of all, they would tell stories. (It's possible I decided I wanted to be a writer listening to Dave Shoemaker tell the one about Naked ▶

Man streaking through cadet area.) When I was eleven years old, Matt Kapinos smeared camouflage on my face and taught me how to march, handing me a broom to use as an M16. Female cadets mentored me through an organization called Young Life. At football games, West Point's cheerleaders, also known as Rabble Rousers, let me on the field and lifted me up in the air. In the summers, my friends and I would sunbathe at Stillwell, watching helicopters fly over with cadets in camouflage hanging out the side.

I tell people that growing up at West Point was like growing up at Hogwarts. I knew that I was witnessing magic. During those years, it was the beautiful, athletic, confident women that gathered in our living room that intrigued me the most. Could I be like them someday? Could I be that brave?

In *East of Eden*, John Steinbeck paints a picture of his hometown of Salinas, California—its landscapes, its smells, its sounds, its people. Once I became a writer, I grew jealous of his muse because my childhood home was never fully mine. I was a bystander, a tagalong—a "dependent" (at least that's how the Army categorized me). Even as I contemplated writing about West Point, I hesitated, fearing that I wouldn't do it justice. How could I write about West Point when most of my experiences were from the outside looking in? How could a girl with no class ring touch the long gray line?

And then, in 2013, a voicemail message landed on my phone that changed everything.

A friend and West Point graduate called out of the blue. She'd read some of my writing and wondered if I would be interested in writing about women at West Point. "We all have so many incredible stories to tell," she said, and I knew she was right. I'd lived at West Point long enough to know there was plenty of material for a book, if not ten. At just the right moment, she invited me to lift the curtain and re-experience those years through the lens of female friendship. She invited me back in. I remember raising my eyes to the roof of my car—my hands too— and saying out loud, "Well then. Here we go."

The next four years (Yes, FOUR YEARS, people!) were a slog, to say the least. It still cracks me up to think that I'd expected to knock this novel out in eighteen months, tops. But writing a novel is nothing like writing an essay for a newspaper or magazine. I started by interviewing dozens of women about their experiences at West

Point and as officers, taking copious notes and recording every word. Many of those women had since gotten out of the Army, and were serving as stay-at-home moms or working in the civilian world. They were breathtakingly vulnerable about it all—the good, the bad, the ugly. Some wished to stay anonymous, others were happy to attach their name to their stories. Most had deployed at least once, if not multiple times. All of them had lost a friend, a classmate, or a spouse to the wars in Iraq and Afghanistan. More than once, as they shared their stories over the phone, I found myself in tears.

My hope is that *Beyond the Point* does justice to their stories in a way that is relatable to everyone, not just those "inside" the military community. I know that I've only scratched the surface of their experiences—like skipping a stone across a deep reservoir. But I hope through this book to help them feel a bit more understood. Unfortunately, as it stands, the majority of the stories we hear about women in the military focus on nonfiction accounts of sexual assault or the pioneering women who were "firsts." The first female general. The first female Army rangers. And while those stories are harrowing and inspiring, they also create a sense of distance between the average American woman and the picture of that woman in uniform. Those "first" stories might inadvertently discourage younger women from serving, thinking they aren't intense enough to join the military. But that couldn't be further from the truth. The reality is, the Army is full of women just like you and me. Women that have hopes and dreams and friendships and relationships and chipped nail polish and an addiction to Madewell. The world deserves to see more women in uniform in pop culture.

Writing this book has changed my life. The women who made these pages possible are not just interview subjects; they are my friends. They've taught me what it means to go to battle together—in fact, many of them have gone to battle for me, both in my childhood, and now, in my adulthood. And I am forever grateful. ᴄ᠆

# Photos and Interviews with Women of West Point

The following are taken from the author's interviews with Mandy Psiaki (class of '06), Charlsey Mahle (class of '04), and Kristin Jenkins Gatti (class of '03).

### (1) How did you decide to attend West Point?

*Kristin:*
I decided to attend West Point for two reasons. First, I didn't know what I wanted to do with my life, and at the time, the Army's motto was "be all you can be," so the Army seemed like a good place to figure out life. I didn't want to go to college and schedule my days around getting ready for a frat party. (Although now that I'm nearly twenty years away from having made that decision, I really wish I had been able to plan my days around getting ready for a frat party—at least a few times!) Second, my dad was very sick with cancer, and he wasn't working enough to pay for college for all four of us kids. I knew I needed a scholarship of some sort.

What I didn't know was what West Point was really like. Unfortunately for me, I went for a candidate visit during April of my senior year of high school, after the plebes had been recognized, so I didn't see any of the yelling or the intense moments to come. I saw springtime and the Hudson and smiling cadets leisurely walking to class on a Friday afternoon. It was really kind of nice. The plebe girls I stayed with helped each other iron their uniforms and chatted about the upperclassmen while they shined their shoes. It seemed all right. I think those memories helped me get through my own plebe year. I knew what was on the other side of recognition. (By the way, I think my mom stayed with your family that visit, and a few times after I went to West Point. We are very grateful for your family's hospitality!)

Courtesy of Kristin Gatti
*Kristin dodges the "Ring Poop." After receiving their class rings, juniors (cows)
have to dodge plebes on their way back to the barracks to sign out for the weekend.
Plebes surround them and shout, "Oh my god, ma'am! What a beautiful ring!
What a crass mass of brass and glass! What a bold mold of rolled gold!
What a cool jewel you got from your school! See how it sparkles
and shines? It must have cost you a fortune! Please ma'am,
may I touch it? May I touch it please, ma'am?"* ▶

**Photos and Interviews with Women of West Point** *(continued)*

*(2) Did anyone try to discourage you from your decision to attend West Point?*

*Mandy:*

I remember vividly being interviewed by one of South Carolina's senators, and at the end of my interview he said, "I would recommend you pursue becoming a pharmaceutical sales person." At the time, I was pretty offended and wanted to say, "I appreciate your input, but I am here because I want to go to West Point. I am not seeking career guidance." I felt like I was not taken seriously because I was a female.

Courtesy of Mandy Psiaki
*Mandy arrives at West Point for R-Day.*

*(3) Do you have any memories about a time in your childhood when you realized that you had a different gear than the other kids around you? Over the course of your life, how have you felt about your confidence, and what have you done to enhance or subdue it?*

***Charlsey:***
I was raised in a very positive-thinking family. My parents always looked on the bright side, so negativity rarely crossed my mind back then. I was a multi-sport athlete, and I think that really built my confidence. I was also kind of a "comeback kid." My dad was in prison from when I was born to when I was about six, facing serious drug charges, so doing well in school, earning a spot on the team, and making good grades were all a part of my story as the comeback kid. I had an amazing stepdad, stepbrothers, and several other family [members, and] friends and teachers who encouraged me and helped me make a path to success. My confidence has almost always resided in the idea that I can do anything with Christ. And I've also always felt that if I made it *this* far coming from *so* little, *what can stop me now*?

Courtesy of Charlsey Mahle
*Charlsey loading a mortar round during Cadet Basic Training, summer 2000.* ▶

**Photos and Interviews with Women of West Point** *(continued)*

*(4) Many women have shared that while at West Point or in the Army they felt pressure to prove themselves physically in order to gain the respect of their male peers. In your experience, is that true?*

*Kristin:*

The male condescension at West Point was kind of a shock to me. As we worked to solve problems in Beast or Buckner, if a woman came up up with an idea, it was rarely accepted by the men. I came into this world fighting, so it was really hard for me to shut up. I was 5'1", blond, maybe 105 pounds—when I would run my mouth about a better way to do something, I got the eye rolls and sarcasm from the men. Maybe I deserved it, but I can't help but think if I had looked different, I would have been taken seriously.

Courtesy of Kristin Gatti
*Kristin's cadet portrait, 2003.*

*Charlsey:*
Oh that's absolutely true. I feel somewhat traumatized from the pressure to be thin and super fit at West Point. The Army wasn't quite so bad in that regard—there's more grace there, but not at West Point. The name calling and degrading of women at West Point really makes women want to be fit and not "one of those" kinds of female cadets (unathletic, out of shape, a disappointment). I suppose in the end the pressure from the men helped me cross the finish line. I never wanted to be known as a girl that couldn't hack it, so I pushed myself no matter what, so no man would ever see me fail.

Courtesy of Charlsey Mahle
*Charlsey with her Beast squad, Cadet Basic Training, 2000.* ▶

**Photos and Interviews with Women of West Point** *(continued)*

*(5) What are some of the rules and standards you remember hating about West Point that make you laugh now? In what ways did you and your friends get around the rules to have fun?*

*Mandy:*

There are almost too many to name. I remember hating the fact that I was supposed to wear my hair in a perfect bun. When I went on a run I had to wear all cadet-issued clothing including the gloves and hat, even though they were bulky and not effective at keeping you warm. I also hated the fact that we had to leave the door to our room open during morning inspection, even if we were trying to study to prepare for a test. Additionally, as a female you never had an opportunity to pick your roommate because there were so few women in your class in each company, so you were generally assigned whoever was available.

I often broke the rules on cold-weather gear when working out on my own time. And we were only allowed to have a small amount of civilian clothes, so instead of keeping them in the barracks I left them in the volleyball locker room where I would not get caught. One of the things I liked to do when approached by an officer about something I was wearing or doing that was not aligned with cadet standards was say, "Sir/Ma'am, can you repeat that?" I always thought if they had to repeat themselves they may realize how dumb they sounded when confronting me.

Courtesy of Mandy Psiaki
*Mandy's cadet barracks room during Cadet Basic Training, 2004.*

Courtesy of Mandy Psiaki
*Mandy (third from the right) and friends leave campus for an afternoon lunch in Highland Falls. Tim Cunningham (third from the left) tips Mandy's hat. First Lieutenant Timothy Cunningham died on April 23, 2008, when his vehicle turned over into a canal in Golden Hills, Iraq.* ▶

**Photos and Interviews with Women of West Point** *(continued)*

## (6) What is one of your favorite stories from training at Camp Buckner as a yearling (sophomore)?

### Kristin:

So there we were, two squads from my Buckner platoon, on foot in the woods, head-to-toe in our battle gear, completely lost, and led by our very incompetent cadet platoon sergeant. He starts to hear a loudspeaker far away and he's convinced we have walked back towards Camp Buckner proper. He thinks the loudspeaker is Guard Room making routine announcements. We move towards the sound. The path gets harder to follow and the brush gets thicker and thicker. Of course, I can't keep my mouth shut, so I start loudly complaining that we are lost and need to turn around. The platoon sergeant gives me some sort of "if you make another peep, so help me" kind of rebuke. (See, I'm not much of a soldier.) Then we hear the loudspeaker start up again and it's a lot louder. The voice on the loudspeaker says, "go ahead and secure one ten-round magazine and lock and load your weapons!"

We all immediately freak out, realizing that we are BEHIND THE FIRING RANGE! The new cadets in basic training are firing. All of us hit the dirt and we hear the sound of M16 fire for several minutes. We wait until we hear "no brass, no ammo, sergeant!" (which means that any extra rounds have been turned in—the range is closing). So, we get up, dust off, and start walking towards the range. We emerge through the wood line. Another cadet sees us and announces, "Look, new cadets! These are yearlings!" It was hysterical. (New cadets don't normally see any yearlings until after the summer is over, because the cadre is made up of only cows and firsties.) Typical Buckner. Getting yourself into tricky situations and then having to wiggle your way out.

Courtesy of Mandy Psiaki
*All camo'ed up at Camp Buckner.* ▶

**Photos and Interviews with Women of West Point** *(continued)*

*(7) What job did you do during your deployment(s)? What were your expectations of deployment (Idealistic? Skeptical?) and how did the reality differ from your expectations? Did you feel that you made an impact?*

*Charlsey:*

I was working as the headquarters company commander for the Special Troops Battalion in 4th Infantry Division. Basically, I was part of the support staff for the division commander. My boss was a little off his rocker and had all kinds of bogus ideas about how to keep morale alive and inspire people during the deployment. He came up with an idea to have a 4th of July "fair" of sorts on the grounds of the division headquarters. He wanted to have camels there that people could ride. So it was my job to find the camels. We housed them in our motorpool for a few days before the 4th of July and then debuted them for the fair.

It was nuts. We had NO idea how to deal with camels, or what to feed them or anything. My soldiers got such a kick out of it, but when there were people losing their lives out there and encountering danger and gunfire everyday, it really felt odd for this to be a part of my job. I did *lots* of things along those lines, like dress up like a turkey for Thanksgiving, take care of a pregnant race horse for a general, and countless other things that people would never expect to do during a deployment.

*Mandy:*

I was a finance officer and essentially ran a bank that had an $11 million cash holding limit. I paid out $56 million in Iraqi dinar and U.S. dollars while I was in Iraq. The money was used on various projects—anything from road improvements to reimbursing an Iraqi for a farm animal that we injured unintentionally.

One of the most impactful things I did while I was deployed was work at a burn clinic for Iraqis that was sponsored and run by American medics. Almost all of the burn victims were women and children (mostly girls) and that is because being burned was a form of punishment and something that men would not do to other males. There were little girls who came in that had been dipped in oil and had burns all the way up their legs. The craziest part of all is that oftentimes it was their fathers who brought them to the clinic. It was hard for me to understand how someone could hurt a child and then ask for medical help. But we helped anyway.

Courtesy
Mandy Psiaki
*Counting money for
disbursement in Iraq.*

Courtesy Mandy Psiaki
*American makeshift burn center
outside of Mandy's FOB in Iraq.*

Courtesy Mandy Psiaki
*Mandy with patient
in the burn unit.* ▶

**Photos and Interviews with Women of West Point** *(continued)*

*(8) It's safe to say that every cadet who has attended West Point in the last decade has known someone who was killed in action while serving in the wars in Afghanistan and Iraq. Tell me about a friend that you lost.*

*Charlsey:*
Emily Perez was a plebe in my squad when I was a yearling. She was so smart, ran track, tutored all kinds of cadets in different subjects while we were at West Point. She was the first African-American cadet sergeant major at West Point. I was in Iraq when the notification that she'd been killed in action came across the wire. It is such a shock in your body, when you lose someone that was so alive and vibrant. It was so shocking. I felt so alone—but unfortunately, we were taking so many casualties in [2006–2007] that it just became another day's list. It sounds so callous, but in that environment, you can't stop working. You just have to keep going. I think in all of those years, I only had the chance to go to one memorial ceremony.

*Mandy:*
I lost one of my best friends, Tim Cunningham. He died on April 23, 2008, in Iraq. I was also deployed at the time and was hoping to come home for his funeral because I was requested as part of the Red Cross message, but I was told by my commander that if I made the trip I would not be able to take R & R.

At the time, I was on a very small base called Forward Operating Base (FOB) Scania, which was a truck stop along Main Supply Route Tampa. There was only a battalion-sized element at the FOB so there were no other female officers and only one other West Pointer. Thankfully, the West Pointer happened to be my classmate and knew Tim. He was not typically someone who was very emotional, but he was a great support during that time.

Courtesy Mandy Psiaki

*Friends hanging out during their college years. In this picture, Mandy Psiaki is holding Conoly Sullivan. Tim Cunningham is on the back of Mandy's future husband, fellow West Point graduate Dave Psiaki.* ▶

**Photos and Interviews with Women of West Point** *(continued)*

*(8) Women in the military often get a pretty two-dimensional representation in pop culture. What do you think the stereotype of a woman in the military is today? Do you think a change in perception is needed? Why?*

*Mandy:*
From my perspective, the view on women in the military has changed a lot in the last sixteen years. However, I still believe as a culture we see women in the military as masculine, hard-core, mean, and not family-oriented.

Prior to visiting West Point, even I assumed that all women at the academy were tough and rough around the edges. As a result of my visit, I quickly learned that they were very driven, smart, pretty, and athletic. They all had attributes that I admired, and I was drawn to be part of their sisterhood. They were going to push me to be better in all areas of life, and ultimately that was what I wanted to gain from my college experience.

I would love to see society embrace the fact that there are very strong and beautiful women who are and have been in the military. ⤳

# Reading Group Discussion Guide

1. The novel opens with Dani, Avery, and Hannah each choosing to go to West Point for very different reasons. What are their motivations, and how does that set them up for disappointment (and redemption) later in the book? How did you decide where to go to college? Do you have any regrets?

2. The book cycles through each character's perspective. Did you have a favorite? Why?

3. Have you ever visited the U.S. Military Academy at West Point? What were your perceptions about that place, and what have you learned about it through the lens of these characters that you didn't expect? How do you think you would have coped with the rules and standards of life at West Point as an eighteen-year-old?

4. The girls' basketball coach, Coach Jankovich, continually makes life at West Point even more difficult for her players. Have you ever had a coach or boss that operated out of fear and paranoia as she does? Is she the villain of the book? Or is something else (time, distance, war) a greater villain?

5. Dani, Avery, and Hannah all pursue love and relationships with men in very different ways. Do any of them handle them well? Should they have done things differently?

6. Dani's injuries set her life on a totally different path than she'd expected. How does she cope with that change over the course of the novel? Do you think she found her true path in the end? Have you ever had a moment in life when a career path closed? How did you find a new way forward?

7. For most of the book, Avery is stuck in a pattern of choosing the wrong men—one of whom even ends up going to jail. Is she a victim? Or is she responsible for those relationships?

8. Hannah makes many of her choices in this book out of a sense of faith and duty, believing that it will all be worth it in the end. In the last scenes of the book, when she confronts God, do you believe she is losing her faith? How have you coped with your ideas of spirituality, when confronted with loss and grief? ▶

**Reading Group Discussion Guide**
*(continued)*

9. The girls prove to be essential friends—the kinds that help carry you through the darkest days of life—as they're each facing their own crises. In what ways do they show up for one another in the pages of this book? What can you learn from their friendship, in the way that you relate to your friends moving forward?

10. Do you still keep in touch with your college friends? Why or why not? What about West Point set these women up for a stronger bond? ⟿

Discover great authors, exclusive offers, and more at hc.com.